Passing Strange

Passing Strange

A

NOVEL

Sally MacLeod

RANDOM HOUSE

NEW YORK

Copyright © 2002 by Sally MacLeod

All rights reserved under International and Pan-American
Copyright Conventions. Published in the United States
by Random House, Inc., New York, and
simultaneously in Canada by Random House
of Canada Limited, Toronto.

RANDOM HOUSE and colophon are registered trademarks of Random House, Inc.

Library of Congress Cataloging-in-Publication data is available.

ISBN 0-375-50613-6

Random House website address: www.atrandom.com

Printed in the United States of America on acid-free paper

24689753

First Edition

Book design by Jo Anne Metsch

In memory of my father,
Jack MacLeod,
and for Marcus

When I did speak of some distressed stroke
That my youth suffer'd: my story being done,
She gave me for my pains a world of sighs:
She swore, i' faith, 'twas strange, 'twas passing strange,
'Twas pitiful, 'twas wondrous pitiful . . .

—Spoken by OTHELLO
from the play by William Shakespeare

Passing
Strange

The terrace is freshly swept. Behind me I feel the house looming.
The debris from the storm last night has disappeared, the yardman
having done his usual masterful job this morning. Since then a dozen
more pine cones have dared to drop onto the grass. A few magnolia
pods lie here and there like unexploded hand grenades, accenting the
compulsory tranquillity. These lawns might be attached to a sanato-
rium rather than my husband's house. I'm not complaining. Life with
Warner is very sheltered, very snug. The light right now is golden, per-
vasive, perfecting everything it touches.

This is where I would start if I could, in the South. On the day I arrived, driving through the fields wearing my tight new face like a
badge stamped out of platinum. That day seems even more distant
than it is, stranded back there at the end of the old millennium. Only
twenty years ago, but everything that happened then seems historic,
which makes me feel even dustier, and yet reassured, as if my real life
is still intact there, safe in that last, safe century.

I don't know if I'm old yet. I can't tell, having spent so much time
chasing youth by redefining old to mean older than me. If I feel young
it's only because I can't remember what youth was like, although being
this age isn't quite the horror I always imagined. Being ugly was far
worse. And now I have to go back and examine that small desperate
person preening at the wrong end of the telescope.

I wish I could at least envy her the joy she hasn't glimpsed yet but
I can't do that, any more than I can cry out to warn her. What I need

now is someone to cry out a warning to me, to stop me from going on with this. I dread discovering how threadbare my story is, worn away in those places my memory has already visited too often. It will probably just fall apart in my hands.

I had to drive into Atlanta to meet Warner's train this morning, one of those dark muffled mornings with the mist hanging in the fields. When I got into town I was too early and spent the extra time cruising through those endless blocks of little wood-frame houses. It was drizzling by then, and they all looked as substantial as soggy cardboard. But one caught my eye. The front yard was marked out with string, the beginnings of a wall, and standing in the open doorway was a young black man. He had set his mug down on the porch floor to work on some small tricky thing he had in his hand. Maybe it was his intensity, the compact seriousness of his lowered head, but I knew him. I knew about the plate of fried breakfast he had just eaten and the smell of his soap and the way his back had looked as he shaved, the skin shining with that strange iridescence. I even had the warm powdery feel of his sheets. Just like that I apprehended him, as I drove on down the wet crummy street.

I

ONE

Do our faces belong to us, or do we belong to them? And what happens when you discard one face and take another? One must be a lie, but which one? When I was thirteen there was no confusion about any of this. The face in the mirror on the medicine cabinet was mine and I was its slave.

She was its slave. I can see her, Claudia Isham in 1978, locked in the bathroom of that little brick house, surveying herself warily in the clinical fluorescence. She has just discovered she can make her features respond to her will. By concentrating acutely on the narrow space between her eyes, she can pry them a little further apart and keep them fixed in that position while she directs a gaze as hot and quivering as a beam of mirrored sunlight at her mouth. This reveals the subtle contours in her thin upper lip where it meets the runnel coming down from her nose. Unfortunately the runnel is very short, pulling the mouth too close to the nose and tacking it there in its cruel overhang, but Claudia can cure this. She tips her head back slightly and slackens her mouth, which then drops lower. This angle also benefits the too distant relationship of her eye to her eyebrow and by foreshortening the sparse hairs of her brows collects them into a more precise shape. The eyes themselves are dramatic (her mother's word), like two gray-blue marbles pressed into wax. With an effort, Claudia subdues them by holding her eyelids at half-mast.

Overall, then, a long oval face, bisected below the high skeletal brow by a nose so overgrown and translucently bony it doesn't quite seem to belong on a face, it looks uselessly large, and unwholesome; in fact breathing is somewhat difficult, always a slight stuffiness there. There is no chin. Claudia's profile, which she gingerly inspects every few days with her hand mirror, reveals just a hint of convexity in the line that slopes down from the lower lip into her long neck. A detestable brown mole sits above the left corner of her mouth, and two smaller ones float on the blue-veined skin of her right temple.

It's not a crude face. The fine-grained luminous skin suggests a rarefied obsolete elegance, as if a Victorian bonnet trembling with ostrich feathers might help. But like every face, this one is in service to the single message it wants to broadcast at a glance. The message here is *Watch out*: this one is not one of us. Claudia's features, huddled around her hatchet nose as if in commiseration, instantly reveal her as a person exempt from life's more gratuitous delights; love at first sight, for instance. She has been congenitally handpicked to live among the other solitary campers-out crouched at the outskirts of life on their queer human haunches, warmed by small twiggy fires. There is no cure. But then, there's *no problem!* She's not crippled, or dying of a rare disease, or retarded. There's nothing really wrong with Claudia, which is why sometimes, cringing with guilt, she longs for a much worse handicap, one she could triumph over someday, to the sound of gasps and a soft explosion of relieved applause. What she has is a nondisability, not even mentionable, except via catcalls and jeers and those moist belches the boys deposit in her ear. It could be worse. Of course it could. She *knows that*. She also understands that when people try to be considerate and ignore her condition, they can do it only by ignoring Claudia herself.

Hair is shoulder-length and light brown, quite thick and wavy. Nice hair. Some days as she walks home from school, she hears a car bearing down, the honking horn mingling with the predatory cries of boys lured by the sway of her hair above her slim back. Furtively embracing the deceit, she nurses her vanity until the car pulls abreast of her profile. A sliver of silence. Then the first wounded howls, reaching a crescendo sucked away in the squeal of burning rubber.

Still, there are good days in front of the bathroom mirror. Sometimes Claudia approaches it with a ruthless asceticism, exposing herself to herself to test her true mettle. Occasionally while reading or thinking, she paralyzes her face in mid-thought and carries it to the mirror carefully, like a dish of water, and sees a delicate radiance shimmering there. There are times when she even feels an affection for her mirror-self, the fuzzy indulgence you feel for a friend you're starting to outgrow. Seeded with nostalgia, these moments can bloom into hope. One day she'll lose the face of this queer person, this stand-in she mistakenly loves. It can happen. It happened to Buddy Rasmussen, the town runt, who grew a foot and a half in his last two years of high school. Buddy probably earned it, by not caring, by not being so vain. Claudia could forget herself too, she thinks, if she could live in a world without mirrors. Oh! She can invent one! She scuttles sideways like a crab in and out of the girls' room at school, brushes her teeth over the bathtub, uses all sorts of caginess, enjoying the negative force field between herself and the mirror. A week goes by, two weeks, and then one morning she opens her eyes, blinks at her empty hamster cage, and knows something is different. Her alarm radio snaps on, offering "Wild Horses," her all-time favorite song. Claudia's eyes close and her body relaxes into pure gracefulness, recorded automatically by the hidden camera in the ceiling. Avoiding the bathroom mirror, she advances into a day whispering with portents. *Everybody* looks better. Diane Yevick's skin is almost perfect and Sandy Paley's gums barely show when she smiles. Claudia's posture grows ever more upright and willowy as the clues keep accruing. There's ravioli on the lunch menu, and then in English class, just before they all sit down, Mrs. Colburn looks at her with mild alarm. Oh, Claudia, she says, there you are . . . I didn't see you.

No one says a mean word. The cloud of suspicious spite that usually follows her around is gone.

When school is over she doesn't race home. She saunters, letting her hair swing, using every leaf and pebble to beat her mind into emptiness. She wings a smile at their disheveled neighbor who drinks, standing out in her yard next door. Inside the house, she ambles upstairs to the bathroom, locks the door, uses the toilet—wiping herself daintily, as she always will from now on—and even manages to tear some dead leaves off the philodendron before stepping up to the mirror and snapping on the light. She does indeed look different . . . worse, much worse than she remembered. She and her mirror image strain at each other like two puppies gagging pop-eyed on their leashes.

Okay. She will retreat from hopefulness. She'll bide her time; watch and wait and sharpen her observation skills. There are books, she'll keep reading. (Having already decided that since only plain friends are available to her, she'd rather have none.) She'll live in that exalted book world of high moral purpose where the important things are always the same—courage, loyalty, imagination—and have nothing whatsoever to do with appearances. Except of course that the heroines in her books are at least presentable and often spectacular. Claudia prefers them to be beautiful because then when she reads she's beautiful too, not as if she's imagining it but remembering, like a quadriplegic who somersaults through her dreams. She keeps reading and waits for that feeling to come, when her face is as lucent as glass and behind it her spirit thrives in splendid self-perfumed isolation, unique as a hothouse orchid.

So. All very simple. Life was pure and doomed. That ended the summer I was fifteen.

Daddy was hot by the time he finished screwing the full-length mirror to the back of my closet door. He sat back on his heels and gazed at it, then at me, then at the mirror again, his pouched eyes simmering with encouragement, as if he had just installed the instrument of my transformation.

"Okay kiddo, all systems go."

He pulled a gray dishcloth out of his back pocket, huffed on the mirror, and started to polish it, his bald sunburnt head bobbing at the level of my pelvis. His zeal was peeling the skin off my teeth.

"Daddy, that's fine. Really great. Thanks."

"Righto, Claudie." Just for a second his eyes met mine, and then I was alone.

A cool breeze knocked the curtain into the room and the promise of rain shrouded the house. Down the hall the toilet flushed, followed by my father's slow footsteps going downstairs and his voice calling for my mother, sounds of the ordinariness that had produced me and my life and this moment. The room had darkened into a grotto. Rain spattered the bushes under the window as I snapped on my ballerina lamp.

In front of the new mirror I took off my sneakers, jeans, shirt, bra, pants, and socks, exposing my body piece by piece, making it whole, magically assembled. I knew certain foreshortened pieces of myself from the bath and the shower, but the complete view I might have had in dressing rooms had always been prevented by the fear of my mother barging in. It must have been fear of the full catastrophe that always kept me away from her own full-length mirror.

So here was a naked stranger, patiently waiting, her feet rather bluish and bony on the braided rug. But the ankles were trim. The calves had a nice shape, the knees were chiseled, the thighs were as white and harmonious as swans' wings. Where they joined, a smudge of hair hovered over the little cleft. I looked at my small round breasts, no longer familiar but conniving now with hips, thighs, and pubis. I knew this body was beautiful. It didn't seem that much of a surprise. Swiveling and swaying, using the hand mirror, I took an inventory of my parts. I gathered my hair in one hand and twisted for a view of soft muscled back and the long neck, unmistakably—lift the hair higher, yes—the neck of a pretty girl. In an ecstasy of slow motion she splayed a pretty hand over her rear, as pert as a peach, then turned back and canted a hand on her hip and posed and vamped, testing all her lines and volumes, drawing herself using a lover's eyes.

Where was I? I glanced around with the polite disinterest of a visitor, blinked at the bookshelf and the Chagall poster, and opened the closet to find a bag of winter clothes. At the bottom was a long black mohair scarf, which I wrapped twice around my neck, flinging the ends over my shoulders. I kicked the closet door shut and leapt gazelle-like to the bureau for my sunglasses, put them on, and improved my costume by nudging the scarf up over my nose. Holding it there, I skittered to the record player, set the needle in place, and stomped back to the mirror against the opening drums. *Well, I bet you're wonderin how I knew, bout your plans to make me blue. . . .* Whoa, funky! I moaned in my head as my brain rolled under the wheels of the song and I danced, hip-grinding, arm-slashing, head-snapping like the sisters on *Soul Train* until I was seized by the certainty that I was beautiful all over, ripped the shades off, gawked, slapped them back on and kept dancing, thrashing my hot self, enraptured, self-mesmerized, sexed.

Twenty minutes later, wearing a cotton bandanna to hide the rash from the mohair, I strolled out into the side yard. Daddy was on his knees, trying to prop up his sodden gladioli.

"Who's my honey?" he said absently, busy with his wooden sticks.

"I am," I lied. My rumpled father had become a sweaty crouching beast. I turned away quickly before he looked up, then I coasted away through the fragrance steaming out of the earth, coasted all the way to Church Street, guarding my beauty, splendid and imperious under my clothes, hoarding myself against several averted glances and one of the angelic smiles old ladies always produced. None of it mattered now. That night under the covers my slippery fingers tempted the provocative beautiful stranger and rewarded her again and again.

I would be two people, body and head, with an invisible seam at the neck. A monster for sure. I was just about ready for Dan.

TWO

I SAW A BOY BOUNCING. He was coming toward me in the crowded hall, a head with thick brown hair cresting the other heads. He was walking on the balls of his feet, like a satyr up on his hooves. With a toss of his head he pranced past me, leaving an image stamped on my eyes of a large face he carried high, like a shield. That was him, I thought. That was the boy from New York City who had managed to get himself kicked out of Stowe Prep, last stop for screwed-up rich boys, so that public high school was his family's last hope. He was living with an uncle who was an executive out at the IBM plant. All this was generally known about Dan Dryburgh by now, even by me. But despite not sharing any classes with him, before long I knew much more. I had seen him slam his locker door and run his bitten fingers over the air vents in a forlorn caress, I knew he felt blighted and exposed in such a proletarian place. The school's five cinder-block buildings and connecting ramps must have felt like a factory to him. I watched him trying to shake off his apprehension with a defiant gulping half twist of his head. Then, once he began to merge into the clique of other rich kids, that twist dwindled into a different nervous habit, useful for tossing his floppy hair out of his face. Finally it became a gesture of dominance, the hair-toss preppy power statement, but I could forgive him that, because by now I was almost sure he was using the gesture to parody himself to me. That was our little joke. He knew I was watching him but he wasn't going to let on. We were in contact.

Some days Dan left school at lunchtime to go get a burger, usually with his stumpy bowlegged friend, Gary. If I saw Gary waiting
for Dan by the front door, I could usually get to the window overlooking the parking lot in time to see them off. It was nice watching
Dan go, giving me time to relax, forget about my hair, and just an-
ticipate, beaming him my loving patience so that when he finally
came back, it was to me. Often during the day there would be a
warning, a little stoppage in the air, and there he would be, disappearing through a doorway or laughing with Gary in the stairwell. I
shuddered with the knowledge that I could make him appear. He
was the secret that held me at a remove from the crude and obvious
meaning of things, and the vulgar mundanity all the other girls
craved. A nascent superiority was glowing in the pit of my soul like
a fire at the back of a cave. In my journal that year I composed a
prose poem for Dan.

> Yours is a *je ne sais quoi, un vrai tendresse.* I watch you walk the
> lean streets, I watch you twist in your sheets. I listen to you breathe.
> You know who I am. Your spirit roams out over the town, a miasma
> of love. Sometimes this cliché world is so hard for you, you want
> to run away and prowl by the sea's throbbing breast, but love waits
> for you in this small banal town. Love dares to speak its proud vir-
> gin name and laugh and scream. It waits to cry and moan and lie
> with you in the tall dew-speckled grass.

I was content suspended in yearning, shivering like a spider on
my web every time Dan passed me in the hall. His other body I carried in my head, undressing it and laying it down beside me so
that his breath polished my face while I was sleeping. When I woke
up his face was beside me on the pillow and when I got to school
he was there too, waiting for me. His underestimation of the sheer
muscle of my love made me love him more. He was mine, and
when he was ready he would know that he loved me and I would
burst into beauty and he would take me away. Be careful what you
wish for, they say, but even my fairy godmother would have seen

this as an unassuming little fantasy, expedient, not dangerous to anybody and certainly—here she would smile indulgently—certainly not Dan.

His girlfriend that spring was a cheerleader named Emily. She had muddy hair trickling around an agitated face whose energy came to a point in her shiny nose. Her ears tended to poke out of her hair. She was like a girl fox in a cartoon, calculating and twitchy. Once when I was using the girls' room she came in, and I watched through the crack in the door, revolted and enthralled as she combed her hair, silkily, voluptuously, lost in a dream of herself. Her complete unawareness of her flaws infuriated me further.

The night I decided to track them down was the first mild Saturday night in May, a sure thing. I was under the electric lines, tucked down in a pocket of erosion around the concrete base of a pylon, using the sloped earth like the back of a chair. Around ten I heard the first car of the evening approach, Dan's Mustang. It rumbled onto the bare dirt under the electrical lines and stopped not thirty feet away. The breeze it stirred glided into me.

The noises started immediately. His voice suddenly. "No, I'm in *pain* here."

"Oh Danny, I know."

"Em, just *look* at it."

Cautiously I shifted my weight off one buttock and accidentally dislodged some small stones.

"No." Long pause. "No, I'll be sick like last time."

"That wasn't anything, that was a reflex."

"Duh. Cause it's not supposed to *go* there." Her unbearable coarseness. I ached for him. Minutes went by.

"Em, can't you use your whole hand?"

I can wait, I thought dully. This too shall pass. I lay my head on my knees and thought, I could die up here and they wouldn't find me for days. The thought loosened my bones.

"Wait. Something's . . . I'm not kidding. *Listen.* Over by that cement thing. What the . . . oh fuck, it's *her.* How'd she *get* here, she lives way the hell over—"

But I was up and gone, into the woods, ablaze in Dan's head-lights, my feet barely touching the stony ground.

He knows where I live, I wrote in my journal. *He will come.*

The following Monday night he was there on the front stoop, staring at me through the screen door. Gary was beside him, his car was pulled up crookedly at the curb. Standing under the yellow porch bulb, Dan was like an idol of himself, his cheekbones and parted lips like molded gold above the familiar faded football shirt.

"Lookit," Gary said. "He wants to talk to you."

"Yeah. You know, you gotta stop doing this." And then, lower, trying to sound threatening, "I know your name."

"Claudia." I was serene, drugged by the intensity of Dan's attention.

"Yeah well, that's great," Gary said. "But you know what? It's illegal to go around bugging people. You're like a *vampire.*"

There was a silence. I broke it by inviting them inside.

Gary winced up at Dan. "No way."

Dan took Gary's elbow and hustled him down the sidewalk toward his car. They conferred urgently for a minute—Dan took hold of Gary's elbow and Gary yanked it away—and then Dan walked back alone.

"Ten minutes . . . *be* there!" Gary yelled from the curb.

As Dan stepped into the hall he fumbled in his pocket. "You put this in my locker," he said, pulling out my note with just the one word on it, *Tonight.* "Nobody home, huh?"

He was in the living room now, standing by the mantel where I had just switched on Daddy's beloved old lava lamp.

"People always think these are obscene," he said.

He seemed riveted by the lurid orange blobs, then he suddenly threw himself down on the love seat. He looked disturbingly large. Standing in front of him I felt like a wavy tube of sunlight shot through with smoke. I ran through my selection of drinks. His hands thrummed the love seat arms as he scanned the room, the imitation Delft plates, the carved eagle ashtray, the model aircraft carrier.

"Yeah, okay, Coke."

The bleakness of the kitchen warned me he might get away. I poured Coke over ice and hastily removed three sugar doughnuts from their cellophane and arranged them on a gold-rimmed plate. Reentering the living room I noticed how the furniture had enclosed him, trapping him naked inside his clothes. He accepted the Coke and a doughnut, and I put the plate on the table beside him and finished arranging myself on the other couch, looking up just as he wiped some sugar off his upper lip.

"So. I guess you're hung up on me. Like, no mercy, right?"

A vestigial head twist. I smiled to put him at ease but he missed it, he was frowning at the fireplace.

"You know," I ventured softly, "I don't exactly bite."

"Yeah, like I look really worried." He wouldn't look at me.

"No. I know you're not."

"I guess you know a lot."

"Certain things I do. Things about you."

"How to freak me out."

"I'm sorry. That was a little bit . . . immature."

"Fucking A right." He was drumming his hands again.

"It's not silly to feel like this though. It's not." The drumming stopped. He finally turned his head and looked at me.

"Yeah, but why me? What's that about?" Mimicking nonchalance, he flung an arm over the back of the love seat. His uneasiness was plain, as if he had just broken out in a misty sweat. "You sure stare enough."

"I have insights. That's how come I know how strong you are. You have a very intense psyche. Your nature is very unyielding and resolute." I had written all this in my journal. "But you can be soft too. Because of all the doubts you have."

"Nope. Fraid not."

"Doubts only happen when people think about what's going on.

Lots of people think everything's fine just like it is, but you're more perceptive. That can make you depressed but not really malcontent, I don't think."

"Whatever that is."

"Chronically discontented."

"Yeah, well. It's a shitty world. Basically people are fucked. Like any minute, bang, your brain just blew up."

When I got up he didn't budge, and avoided my eye. When I sat down beside him his body felt wooden with longing. Very slowly his extended arm drooped onto my shoulder until his fingertips dangled just above my right breast, bare under my shirt. My nipple melted upward into his hand.

I began very quietly.

"I have this feeling, I think it might be a memory, of us being someplace foreign. Maybe Italy. The street opens out into this gigantic square that's packed with people and the sky's full of pigeons, you can't even see the sky, it's full of wings thrashing. It's dark like before a thunderstorm, it's macabre. We love it." I nestled deeper into his shirt's cotton smell. "The weird part is, we might still be there, having a memory that we're in this room." His hand squeezed my breast and the lava lamp oozed, a thick voodoo candle on the altar of love. "Our thoughts are like those pigeons, leaving our heads. They're flying out. I can hear your thoughts. I know you can hear mine. Don't be afraid." I put my hand on his thigh. "Say whatever you want. You can tell me things."

His hand had died on my breast. Quickly I lifted up his other hand, buried my face in his palm, and inhaled.

"Wait, wait. Hold it. Do you even get what's going on here?"

I returned his hand to his lap and touched the denim-crusted bulge. I tried to wedge my hand gently between his thighs but he clamped hold of my wrist and pulled my hand out and held it, like a claw grasping at air.

". . . don't fucking believe this. *I'm* screwed up? I'm *depressed?* Gimme a break. What're you, sex on a stick?" His eyeballs looked swollen, his breath blasted me. "Who's doing who a favor here, you got any clues?" He threw my hand down and turned an edge to me, withdrawing, getting away.

"You are. *You* are, Danny. . . ."

His hands were at his belt, tearing at the buckle. When he turned back to me my blouse was undone. I slid off the couch onto the floor, onto my rucked-up skirt, and teased it higher. I had rehearsed in this light, I knew my skin looked like a river of cream. I pulled my blouse open to show him my breasts. His feet stepped over me and crossed the room and the light went off. He was unzipping as he came back. I was spread on the rug now, brazen in that light, cupping and squeezing my breasts for him. *Look at me.* He knelt and I saw his long pale penis crouching in the dark V of his open fly and my legs opened for him, just a little, showing him, and his hands came down and slapped at my hips and he rolled me over onto my stomach. Then he was climbing over me, straddling me and tugging and lifting until I was folded in front of him, my bottom in the air and my face ground into the carpet. He groped me roughly with one hand and then stuffed himself in. It burned, like a long rope drawn through raw weeping flesh.

As soon as he withdrew I collapsed onto my side and got my skirt pulled down. There was a silence, then the swishing sound of his pants. I heard his belt buckle jingle. He stepped over my legs to get to the door.

Oh, but that was all right, I would allow it. I lay with my head on the fireplace rug and I thought, Yes. I understand. It was my fault, *I scared you.* I could save both of us, my forgiveness would keep us cleaved together. We had infected each other, we were joined in a disgrace so intimate it was sacred. It was ours. We could build on that. I would just stay out of his sight for a while. I managed to do that, and then suddenly I didn't have to, he was gone. He left three weeks before the school year ended. He was back in New York City, people said. Yeah, where he belongs, somebody muttered, and I felt proud of his irrefutable glamour, which was still flourishing in the moistness of my body. I could taste it on my lips. Then it began to metastasize into patches of lust that glowed all over me. Even my wrists ached sometimes, as if they knew how much my hands were longing for a boy's bare skin.

Duncan showed up in July. He was on his way to a science summer camp with my Uncle Ham, his new stepfather, who had let him drive the whole way from Pittsburgh. I watched Duncan step out of the car, long-boned, hair too short and lank, revealing an earnest sunburnt neck. He was wearing a drip-dry shirt and too small shorts and sandals with socks. Spittle collected in the corners of his mouth when he spoke. Mostly he didn't, but as we shared the love seat before dinner I noticed that when he did muster up something to say, his manner was polite and collected. On the inside of his thigh there was a small birthmark like a clover. His IQ was 182, I had overheard Uncle Ham telling Mom in the kitchen; in return she had divulged my PSAT scores. It had been announced to me only a few days before, with a certain fanfare, that she and Daddy could afford to send me to the University of Vermont; as Duncan and I sipped ginger ale we were encouraged to elaborate on our college plans. I knew that after dinner he and I would be urged to go for a nice ride.

He drove tersely, all elbows and knees, eyes straight ahead. After a while his anxiety began to relax me. I decided to suggest a viewing of Camel's Hump. As the macadam road dwindled into dirt, he cleared his throat and said rather gruffly, "What's this?" Then he saw the power lines, and the dirt road broadening into a patch of dust, and he knew exactly where we were. The car rolled to a stop and Duncan pushed his face closer to the windshield to admire the mountain's cleft shape looming behind the dusky hill in front of us. He said, "Oh yeah." Neither of us said a word as I climbed over the gear shift into his lap. His long arms clamped around me. I shut my eyes and let his tongue enter my mouth solemnly, proficiently. His hands, which had sat like lumps of cement on either side of his plate, were efficient and slow. We flowed quietly toward the event and when it was dark enough we moved into the backseat. It was awkward because of his height, he had to leave the door open for his legs, but as if to make up for this indignity he attended me painstakingly at the other end, moving his lips over my face in long nibbling caresses. If he noticed my tears, and he must have, he disregarded them with a dignity that seemed to include me. His intensity was un-wavering, and singular, it seemed like his own. He even whispered my name at the end.

When we got back to the house everyone had gone to bed. I sat in the kitchen and watched Duncan finish up the leftover pie, then we kissed at the foot of the stairs. In the morning I got up just in time to help wave him and Uncle Ham back into the car. Duncan was gauche again, his shorts bunched up in his crotch, off to his science camp, and then to MIT, and California, and a wife and a Down syndrome daughter. He's a millionaire now, from designing software. The first of my raw, brainy boys.

My lovers at UVM all studied some form of engineering. The exception was Richard, who was intent on ob/gyn despite, or maybe because of, his terror of women's bodies. His hands twitched on me like damp butterflies, but we spent hours together in his stale room with the blinds drawn, and when he laid his head in my naked lap, hoping I might endure a little more of his anxiety, I noticed how it neutralized my own. I felt womanly and whole trying to distract him, dragging my nipples over his bristling red hair. I was efficient that way in those UVM years, like a nurse rustling from one patient to another, naked under her uniform. This wasn't what I wanted. I was studying art history, I wanted an artist, somebody who would recognize me in his bed, pallid and arresting in my long-necked Modigliani way, but the art students were all killing each other over the prettiest girls. My anxious lonely lovers were nice to me, I think they all became anxious decent men. I didn't scorn them for being unbeautiful, any more than I scorned the boys who passed me over for nice-looking girls. I was still devotedly forgiving Dan, carrying him through my life, my graduation, my job at the paper, more lovers, wearing him like a lesion that, left undisturbed by my memory for more than a few days, might heal over without a trace, and that I couldn't have borne.

THREE

THE GALLERY THAT night was hectic, overawed by its reputation as Burlington's trendiest. Outside the streets were creaking with cold, it was the first hard freeze of that winter, inside the windows were streaming. I had come with Kat, lost her in the mob, and was standing out of the way against a wall, wishing I could see more of the pictures. They were huge graphic simplifications in oil of the kind of photos favored by *Vermont Life* magazine, blue shadows draped on snow, but somehow this exaggeration wasn't crass, it seemed respectful, almost reverent. I had spotted a couple familiar faces—my old art teacher done up in a turban, the guy the museum had hired instead of me, who appeared to have reinvented himself as a lounge lizard—when I saw Dan, and instantly rejected him as a crude impostor. A trick of my mind. This man was fleshier, with heavier eyebrows and shorter hair. And then my view of him was lost, obscured by bodies. When I saw him again he was closer, elbowing his way toward me carrying two glasses of wine, and not bouncing. His walk had calmed down but his face was a mask of animation. I knew that looking straight at him would be as dangerous as looking into the sun. He was wearing a blue shirt, some variation of denim, with bone buttons. He pushed a glass at me.

"Claudia! God, what a scene, huh? Is this stuff any good? I don't know squat about art!" An easier grin than I remembered, more fluid and toothy. "So how've you *been*?"

I felt sick. Naked. I was lying on my parents' floor, breathing the dirty tang of the hearth rug. He thrust his head closer.

"I was just thinking, I'm gonna pass out here if I don't get something to eat! You want to come?"

I knew to say as little as possible, to find my coat and slip away without alerting Kat, to fold myself gracefully into the miniature car. At the Ice House it was noisy too, with a big Friday-night crowd. Our conversation seemed to drift on the din like chunks of debris while I waited, submerged, breathless, watching his hand peel the napkin from his wet mug and then stick it back and a minute later unpeel it again. Everything was so odd that a murky reckless normality had set in. Luckily our inexhaustible main topic was all the changes that had happened in Burlington.

"How'd this town get so shit hot all of a sudden?" he said, and I laughed.

"It wasn't sudden, it's been years since you were here!" Risky. I didn't care.

"The buzz is incredible."

"Caffè latte on every corner. That appeals to you, does it?" I heard my voice flirting.

"But that stuff back there at the gallery. That was some real shit, wasn't it? That was like paint by numbers."

"I know. Like, get a *camera!*"

He was showing me a broad, rather fixed smile.

He'd been in Burlington a month, working as the sales manager for a kitchen gadget manufacturer based in North Carolina. Even this didn't seem peculiar. Why shouldn't he sell people can openers, such a nice-looking, amiable guy? My memory had swallowed itself. His big fidgeting hand was a stranger's hand. A very small portion of my mind "knew" he wasn't quite what he seemed; breezy, alluring, yes, but also tricky and wounded and opaque. There was something wrong with him but there was something wrong with me too, we were playing it back and forth to each other, cracking it open with our smiles. Then in the car as I felt my thighs drawing his gaze from the road, my face seemed to come loose and float into the rushing dark. I stayed faceless for hours. He was that good. We tore at each other, torturing our young ghosts. But he couldn't stop, he was frantic. Becoming satiated underneath him, then exhausted, I began to see that he must have used other plain women over the years, trying to ignite some dank moldering frustration, casually hurting women and refining his easy power until it had slackened into this rather obvious skill. That was what was left, that and now this appetite for me, the prototype. She had shocked something awake in him with the monstrous purity of her girlish desire. It was her he was fucking now, sanding her forehead with his jaw. He was grinding away at the bottom of himself, groveling in his self-despair, wallowing in it. Of course it made him more beautiful. The shaggy sweat-clotted hair, the heavy mouth ripe with oblivion.

In the morning when I woke up he was already awake, propped up on his pillows, unaware I was watching him, thinking that his face looked like it was a half size too big. I wanted to reach up and pinch the chiseled upper lip and peel the skin back over his nose like latex. He was staring at nothing, other than the far wall, artfully plastered like all the walls in his drab expensive new condo. I watched him run his tongue over his upper teeth. He was adrift, doubting his life. He was wondering what was wrong, why he was still lonely, why *I* was there. But he had half accepted it, there was an aspect of submission, even defeat. I saw I could have him now. He closed his eyes and curled himself around me, and when his hand slipped between my legs I lifted my mouth to kiss him. I made the kiss lazy and provocative, a reward for all our years of heroic endurance, and felt a current of mutual congratulatory indolence run through our bodies. When his hand moved on me it seemed weighted differently, loaded with solace. The menace of pity. I was his wounded bird. He thought he was rescuing me, but I thought I was rescuing him. Symmetry was in place. My "forgiveness" of Dan could be stored away in a far corner of my mind like a bizarre souvenir.

I wasn't as manipulative as I sound, I was drowning in astonishment. People go on about desire tragically misconstrued as love, but when I remember our feverishness that morning, I can't separate my desire from my gratitude.

We went back to the Ice House for brunch. With one eye on me, Dan ordered half the menu, and I saw that my relative poverty stirred him, as if he thought I needed building up.

The idea of leaving Vermont might have been brewing in me already. Dan had said his company was based in North Carolina; I was probably already hoping he could move us down there and save me from the contrived crowded place Burlington had become. I had no idea then what the South was, other than a hot place full of religion. Looking back now, I see Dan and me tumbling out of the Northern sky toward the baking fields, innocent as snowflakes. Even then we were already falling.

Neither of us really knew how to talk. We felt we had to try, but anybody eavesdropping on our early conversation would have noticed we were more intent on camouflaging our true childhoods than on sharing them. I contributed memories that would depict me as a creative only child who had always been too preoccupied with her precocious imaginative life to notice, much less care, how she looked (trying to imply that Dan obviously operated on the same lofty plane). Dan served up stories of gross practical jokes perpetrated at his various private schools, stories about seducing Dalton girls on the roof right above his parents' penthouse and getting "ripped" on bad-ass uptown grass.

"So you were a real city kid." I was emphasizing my rural side, which was easy since I'd been out of New England just once, to New York City with an art history group.

"Oh, big-time."

"Were you one of those New Yorkers who can't drive?" A bad lapse: I suddenly remembered his vintage red Mustang.

"Nah, not that bad. But whenever my parents made me go out to Southampton I always fell asleep till it was over."

"Too much oxygen."

"Plus it's a hard place to score, at least it was then."

"Oh dear."

"Well, not that hard."

Dan slung his anecdotes at me like sandbags, trying to balk my curiosity, but he needn't have worried. Having realized that his teenage anxiety had never found a voice, I didn't mind, because it meant he would never try to encourage any confession from me. While other couples our age were trying to dredge each other's psyches, Dan and I had mutely pledged to leave each other alone. I told myself what I had to do was monitor my mouth and make sure that some night after a fourth glass of wine nothing dribbled out, nothing remotely self-pitying that might suddenly reveal to Dan how lonely and watchful and queer I had been. I had to hide that, I had to scavenge every possible advantage out of our disparity. Anything to redistribute the lopsided weight of our load.

Although sometimes Dan hardly seemed aware of my looks. We went out, people saw us, but Dan acted as if he were oblivious to the way they exchanged looks like thunderclaps behind our backs. It's disturbing for people when couples don't match, unless the imbalance explains itself, like a wealthy old guy with a very young woman. (It doesn't matter what other, invisible trade-offs are going on, nobody cares about them.) People certainly didn't want to see us, we were Beauty and the Beast with the genders reversed. Chaos was at loose in the world. Confused, needing an explanation, people always managed to find one, always the same one. Every one of Dan's sales reps, meeting me for the first time, rolled an oily gaze down my body and back up again, presuming he had just X-rayed the secret of my stupendous success. One even tried to compliment me on my prowess with some funny eye business, a little salute, while his girlfriend's gaze dropped to my belly, hoping to confirm that Dan had been trapped. And yet there were times, I admit this, when just thinking about the crudeness of people's assumptions could torch my desire for Dan.

I fretted for weeks about how to introduce him to Kat. He was bound to see us as a pair, a set of gargoyle bookends. All he knew so far was that I met up with an old friend from UVM now and then, a textile designer. All Kat knew was that I had a new boyfriend. But I had downplayed this, to imply it wasn't serious. She would never have imagined it was anybody like Dan. As the weeks went on my fear that Dan and I would bump into Kat downtown became intense enough to mutate into hope that we would. And one Saturday afternoon we were down on the lower level of the mall when I saw her magenta parka. She was studying an aquarium in the pet shop window but as she turned away I lost my nerve. I tried to steer Dan out of the way, around the other side of the escalator, and thought we were safely past her when she called my name. She was waiting for us to come over, with her soft freckled face like a gnome's and her hair standing up in those copper feathers. I saw she had the wholehearted liveliness of a doughy plain little boy. I saw also that she wasn't as plain as I was. I managed an introduction and she and Dan shook hands with businesslike vigor, as if to confirm their mutual importance to me.

I tried bolstering this solidarity. "Well. I guess we're all cruising."

"We're bored," Dan added. I saw Kat register his proprietary tone, saw her register that we were a real couple.

"We only got up an hour ago," I said. I knew this was going too far. Kat knew it too.

"Tell me," she said to Dan. Her face was sparky. "Should I buy an aquarium?"

"Absolutely," he said.

"Really? Could you come inside for a minute?"

Without a peep Dan followed her into the pet shop. I trailed in and looked at the rabbits while they stood in the dark aquarium area and pointed out fish to each other, silhouetted against the tanks in their big parkas like astronauts lost in a phosphorescent universe. Their ardor finally attracted a salesman, which was when Dan

excused himself, patting Kat on the shoulder, wishing her luck.
I glimpsed the edge of her face as she said good-bye to Dan—
she looked enchanted, either by the fish or by him—and then she
looked around for me and gave me a distracted wave.

Out in the mall Dan walked faster, she had altered his metabo-
lism. I kept up with him and waited. Finally he said, "She's a goof,
I like her. She looks like one of those dolls made out of a dried
apple."

I wanted to scold him. Oh Dan, that's *terrible*, I almost said, but I
managed to hold it in. I couldn't fault him. He had passed. He *was*
a good guy, he was what he seemed.

"Hey, should I buy her an aquarium?" he said all of a sudden.

"No!" I laughed. "She's got money."

The next time I saw Kat she asked about Dan, in precisely the
same casual voice I had when I first mentioned him. "He's nice, I
like him." She mustered up a bit more about his energy, etc., and
then changed the subject. There was no voice casual enough for Kat
to use if she had wanted to add anything along the lines of "He's easy
on the eyes." Which she didn't. Dan's looks were off-limits. Even a
brisk "Nice-looking guy" would have implicitly referred to the mi-
raculous aspect, and Kat wouldn't do that. It wasn't tact exactly. Kat
and I never discussed our own looks, or referred to them in any way.
Maybe other plain young women crack loud knowing jokes, but we
never did. That silence stood at the center of our friendship like a
hollow tree where we left secret notes for each other.

Two months after that, early in February, I was in New York to meet
Dan's parents. Trying to remember that night doesn't take much effort, it pours back at me. The golden warmth of the lobby as we
dashed in off the street. Our creaking ascent in the paneled elevator,
with Dan squeezing my hand too hard, which only scared me more.
We knocked and waited in front of their apartment door with its little peephole, through which I could feel his parents' dismay extruding like a long needle. My terror deepened when the door was
opened by a maid, a small Asian woman. She bustled our coats away

and then his parents appeared through an archway, keeping their eyes under control as Dan introduced me. Maybe there was the faintest clang of manners slamming into place, maybe a gauze of coolness blew across their eyes, but they were deft, Ping and George, a couple of old pros in their matching pewter hair.

There was a spicy pinkish smell in the living room. It was probably a discreetly placed bowl of potpourri, but as Ping directed me toward the sofa I thought I must be ingesting vapors of pure luxury generated by the crackling fire and the needlepoint cushions and the roses spilling out of an old silver pitcher. Little porcelain pillboxes cluttered the inlaid table by my elbow. Over the mantel was a huge pastel portrait of Dan and the older brother he mentioned sometimes, always saying his name with sarcastic grandeur— Garfield; I knew there was something there, jealousy probably, but here they were just chubby toddlers rendered as spun sugar, Danny's hand a little starfish on Garfield's blue velvet knee. After the maid had brought me champagne, Ping in her gravel voice launched into a lengthy reminiscence of family skiing holidays in Vermont. As I smiled and nodded, the sense drained from my head. With a benumbed thrill I realized she assumed I skied too, or else was pretending to. Dan and his father stood by the fire talking in a mutter, ignoring us.

The white-clothed dining table was a little big for four. Ping, after pausing a moment to glimmer in the candlelight, pressed a foot buzzer whose echo I could just detect in the kitchen, and a different maid appeared. The salad she set in front of each of us was like a Kandinsky painting, the various layers stippled with herbs and garnished with crosshatchings of slashed scallions. I glanced at Dan beyond the candlesticks. While his parents pretended not to notice, he was editing his salad, removing everything that wasn't lettuce until he had a delicate compost heap at the edge of his plate; scallions, olives, radicchio, radish, and carrot curls. I knew about the food problem, there was a list of foods he refused even to try, but since I was sure he ate carrots I assumed he was pressing the point, whatever it was. He was sulky, shimmering with distaste. Plates of shrimp with eyeballs had appeared. Ping was twinkling at me from

under her bangs. George was refilling my wineglass. Try this Sant-
Estèphe . . . lovely stuff, you'll like this. Ping and George started trad-
ing desultory observations on New York's deterioration, their
detachment implying that New York lay somewhere on the far
side of the moon. Two small bony birds in a bloody puddle were
brought in, as I tried to remember Dan at the hotel two hours before, growling and ravishing my belly. Dessert, garnished with a fat
sliced-strawberry heart, was pink ice cream in chocolate filigree
cups, exactly like breasts in black lace. Dan gobbled it like a child.
A familial chumminess seemed in place as I excused myself and ne-
gotiated the long hall to the powder room.

In the aromatic overheated halogen glow, I immediately fell
under the spell of being alone with myself. A tortoiseshell kleenex
box cover gleamed against the green marble counter with a magnifi-
cence that was almost sinister, the square taps were like hunks of
gold cheese. My face in the mirror was new, plumped by the wine,
the eyes smoky with confidence. Striking poses, fingering the towels,
poking through the emollients and soaps and little vials heaped in a
gold basket lined with monogrammed linen, I stayed in there too
long. Then I dawdled in the hall among the photographs, a long
glassy tapestry of them, framed in silver and burled walnut. George,
vital and ruddy in espadrilles and a striped shirt like Picasso's, toast-
ing the sea from the prow of a sailboat. Garfield aged around ten,
bareback on a white horse and blurry with glee as Ping, sitting behind him, leaned forward and nuzzled his neck. Lots of pictures of
the family with various friends, posing with tennis rackets or lolling
on rustic porches. On Christmas mornings they opened their presents wearing neckties and pearls. Creeping back up the hall I noticed that Garfield was omnipresent but I had to look hard to find
Dan. He was often sliced in half by the picture's edge or his head
was down, and when both brothers were photographed together, it
was always Garfield at center stage. In one picture Dan, looking
about eight, was standing beside his mother on a lawn. Ping, in narrow pants tucked into tall boots, her beauty stamped into planes as
graphic as a woodcut, had her arm around him. His fingers were

clenched around his thumbs and he was holding his head at a forty-five-degree angle away from her, and not smiling at whoever was casting that long shadow on the grass. As I leaned closer to examine Dan's discomfort I heard his voice in the living room.

"No. Nothing like that. I just said, it won't *be* a big wedding."

Who exactly was getting married? I had not been asked.

"Well, I think you're wise there." George, keeping his voice down. Did his tone hold a whisper of sarcasm?

"You know . . ." Ping growled quietly over a tinkling of ice cubes, "she's so extreme, she's almost *almost* chic."

"Hmm. I think you mean kitsch, don't you, darling, in that floral print? The shirt itself's not bad though."

"I bought her that." Dan, interjecting loudly.

"Daniel?" his father said. "Let me be frank. I can't say we're over-whelmed. Not with any of it, I might add. But I think if you're intent on this, the least you can do, and I mean this in all seriousness, is get her fixed up."

"Darling, he's right. Daddy knows. She couldn't be nicer. I see what she has, darling, there's a quality there. It's just not terribly apparent, is it, with all the distractions."

Dan said, "Oh yeah? What distractions are those?"

"Darling. She just needs her nose done, maybe a very small chin implant. Different hair, something short and fluffy. Blond. I'd *love* to see what Leonard—"

"Dan, don't look at your mother like that. She does have a sharp little figure, I noticed. Very sharp."

Ping made her voice intimate. "Darling, you know she'd be thrilled."

"Just like you were when that guy screwed up your lift and you wouldn't get out of bed for three—"

"*Dan.*"

"Oh George, it's all right. Danny, it's not as if she doesn't *know.* I'm sure she looks in the mirror."

"Not often, I bet. Anyway," George said mildly, "what's she done, fallen into the head?"

"Darling, go see."

Danny stopped short when he saw me there in the hall, cringing. He stared and I stared back, pleading mutely for him not to look at me. Something moved between us, a breath of kindliness for each other. In the living room George cleared his throat.

"Ping. Dearest. This is *Daniel.* You know what he is." A pause. "He's not *serious.* She's a specialty item, she's good in the sack. She'd have to be, wouldn't she. Christ."

Dan came at me and ground his mouth against mine, as if he were trying to erase my lips. He detached me from the wall, led me to the closet, and grabbed our coats, rattling hangers, making a lot of noise. No one came out. In the elevator we worked to avoid each other's eyes in all the polished brass and then we were in the cab, tearing back across town. I couldn't bring myself to sit close to him.

"So how'd you like em?" The streaming light was lashing Dan's face. "How'd you like all that happy horseshit, wasn't that great? Come over here. Fuck em. Fuck em all."

Danny, what did you expect? "They're all right. They're okay. It's fine." I couldn't bear talking about it. I wanted to put my hand over his mouth.

"It's nice having stuff you can count on. I *like* knowing they'll always be the assholes of the universe. They don't ever let you down, you know what I mean? Hey, Claud. You in the corner. I said, come *here.*"

He was pulling at me. He needed me. I slid over and let him cuddle me hard against his cashmere shoulder.

Rich people are different, I told myself. He had had to perform that idiotic ritual. He had been brave to drop me into that airless black hole and then carry me out intact. I did know he had flung me in their teeth, I grasped that, but that was because he had needed to show his parents he was mature and capable of real love. He was less superficial than they were, more *original.* Maybe he had wanted to show them what real love looked like, while managing to forget how much of it they'd always given Garfield. Peering deeper into Dan's neediness, I even considered the possibility that he was using me, ostentatiously valuing me to prove his own worth to himself. If anyone had ever dared to ask me what was in it for him, I could have composed a long involved list. The list had grown nicely since that first morning in his bed. And diffusing all of this like a thin lilac fog was the possibility that Dan didn't actually see me the way other people did. He had at first, but he was half blind now, disabled by love.

Back in Vermont I bought the most expensive notepaper I could find and composed a mewling thank-you note. Three weeks later on our honeymoon in Montreal, Dan sent Ping and George a hotel postcard with two curt lines announcing what we'd done. When we got home Ping's presents were waiting, a sterling platter, a carton of monogrammed towels, and two sets of linen sheets, necessitating another thank-you note. That fall, anxiously anticipating Christmas, I got hold of a Tiffany catalogue and picked out some small silver items and got Dan to okay them. On Christmas Eve their present to us arrived, a bouquet of two dozen red roses and a printed card that promised a lavish bouquet every month for a year; I sensed Ping trying to appease me and was secretly pleased. The next day they called. The phone call, an annual tradition, was a parody of family gusto, with Dan stiffly jovial for three minutes before he hung up with the furious relief that always bestowed a febrile festivity on the rest of the day, spent with my parents around their ancient tree from Woolworth's with the grungy sprayed-on snow.

Dan always expanded in that cramped little house, but at Christmas he was a colossus of cheer, thumping Daddy's back and kissing Mom's head as he doled out their presents. That first year it was a goose-down comforter and their first cordless phone, among other things, all of which they accepted with the same bashful grace with which they had welcomed the miracle of Dan. It was as if deep down none of it was a surprise, just a continuation of the happiness I had always brought them. I was glad they liked Dan but I was naive enough to think their affection might compensate him for his own missing parents. The whole time Dan and I lived in Burlington,

Ping and George never visited; Dan would never invite them and they never invited themselves.

Of course Dan's money also contributed to our married style. Dan was like a fifties bride, he believed in the consumerism of marriage. The few items I brought to the condo from my apartment disappeared in the glut of acquisitions our union apparently required. "We need this," he would cry, hustling up to me in the store bearing a new style of grill pan, and I came to understand it was a cry of love. He was never profligate, I think he was just uncomfortable with the way money is invisible until it's spent. Like most people Dan always preferred the material to the abstract. "Money's so exact," he explained to me once when I kidded him about looking so happy when he was paying bills. It must have given him such pleasure to equip our new life with the kind of things that look expensive because they are. So I forgave him his inherited money and his disregard of it; he could never appreciate what it was like to be rich, he just was. And anyway I was learning how to be his accomplice in exquisite consumption, having decided that, given our other, more glaring inequity, it would be churlish of me not to.

My first contribution to our life as a couple was probably my suspicion that we weren't ever going to have too many mutual friends. We would have to work around that. If I was supposed to be the sensitive one, maybe I could be more so, especially to Dan, sensitive but not too complicated. I was taking a watercolor class when we met up again, and when he was so enthusiastic about my stillborn still lifes, I let him believe they were good. When he referred to me as "artsy" I never cringed; he had managed to find something exotic in me, something that gave him a little lift. ("Claud gets through three books a week.") I was grateful for Dan's conviction that life was a bunch of great moments you could string together like big colored beads on a very long string. His affluent conformity would cocoon me while my imagination slipped away to those places he couldn't go, even when he was stoned. The idea was that we were two tracks of a parallel running gag. We were one of those couples who figure out how to use their dissimilarities, who make fun of each other to preempt any real discussion or argument, lathering incongruity into sexual glue. We worked in a vacuum, we hardly saw anyone outside of work, but when Dan was opening another bottle of wine on a snowy night in front of the TV, we seemed in sympathy with each other, and our marriage was an intelligent and unique choice we had made.

But then, the second winter it was, he wanted a baby. We were snuggled on the couch, sitting through a Pampers commercial, when he said in a small sly voice, "Claud? I want one of those."

"You can't have it." I said it instantly, lightly. I felt winded.

"Why can't I?" he whimpered. It was supposed to be humorous.

"Because *I'm* still a child." Referring to the one thing I shouldn't have, my age. I had just turned thirty-two. Sure enough, when I glanced at him he was complacent. I put a tease in my voice. "You just want what you see."

"No I don't. We're married. I love you. Blah blah." Eyes on the screen. His hand creeping over my thigh. Starting to grin now, confident of success, of scoring. He was fumbling under my shirt, pulling my bra down. He squirmed around to lay his head in my lap and pushed my shirt higher. Raising his head, he fastened his lips to a nipple and started suckling. He groaned, mmm mmm, but his eyes were open, rolled up at me, his whole face fat with craving. He was demanding my desire, guzzling it out, and I could feel it trying to let go. I was thinking, This is natural . . . he does love you and he knows what he's doing, he's not all twisted and paranoid like you. We wrestled together and I was straining to meet him, straining to be happy, to *deserve* him and be right there where he was. Already I felt alone again, abandoned, as if Dan and his baby could just go on without me somehow. And then Dan was lying beside me, all floppy, rolling his head against my shoulder and making goo-goo eyes, and I was all right, I was back with him and we were normal, as normal as any two people contemplating such an irrevocable, terrifying thing. The room had settled back down. It was true what he said, it *was* time. There would never be anyone else. He was the right man. I thought, He's great, he's so blunt and natural he can still catch me off-guard. I could even imagine the baby there with us, a warm wriggling body lying on Dan's tummy, drooling nectar. It was okay, I was almost ready. I would give up my birth control next month. Once the reality of it had sunk in, I told him. He was quiet, he just grunted softly, gracious in victory

FOUR

W E WERE THE only people waiting that morning to see Dr. Kurth. Blue floral curtains cast us into a serene gloom guarded by hulking pieces of furniture, giant wing chairs, deep sofas, an antique armoire. The music was ersatz Bach. A coffee table was decorated with glossy reading material from which Dan had selected a Hammacher Schlemmer catalogue. He was beside me, legs spread, resting his feet on his heels, as relaxed as if he were slumped on our sofa at home. I noticed we had heedlessly marked the expanse of plush new carpet with our footprints, like animals crossing snow. In a distant corner a huge potted palm danced, battered by an airstream from the heating system. Dan, studying the catalogue with his usual look of haunted expectation, didn't see the nurse come in, a woman with a flat round face, bland as a bread roll. She blinked at me and went away again.

"This is cool, we should have one of these," he murmured, turning the page and excusing me from having to ask what the thing was.

Dan's looks had grown stronger. Even in high school he had had that decorative fineness, but since our marriage my attention had burnished him. Like Princess Diana during her epoch of mass adoration, he had come more into focus. The classic oversized features, the bruised deep-set eyes, the slightly puffy upper lip, they all added to his aura of spoilt inscrutable innocence. All that thick hair. He should have been truly handsome, the promise flickered behind his face like a loose lightbulb but never caught and held. If it had I would have seen it because I never stopped watching Dan. When he was asleep I liked to study the luxury of his face and try to imagine what it might feel like from inside. That day in the waiting room I was stealing my usual glances sideways, dosing my anxiety with glimpses of him. The shape of his knee under the sand-colored corduroy. The back of his hand, eloquently carved with the veins carrying his clean robust blood to his heart.

We waited a good twenty minutes before the nurse called me in. I followed her down a narrow hall into the consulting room.

As soon as I saw Dr. Kurth I understood I had been anticipating somebody like Jeremy Irons. This man was squat, only an inch or two taller than I was. His skin was sallow, his fleshy pendulous earlobes were sooty with fuzz. But when he took my hand and pressed it between his, I saw the warm liquid eyes of a friend, their interest in me intensified by the extremely thick lenses of his glasses. On my next visit, after showing me the inserts he would fit inside my face, even encouraging me to hold them—"Go ahead, experience them, they're yours"—he would look me over in such close-up I would dare to stare back through those lenses into his magnified pores, like tunnels boring into his skin. Mint-breathed, gallantly solicitous, he would rub my cheeks under his spatulate thumbs, intimately aware of the secret layer of me he was practically touching.

But all that was still to come. During this first visit—with Dan still out in the waiting room—Dr. Kurth was just genial and authoritative as he explained my best options. They were a septorhinoplasty (a nose job that would also make my breathing easier), an augmentation mentoplasty (chin implant), and malar implants to give me cheekbones. This could all be done at the same time and it would take four to five hours. At this point he stepped out in the hall and summoned Dan in. Dan sat down in the leather armchair next to mine to absorb the small monologue Dr. Kurth had launched from a friendly perch on the corner of his desk, while my attention attached itself like a leech to his stubby leg. It was dangling in an improbably debonair manner and a hairy yellow bruise was showing above his sock. His subject was *the imperative of the human visage,* a phrase I must have retained from the brochure we took home, because during his patter I was in a trance. I had already absorbed all I needed to know, which was that Dr. Kurth wasn't remotely like the cosmetic surgeons who wrote the chatty paperbacks I had been reading. He wouldn't ask me to bring him examples of my favorite nose ripped out of magazines. Dr. Kurth knew what I wanted, and I knew that, and he knew I knew. We were like future lovers just entering the first thrall of mutual recognition. The satisfaction of all his other women clung to him like wisps of perfume. And he was a very good doctor, there was no danger here. His various diplomas were hanging on the wall. His shoes were expensive loafers with tassels. His silver cuff links winked at me above his beefy hands, packed with compassion and expertise.

He wanted to know if Dan and I were both "okay" with the idea of surgery. Oh yes, we murmured as one. That wasn't good enough. Whose idea had it been? Dan kept mercifully quiet. As we sat waiting for me to volunteer the necessary admission, I realized I didn't want to sound *vain.*

"Claudia?" Dr. Kurth prodded gently.

"Yes . . ."

Apparently that was enough. We moved on. Summing up, Dr. Kurth told us what not to expect. He was talking to Dan but gazing at me in an indulgent ruminative way.

"I think what Claudia will find is that she's quite unchanged. A little tuned up, a touch more confident. It may give her a little psychological lift, but it won't affect whatever is essentially her."

Did he *believe* that? "Yes," I said. "Good."

Dan, in his firm buyer's voice, asked Dr. Kurth about his fee. I remember a figure just under ten thousand, which didn't include anesthesia or any of the other hospital expenses. "Fine," Dan announced. "No problem."

"I think we might be done here." Dr. Kurth edged his large bottom off his desk and Dan and I stood and shook his hand. We were all grinning like fools. As I stepped out into the hall, I was reentering a world that was so changed it made me light-headed. There was a vivid brimming significance about the office cubicle where I arranged my next appointment with the bread-roll nurse, wondering if Dr. Kurth couldn't do a little something to improve *her.*

After lunch downtown, Dan went back to the office. I called the paper and made some excuse and went home, feeling ragged. I tried to confer with my face in the mirror but it was as innocent as a blank piece of paper, it wouldn't give me a sign. I got the tequila out, poured a shot, and lay back on the sofa, my intention being to review all the worst moments of my vanishing life. I let it all come. Patti Dean, blond and wholesome as Heidi, making me her pet on the first day of grade school. The ballet recital. The interview for the museum job. I was trying to avoid thinking about how I was going to tell Kat.

A restaurant was not the best place to break the news, but it was the only way I could gracefully manage to get a drink in me beforehand. Once we were at the table I regretted the public nature of the place where we sat on display with our faces, Kat's dented ping-pong ball and my egg with a nose. For one moment, as our plates were set in front of us, I decided I didn't have to tell her. Kat for some reason was almost dressed up, with a new linen shirt on under her Fair Isle sweater. I admired it. We were always elaborate in our attention to each other's clothes.

I called it a nose job.

Kat's fork paused in midair. There was a tidy pause, a small one, calculated to honor the *small* news. I saw that she knew I had understated the case. Lied, in fact.

"My God. Claud. That's great." She put down her fork, swallowed, took up her glass, and had a sip of wine.

"Yeah, well. We'll see." I said this as darkly as I could.

"No, that's great. God. Go for it." She had some more wine. "Just in time for your move." I knew she hadn't planned to say anything that bald. "The move down south." She was floundering.

She asked questions, wanted to know when it would be, who the doctor was. For a while she was matter-of-fact, listening well and smiling convincingly, and then I noticed a certain crooning aspect had crept into her voice. "Oh, it's *always* been a good hospital, everybody says so." As if I were the one who needed reassurance and encouragement, when it was *Kat* who was changing, growing more and more desolate as my big train huffed away and left her standing there alone on the platform.

We only ever spoke about it again one other time, about two weeks later. We were in her apartment, just back from a shopping trip that had been her idea. She was curled up on her bed, making me try on the sweater she had insisted I buy, a black angora job with little silver buttons, fluffy and close-fitting, guaranteed to draw attention to my breasts and then bounce it straight up at my face. I got the sweater on and looked at Kat.

"Undo another button," she said, and I did. I also let some hair flop forward over my face. When I looked at Kat again she had a finger pressed to her lower lip. I knew I looked lurid and desperate.

I cocked my hip miserably, hoping to seem merely desperate for her opinion.

"Oh yes . . . definitely." She was pretending too. Her eyebrows were up in her hairline and her eyes glinted, her shrewd-troll look. I hated her for it. Everything I couldn't say to her was screaming in me.

"What," she said quietly.

"Kat, it doesn't *mean* anything. You know that."

She got up off the bed and came up close and put both her arms around me. She smoothed my hair down in the back, like a mother. We were maladroit and groping, our foreheads bumping, trying to hug and trying not to.

"I know. It's okay," she said.

We stepped apart and I turned away and pulled the sweater off and Kat took it and folded it back up into the bag.

Being photographed by Dr. Kurth's nurse was gratifying, with a dash of the specialness that attaches to being ill. The implication was that my problem had been diagnosed and the rest would be easy.

The big black-and-white prints, one frontal and one of each profile, have the stamp of infamy, like morgue photos, intimate and cold. I haven't looked at them in twenty years but I take precautions with that manila envelope. Right now I've got it taped to the bottom of the chest in the hall, well hidden but accessible in case of a fire.

I was feeling fairly well organized as the surgery approached. I had stopped working, my last day at the *Free Press* had been exactly five weeks before we were due to go south. I hadn't said a word to anyone there about the surgery, which was timed to give me just enough time to recover at home, do a bit of light packing, and pick up my last check (if I found the nerve, otherwise I would ask them to mail it) before we left. During the last few days before the surgery I started dismantling the closets. I was being very busy, trying hard to never quite focus on what was coming. I was trying too hard. There were bad dreams involving surgical waste. Horrible wet slop in a bucket, still moving. One night I dreamt my whole head had been removed, taken away, and stored in a locker. At least she'll get some air, a woman's voice said. I kept thinking there needed to be some last-minute documentation; my head computerized into gridded contours, rotating on a huge screen for an illustrious audience of doctors taking notes in the dark. Other times my agitation just collapsed into a gooey quiescence that was worse, when I brooded on how this could have happened. How could it all have gone so far? There was no going back now . . . back to *what*? I ricocheted between past and future, with no oasis in the present where I could draw breath and think calmly and make the decision again with my real brain. My most lucid moments were probably the flashes of certainty that what was about to happen amounted to theft. I was getting compensation I hadn't earned. Getting my way. Getting even.

And what was Dan thinking? Dan, whose idea it had been.

Did he rehearse what he was going to say or had it been in his mouth for years, squatting like a toad in there? Or was he just drunk? We were both throwing back the margaritas, juicing up our excitement about the transfer to North Carolina and tamping down our personal misgivings. Dan had wrapped his necktie around the blender and his sock feet were up on the table, straddling the little TV. The news was on. I was laying fish in the steamer when I felt his eyes on me and remembered I hadn't even combed my hair when I got home from work. I went to freshen up and hurried back to check on my fish. As I lifted the steamer lid Dan said it. He had to raise his voice over the TV.

"Hey Claud, new life and shit! Let's go all the way, what d'ya say? Let's get you fixed up!"

His father's very words coming out of Dan's mouth in our kitchen. My self-disgust ignited like tinder. I thought, idiotically, *He does know what you look like, he's known all along.* I poked my fish and set the lid back on the pot. I opened the fridge and found vegetables. Tears were coming, in a minute there would be a flood. I couldn't let him see me sobbing with joy. I didn't want either of us to have to endure that. I wanted to show him a thankful, sincere smile.

He got up a little unsteadily and came over to me. He was wearing a crooked face himself.

"Claud. Look at you." He grabbed my elbows and started wobbling my arms, turning my hands into rubber flippers. "You're *wasted*!"

I think that was nice of Dan. Decent of him. I'm not sure.

A second later it occurred to me I would be under extra pressure now to get pregnant. I couldn't hide my pills from him anymore. I would throw them out tomorrow, in a brave-new-world spirit. I could be honest if I were . . . different. Different was all I was daring to hope for.

And I did do it. I flushed the pills away, emptying the packet ceremoniously into the toilet, one by one.

I couldn't ask Dan why he'd brought it up or, more to the point, why not sooner? I would rather have cut my legs off. Not that he wanted to be asked. After that night he had thrown up a wall of indifference, draped in jaunty solicitude. He insisted I take a room at the hospital the night before the surgery and was there to help me get settled. When I came out of the bathroom he was bouncing on the bed, to test it. He had wanted me to see him doing this. He moved over so I could get in.

Behind him in the hall two young nurses were conferring. One was brunette in that plump uneventful way, the other was a blond Swedish type cheekboning her way through life, with scraped-back, don't-have-to-care hair. With their arms crossed over their chests, they kept glancing in at us. Their tribal instincts were aroused, I had snitched one of theirs. I put my hand on the back of Dan's neck, which made him lean in for a kiss. When I looked again the nurses were turning away in disgust, but as I flopped back on the pillow my vengefulness curdled. I had just smelled the hospital sheets.

"I'm going now," Dan said.

I was quiet.

"You want me to kiss your nose good-bye?"

"No. I'm fine," I said brightly. "You go. Good-bye."

He was getting up, pulling his parka off the chair. Once he left no one would see me again. Not Dan, or Kat, or my parents, who had always loved me *exactly the way I was.* I couldn't do it. I wanted to run to the mirror and apologize to the face I had been about to destroy. I was halfway to the bathroom when Dan grabbed me and tussled me backward onto the mattress.

"What's this now, you think you want to go home? You gonna change your mind? I don't think so, so just don't *do* this, all right? I've got enough shit on my plate with this move."

"I know."

I wasn't really contrite, I didn't care. I had suddenly traveled away from Dan into some long fuzzy tunnel of anticipation. It felt like my own skin.

"You know, this isn't exactly open-heart surgery here," Dan said, and a sense of the pure *triviality* of what I was doing slid through me like a flag unfurling. I would be fine. I was already healthy, I could only get better. Dan saw this, saw something. "Are you calm now?" He sat back down on the bed. "Anyway. I *love* you, all right?"

"I know. But then, you're crazy." I was crazy too now, I was oozing with hopefulness, smiling up at Dan to get him to smile.

"Crazy, yeah. This is true." But his smile seemed a little remote. Something stirring in there.

"You always have been." Beyond Dan's shoulder the blond nurse wandered by to check if he was still there. "Everybody knows that," I teased feebly, digging.

"Yeah, really . . ." He had a wormy inward look. "Some guy even said some shit to me once."

"What shit, what guy?"

"Oh . . . you know. Nothing much."

He was staring hard at my shoulder, waiting for me to help. "Where was this?"

"In a men's room. I had to . . . you know, *enlighten* him."

"But what did he say?"

"I forget. You know what I told him? That you were a real person, a *human being*, for fuck's sake. What a bozo. Okay. I'm outta here."

His last kiss was perfunctory, grudging, he was already regretting his confession. Then he was gone.

A *real person*. Oh Danny.

But that's exactly the way tactlessness functions, like mutant tact, deploying material that, aimed at a different target, would detonate as praise. Dan's defense of me would have flattered a pretty girl (my God, she's pretty *and genuine too*?). I understood that. I knew his attempt to justify my existence was not only chivalrous but obligatory, that there was an aspect of me that was sufficiently unreal to require some explanation. Which meant, by extension, that the surgery would make me less unreal. Therefore, paradoxically, more real. I stared at the plastic pitcher on the windowsill and tried to decide if it would look different tomorrow. Of course it would. So would the whole wide world. I would finally stop trying to ferret out everybody's physical flaws, discard my odious inverted vanity and become, by a magical irony, less vain. Good qualities—my dignity, my *acuity*—would survive the operation but they would show more, and as people would see the best of me, so would I of them. Pure benevolence would slosh back and forth in a great tidal flow between me and the rest of humankind.

You lie there waiting. In the limbo that follows the surgery, you don't have a face, just a parade of half-glimpsed conceptions, phantasms with features that fester up from the druggy swamps of your mind. After a few hours of that you're exhausted from not knowing, longing for a glimpse of your reflection in the TV screen or the spoon on your tray. When I managed to make it to the bathroom mirror, there was nothing to see but the tape bindings and a big plaster bandage, but I decided this was all right. The splint-like straps of tape provided a degree of decorum and privacy. My nose ached, but it wasn't excruciating. My cheeks were numb, my chin just felt sort of stretched. I slept off and on, never catching sight of either of the two nurses, and then Dan appeared in the doorway. He blanched, glanced back in the hall as if for help, and an old grandmotherly nurse came in and stood by while I got my clothes on. Dan put me into the car and drove me home.

All I had to do was tend my condition. Rinse my mouth with salt water, lie down with frozen tea bags on my eyes. It was forbidden to bend over so there wasn't much I could do to prepare for the big move except clean out a few drawers. I spent a lot of time pacifying Mom, poor Mom, who could empathize with a broken flower that wouldn't make it into the bouquet or the last uneaten cupcake on the plate. Her sympathy was devouring. Kat wasn't a problem, she knew I would call her when I was ready. All I could eat was soft food, mashed potatoes, white rice, chocolate pudding, all Dan's squishy favorites. The horrible food was a new bond between us. For Dan I think my inflated face was also a connection, something tender we were hatching together, like a fetus. Excused from my usual life, I allowed myself soap operas, entranced by my inability to compare the actresses' cheekbones to mine. As I lay there sedated by their giant close-ups, my hand wandered to my chin and tried to introduce the fact of itself to my sluggish brain, which responded with its own images: the inserts glowing under my skin like radium, the inserts lying pristine and perky on the floor of my coffin amidst all the maggoty rubble.

On day four Dan came home at lunchtime to take me to get the packing removed. I was out in twenty minutes, reeling from Dr. Kurth's instructions. He had said I should remove the tape myself after no more than a week. The stitches in my cheeks and chin would dissolve. He had also reiterated his advice about no sex for two weeks and then "very cautiously" for the week after that. I was worried for Dan but as the days passed I saw he didn't mind, and I didn't either. I was in a wasteland of expectation where nothing could breathe, certainly not desire.

One night during the second week—I was still taped up—Dan shook me awake, muttering something. My arm was tingling, I had been stroking it in my sleep. What are you *doing*? he said, disgusted but immediately asleep again. I lay awake with the light coming in from the bathroom, reflecting off my tape, throwing an insistent hygienic whiteness into my eyes. I was thinking the narcissism might be a good sign. My body was caressing itself out of some precocious cellular awareness: I was becoming truly desirable. I was like Frankenstein's bride, blinking and starting to believe she was alive. Which would make Dan my creator. I looked over at the gray lump of his shoulder. I pictured him writing out the check to pay for my surgery, a green one from his trust fund account. He was so safe, fortified by his act of largesse even when he was asleep, while I was stranded in limbo with my anticipation burning holes in my brain. I tried summoning up comrades, sick people lying awake in dark hospital rooms with bigger problems, like death dripping from the ceiling, but it didn't help. Then a vaporous impression of the South sifted over me, hot and damp as a greenhouse. Spanish moss swayed around the bed, I heard crickets and saw black people, and for the first time in years I remembered the little black girl. My first black person. She was sitting at the table in the principal's office, dressed in red. She had her back to me but I saw her fuzzy head, her severe parting and tight pointy braids. I could easily have missed her, it was sheer luck that I was out there in the hall, working on a mural for spring. I was doing jack-in-the-pulpits, at which I excelled.

She was working in a coloring book. A crayon was on the floor under her chair, and I went in and picked it up and handed it to her. She said thank you, barely glancing at me. I sat down, uninvited, but the woman who worked in the office was there, Mrs. Sample. She smiled and nodded and I saw I was being quietly, secretly, encouraged to keep the visitor company. She tore out a page of her book and passed it across to me. I set to work drawing on it—I scorned filling in lines—while I stole peeks at her hair, her red corduroy jumper embroidered with hearts, her wide mouth and nose, her two-tone hands. She knew I was looking, she was permitting it. She was cool under my eyes, but I knew that coolness felt hot inside. I wanted more of her, and found it: frosted blue nail polish that was almost all chipped off. No one else would have noticed that but I had. The whole room felt smooth and light, there was a glow, which would have been the undistilled seventies beneficence of Vermonters for any black person miraculously discovered in their midst. Teachers peeked in at us and smiled. She never looked up. She colored as if her life depended on it. While she worked she canted her head one way then the other like a sticky metronome, a show-off trick I hated normally. Not hating her for it made me like her even more. Then I sensed her mother in the hall, and as her bulk filled the door I immediately signed my drawing and rolled it up into a scroll; for some reason I was afraid of the mother. I handed the little girl my drawing and was trying to leave when I felt her poking my shoulder. She handed me her torn-out page, folded up small like a note. I ran to the bathroom to open it. It was signed too, but so lavishly I was stung. Hers said, From your friend, Joyce.

I don't know what they were doing in Burlington. I saw them an hour later from the school bus, they were coming out of a UVM building, picking their way down the messy sand-strewn steps toward the taxicab waiting at the curb, a novelty in itself. They were completely unaware of me, I had been forgotten. But that night, remembering them as I lay there being afraid of the future, and my face, and the South filled with beautiful women, Joyce glanced up and saw me on the bus and waved. She forgave me my stingy signature, my curiosity, the way I looked. She probably didn't even know I was ugly. In her gentle aplomb she was perfect, complete, a little effigy of herself that I could tuck away and take with me to North Carolina, and everything would be fine.

FIVE

THREE WEEKS AFTER the surgery, when the dirty tape on my face was gummy and frayed, Dan said it had to come off. A commercial had just interrupted the movie we were watching in bed. "Come on, up you get. I'll see you in the bathroom. I want to make sure he didn't just beat you up and send me the bill."

He came in after me, lowered the toilet seat, and sat down. I just stood there in front of the mirror, stiff with terror. I knew this was it, there was no way out now, but nothing happened. My hands wouldn't go to my face. Dan stood up without a word and stepped between me and the mirror and got hold of the tape by my left ear. *You know there's a chin there, you know that.* I tried to get ready, taking deep breaths, watching the back of Dan's head in the mirror. I felt the tug of the tape leaving my face. Dan stepped back and I thought, *It's okay, I'm ready.*

I heard a wounded croak. I glanced at Dan and noticed in a detached way that he looked frightened, eyeballs skinned, features slack. Looking back at the mirror, I saw that the woman was familiar. Those were my lips. I licked them. That was my forehead, but somehow it was smaller. And my eyes. They were farther apart now. The nose was small, very small. There were cheekbones.

I was gone.

"Claud? Holy shit." Dan was hoarse. "Geezum. This guy . . ." We were both staring, frozen. "Is he like a genius or what? . . . *Say* something. Can't you still *talk*?"

Either he was desperate to believe what he was seeing or desperate not to. "What d'ya think? *Claud?*" I remember a frantic note in his voice, as if he needed to make sure this person answered to the same name.

He was beside me now in the mirror, drained, anxious, ready to leave this moment behind. I watched him take a step back and angle sideways, getting ready to high-five me, I think, when he suddenly noticed how the woman in the mirror had locked her eyes onto mine.

Poor Dan. There were no words for it. "God, what an improvement"? I didn't even have any words in my *mind* yet. I think I didn't quite understand.

Two days later I slipped out to the *Free Press* where they had my final check waiting. I could tell the girls at the front desk had seen me coming, they were trying too hard to occupy themselves as I walked up the hall. When they finally raised their heads they both blinked, hard and fast, then came that mincing smile people wear when they've just spotted a celebrity in their midst. A split second later they both managed to look almost nonchalant as they tried to frame compliments, but nothing too flatulent, nothing that would suggest there had ever been anything *that* wrong with me. (Gail's tremulous solution was "Looking good, Claudia.") My job as the celebrity was not to notice them making bug eyes at each other as I walked back out.

The only people who didn't perform this sequence were the ones who didn't even recognize me. At the Food Fayre the checkout girl did a double take when she saw the name on my check. That was fun, I even told Dan. The next time I went there the word was obviously out and a couple of the checkers threw me shy little sidelong glances of congratulation, wanting me to know they knew and they were glad. No one minded or objected, that was the shock. There was no argument. Who ever argues with a face? A face is a fact. People accepted it, even people at work, who knew me, who *knew where it came from.*

Dr. Kurth had mentioned this, calling it the psychology of change. The only person this magic excluded was me. *Was* I pretty? As a girl

with a pretty face, was I thus now a pretty girl, the way a large dog
with brown fur is a large brown furry dog? At home I was enjoying
catching Dan stealing looks at me but in public I slunk through
those first days with my head down and my sunglasses on. It wasn't
enough. *"Hey!"* I remember the exact boyish yelp, like a rip in the
air. I was loading my grocery bags into the trunk. "Hey! Over here!"
I remember the slow helplessness of my head lifting and my eyes
skidding over the sea of car roofs. He was wearing a red ski cap, a boy
years younger than me, wailing as I got in the car and slammed the
door. "Wait, where ya *goin? Don't go yet!"*

From Ping, surprisingly—maybe she had been alerted by a terse
postcard from Dan ("Claud fixed")—came two dozen lilies, followed an hour later by a UPS delivery, a shiny black plastic designer
makeup kit the size of a laptop. The card said, "Darling, so pleased
for you! Pix ASAP?!!" Composing my thank-you note, in which I
promised I'd have Dan take some pictures as soon as the swelling
went down, I had a nice image of Ping in her living room, eagerly
checking her mail every day.

At home I was too busy now to keep running to the bathroom mirror, I took the mirror from over my dresser and propped it on the sofa
in the living room, thinking I'd assimilate the new face by repeated
exposure as I went back and forth. I couldn't have guessed how it
would hide in the mirror like a wild thing waiting to leap out of its
cage at my head. Every few hours I stopped and called my mother,
to forestall my long-overdue visit to her and Daddy. I organized
books and emptied closets, searching out old photos of myself to destroy. There weren't many. But in a box under the bed I found our
wedding pictures, just Kodak snaps in a drugstore mini-album, making me wonder for the first time why Dan hadn't wanted them en-
shrined in a leather album. I noted the understated splendor of the
groom and the tacky excess of his little mouse-bride with her puffy
homemade dress and her too many flowers. What was going on
here? In one shot she was in profile, beaming at him from under a
bridal hat that was like a mushroom swaddled in cobwebs. I could

feel my heart breaking for her. But weaseling through that sadness were the first cagey stirrings of elation, and worse. *Joy*. Which I tried to beat back. Joy was wrong, it sneered at whatever joy that little mouse had known. Surely she had known some, but *how?* And yet here she was on her wedding day, flashing a blinding smile. Pictures don't lie. She must have been ecstatic on this most ecstatic of days?

Of course, she was agreeing through teeth that seemed gritted. *Look at him!*

Well. If that's all you want. Has he got any brains, is he . . .

He's a good man. . . . He's just a little screwed up, he needs me to help. . . .

I saw the possessive way her freshly bejeweled hand was resting on his arm. Now her plain face had turned sly. *. . . and rich enough to buy me something I want.* I turned the page over. In the the next picture the bride and groom were just another mismatched couple — aren't they all? — with every right in the world to tear down the court-house steps together into the great unknown. I flicked through the rest of the pictures, buried the album in a box of underwear, and went to the mirror in the living room. Correcting my harried ex-pression and trying to suppress the disbelief that still flared in my eyes, I was turning away when I just glimpsed, as if through a crack, that crippled pride I had always kept so diligently hidden.

When I told Dan I was going to visit my parents without him, he acted a little peeved. I tried to joke. "Honey, this is just for us tonight. Only gene-pool members are allowed."

"Yeah, you said that already. I just don't get why."

I didn't tell him that having spent years listening to the exhaust-ingly casual way my parents had delivered all the beauty homilies — can't judge a book by its cover, beauty's only skin-deep — I needed to be alone with them when I brought them the incontrovertible evi-dence that I had never believed a word.

Not that my mother had either. Maybe mothers think their chil-dren are blind. A thousand times I must have watched her run the lipstick around her mouth and grind her lips savagely together and blink her satisfaction at the mirror, holding the moment just a little too long. My poor mother. I can picture her, dutifully searching her own even features for a clue to what could have gone wrong; she would have wanted to assume full responsibility. (Or maybe not. I like to think she called in some help, and blamed her mother-in-law's nose; maybe she guessed her father had worn a beard his whole life to hide a weak chin, a version of which he bequeathed to Uncle Ham.) I do know she suffered as she marked my progress, waiting for me to grow into my glamorous name. All that sewing she did for me, the endless fittings and the stabbing of pins and yanking of the cloth, when our hopefulness would condense in a little miasma around my head. Years she spent at it, curling my hair, sending me off to neighborhood birthday parties dressed to the teeth, equipped with lavish presents I gradually realized she and Daddy couldn't afford.

Was she protecting me from the world, or the world from me? Crying, *Honey, look!* at every sunset, every snowdrop and clipped poodle, begging me to notice the world's beauty in all its glorious particulars, as if she understood that looking out at the world is the only antidote to being looked at. Maybe she did understand, except that with every repetition of the sacred truth that looks didn't matter she was just reinforcing how much they did. She couldn't win. Sniffing the future for threats to my composure, she contaminated it with her dread. I suppose she must have turned to God about this, but while he was advising her on the redemption of suffering (ours— hers and mine) she would have been arguing back at him, defending her right to pace like a she-wolf at the mouth of her lair, determined to be ready for the moment when I would discover how different I was. She didn't know it had come and gone.

She must have known about Patti Dean and her dominance over me, but she couldn't have dreamt its cleverest manifestations. Kids are way too smart for that, they know just how far they can take it. That kid Timmy on Church Street that day, an elfin ten-year-old shooting my mother a precisely calibrated smile. *Hi, Mrs. Isham!* She was disarmed. *Well, hello there!* Then while I ignored him he turned the smile on me. *Hi, Hazel!* When he was safely past my mother looked down at me, laughing. *Hazel?!* Short for Witch Hazel, one of my tamer nicknames. She had no idea. She couldn't save me. I would sooner have died than told her there was anything

I needed to be saved from. That would have revealed I knew the thing I wasn't supposed to know. I couldn't do that. Everything was going to be fine. It *was* fine. So we guarded each other that way, my mother and I, and ourselves.

That night as I was driving over to my parents' house through a slush of new snow, heading for the pot of tea my mother would have waiting, I was envying her, wishing I had something that straight-forward to give her in return.

My parents didn't come to greet me. As I took my coat off in the hall I heard whispering from the living room. They were letting me make an entrance. Struggling with my boots, I wanted a bag to put over my head, I felt preposterous, but when my mother called out, *Hi sweetie, we're in here!* with that quaver in her voice, it re-leased a jittery little jet of defiance, which helped. I stood up and walked into the blaze of overhead light where they stood waiting side by side.

I stalked up to them, crazily, right up close. My mother's small blue eyes stared, blinked once, and overflowed. Twigs of wetness shone on her powdered cheeks. She pressed her trembling fingers over her eyes for a minute. I wanted to do that too, my face was on fire. Daddy was very flushed. My mother looked at him, fingering her collar, silently beseeching him to say something. He pulled thoughtfully on his nose.

"Well now . . . that's a relief. I reckon you're still pretty to me."

I made a little snorting chuckle and my hand rose helplessly to my nose, a bit too forcefully. *"Ow."* We all laughed at that, Mom through a fresh burst of weeping. Then carefully, clumsily, we jostled into a brief embrace. When Mom disengaged and backed away to get another perspective, she bumped into the coffee table. We all laughed again as she sniffled off to the kitchen.

Daddy and I stood listening to the sounds of tea-making. We heard Mom blow her nose. The atmosphere around Daddy and me relaxed, becoming conspiratorial, almost festive. He was already at ease with the new brown dog. I barked once or twice in my head.

"She's discombobulated, worrying about you and all," Daddy said. "But it's over."

"Well, now she's worried about how you'll be living down there and she won't be able to remember what you look like."

There was no answer to that. I removed myself to the couch and Daddy settled into his old grubby recliner. The room's familiarity almost obscured it, but now that the moment of revelation was behind me I was feeling a pious obligation to try to really appreciate the old place. I pondered the imitation Delft plates, newly relocated to a shelf Daddy had built into the brick wall behind the television. I tried to remember when his lava lamp had finally been retired.

"That doctor knows his stuff," Daddy offered.

"No flies on him," I rejoined.

"Nobody'd ever accuse him of going to school for the lunch." There was a pause. "I guess you probably still feel like your old self though."

I would sidestep this. "Daddy, you know how many rhinoplasties this guy does a month?"

"That's the nose? Ten?"

"Fifty," I guessed.

"That's a lot of happy noses. Happy pockets for him too, I reckon."

"You bet."

I returned Daddy's smile, and felt the room contract and squeeze my breath back into my bursting heart. Easy easy *easy*, being here. Too easy, sitting here now after those long years. I glared at the hideous plates I'd known all my life and the reason for the difference between that life and the new one shriveled and withered in me like a salted slug. I wanted to grind it under my heel. A prettier nose? More *chin*? I wanted to howl and rage and smash up the furniture.

"Funny thing is," my father ventured, "you don't look all that different."

"Daddy, what are you, *blind*?"

The tea tray approached, clinking. Mom edged through the door with three stemmed glasses and a bottle of supermarket champagne on the tray, along with the tea and cookies, but I was too sodden to cry, *Oh champagne!* or even stand up to help her. With a ladylike grunt she set the tray on the coffee table, a maneuver made trickier by the Polaroid camera hanging around her neck.

"Sweetie, I know I'm a nuisance and all, but . . ." She glanced at Daddy, who was gaping at me, mouth open. When he saw me looking at him, his eyes skimmed over to Mom. "We're just not going to have enough time to . . . get used to the . . . your new . . . how pretty you . . ."

"I can't be photographed for another three weeks." Daddy was getting up to uncork the bottle. "Doctor's orders." Mom looked stricken as I held up my glass. "Mom, I'm kidding, it's okay, go ahead. Fire when ready."

It *was* okay. It was great. Could there possibly be a bigger, brighter, more American Kodak moment than this one?

The cork popped, the champagne foamed. We lifted our brimming glasses. We waited a moment but no toast came. We drank. Mom put her glass down and started fiddling with the camera, a recent birthday present from Dan. The perfume of his money wafted agreeably into the room.

"Danny's taken lots by now, has he?" my mother said, leaving the other question hanging: What does he *think*?

"Nope, you're the first."

"Oh gosh, really? Okay, I'm all set."

"Wait." I didn't want to be holding a glass of champagne, celebrating myself, it would be grotesque. I set the glass on the tray. I didn't want to be sitting down either, peering plaintively up at her. The flash burst. I was blind, caught in a green dazzle as the Polaroid ground through its procedure. Mom plumped down beside me. I could just make out the white square she was balancing on her knees, as its blankness, like mist burned off by the sun in my eyes, dissolved into nostrils and eye sockets and the shadings of . . . a face. Not gorgeous, no. Pretty. Quite pretty. Officially stamped with the unequivocal authority that prettiness confers. It was all true. The shortening of the nose had released the eyes into a more comfortable relationship, and the mouth no longer had to scrabble up under the nose to keep from sliding into my neck. It was safe now and looked it, relaxed in a modest half smile ideally positioned between the smooth chin—was that the hint of a cleft?—and a very short but refined nose. Even the nostrils were well cut and almost

haughtily elegant in their reference to the upper cheeks. All the features referred to each other. This was the "facial harmony" Dr.
Kurth had talked about. No part was out of sympathy with the others but the whole was more than the sum of its features. I could see
why people had believed it. I believed it. This woman had been in
side me, sleeping, patiently waiting for the kiss of the knife. All my
life the despised mole above my mouth had been her beauty spot.

Glancing up, I caught my father's warm wet eye. When I looked
back at the Polaroid, it looked even better. Mom had fished out her
glasses and was bent over it, holding it pinned to her knees as if it
might fly away.

We made small talk. I told them my car was being driven down by
a student Dan had hired, which led on to a discussion of the route
and how long it would take to get there. We had innately grasped a
rule we hadn't known existed before. The surgery was not to be referred to now, or ever again. It had not happened, there was no after
and no before.

Before I left I went up to my old room on the pretext of picking
something up. I stood in the light coming from the hall, in front of
my old mirror on the closet door. All I heard from below was silence,
the sound of them communing with the spirit of their lost ugly girl.
My mind was silent too, unable to form any apology that wouldn't
blame them for a crime they hadn't committed. The face was different again in this half-light, the cheekbones sharper, the eyes hol-
lowed in alabaster. Behind me the light sprawled across the bed
where that girl used to sit with her books, waiting, trying to be profound, poor child, so doggedly hopeless. She was staring at me, daring me to do what I had done.

At the front door Mom started losing it again. My father put his
arm around her shoulder and gave her a rather absent hug and
stared at me with cloudy eyes that might have been remembering
the years he'd spent trying to build a big love-filled future for me in
his head. It occurs to me now that maybe his fatherly hopes had
even driven him, just once, to try to imagine himself happily in bed
with somebody as unappealing as me.

My father clasped the back of his neck and said what he always said. *Be my good girl.* My mother leaned forward and kissed my face reverently, like someone in a movie pressing her lips to a framed photograph.

Dan was in the hall when I came in. "So?"

"They were speechless."

"Fuck. I wish I'd *been* there. Claud, you know what? You look really wiped."

I went into the bathroom, locked the door, brought Ping's makeup kit out from under the sink, and pried one of the little foam-padded sticks out of its slot. I obliterated my timid eyeliner with kohl and blended it in, then used some eye shadow and lipstick and blusher. I put eye shadow on the bone under my eyebrow, blending one shade into another, using the brushes now, and my little finger. I made a few attempts at outlining my mouth with a pencil before it was right, working intently, trying to paint my face into permanence. Dan was snoring when I came out, veneered in makeup. I got into bed, carefully face up, like a mummy, and then I cried. I could feel the greasy color running into the pillow. My whole face was dissolving with a fierce bitter relief. That was easy. But my gratitude was still balked, dammed up in me. I didn't know how to discharge it.

In the morning I called Kat. She had told me she'd be home but her machine answered. I left a message and then went to Dr. Kurth's office for the "after" photographs. The nurse was gruff with me, disgruntled that it was too soon for them. When I got home there was no message from Kat. She knew I was leaving the next day, she didn't want to see me. I knew this with some certainty, because I didn't want her to see me. Confident she would be screening her calls that night, I called after dinner and told the tape good-bye. I promised to write. I can see her standing there next to her drawing board, listening. Her mouth is a thoughtful little pucker and her eyes flick here and there around the room where we spent all that time together. She wishes me well but she can't afford any tears.

SIX

WE DIDN'T HAVE a place to live waiting for us in Beasley, we just sailed down there, the second week of March. I have to admire Dan for being willing to make the change. I have to admire him for working at all, when he could have supported us both off his trust fund. My own plans for Beasley were unformed, I hadn't been able to concentrate on specifics yet. After so long at the *Free Press*, I wasn't in any hurry to find graphic design work. Dan had some idea I should write and illustrate books for children, an idea that vaguely repelled me, although I never said so.

As Dan raced us along the interstate, coaxing hiccups from his new radar detector, I was busy trying to provoke a reaction from every male driver we passed, staring at the side of his head until the split second he felt compelled to glance over at me, when I immediately averted my gaze and waited to feel his attention suck at my cheek. Once I had this down, I decided to initiate eye contact for the first time since I was six, lifting my gaze like a double-barreled shotgun. The guy was middle-aged, with a pockmarked dilapidated face. Did he cringe? God no. He didn't smile either. This was serious. We were coupling, our entwined eye beams taut as a rope that shuddered with every reluctant glance he had to make at the road. Finally as Dan passed his car the rope stretched and snapped and my eyes stung with tears. Who were all these men, *where had they been?* But of course they'd always been there, it was me who'd been missing. I faded, I disappeared again for a minute, but then Dan, extracting an Oreo from the bag on the dashboard, brought me back. I emptied my mind. I watched a scrap of paper riding an updraft. We were sailing up a hill, rapidly overtaking a lumbering van whose driver, wearing a moth-eaten fur hat, was thrusting his head in a geeky way and grinning sideways at our car. I finally comprehended he was pretending to urge his old van faster so he could keep me in view. His passenger—ponytail, equally big grin, kind of like Dan's horrible old friend Gary, *was* it Gary?—leaned past him and blew me a kiss. In my memory they have a grisly charm, like a man with two goony heads.

We stopped for the night somewhere near the Delaware Memorial Bridge, a Holiday Inn. In the lobby on our way to dinner, something was lacking ... the frisson our combined effect had always produced. An older couple checking in at the desk threw us a glance that was blandly cordial. So this is what it's like, I thought. It was like nothing, like being dead and discovering you really can walk through walls. My face felt shellacked. I concentrated on the back of Dan's head as we went into the dining room. When the food came I ate decorously and tried to avoid looking at the man sitting alone behind Dan. He was glancing from his food to me, back and forth, using his eyes with the finesse of a kid whacking a ball against a garage. For years I had watched men do this to women, but now I was having a hard time believing I was the woman. If it were me, I would know what to do about it, I wouldn't be trapped like this. Ignoring this man's attention took every fiber of my concentration. I used the fake chrysanthemums, Dan's parsley, anything, not to look back at him. Finally the waitress was taking his credit card, he was leaving. A few minutes later, as if his desire had been carried to me on spores, I wanted to be upstairs in bed with Dan.

I was ready when he came out of the bathroom. The only light was the TV, with the sound turned off. Dan crawled toward me over the foot of the bed while I peered at the mirror of his face and waited for him to tell me how good I looked. But then a different thing happened. I told him.

"You are my beautiful man." Naked, the vein pounding in his forehead, he was no more beautiful than the last time we'd made love, but I had had more to protect then. "Where'd you come from?" A knot was unraveling, a new generosity opening in me. "Who *are* you?"

"Your husband. Remember?"

"Oh not mine, you *can't* be."

He was kicking away the sheet, smearing the nightgown over my hips, thrusting a thumb in.

"Danny?"

He was knocking my legs open with his knee. "That's me."

"Let me catch up. Just give me a minute, will you?"

But he was in, riding, eyes shut. I bucked obligingly but I was tepid now, remote and alert. I could feel the TV light on the new shape of my face, pristine as a snow-carved landscape. He would look in a minute, his eyes would open to confirm the outrageous thrill of his dick inside a new wife. They did finally. Like car headlights his gaze angled over the headboard, the pillows, and the top of my head, which was being ground into the headboard by his thrusting. I followed his progress, waited for his juddering finish, his ostentatious sigh as he rolled off me. That was familiar at least, his obvious contentment.

"Love you."

"Love you."

Over and out. He would look next time.

The next day I was too peaceful for yesterday's game. Now I was concerned for the other people on the road, alarmed by their frailty as they hurtled into their haphazard futures while mine was so secure. Sunlight swam through the car and pooled in my lap.

When the first exits for Richmond, Virginia, appeared, Dan confidently chose one that dropped us into weed-choked dereliction. "Shit. No problem." He aimed the car at a distant cluster of skyscrapers and drove quickly through streets lined with decomposing brick row houses, patrolled by small groups of black men. Soon we were among office blocks, searching for what finally presented itself

as a green awning over an oak door flanked by potted palms. We put
the car in a lot and walked back along a main street thronged with
lunchtime crowds. It was ten degrees warmer than it had been in
southern Jersey, and the air held the mildewed tang of moisture
drawn from cold cement. Real spring sunshine bore down on the
long smoky vista of silhouetted heads. Most of them were black.

There were more white people in the restaurant, but not many.
As we settled into our booth Dan said, "Okay. Spot quiz. Tell me
everything you know about black people. They dance really good,
right?"

I ignored him. He knew how few black people there were in
northern Vermont. Our waiter was a light brown man about our age,
with an impassive face. He was trim in his uniform of white shirt and
black slacks, ready with his order pad. When Dan told him I wanted
clam chowder and a side order of potato skins, he pinched one eye
shut.

"Those skins can be kinda nasty," he said.

"How so?" said Dan. Without looking at him, I knew he was trying to catch my eye.

"I think what she wants is some fries."

"I do?"

"What's the matter with the skins?" asked Dan.

"Yeah, you do. . . ." He was looking straight at me now, tapping
his pad, suppressing a smile.

"*Thank you.*" Dan flicked his napkin into his lap. "Christ
Almighty."

When the waiter brought the food he set the fries down with a
minute flourish Dan missed. Watching him walk away it occurred to
me he might be descended from slaves.

Back in the car I worked out the numbers. It was conceivable
that his great-grandparents had been born during the Civil War or
shortly after. His grandmother could still be alive, propped in front
of a nursing home TV, listening to some black reporter talk about
cyberspace while old family slave stories flickered like guttering candles inside her head. This telescoping of time flavored our departure

from Richmond. It made the mirror-clad corporate headquarters and outlet malls look phony, rudimentary, as if they'd been thrown up in a hurry to distract from the appalling past.

Just below the North Carolina border we exited at Roanoke Rapids, onto a two-lane road of old tar-stippled cement that would cut straight across to Beasley. The change livened Dan up.

"Hey, li'l Sis." He was trying out his Southern accent. "That thar's what we call King Cotton."

The vast field of brown leafless bushes looked as if it had been sprayed with wet kleenex. We didn't know it had been harvested the previous fall. White blobs still clung to the acreage of bushes stretching to a distant line of trees, a vastness of cotton, waiting for the pickers my imagination was supplying, women in long dresses with babies on their backs, and men in straw hats, hauling their sacks down the rows as they bent over the plants, oblivious to the great black birds drifting in the haze.

"Hot *damn*, honey, lookit the sahz of them crows!"

Dan lowered our windows and the yeasty warmth of the fresh-plowed soil poured in. We were on the great coastal plain now, flatland sectioned into fields and huge tracts of pine. We shared the highway with local pickups, and eighteen-wheelers hauling shaggy lengths of pine as long as telephone poles, thundering at us with their blinding chrome and raucous bumper stickers. DIXIE AND PROUD! TRUCKING FOR JESUS! Four-square to the road the old abandoned wood-frame houses seemed to hover over the land, an illusion induced by foundations that were just neat stacks of brick at each corner. They were beautiful stark houses, mostly two-story, with pitched tin roofs and front porches that ran their whole width. The one-story version, little more than a shack, I knew from one of my favorite paintings: a still night out in the fields, the doctor's Model T pulled up in the dirt yard, the door standing open and inside in the yellow light a wizened black woman tucked up in bed, waiting for the chariot being drawn down from a boiling purple sky by a team of winged horses.

A dry landscape, archaic, heat-preserved. Rocking chairs oblique to the point of collapse waited on porches for people to come back. Ancient oil drums wept rusty streaks onto their sun-bleached wooden cradles. Here and there an outhouse had survived, or a sagging barn with its dark rhomboid mouth revealing the shadowy husk of a car. Some houses had lost chunks of their porches or were smothered in vines but most were intact, as singular and sincere as black-and-white photographs of themselves. Even their yards seemed frozen in time, accented with a funereal cypress or two, or a camellia dropping blood-red petals onto the bone-colored grass.

I speculated on whether these houses might still have furniture in them.

"Oh sure," Dan said. "Early American corner cupboards, Fiesta ware, Maxfield Parrish —"

"Old *stuff*, I just meant. Belongings. It's like people just went. Where'd they all go?"

"Snakes. Rats. Spiders as big as your hand."

Suddenly, on a cratered porch, we saw two little black kids tumbling over a gutted armchair.

"Dan . . . people are living in there."

"Bummer."

And then another faded little house, with a car parked out front and out back work clothes blowing on a line.

"I see it," he said. "No need to get dramatic. People are poor here like everywhere else. It's not *all* like this." But his reassurance held a querulous note; if we did find ourselves swallowed up in this decrepit simplicity — I knew how unappetizing it must look to him — it would be my fault.

Almost since we'd been married I had been encouraging Dan to try to get a transfer out of Burlington. Dan would have stayed forever. That was one of the differences we tapped regularly, my gloom and his glee about the huge branches of upscale chain stores, the availability of twig furniture and carpaccio and French shaving soap. He seemed to think this was still the real Vermont. *Geezum crow*, he said every other minute, and when I pointed out that while *I* knew he was using this euphemism ironically, most natives didn't, and it just made him sound hickish, he laughed. I know I was sour. I was always pining for the days when plain perfect things — leather-bound books with blank vellum pages, linen nightgowns — had just existed, in nature, as it were, not as merchandise designed to make people feel discerning and superior. I tried to admire Burlington's cele-brated metamorphosis but to me the town was a theme park (Real New England College Town) full of bouncy affluent Vermont-ized intruders wearing distressed Gap ball caps to confer on themselves a fake history of New England summers. The worst part was the way the real Vermonters aped them. I would sooner have died than use the term *leaf peeper*. I resented all of it. It was as if Burlington's vul-gar self-consciousness was always trying to make fun of my trying to be aloof and special and high-minded.

A new setting was what I needed, and here it was. In North Caro-lina time seemed to have just plodded on, without taking any cute shortcuts, aside from the trailers parked beside the old farmhouses they had been hauled in to replace. Instead of the tracts of artful half-million-dollar houses that had eaten up all the fields around Burlington, there were mobile homes everywhere. There were cor-roded streamlined models, and long rectangles fastened with car-ports and decks to pristine lots featuring birdbaths and gazebos, and the latest variations, masquerading as ranch houses. Ranch houses were the predominant architecture. The ones I liked best were long and low, set way back from the road amidst towering pines whose random elegance suggested columns decorating a stage. Each tree rose from the exact center of a huge mound of raked-up needles, this laborsaving meticulousness investing the house with a succinct glamour, like a mini–country club. Similar grandeur was supplied by all the sculptural plants, the spiked yuccas and fans of palmetto, though their lavishness was offset somewhat by a planting style whereby front walks and driveways were lined with identical shrub-lets, as evenly spaced as if they'd been drawn in by a child. On lots as flat as tabletops these houses rolled by. Inside, through storm doors that were just big panes of Plexiglas, I saw glowing TVs and a woman blow-drying her hair and a child sitting on its yellow plastic potty. This seemed to be a place without secrets. I thought it might be short on the sort of snobbishness that encourages sequestered habits. A typical stretch of road might present, along with the ranch houses and trailers, a whopping brick showplace fitted out with stained-glass windows and Greek statues, directly across the road from a body shop disgorging oily car parts. The democratic flavor was tinged with a formality hallowing the glorious past. Even the most ramshackle brick shoe box had vestigial pillars and a porch, sometimes carpeted, offering a hospitable symmetry of plastic chairs and urns.

It was all so unaffected. The shutters nailed up beside windows were cheerfully fake, the cement lions guarding trailer-park driveways were just droll and good-natured, not pretentious. Also droll were the plaster life-sized collie dogs chained to front porches, though I wasn't sure if they were there to welcome visitors or ward them off. Bare bushes were studded with big plastic Easter eggs and there were more American flags flying than I had ever seen outside a parade. Front doors were rarely left undecorated, but the straw hats and dried flower wreaths that had always depressed me in Vermont struck me as more sincere here. Even the nylon banners, an epidemic of butterflies and golf balls and Snoopy cartoons, seemed somewhat more justified by the sunshine backlighting their lurid purples and lime greens. The ribbon clusters (pink or blue) that people stuck on their roadside mailboxes to celebrate their new babies reinforced the impression that living here involved everybody in some type of party. Such well-ordered conspicuous solidarity must mean contentment. Maybe happiness. Certainly everybody seemed in agreement that generally life was okay and they were all doing just fine.

Dan wanted a soda somewhere along in here. We veered off the highway into an eerily authentic-looking little town, like a set for a period film. There was a dusty storefronted main drag, a pool hall, a tired luncheonette ornamented with an archaic round Coca-Cola sign. Two women walking along the street were wearing dresses. A black couple holding a baby peered into a closed jewelry store. Dan pulled into a corner gas station with an old rickety canopy protecting the forecourt, and I swung myself out into this scene, pulling off my sweater to get some sun on my arms. Across the street was a plain brick building with a deep tin-roofed porch and a wooden sign over the front door that said TOWN HALL. Beside it in a little grass plot was a granite plinth neatly ringed with pansies. A young Confederate soldier stood on top, carved in pale gray stone. While Dan fed the Coke machine I went over for a better look. The soldier's square-toed boots were just level with the top of my head With his canteen strapped across his chest and his rifle held at the ready, he stared over my head into hope and glory. Dan came up and handed me a cold can of soda.

"What's weird about this?" I said.

"Nothing. Don't you love that uniform? I had one of those canteens."

"Have you ever seen a Civil War monument in the North, where they actually won?"

"Hey now, li'l gal. We mahta done lost the damn war, but we fought *hahd.*"

Dan followed me around the plinth as I read the inscription out loud. " 'This monument erected by the Addison County Monument Association. A.D. 1902.' Dan, this list of soldiers this is in honor of? They're mostly the same guys that are on the monument committee on the other side." I scoured the area for a human target for my scorn. A heavyset guy of about twenty-five was just lowering his rear end onto the town hall steps.

" 'The Confederate soldier' "—I read loudly off the back of the plinth—" 'won, and is entitled to, the admiration of all who love and honor liberty.' Hmm. Do you think that might include any of the you-know-whos?"

"You're being an asshole."

" 'In appreciation of our faithful slaves,' " I read. "Oh. That's okay then."

I peeked out to check on the guy. Nothing was moving but his cigarette smoke. "Let's go," Dan said.

The guy was unfolding himself from the steps.

"Hey!" he called lazily. "Y'all ain't from around here! Where y'all from?"

"Vermont!" we cried as one, trying to warn him we were too alien to approach.

"Ver-mont." He was in front of us now. His eyes were like patches of clear blue sky. "Is that purty up there?"

"Sure is." Dan had relaxed.

"Lots of mountains," I volunteered.

"Yeah, I heard that," he said dubiously. "I heard it was purty." He stuck the cigarette in his mouth and spoke around it. "Ashley Tetterton, Jr." He stretched out a hand. Dan took it and introduced me. Ashley pulled the cigarette out. "Ma'am." During his ponderous once-over his gaze settled for an instant in mine and I could feel, like a caul on my face, the prettiness I was automatically submitting to him.

"Did you grow up here?" Dan was asking. I knew he had forgotten the name of the town.

"My kin's all over in Palmyra."

"Oh yeah."

"That's twelve miles and a bit."

"Any palm trees?" I quipped.

"Well, I'll let y'all get on with your visit. Y'all see that white tree over there, looks kinda like a flame?" We followed his gaze. "That's what we call a Bradford pear. Ain't that somethin? I bet y'all never saw anything like that in Vermont."

"No, we never did," I said.

"This whole county where we're standin? This is the purtiest spot in God's whole kingdom, and y'all are real welcome here anytime."

"Thank you," we chimed.

He nodded again in his mannered way, releasing us, and turned and ambled on up the street. As we walked back to the gas station I saw him climb into a pickup with a green bumper sticker. TOBACCO MONEY PAID FOR THIS CAR.

Back out on the road, Dan and I were quiet for a few minutes. He finished my Coke. "Decent guy," he said finally.

"Maybe."

An eighteen-wheeler roared past like a bull chasing the Confederate flag on its grille. "You know, Scott loved it down here. I told you what he said about the race thing."

I couldn't remember who Scott was.

"Scott Godden from the office, who was *down* here last year. The whole race thing's a non-issue. The whole town's very cool, they're all happy campers. Scott says it's because they go to church all the time, even during the week. I think it's on Wednesday night. Going to church is a fairly big deal."

"Like, how big?"

"We just might want to go, that's all."

"Or what, they'll paint an X on the door?"

"Okay, granted, it's a little spooky through here, but Beasley's gonna be fine. It's a nice little town and I want us to, you know, dig in and make some friends and be normal. Have more of a social life maybe. You know? The idea here is to try to blend in."

This was more of a declaration of intent than I had ever heard from Dan. I was struck by it. I knew that in my squalor of selfishness I had never thought hard enough about what his ideal life might be. "I want that too," I said.

"Yeah. Good."

"I really do."

"This is where it'll happen, you know." The baby, he meant.

Yes, I thought. It probably will.

"But Danny. If we could just . . . I just want to . . ." (why was it so hard to say?) ". . . you know, if I could just be like I am."

"That's deep."

"I don't want people to know about . . . the surgery."

"Oh. Well, okay. I don't know what the big deal is, but that's fine by me. Anyway. You're all set now."

"Yeap." You owe me one, was what he meant.

He may even have suspected I'd been holding out on him.

SEVEN

V ERY REVEALING WHAT the eye chooses first in a new place, and what it will try to ignore for as long as possible. There were churches everywhere, they sprang out of the land like tricks in a pop-up book. Red-brick Norman Rockwell churches with huge parking lots and various annexes all ramped for wheelchairs, little shacks in the woods with two sticks for a cross. There were handsome old wooden churches with historic markers, windowless cinder-block bunkers with smoked-glass doors, and requisitioned gas stations with their windows covered in stained-glass contact paper. All the usual Protestant denominations were there, along with some new subclasses of Baptists, one called AME Zion. Their names relied on the same words—Redemption, Loving Union, Holiness, Love, Peaceful Union, Faith and Trust, Peace, Holy Peace, Victory Faith and Love—a poetry of promises flowing by. The bigger signs also bore epigrams spelled out in block letters. LIFE IS SHORT, DEATH IS SURE, SIN THE CAUSE, CHRIST THE CURE. Or, TRUST IN GOD AND PRAY, WATCH YOUR WORRIES GO AWAY. But it was the hectoring ones I responded to. SLOTHFULNESS DID NOT MAKE THIS NATION. GOD KNOWS THE LAST TIME YOU PRAYED. Ah yes, I thought, sinking reverently into my old religious revulsion, silently, so as not to alert Dan.

Dan always thought my disdain for church was melodramatic. After telling my mother he was an Episcopalian, he learned I had been one too, until I was fourteen. He was never curious enough to ask what happened and I doubt I could have explained it, certainly not then.

Sunday school was fine. Five years old, installed in the cozy clanking oven of the basement while my mother was upstairs, I was smitten like everyone else with good handsome Jesus sitting on his tree stump, beckoning the children to come unto him. I loved the movies with the people in pastel robes rolling the boulder away from the mouth of the tomb and gasping. During the week my mother reemphasized the message I was getting on Sundays, which was, *Mommy and Daddy love you, Jesus loves you, and God loves you,* but soon I was picking up a melodious subtext . . . *just-like-you-are!* When kindergarten started and I sensed I was actually less lovable than I could have been, I just loved Jesus more. Then I noticed how unremittingly, long-lashedly, winsomely pretty the children he beckoned always were. But he was too handsome not to forgive, and anyway by then I was in first grade and Patti had made me her pet and I was swept away on the wings of her rather temporary love.

Miss Kehoe was one of the Sunday school teachers for the second and third grades. She had thin chapped lips and wilted shoulders and big unbrushed roller curls I liked to imagine sticking my finger in. She wore spike-heeled sandals, even in the winter when she had to bring them in a purple velvet fur-trimmed pouch she'd made. Every Sunday she let me stand next to her chair in the coatroom while she tugged off her ugly rubber boots and buckled on the sandals, tweaking out the toes of her stockings so they wouldn't snag on her painted toenails. I spent most Sunday mornings shadowing her, which was why, during a conversation she was having with the other teacher, I crept up behind them just in time to hear Miss Kehoe, her curls wobbling dolefully, say, ". . . that little Claudia Isham, that poor little thing."

After that I didn't discourage Miss Kehoe's efforts to include me (oh no, far from it) but I was on guard now for the charity the other girls aimed at me like poison darts, always with one eye on Miss Kehoe. "Oh Claudia, your shoes are so *shiny!*" "Miss Kehoe, Miss Kehoe, look at her bunny barrette!" This had a more pronounced flavor than the interest I generated at school, since the girls here had to curry not just the teacher's favor but God's. The hard part was resisting the temptation to just give up and sink into their plushy pity. The allure of being pathetic seemed to shine at me from deep in their heads. To withstand it, a new tough part of myself appeared, or rather didn't, because I kept it stored in the place I dimly sensed was the part of me Miss Kehoe wanted most. Now when she quizzed us about baby Moses, and the loaves and fishes, and the burning bush, I liked the distance between looking zealous, my arm straining in the air, and feeling this cool hidden detachment. Withstanding the pity lurking in the girls' Christian charity taught me that pity was a power certain people had. After another couple years I could sense that the girls didn't even know their compassion was flawed so, quietly, eagerly, I pitied them.

My disregard for all the goodwill on offer wasn't completely airtight. Now and then I relapsed. What I wanted was to be pitied by God. That would be different. I sensed possibilities here, opportunities for revenge. At some point the idea took hold that if I *was* pathetic, maybe I did deserve some reward. The meek shall inherit the earth and all that, I knew what that meant. Maybe I could be God's *secret* pet. As I waited for special customized goodness to settle over me like a veil, I knew it would only happen if I didn't keep looking up and watching for it all the time. Goodness was something you had to sort of stumble backward into, while you pretended to be busy doing something else. It didn't count unless you could be good without knowing it, unselfish and innocent and funny, like my cat Tuffy. If you knew it, it didn't count. But how could you even make the effort without knowing you were trying? I was getting a little ground down by all this when an epigram suddenly jumped full-blown into my head one day on the school bus. *If you think you're good . . . you're bad; if you think you're bad . . . you're good.* This I liked. I knew I was bad. I was crammed full of bad thoughts and I lied regularly. But then this benediction suffered its own collapse. I knew I hadn't really been given permission to lie awake at night imagining Patti, smashed in a car crash, lying in a body cast and sobbing through her bandages at her only visitor, me.

My confirmation came and went. I remember trying to summon

up a bit of false humility, appropriate to the best memorizer in the class.

Who knows what stopped my bartering with God, unless it was spending more time upstairs in church, startled into fresh waves of revulsion by the crumpled grown-ups on their knees, plea-bargaining in whimpers only senses as acute as mine could recognize.

Finally, at fourteen, just sensing the true nature of my predicament, I tried again with Jesus and was heartened to discover that my suffering paled next to his. I was also aroused by the public aspect of his ordeal; it wasn't hard for me to summon up the sound of the crowd jeering "King of the Jews." I used to think, how great not to be suffering! Except I was. My distress and isolation, approaching their zenith, would not allow Jesus' suffering to eclipse them, and in this refusal Jesus himself got eclipsed. I might have been stricken one more time by my failure to believe, and been saved again, but I wasn't. I was exhausted by now. My pride seemed to have snuffled permanently into the daylight, like the runt of the litter, over-endowed with survival instinct. All I had was the conviction that no one — *no one* — knew what I had to endure.

And then a true fellow sufferer appeared to me in the school library. Somebody heroic and humble like Jesus, and Jewish, but female, and not pretty. Anne Frank. I cherished her. When I discovered her diary, I was only a year younger than she had been when the Nazis ripped her family out of their hiding place. My sorrow for her was overpowering and unconfused, and my goal was simple. I would live the rest of her life for her, in exchange for seeing the whole world through her shrewd grave eyes. I knew I could do this because her private voice could be just as disparaging and picky as mine. I pored over her descriptions of the other people in those cramped quarters, the dentist who fouled the air of her bedroom, the repellently transparent Mrs. Van Daam. And then with Anne's guidance I understood and forgave them like she had. I noticed how even her religious feeling, her hopefulness for the Jews who would survive to carry forth, seemed born of loving kindness, without a grain of self-interest. "The unbosomings of an ugly duckling," she called her diary. I would not forget her. I would *be* her. I told her that, in the mirror. I warned her I might change physically, I might not always look the way I did now, but it would only be the most superficial transformation. I would always be a refugee, like her, one of the exiles fate had chosen to penetrate lovingly and unflinchingly the precarious heart of the truth.

Dead animals everywhere, I remember, that day in the car. Dan had to swerve to avoid a big black Lab lying not quite off the highway, bloating in the heat, one leg lifted as if to summon help from a house not twenty yards away. "Some serious roadkill down here," he allowed.

Since we left the interstate there had been, besides anonymous entrails, the bodies of a cat, a raccoon, even a small doe. Human death went less unremarked. Huge cemeteries sprawled by the road, the headstones decorated with plastic flowers attached to the tops, like big gray cakes all from the same bakery. Out in the fields were the older cemeteries, a few tilted stones thin as old soap, guarded by a single black cypress. Curious, all of this, to Northern eyes, but even odder was how familiar it was starting to feel. An impossible nostalgia was creeping into me. It wasn't fragile like déjà vu. It was like engaging with a book, when your mind starts muttering yes . . . *yes*, traveling out to meet the writer's mind until you're convinced that all these wise things he's telling you have been in your head all along. Just like that my mind rushed into the land. Here was a prison farm. Sure enough; long wooden barracks and barbed wire and lots of black men resolutely lounging. The road passed through a real swamp, with gray tree trunks standing like elephant legs in the green slime, and I knew them too.

Part of it must have been the first excited identifications of Southern symbolism, all the venerable clichés. You'd have to be dead not to respond to your first Spanish moss, or the first great blue heron—we both spotted it and cried out—regally inspecting a drainage ditch. But the fake collies too, and the yards dressed up with jugs of colored water, all of it was getting to me. And an old black woman who was standing out on the road by her mailbox, a bent twig in an orange quilted bathrobe, expressionless as we came toward her and then just as we passed her face flashed a smile of pure girlish joy at me.

We edged deeper into greenness, the saturated blue-green of some early crop, lying in fields curtained with woods that seemed to swing open as we passed, to show us what was here in all its modest grandeur. The burnt black shell of a tree rippling with new ivy, or a tobacco shed with a rusty roof so orange it vibrated against the green field, this violence softened by a nearby apple blossom. The woods far away were a sheer wash of yellow-green, but close by the road I could look in and see the tangled snakes of vine dangling in the sun-speckled undergrowth.

"I didn't know it was this flat," Dan said.

"No mountains to get in the way of the view," I said, rushing to commiserate, wanting him to be quiet so I could hoard it all to myself. "We'll get used to it."

To me the flatness was tantalizing, urging my imagination through the hazy sunlit slits in the distant woods to the ocean I knew was shining beyond. The land itself was as level and enigmatic as water and I felt like a swimmer standing in it up to my nose, getting ready to tuck my legs up and just glide.

The approach into Beasley was a modest mess. Car dealerships, fast food, a few small billboards. In the midst of this Dan spotted a trio of historic markers and pulled over so we could read.

ATTACK ON BEASLEY Town taken by Federals, March 1862. Confederate efforts to recapture it failed, 1862 and 1863.

SIEGE OF BEASLEY Confederates failed to recapture town March–April 1863, but held it March–November 1864.

BURNING OF BEASLEY The town was burned and shelled by evacuating United States troops in April 1864.

"Okay, I give up. Let's go home," Dan cracked.

The war was the reason so few houses in the little historic district boasted antebellum dates on their wooden plaques. Mostly their dates testified to a burst of postwar activity that had long since slowed to a crawl, having produced a nice variety of wood-frame houses with deep, inviting porches. Generally they were painted white but here and there someone had gone for pale salmon or lavender. Edging these few square blocks was a main street that constituted most of the commercial downtown. It was half dead, half alive. Among the empty storefronts were two surprisingly smart ladies' dress shops, a Christian bookstore, a window crammed with dummies' heads—brown ones, modeling wigs and very fancy hats—and three jewelry stores, all having sales. One of the two pawnshops still had its original gold balls. There was a defunct movie theater with a bulb-studded marquee. Strategic to the door of the drugstore, almost dwarfing it, was an old step-on scale, maroon and cream enamel, luscious as a vintage Chevy, suitable for weighing untoned bodies nurtured on marshmallow candied yams and pecan pie.

"Place is a throwback," Dan muttered. "Scott Godden must be cracked."

"No he's not," I scolded. "Not a lot of sushi here though, I don't think."

"No shit."

Dan cruised the wide quiet streets. We passed a spectacularly pretentious brick courthouse, a fire station with a United Way fundraiser thermometer, and probably half a dozen churches, and then turned onto a little parkway that ran beside the river, the Pamlico. It was spanned at this point by an old cement bridge perhaps a quarter mile long. Beside the wide paved promenade a long row of cherry trees bloomed. A white man sat fishing, his rear end drooping over the sides of his camp stool as he stared across the tea-colored water at green wetland. An old wide-bodied car was parked at the curb with a black woman sleeping inside, openmouthed, a book splayed on her chest. There was nobody jogging, nobody tossing a Frisbee to a golden retriever wearing a red bandanna. Dan cruised stoically on. There wasn't one "hand-carved" sign. There was no trendy signage at all, just that arcane, almost counterfeit artlessness. It was like a

town in a fifties sci-fi movie, right down to the battered silver water
tower that always seems like an ominous prefiguration of the flying
saucer due to land in an outlying cornfield. In the golden languor
hanging over the streets there was a strange loaded intensity like the
thickening before a storm.

Dan was getting morose. We stopped at a light and watched a
large black man wheel slowly by on a very small bike, sawing the air
with his knees.

"Never saw one on a bike before," Dan sniffed, expressing his disdain for a town so small-time it denied black people cars. "You *like*
it."

"Oh honey, it's got charm. It's going to be *fine.*"

We found Dan's new office out on Route 17 between a mobile
home dealership and an eye clinic. He turned into the parking lot
and nosed the car up to a railroad tie. When he turned off the engine we heard the syrupy flap of an enormous American flag. The
building was a low-slung contraption with a brown metal mansard
roof and double smoked-glass front doors etched with an insignia of
crossed barbecue fork and spatula. The plant out back was as big as
a small aircraft hangar, in turquoise corrugated steel. Our anxiety
dispelled by the future made visible, we were chewing on this when
one of the double doors opened and a young woman backed out,
fluttering good-bye to somebody inside as she executed a tidy pivot
in her high heels. Her silver-blond hair was pulled into a puff at the
crown of her head. Her navy blue dress was full-skirted, with a fitted
torso dominated by a white lace-edged bib, which she held tacked
against the breeze. Her makeup was masterful, if thick. After Vermont, where anything beyond lipstick and a little powder had been
verboten for years, her face seemed to have the cat's-eye immobility
of an alien's. She might have arrived on the flying saucer. A gob of
sunlight gleamed on her lip. Dan had gone very quiet.

"How come you never wear a dress?"

The gold-trimmed buckles on her pumps, her twinkling earrings
and little gold rings, it was all beating out rhythmic sparkles as she
strode across the gravel. Her level of grooming was so inspired that

my eyes, tuned by this precision to their sharpest focus, consumed it all at a gulp, even the candy-floss fingernails. She unlocked her car and got in, paused to get a cigarette lit, and hauled out, spewing gravel and dynamically exhaling with a complacent chin-thrusting snort. Her jaw was too big.

While Dan drove around trying to find the Holiday Inn, I was thinking about clothes. I might consider a dress. A sundress, black, with spaghetti straps, the style favored by Tennessee Williams's bad girls. Maybe some backless sandals, to make that tawdry slapping sound. Jewelry. I had always been so cautious in that area, but now I was entertaining the possibility of pearls, a long rope I could fondle as I lay back moist and sultry among delicately sweat-stained linen cushions. The future was collecting itself inside the tall cool walls of our house. I could see the dark polished floors and smell the redolent gloom of the past, barely disturbed by the breeze from the ceiling fans hovering in every room like tropical moths with huge dust-furred wings.

The real estate agent was a very affable fortyish woman named Mary Rose. Right away she grasped that Dan and I were snobs of two different species. I wanted an unmodernized antebellum house, Dan wanted a new one but refused to live in a development, no matter how "mature." He had also rejected the historic district as poky, though I too had been a little deflated by the seediness around its edges, where the porches full of wicker furniture and asparagus ferns gave way to stoops crowded with old tubular chairs and bagged collections of tin cans. We had both been quietly offended as Mary Rose drove us around Lynwood Landing, a jumble of mock Tudors and "planters' houses" and French châteaus, each giant stairwell window flashing an icy sheet-like glare that gave the lie to its plastic stick-on mullions. It made me think of a huge display of show food I had seen once at one of Dan's trade fairs, a smorgasbord of tortes mortared with chocolate cream, salmon dressed as mermaids in pastry scales, all of it coated with some preservative gelatin goo to

make the details glisten in the hot display lights. Here sunlight was
providing the finishing touches, bouncing starbursts off all the brass
carriage lamps and chiseling evergreens so kempt they looked artificial.

By the time she delivered us to the strip of riverfront, Mary Rose
was thoroughly sick of us, I'm sure, but still managing to draw energy from her own blinky niceness. She pulled into a circular driveway and turned off the car to let us steep in admiration. It was
another planter's house, apparently brand-new; white frame, with a
sharply pitched, very thickly shingled roof extending out over a nice
deep porch. The columns were rather dramatic, being freestanding,
without railings. There was a problem with them, which I had to
work out. Albert Speer, when he designed all the Third Reich buildings, had tried to give the columns more totalitarian oomph by
eradicating the subtle classical bulge, but these columns erred in the
other direction, bulging a little too ardently in their yearning for the
Old South. They were a touch squat.

The front door was equipped with brass kick plate, letter slot, Colonial knocker, and a beveled octagonal knob. The alarm system was
complicated. Once inside, we stood momentarily dazed by the
clean river light shunted down the central hallway and boxed in the
symmetrical set of empty creamy rooms. Dan followed Mary Rose
back toward the river while I stayed in the hall and absorbed the
thick crown molding and the echoing yardage of pickled floor. At
the back of the house I heard Dan's voice rumble and Mary Rose
cried, "Oh don't you just *know* it?" and they both laughed. The
brass chandelier over my head burst into electric flame and went
out again, stripping away more than light, leaving the neo-Colonial
space domestic but bleak, like an unoccupied cage at the zoo. Suddenly I felt robbed of the soulful life I hadn't lived yet and never
would in this tricked-up showplace. I could detect the presence of
my older, groomed, mediocre self lazing around upstairs, doing her
cuticles.

In the living room I found Dan and Mary Rose in front of a fireplace with a tall ornate mantelpiece. Dan was toeing the oiled sheen

of the very blue slate hearth. "Just two months," Mary Rose responded to a question I hadn't heard. Dan began opening cupboards built in next to the chimney breast. "You could stick a darlin little bar in there," she added.

"What's the deal though?" Dan said. "Why'd they leave so soon?"

Mary Rose threw me a glance. "An accident of some kind? The wife . . . now, did she drown?"

Dan looked up sharply. "In the tub."

"No no." Mary Rose was peering down at the knot in her scarf. She gave the scarf a tug. "In the river. I believe that's what we heard."

"It was an accident," Dan said.

"Oh yes."

"Oh boy. What a shame. Claud, why don't you scope the kitchen? I'm gonna run upstairs."

"He likes it," I told Mary Rose unnecessarily. We could both hear the proprietary weight of his tread on the steps.

"But now what about *you*?" she asked mournfully. "Still too new?"

"No, it's pretty. She drowned?"

"Oh . . ." Her worriment festered. "Well, y'all'll probably just hear anyway. She took her own life."

"In the house?"

"I am so sorry. Downstairs powder room. Isn't that awful, she really was in the tub at the time. The powder room is unusual, it's a full bath."

Striped lilac wallpaper, black-and-white tile checkerboard floor, a room as cheerlessly spotless as a microchip lab. The tub was a curious mushroom color. I sat on the edge and tried to see what she would have seen lying in the pink water as the light was thinning; maybe the louvered doors under the vanity, with their porcelain knobs shaped like scallop shells. Mary Rose wouldn't come in.

"We have another listing *very* much like this," she said from the doorway. "Almost identical. They're from . . . you know, master plans. But now, Claudia, the other one won't be on the river."

"No. But . . . we don't have to tell Dan."

"Oh, I was hopin. You know what this home needs? Love and affection, that's all. Just some ole TLC." Pause. "Such a sad dreadful thing."

"Did you know her at all?" Lured to the mirror, I began fussing with my hair, trying to disguise an overwhelming desire to just stare.

"No, I never did. But she went to church with my friend Audrey, and I know she'd been on their prayer list twice, so there must've been somethin. But what do you *do*? I think it might've been a problem with drink. I do think you're smart though. Dan doesn't want to know about all that."

In the mirror Mary Rose appeared beside me. As I watched she made her mirror face. Her eyelids drooped and the bright good girl dissolved into a hollow-cheeked siren who simpered for an instant and then blinked herself back, plucking at her hair. "Oh, if I'm not a *wreck*?"

"No, you look great." To prevent my own features from doing that, I was keeping my eyes glued on her.

"Oh, you're so pretty, what do *you* know?" she cried, turning away. I barely had time to ooze into my own secret face before she called me to come out and admire the river.

I figured Dan would eventually find out his new home bore a small indelible stain but I didn't think the pragmatist in him could fault Mary Rose just for doing her job. But two months later at a barbecue, someone assumed Dan already knew and mentioned the suicide. Dan played along but in the car going home he was furious. Mary Rose had swindled him. He was squeezing the wheel, his knuckles were coming through the skin. Finally I said, "Dan, she didn't. She told me about it." That calmed him down. It was not wholesale humiliation after all, it was just the fault of his wacko wife who was always attracted to anything morbid.

"What *is* it with you anyway?" he said as we swerved into the driveway.

"I just thought if you knew, you wouldn't want the house. I was trying to save it for you."

"No you weren't. Just tell me. I'm curious. What is it about all this shit you get off on?"

"What shit?"

"You know what I mean."

He meant I lacked the proper sensitivity to certain things, like the surgical procedures I liked to watch on cable TV, the C-sections, breast reconstructions using recycled stomach fat, brain surgery where the patient can talk while the laser scorches his brain. Once while I was watching a kidney transplant, Dan groped through the bedroom with his eyes shut.

"Dan, when the doctor squeezes it, it makes urine!"

"You're a total sicko!" he yelled from the bathroom.

But it never felt sick. It felt prudent. I needed this misery—Auschwitz bodies stacked like firewood, teenagers brutalized by Tourette's—to serve as a form of self-inoculation. My superstitious, if not religious, belief was that if I refused to run away from horror, horror would never find me. I was in agreement with the Buddhists who say that thinking too hard about the malignancy of life delivers it to you, but I took a more offensive approach. I tried to find evidence that the most unendurable circumstances were completely routine and then deprive them of their power by inspecting them while I ate a sandwich. I wonder now though if Dan wasn't right when he accused me of using my predilection like a bludgeon.

I'm thinking of that long-ago afternoon at Patti's. That silent spooky house all done in white with plastic covers on everything. Just the four of us, Patti and her henchmen Macy and Charlotte, and me, by special invitation. I was the one who had to get up on the wobbly bar stool and then step gingerly onto the mantel and extract the forbidden book from the top shelf. I was the one who had to turn the pages. It was a heavy medical textbook—her brother had been in med school once—packed with photographs of congenital deformities, mercifully in black-and-white, most of them. Some babies were pickled in jars but many were alive. There were webbed hands with three fingers, babies missing their eyes or noses. Toddlers with their limbs or their genitals swollen into shapes that reminded me, shamefully, of animals made from twisted balloons. Behind me Patti risked peeps around my head, and behind her Macy and Charlotte were cringing and snorting. With each page I contained my

own horror, swallowing it and managing to keep it down, always trying to impress Patti. But somewhere inside my faked aplomb I was
genuinely repulsed by her snickering. *How dare she?* I understood
dimly that she was afraid but the more she gagged and puffed her
breath on my neck, the more mute I became; stoic, almost prim.
Then I began to feel dully but steadily enlarged. She didn't know
what I knew, which was that every baby would have been normal except for one mistake. I knew this because of the tiny tiny little—
thank you, God—*tiny* mistake that had happened to me. But now
my nonchalance was starting to bother Patti. She summoned Macy
and Charlotte away to help her fix some snacks. I sat on the couch
and turned the pages faster, trying to cram in more of the horror that
might have been mine, while I appeased it with my swooning thank-
fulness that I hadn't turned out any worse.

As they came back in with the Cokes and Twinkies, Patti's cheeks
were patchy, her blue eyes bright as two hard candies.

"Don't keep looking at that. You have to put it back before my
mother gets home. Go on . . . *do it.* Then you can have your *treat.*"
She held my Twinkie behind her back. Macy tittered.

"You better . . ." Charlotte warned, keeping an eye on Patti. "Witch
Hazel. Stinkhole."

"She's not *doing* it. . . ." Macy sang.

I got up from the couch, holding my thumb in the book, walked
over to them, and cracked the book open. The picture was a full
page in color, a living boy with a defect that had split his face like a
fig, the half-healed flesh sprinkled with baby teeth like exploded
seeds. There was a forehead with a cowlick of brown hair and the
curve of an eye socket. He didn't have hands or feet, just little cloven
stumps, and bulbous genitals. Macy's eyes were clamped shut. Charlotte blundered out into the hall. Patti burst into tears. Horror-
stricken, I ran to the bathroom to get her a kleenex.

So yes, maybe I was guilty of hectoring Dan. I certainly didn't
approve of his own strategy for keeping the horrors at bay. Dan liked
to lump them together, he refused to distinguish between, say, the
"horror" of lifesaving surgery and the "horror" of suicide, as if blanket contempt for every possible way of being a victim would make

him invincible. He watched, and snickered over, a lot of tabloid TV, which I always shunned. But he was right on one point: I didn't mind about the powder room. The first two or three months we were there, I would find myself stopping outside the door, as if I might hear that woman inside, splashing quietly. To me her grief breathed some life into that perfect cold sunlit house.

EIGHT

COLOR WAS WHAT I wanted for the house, ochers and mint greens, fresco colors that would individualize the rooms in all that disorienting light. But then Dan, insisting he had spent his childhood in a maid's closet, became convinced that colorlessness was necessary to fulfill his one requirement, which was that the house feel *humongous.* That meant color was out. So then I thought about "amusing" wrought iron chairs and fanciful couches, oddments bobbing in all that pale space. Our old furniture was about to be thrown out anyway, the old beige sectional pieces. In all that sunshine they were suddenly grimy.

But oh the beauty of the river in that light. The kitchen and dining room and our bedroom and bath all looked out on pine trees swagged with Spanish moss; such peculiar stuff, like the fossilized exhaust of some unspeakable night-flying creature. Beyond was the wide water, wider here than in town. The opposite shore was densely wooded lowland, with three summerhouses positioned nicely off-center in a clearing downriver, toward the Sound. Our long, somewhat rickety dock obviously predated the house. The lot was big, almost half an acre, with evergreens and some azaleas and a lawn of tough spongy grass that sparkled like cellophane. Every morning the river was a surprise. It might be blue and benign, or muddy-looking, with a dirty metallic skin on it. Sometimes it was a sheet of glass crawling with smoke. One morning I was in the dining room when Dan called from the kitchen, "What the fuck? Claud, come here quick!" and we stood and watched as a gust of golden dust draped itself on the breeze, a long chiffon scarf twirling past the window.

"Geez," he said, "what a weird place."

"It is, it's a circus." I was still trying to withhold my full enthusiasm from Dan.

" 'Thank you for bringing me down here, Danny.' "

"Thank you."

"Kiss please."

When the dogwood blossomed its shape was familiar but not its vehement profusion, and then the azaleas arrived, like discordant blasts on a Wurlitzer organ, magenta, Chinese red, coral. Ours turned out to be a rare fluffy white. The wisteria was decorous to begin with, trained to froth up in little fountains in people's yards, then it burst out wild in the woods, dripping from the treetops and phone poles. Meanwhile everybody in Beasley acted as if this were all normal, not pointing and slapping their foreheads but just being their yakky agreeable selves. (The gold dust turned out to be pine cone pollen, deplored for messing up decks and cars.) And then, as if we were caught in a piece of speeded-up film, it was suddenly full summer. Every day after breakfast I got in the car, hoping to find a new back road that might carry me over a little stream, or a croaking pea-soup creek, or an inlet edged with boats. There was water everywhere, promising, along with the light bouncing around the bowl of the sky and the trucks selling shrimp and oysters at the roadside, that the ocean was tantalizingly close, just a couple hours away. It was all so tangible after Vermont's unattainable postcard vistas of valleys and mountains. These flat Southern distances aimed from the horizon and hurtled over the fields to the edge of the road, inviting me to pull over and get out and just inhale. One morning by a deserted, freshly sown field, I stopped and got out to spread myself on the big churned crumbs of earth. The seagulls swooped, streaking the sky with their affectionate sad cries. I was in heaven. No further benediction was required, but then as I was meandering back to Beasley I went past a barn covered with white block letters, spaced to take up one whole side. MERRY CHRISTMAS HAPPY NEW YEAR MAY PEACE AND LOVE ABIDE WITH YOU I LOVE EVERYBODY DENTON FULLER.

And it was all working. No one suspected I wasn't what I was, what I had *always* been. I had a whole history of prettiness, my prettiness had been accruing since I was born. I had had to forgive Dan his promiscuous grin, now that I knew what it was like when people met your eye, and smiled when they saw you coming, and their welcome swelled your head into a helium balloon that bounced you along the street with your toes scraping behind. Some days the accumulation of all this unearned esteem would weigh on me, and paw at me like the hand of a beggar, asking me for that one small thing I couldn't produce, the truth. I used to fantasize about telling somebody, some nice old saleswoman, while I wandered the malls. For company I summoned up all the other women like me, a whole secret army pacing other malls, stalking their sleek new jowls and boosted breasts in every scrap of mirror.

I still studied attractive women as critically and voraciously as ever, but with considerations that were more practical now. I needed to see what they did. The cleverest ones pretended not to know what they looked like, taking that old "looks-don't-mean-a-thing" pretense to flawless extremes, tossing their frank glances around like strippers working with scarves, knowing how this "obliviousness" contributed to their charm. This was a piece of business I knew I would never be able to pull off. But then I caught an ancient echo of my mother's special coaxing voice, the one she used before birthday parties or on the first day of school. She would crouch beside me and beg, Honey . . . you just be your own sweet self. But of course, now it actually worked. It was especially effective whenever I sensed a man loitering at the edge of my consciousness, inching closer. One little smile, very sugary and dismissive, would short-circuit him.

In the big malls, most of them not more than an hour away, I found the clothes I wanted; solid colors, mostly neutrals. Strong colors and prints I considered ingratiating. I picked out the plainest things, the kind of things people call deceptively sexy, and drove home still fuddled by the after-image of myself dissolving on my eyeballs. The fields were pristine now in their long dotted lines of baby corn and tobacco. The rye was so tall that from the roadbed a tin roof and a chimney looked like a rusty boat floundering in brown waves. The magnolias, trees that seemed too lofty to flower, were studded with their fleshy blossoms like stars, and the kudzu vine had lathered whole tracks of woods into forbidden caves, forcing me to choose which one to penetrate with my eyes as I drove past. I was so aroused, so indolent in those days, as if every drag of my gaze across the land's beauty pulled me deeper into the intoxicating impossibility of myself.

I was disgusting.

The house was coming along. I had to have Dan's approval before I could buy anything, so I brought home some samples of open-weave linen and explained how I wanted it to hang from wrought iron curtain rods. "That's cheesecloth," Dan said, and proceeded to draw a picture of his ideal curtain, like somebody struggling to reproduce a dream image for his psychiatrist. It involved a pelmet with a scalloped edge, covered to match the (chintz) curtains, which were caught in matching tiebacks, every bit of this contrast-piped. It appeared that Dan did care, passionately, about the look of his house. There had to be a "classic" couch covered in a print that was "lively," dressed up with petit-point pillows. Flanking the couch would be two round glass-topped tables with skirts; on top, twin Imari lamps, surrounded by photographs, framed in gold-trimmed Lucite, of us looking sportily and unaffectedly rich.

What Dan specifically coveted was one of those round, gold-framed, Colonial convex mirrors that always struck me as surreal, like the eye of a monocled Cyclops bulging out of the wall. He also needed a liver-red buttoned leather wing chair with an ottoman to match. Catalogues from the swankiest furniture factories in North Carolina littered the house. Every morning Dan dawdled over his toast, turning down page corners. He ordered us a Shaker long-case clock for the foot of the stairs, a Sheraton bowfront chest for the front hall, a massive armoire for the bedroom. At one of the auction houses in Wilson he found a mahogany table that could seat the ten friends he must have anticipated, and a set of Chippendale chairs. Also, with an urgency I couldn't place, he bought some pieces of antique silver; a butler's tray, some little boxes, a cigar clipper, and a pair of grape scissors.

I submitted to a single skirted table and a chintz armchair. There were never any fights throughout any of this, just veiled references as to why neither of us had any taste; not enough money in my background and too much in his. Mostly we struck bargains. When I located Dan's mirror, I was allowed the refectory table I had seen on my first trip to Wilson. Eighteenth-century, beautifully nicked and scarred, it had been hand-waxed and then inexplicably shoved into a corner and covered with English willowware. (I didn't understand what Dan had already grasped; Southerners respond more readily to big-house gloss.) The table arrived in Beasley in a truck and was grappled through the back door by two teenagers, one black, one white. When they had finally maneuvered it around the island and settled it next to the bay window on its stubby legs, it seemed to pant for a minute, lion-colored and glowing, before giving up. "That is some *old*," the black boy said. When he thought no one was looking, he pressed his palm on the table, held it there for a minute, and then inspected it shyly, devotedly, as if he had harvested some secret particles from the past.

By May, with the cherry sideboard installed in the dining room under Dan's mirror, and Ping's house present, a huge Steuben glass bowl, resplendent on top, it was obvious that neither Dan nor I had won the war for the house. The house had won. It looked the way it had always intended, venally luxuriant, like the houses in made-for-TV movies where "ordinary" families suffered their topical psycho-socio traumas. Even the bedroom, which I had tried to hold to a subdued minimalism, was grand in a spiritless way. Dan's trouser press and the de rigueur armoire had turned my old brass bed from Vermont into a "piece." The quilt my mother had given me when we left Vermont, made by her aunt during the Depression, looked like an item from a "collectible heirloom" catalogue. I was ashamed of not appreciating the house but I was more ashamed of the house. I fumed and fussed but everything I threw at it—old breadboards, humble chenille cushions—only made the ostentation worse. The struggle ended when there was no space left to put anything else.

Every bit was occupied, even the stretch of sideboard the sun always gilded late in the afternoon, in this case by a large brass "nineteenth-century" cork-popper contraption Dan had dug up somewhere. The house was also sealed up like a tomb. Dan had immediately subscribed to the local rule: with the first whisper of heat, every window had to be closed. Chilled processed air was venerated with a fervor that must have been instilled by the generation before, who remembered the dawn of air-conditioning.

It was around this time that I stood in the bathroom one morning and realized my own transformation was incomplete. I drove to Greenville and had my hair "lifted"—practically one hair at a time, I felt corrupt and smug—with highlights in a shade called Palomino. It took over two hours. Then it was cut into layers. By the time I had crossed the parking lot, the humidity had plumped my head into a puffball. That afternoon, strapped into a new bikini, face lathered in sunscreen, I went out on the dock to sunbathe. When I closed my eyes, temptress versions of myself swam through the red darkness, encouraging me in this new routine that demanded nothing except that I lie there and wait to get blonder and tanner. I didn't know I had fallen asleep until the dock vibrated against my pelvis.

"Va-va-fucking-voom. Geezum *crow*, Claud, look at your *hair*. Wow. Stay just like that."

He came back with his Leica and squatted down. I was ready. The moves were embedded in my bones, activated by the click of the shutter. I drew one knee closer to my chest, arched my back, corrected the shape of my hand. Dan knew what to do too.

"That's it . . . that's it . . . great. Beautiful."

I licked my lips, cut my eyes away.

"Okay. Something cuter." He was impatient. "You know, Beach Blanket Bananas, Gidget Goes Goo-Goo. C'mon . . ."

The mouth pouted, the nose crinkled. A "defiant" little tilt of my fluffball head and the shutter clicked. Dan had that one enlarged and found a frame he loved, ribbed silver with a little flat silver bow on top. It found its place on the skirted table under the Imari lamp.

NINE

"J UST A LITTLE somethin to help sweeten up your new home!"

This was my first glimpse of Janet Alligood; about fifty, with hair the color of nougat, beaming as she came across the grass from next door. She was youthfully tiptoeing and holding up a pie. "Key lime!" We met in the middle of the yard and stared at the pie. It was very green.

"Our favorite!" I lied.

They were very genial, she and her blond husband, Dick. More than genial. Whenever Janet wanted to donate a pile of her old *New Yorker* magazines to me, or when we happened to be in our yards at the same time, she and Dick radiated a breezy charm laden with gladness that we were qualified to be there with them; apparently we had made the team.

The rhythm of the new life—sunny day after day of it—sucked at us like warm surf trying to sink two stones deeper into the sand. Mingling with the heavy pollen in the atmosphere was an archaic politeness, punctuated by the children's pliant yes ma'ams and no ma'ams. It was hard to imagine these submissive children ever exploding into the exuberant grown-ups we saw everywhere. The communal cheer *was* real, I could hear it now. "Wasn't that *fun* last night?" a woman would cry across Main Street to a friend. Snippets from those days are lodged in my synapses like snatches of tune; a woman table-hopping her way to the Chinese restaurant buffet table and pealing out to somebody, ". . . and I never drive by your *house* that I don't think nice thoughts!" There were simply no strictures against being private in public, not for white people at least. They were as garrulous as Vermonters—real ones—were taciturn. Even men discovering each other in the line at the post office boomed away while everybody else pretended not to hear.

No racial cloud blotted the scene, as far as I could tell. Any older white woman who smiled at a young black boy could generally expect a head dip and a split second of eye contact in return. There wasn't much racial intermingling; so far I had seen just one mixed couple, teenagers holding hands self-consciously on a bench on the Parkway. Obviously the two races interacted mainly at work. But things were very relaxed. White and black guys hailing each other at the gas station mined rich veins of agreement while they pumped their gas. *I hear that! You know it, don't you? Man, ain't that the truth!* The white checkout girl and the black boy bagging my groceries would pester each other, staving off boredom, while I wrote my check and tried to feel as natural as they did, which was impossible. I was unnerved by the naturalness of black people, who seemed barely to notice my color, while I felt unable to disregard theirs, as if in an unguarded moment I might cry out *Oh! . . . your pink palms!* And I didn't like my voice anymore, it was too clipped and haughty compared to the elastic Southern sound, like a song. At the Food Lion they sang it, the older white women, the gals in their pressed well-filled slacks and salon hairdos and gold leather flats. *Hey!* they cried to each other, not *Hi.* "Hey, Etta Mae!" "*Hey*, Jane Lee, how *you* doin?" "Well, I'm *fine!*" they would drawl back and forth on a long high note of simulated surprise. Among the older black women there was more formality. They tapped out a code on each other's arms as they talked in voices so low I couldn't make out what they said. They tended to shop in big comfortable sneakers and often a hat, a hand-knit cloche or a velour beret. Big flat handbags like the Queen of England's dangled from their thin charred-looking wrists.

There was a small Mexican population too, mostly single men who shared houses and sent their wages home. They moved through Wal-Mart in tight virile groups with their thumbs hooked in their belts, their long hair razored into identical haircuts, like blue-black Roman helmets. Occasionally there was a man with a small family, a wife and baby who eyed the vegetables with the same placid stoicism. We learned from Harley that the Mexicans were here to do the work black people wouldn't do anymore.

I hadn't met Harley Swain yet. I only knew he was one of Dan's sales reps, born in Beasley and full of local lore and advice. (I assumed it was Harley who had found Dan a source for his grass; he was smoking less now but he still liked to light up sometimes during the late talk shows.) Dan seemed to like his life at the office. He liked his secretary, Melissa, who turned out to be the well-groomed blond girl in the parking lot. He liked Harley, he liked Harley's wife, Debs-Anne. "She's a real corker," he said. I didn't like the sound of that. He'd met her a couple times now and was keen on the four of us developing a social relationship. I was supposed to initiate it, but I kept stalling. I still felt best wandering around on my own, busy with my Southern research. I was scared of the women I saw around Beasley, women my age but so brutally confident, with a graphic, accessorized femininity that made me feel messy. Smudged. I didn't want to be with them, I wanted to be in Wal-Mart, wandering down the aisles of black products, reading the labels on African Miracle "fade cream" and Raveen Hair Fabu-laxer and summoning up spasms of appalled empathy. I was gorging myself on details, like the small gold plastic crowns I kept seeing in people's cars, usually perched in their rear windows. But only black people had them (why?).

The Daily News, Beasley's paper, was essential reading, especially the letters column, tucked under a bit of daily Scripture. Often a letter started, "As a Christian, I feel very strongly . . ." and then went on to express a dire pessimism about the future of America, like a drumbeat underpinning the mellifluous praise for the latest church bake sale. One woman wrote regular mini-sermons of thanksgiving for her life, other people wrote to vent their spleens, which was generously allowed by the editor. "To whoever sick person stole my tires, I know who you are." After the letters I always turned to the Police Scanner. "Items stolen from the car were Mrs. Smith's MasterCard and .380 pistol." "Cox pushed the money through the bullet hole in the door." One single Scanner might feature as many as three shootings, while more serious incidents got written up separately; a young man accidentally wounding himself, fatally, while he was joking around with his gun; a man rolling over on the gun in his pocket while he was asleep. I labored over names and addresses, trying to decide which race people were. It seemed crucial for some reason. The most pointed hints were always in the obituary section and the essential clue—although it took me awhile to figure this out— was simply the name of whichever funeral home was handling the arrangements. But even with that mystery removed, I liked to savor the names. Cordice, Omar, Joshua, always a few from the Bible. I remember once a woman named Goldenring.

From the paper I learned that violence didn't generally cross the racial divide. The black violence was all about drugs, much of it perpetrated along notoriously crack-ridden Fourth Street. It made the white mayhem seem almost frivolous. A white guy had killed his friend in a snit having something to do with the Super Bowl. Somebody casually shooting from his buddy's pickup on a back road had accidentally blown a little girl off her horse. Then there was a white man who had killed his boss with a shotgun. Most of the capital crimes seemed to get plea-bargained down and were never mentioned again, but that one was actually going to trial. I was agog with all this. The pictures it stirred up in my mind shifted and swam into a pattern that moved with my eyes, casting a dense heightened color over everything I saw. But my *Daily News* bore only a passing resemblance to Dan's. His was more temperate, murmurous with social connections. "Chris Blount accepting a United Way check," he would muse. "I bet that's Mike's brother." Though Dan wasn't immune to the fascination of Southern tradition.

"Get this," he said one day from behind the paper. "Do you know what 'real daughters' are? They're the daughters of guys who fought in the Civil War. They're alive, they're *out* there. The Daughters of the Confederacy want them all to show up at their next meeting. Sounds like fun, huh?"

Giddy in our separate ways, Dan and I were giddy together. The

zippily positive Southern way with negatives—"no, I surely do *not!*"—
made them perfect slogans for our new affability. We found ways to
insert this into conversations around the house, that and the Southern colloquialism whereby *wasn't* collapses into *won't*. "It won't *my*
fault!" We were a little slaphappy with each other in this new place,
like American tourists who've just discovered each other on a bus
in Guatemala City. Vermont was never like this, we laughed greed-
ily. Dan still said "Geezum crow," to what effect I couldn't imagine—
surely people knew it was profane?—but now he had also adopted
the ubiquitous "Preciate it!" He insisted it had found its way into his
mouth because he heard it all day at work, which I believed, because
sometimes when I was talking to the checkout girls my pronuncia-
tion could start feeling chewy.

The South has a special persuasive insistence about it. If I was
a little incredulous to learn that *y'all* wasn't just an idiom cherished
by screenwriters but was absolutely habitual, I was also impressed.
Being Southern seemed to mean being wholly and *sagaciously* aware
of every caricaturized aspect of Southern life and faithfully, ardently,
embracing it. This sounds patronizing but the South can't be patronized. It refuses. We joked about how to disguise being from the
North. Dan thought a bumper sticker would do it, he had his eye on
SAVE THE SOUTH, SEND A YANKEE HOME TODAY. (I never mentioned
my secret craving for one that wasn't specifically Southern: I'M FAT,
YOU'RE UGLY, BUT I CAN DIET.) One day Dan traded in our two Vermont license plates for the single rear plate that was all North Carolina required, and came home with a front plate that read, NEXT TIME
YOU THINK YOU'RE PERFECT, TRY WALKING ON WATER. Another joke.
We laughed.

But then he started seriously lobbying for us to go to church.
Adrift in my new serendipity, I decided maybe my old protestations
were lending my sentiments about religion, antisentiments though
they were, a little too much weight. A more honest expression of my
ambiguity would be a lusty "Oh well, why not?"

So one spanking Sunday in May, in we went to St. John's Episco-
pal Church, its fragrant depths filled with a hushed dressiness I had

forgotten I liked. Heads swiveled at us. A nice-looking older woman farther down the pew leaned out and sparkled at us. I smiled back, crisp in my new pearl-gray linen suit, suffering a spasm of latent embarrassment for my mother, who had always dressed so meticulously for church in those crooked tweed suits she designed for herself. Of course the guilt attached to this memory I could barter my way out of. *Yeah, but Mom, look, I'm in church!* And I wasn't ugly. And no one here knew my father was a maintenance man at GE. It was familiar, all the sonorous old phrases rushing back into my mouth, and dislocating, like being dunked into childhood with all the inadequacies removed. God was still there, making people sit up straighter, but his power had dwindled. He was a polite, cautionary premise you could respond to or not, like the importance of eating low-fat.

Afterward we all stood preening on the sidewalk, beside the delectably pretty churchyard, moldy obelisks and palmettos fanned against lichen-crusted gravestones, overhung by live oaks. People pressed forward—"Nice to see y'all today. Mayhew Watkins . . . hey, how y'all doin . . . and this is my wife, Cyn?"—and then wandered away, snagged into other congenial groups making their way out to the big cars and minivans at the curb, none of which, needless to say, bore front plates that said GOD IS YOUR FRIEND. I was waiting for Dan to disengage himself from a man from his office when I felt a hand gently seize my wrist.

"Margaret honey? . . . It *is* you! Where have you *been,* darlin?" The woman was gray-blond with a thin crimped face, sixty-five or so, in a full-skirted flowered dress. "It must be ten years. You look *wonderful,* darlin!"

"Thank you, but I'm not—"

"Y'all heard about Carolyn." She was trying to free her pearls from a complicated neckline ruffle.

"I'm sorry but I don't—"

"She's in *France!* She married a *diplomat!* Well, you knew she'd do *somethin* like that. And this is your husband." As Dan joined us, she slid me a glance of conspicuous congratulation.

"Dan Dryburgh." He gave her his hand.

"Tassy Rankin! I'll let Margaret catch you up on my news. So nice to see y'all. I gotta run now, John's in the car, hasn't changed one iota! Y'all come *see* us now, we're still there!"

"Who's Margaret?" Dan wanted to know as we walked to the car. The woman was getting into a white Cadillac.

"You're looking at her. Me. Didn't you know?"

"Oh?"

"That was too weird. She was utterly convinced."

"Well, it's no big deal. You don't have to get all screwed up."

"I'm not." But I was. I was confused, and repulsed, by whom or by what I couldn't have said.

"Oh, Margaret, honey, don't be like that." Dan was not quite giggling.

"It's not funny." But of course it was.

"That's what we want," Dan said all of a sudden. He was pointing out a front license plate embossed with three marine flags. He explained that they represented the car owner's initials and signified membership in the Beasley Golf and Yacht Club. Dan wasn't a golfer, or a boater, but he always needed a nice place to go. From Harley he had learned that the restaurant options in town were sparse. There were two Chinese places, a casual place called Julie's, and two or three "family" restaurants with linoleum floors. He had duly checked out the club and decided it was adequate, and the week after church he told me we were all signed up. Harley had vouched for us. I saw myself rocking on a roomy verandah, sipping at my frosty drink while young black waiters with big silver trays tucked under their arms stood by silently.

Alas, the verandah no longer existed. There had been an ornate wooden clubhouse but it had burnt down one night in the seventies and been replaced by a two-story brick monolith. The dining room had a cathedral ceiling, brick walls, and blue carpet. There was a small parquet dance floor and a grand piano. Branches massed in clay tubs sparkled with fairy lights, and high on one wall a blue swordfish was arched, as if caught forever in the act of not quite escaping from a deep brick tank. Strangely, there was only one window on the room's long riverfront wall, so only one table had a view of the marina. One night during the summer we sat at that table, part of a big drunken group. Beyond the manic heads I watched the Spanish moss swaying and the masts slowly tilting in the dusk deepening beyond the plate glass, a view as poignantly useless as a TV left on in a deserted room. The whole clubhouse was like that, hermetic. In the bar upstairs, members drank in a stale chill perpetrated by the pale blue vinyl-covered walls, deprived even of the alluring glint of bottles behind the bar; to circumvent the Bible Belt licensing laws, people had to bring their own bottles, which were labeled and stored in the back somewhere. On the tables were plastic salad bowls Chester kept filled with warm popcorn. Chester, apparently the club's only black employee, was the bar manager. He was possibly sixty, possibly eighty, a dark man with eggplant-colored eyelids, not a lot taller than the bar. People loved him, as much for the humor swimming in his yellowed eyes, I imagined, as for the heavy hand he used for pouring drinks.

We were unsure about the club's black membership. There were never any black people in the dining room or at the pool or, so far as we knew, on the golf course. We had to assume this was due to a fact that was slowly becoming clear. Beasley lacked the black doctors and lawyers and bankers and accountants who might have wanted to join. There was a black professional class—teachers and nurses and administrators, and many ministers—but they couldn't have afforded the dues. It was difficult. We couldn't inquire about club policy concerning blacks without sounding aggressive and we didn't want to offend anyone. I might have been tempted to ask one of the Northerners at the club, one of the retirees, but they were all thirty years older than we were, and even then it would have been hard to work the question into a conversation. Nobody ever really referred to the black population, it just never came up. I made the mistake once of asking Dan why he thought this was.

"A, you don't ever talk to anybody, so how could it come up, and b, what do you want people to say? They're black? They're here?" He was impatient, I had stopped him at the wrong time, on his way out the door to work. "*What?*"

"Nothing. I don't know."

He stepped back inside so he could shut the door. He liked the house icy.

"They *are* here," I said. "They're . . . all *over,* they're—"

"Classic. So you want to move back now."

"No I don't. I just mean they seem . . . at a remove. Don't they?"

"You keep saying you love it here."

"I do. I do love it. It's fine. It doesn't matter."

"*What* doesn't?"

"Go to work."

"Yeah, well. Forty-two percent black in this town. I mean, the stuff they don't bother telling you, right? Course then . . . I don't know." A taunt was coming. "We might not have bothered to come . . ."

"That wouldn't have stopped *you.* You're from New York, you're *down* with the brothers—"

"Is somebody fucking with you?" he asked sharply.

"No. What are you talking about?"

He blushed, almost. He changed tack. "Actually, you know, the race thing's okay, Scott was dead right. I know why too. They're too grateful, they're hardly gonna rock the boat now. Once in a while somebody in the shop cops an attitude but it's rare. Basically these guys are cake to work with. I'm pretty impressed."

"Is that what everybody thinks? What does Harley think?"

"Harley's cool, he grew up here."

When he opened the door I followed him out and the heat toasted the front of me like the breath of a friendly beast.

"Be my guest," Dan said as he skipped down the steps. "Go make some black friends, be the first on your block!" I watched him walk to the car, summery and crisp in his new short-sleeved shirt. By the garage he stopped and looked back. "And Clod-head, listen, call Debs-Anne, will you do that for me? And keep the door shut!"

A couple days later Debs-Anne called me.

"Claudia? Hey girl, you need a *friend*!"

There was no point arguing. We agreed to meet at Julie's, which was in a two-story house overlooking the river. Dan told me happily this was where ladies had lunch.

Cresting the stairs I identified her right away, smiling and leaning into the excitement of my arrival, fingers laced, arms akimbo on the table. I grasped as I sat down that of course she was pretty. *My first pretty friend.* She had a small heart face, framed in glossy chestnut hair cut not quite to chin length and feathered into a point on each cheek. Her thick bangs accentuated her precisely made-up eyes. Her lips—geranium pink—were quivering with suppressed merriment. There was a dramatic stalled moment while I got settled. Without moving my eyes I took in her sleeveless navy blouse, high pretty breasts, tan denim skirt, silver bangle. She had a firmly packed body and one of those necks that are creased as if they're wrapped in invisible thread. Debs-Anne, barely glancing at my clothes, was conspiratorial already. She had expected us to be a visual match.

"It's so nice to *see* you," she said.

"Thank you for calling me. It's great up here. What a view."

"Yeah, it's all right, if you like plastic chairs. Well. What do you *think?*"

"Well, maybe a beer? Can I get one here? I'd really kill for a beer." I sounded gushily unlike myself.

"About this *town.* Listen, it's okay, y'all are gonna be fine, long as you mind your p's and q's." She glanced at a table of women nearby. "Girl, they hated me when I got here." She was stroking the underside of her nose with her forefinger, indicating snootiness.

"You're scaring me."

"I'm *tryin.*" She leaned toward me theatrically. "Course, you know about Yankees," she said ominously. Becoming confidential, her voice got louder. Heads had turned our way. "Two kinds," she said. "The Yankee that comes to visit and goes back home, and the *damn* Yankee . . . he *stays!*" The heads looked away. "Now, I want y'all to *stay,* you and Dan. Don't y'all *go* anywhere." She patted my forearm. "I'm just kiddin. I'm just bein awful."

In the armhole of her blouse a sliver of day-glo turquoise bra glowed. Yes, I thought, she married up, too.

"So what was wrong with you?" I said.

"Well. First I had the unmitigated gall to just show up with Harley. 'What's *she* doin here, messin with my baby boy, why ain't she still back in Hickory where she belongs?' And then of course, my daddy's money won't the right color. And I didn't go to Pearce or St. Mary's. Generally speakin? They treated me like I was his concubine. Okay, it's an old family and all but I mean, don't let's get carried *away*. Actin like they were some old blue-bloods and all, like they had *slaves*. Those are cute earrings. They're precious. Where'd you get them?" I told her the name, a place in the Crabtree Mall in Raleigh. "Oh, I go there," she cried. "We can park Harley Tom at Nan-Darlin's and have us a real time. Oh heck. I'm gonna have a beer too."

Our sandwiches and potato chips arrived and Debs-Anne talked on. I answered a few questions, mostly to do with Dan, how long we'd been married, where we met, and so on. She wanted to know what church we went to. She herself had been raised as a Baptist, "but Harley's Presbyterian so that's not working out real well yet, but it will." I told her about our house, told her I had plans for a children's book, I even told her we were trying to have a baby. But then, in tacit agreement that Debs-Anne was more interesting, we snuggled down into her monologue. This carried us deeper into her stuffy in-laws Nan-Darlin and Eddie (who, to be *fair*, she admitted, were subsidizing Harley as a reward for not leaving town), and her and Harley's two-year-old son, Harley Tom, who was driving her crazy. ("Well, I'm as sorry as I can be, but him and me just don't get along.") Her mouth was prettier than mine, as fresh and mobile as a toothpaste commercial. She touched on the general gossipy drear of life in Beasley, she said people were two-faced. "I'm *tellin* you, girl!" Slangy, dainty, interrupting herself to beam at the waitress or mourn a chipped nail, Debs-Anne was busy with herself every minute, and yet every minute she seemed open and true, alert to some notion of womanliness, some fantasy she'd been consummating since the day she discovered she was female. I was falling under her spell. She exposed herself with such trusting, affable candor, like the kind of hammy actress who signals the audience that she's in on the joke of

herself. I was trying not to watch her freshen her lipstick using a little silver brush, when the check came and Debs-Anne, eyes still on
the mirror, slapped her hand over it.

"This is on me today. But now, you have to show me your new
home."

She followed me back to the house in her car. Her front license
plate was mirrored, with SPOILED BRAT scrawled in teal blue.

In the living room we stood silently looking through to the dining
room and the mahogany table, slick with light off the spangled river.

"This is so pretty?" Debs-Anne said in a small voice, and then
strayed back to the entrance hall. I heard her stop to look at the
clock. "Y'all got some pretty things. . . ." Her footsteps trailed down
the hall to the kitchen as I came in from the dining room. She noted
the marble counters and the refectory table squeezed up against the
windows, unsavory, I suddenly thought, crammed in like a king-sized
bed in a dinky motel room. But Debs-Anne was pulling up a chair.
She sat down and pressed her cheek against the table with her tan
arms spread over it in an embrace.

"I'm gonna just be quiet now and pretend this is my house. Y'all
got a lovely home. I'm serious. And I haven't even seen it all." Her
head came back up.

"Coffee first," I said, and put mugs and spoons on the table and
sat down to wait for the coffee machine. Debs-Anne's face was pearly
in the afternoon light, every mascaraed eyelash etched in place.

"Oh, this is all just so peaceful out here," she said. "It's pretty
much of a dump over by us."

"Oh, it's not!" Dan had pointed out their clapboard house, painted
a chic red-brown with white trim, with a smilax vine being trained
around the front porch. "Aren't you in the historic district?"

"So-called. Woulda been, if y'all hadn't burnt the place down.
Oh, it's fine. I'm just bein ungrateful. It's a cute little house. Harley's
daddy finally broke down and let us have it. It's lookin pretty good
now. Small." She sugared her coffee. "Plus we got a dog problem.
My baby sleeps straight through it but it just about loosens my
screws, dogs goin off all night worse than car alarms, every time a
leaf falls on their nose. Course, people still got em chained up in the

yard like ole coonhounds. The guy across the street's the worst.
Can't hear his own dog barkin three feet away."

"Don't you complain?"

"Oh sure. I go over there to Crane's house. He's always nice as he
can be. Looks over at Sadie, that's his little collie. Gives her this
killer mean look and says, Sadie, you terrible damn dog, why do you
always wake Debs-Anne *up* like that? Like it's the *dog's* fault! Harley
got hot with me about that."

"Why?"

"Oh, cause Crane's got the right, I guess. Harley's real big on individual rights, don't ever get him started, I'm serious. That doesn't
mean he likes it though. One time he took his gun in the middle of
the night and went out in his underpants, said he was goin to shoot
Crane's house up. Came home in two minutes. He and Crane go
back to ninth grade."

"Wait. It's Crane's right to wake up the whole neighborhood?"

"Well . . . to keep a guard dog. Cause of where we are too."

I got up to get our coffee. Behind me I heard the whir of Dan's
new battery-driven pepper grinder. "Oh Lord, look what I did." Debs-
Anne was about to get up for a sponge when I brought the coffeepot
over, flicked at the pepper with my hand, and sat down.

"You mean your neighborhood has break-ins?"

We waited for a jet-ski to skim by. Debs-Anne's eyes had gone
filmy and coy, or maybe just shy for some reason.

"Oh, well, it's a little bit mixed where we are."

I poured out her coffee.

"Well, mostly over on Second Street but . . . you know how people are."

She stretched up her arms and her bangle slithered down. "You
know what I say? There's good people and bad people. People make
too much fuss about all that now. They should just get on with it."

"Well, they seem to. Things seem okay. I'm a little surprised there
aren't more mixed couples."

"Oh, they're there!" She laughed.

"But people around here seem to get along pretty well."

"Course they do. They ought to be glad it's not thirty years ago. My granny still keeps a separate glass for her yardman."

"Oh no."

"Under her sink, been there for years. Thomas comes and she sets it out on the porch and he has a drink from the faucet outside and then when he's gone she brings it in. One time her and me were in the kitchen havin a fight about my skirt bein too short, some dumb thing, and I was so mad I pulled that glass out and ran the water and had me a drink. Watchin her to see what she'd do? I thought she was gonna *die* on me. That was me then, always doin some ill thing or other. Big stuff too. I was vile. And I don't even know what for. No good reason at all."

She had wiped a hand up through her bangs, creating a gel-stiff Woody Woodpecker tuft and exposing a well made-up constellation of pimples. I didn't know what to say.

"My four brothers are all alcoholics. That's their genes. But they're darlin's, they really are. My daddy always says, I got four good kids and one bad one. I'm always tryin to make myself not be so deranged. I don't know. I don't think it's workin so far." She made a little face. "Like, I could *give* a flip. Maybe I'm as good as God made me. You know, you look so cool sittin there. How do you stay so crisp like that? Look at you."

"Oh. Gee, thanks," I said, laughing. "I'm not really." Touching my hair. "I'm a mess half the time. But Debs-Anne." Her confession had loosened me up. "You know, what you were just saying. I heard something at the club the other night, in the bar."

"You sit in that place long enough, you'll hear it all. This is some good coffee, girl."

"This older woman was standing just behind Dan and me. She was talking to somebody about Bryant Gumbel, you know."

"Sure, on that morning show. Now *there's* one. Cute as a bug."

"She called him a nigger. She said, 'I don't like that nigger.'"

"Oh Lord. What'd she look like?"

"Well preserved but matronly. Short white curly hair. She had on a red, sort of Chanel suit and a lot of gold chains."

Debs-Anne was searching her mind. I tried to work out why, having set her on this witch-hunt, I didn't feel shabbier.

"Old . . ."

"Maybe seventy-five."

"See? There you go! That's what I was sayin before, that's all dyin out now. Claudia? I want you to *like* us."

"I do."

I was disconcerted and pleased that I had just managed to say a simple true thing. I was smiling. Debs-Anne was smiling. To break the moment I turned my head to look out at the river and I think Debs-Anne winked at me, a sly conciliatory little wink. Then she remembered her bangs standing on end and tapped them down. "This table is so special," she breathed. "Don't you love all these crazy old scars."

I invited her to come see the upstairs.

Yes, she was affecting me. First of all because she naturally accepted me without turning a hair. I wasn't bitter that because of my new looks she had been predisposed to like me, I had moved on from there. I wanted her acceptance to cauterize the incredulity that was still weeping into me from my invisible wounds. I was also becoming addicted to her conversational style, not just the Southern idiom but the way her self-assurance saturated whatever she said, so that even her racism, which I acknowledged, was nothing she needed to hide: I know what I am, but love me anyway. Love me *because* of it. Like a dare, one I had just accepted. I admit also to being gratified that another of my Southern preconceptions had been confirmed. I had it all covered. What I didn't quite see was how much I'd actually liked that dollop of racism, with its implicit promise of more to come.

That night, hoping to impress Dan with my new fund of local info, I told him Harley's mother was called Nan-Darlin. "As in *Darling*," I said, and waited for him to wince.

He blinked at me across the table. "I know," he said. "I bet she's really nice."

TEN

I NEVER SPIED on black people. They were just there. I sat down on a bench in the mall and they poured past, the boys keeping their faces vacant and doing that limp, as if their legs were different lengths, and the girls, the angular studious ones with their long African bones and taut underjaws, and the loud ones with their hair raked into topknots, jostling and bouncing off each other. Their abundance shocked me, their high round rear ends like lycra-coated melons and their big compact bosoms, and their glamorous heads with the features enlarged to twice the scale of mine, the space between their eyes and their brows painted in iced colors to go with their outfits. Sometimes in the midst of a giggly eye roll their extravagant glances would catch on me and settle, and then flounce away. The hysteria that followed wasn't anything I had provoked, I told myself, but just a continuum of the hilarity streaming behind them like colored ribbons. Mostly they ignored me, making them easier to watch.

I used to feel like one of those trick cameras designed with the aperture on the side, snapping away on the sly. A mountainous black man at a pay phone, his broad listening face trapped in an iridescent mesh of sweat, his eyes varnished that rich yellow-brown. A pale smallpox vaccination on a woman's arm. After a few weeks I was moving in for intimate details, whereas before I would have restricted myself to a stolen peek at her dressed ringlets gleaming like graphite. I did stare outright at the kids. I pretended they didn't mind, and feasted on their small shoulders and their busy heads that I longed to touch, until finally they tried to escape my attention by turning into little statues.

In the little public park near the house, black people fished on the breakfront. Spaced too far apart to talk to each other, they just sat on their lawn chairs and coolers and waited—young men in muscle shirts, old men, old women spread-legged under their long skirts—while I sat in the car behind my sunglasses. Late afternoon was the best time to be there, when a lot of other people parked for a few minutes on the way home from work and contemplated the river, while I watched the fishing people start to pack up, languidly settling a thermos inside a bucket inside a bigger bucket with that fond fluid precision that suggested a confidential intelligence about buckets that I didn't have. They loaded their gear into late-model compacts or else old guzzlers like Grand Ams and Cutlass Supremes that wallowed out of the parking lot onto the road, and in my mind I followed them. A small ranch house, a plastic cloth on the kitchen table, a television on in the other room, kids yelling. The fish are in the sink, slit, their liverish guts puddled in the drain. I hear the theme song for the news as my brown hands reach down and lift a fish, plop it in the bowl of flour, turn it neatly, and lower it into the spitting pan.

I was going in abandoned houses by then. I think that started around the end of May. It wasn't about being restless or bored, because I wasn't. Maybe I had found a novel way to be my usual self, creeping around and feeling invisible. I knew these houses had to have owners somewhere, but they were so invitingly accessible it felt as if the rules on trespassing had been stretched to accommodate me. The first house, a farmhouse, had tempted me for weeks, its rear windows blinking through the trees at me every time I passed until one day I just careened off the road onto a dirt lane that rumbled around behind an old trailer junkyard and there it was, almost dwarfed by a pair of old magnolias. I parked on a little track at the back and got out in the stinging hot stillness, so fragrant with baked pine resin.

Some rotted steps led up to a surprisingly solid porch. There was a rusty screen door and a plain old four-paneled front door. The corroded doorknob wobbled in my hand but then it turned. The wide musty hall had a fairly high ceiling, the walls were unpainted plaster, dinge being the predominant effect. Suddenly I felt unalone, and turned my head slowly and saw just behind me a smooth ashen blob stuck to the door frame, the size of a baby's head. I escaped from it into another room that was alive with these horrible blobs, all sizes, repulsive in their proliferation, which seemed concerted, somehow *willed*. It was like being back in the Shelburne marina in the winter, among the upturned boats with the barnacles fastened to their hulls like disembodied mouths. In the hall were more blobs, with their tubular innards extruding like layers of Pan's pipes, but across a small breezeway there was a kitchen they seemed to have overlooked. The sagging floors had skewed the counters and popped open cupboards containing nothing but dust as thick as spilled flour. Ivy had crawled in under the window by the sink. Weird glittery grit crunched under my feet as I moved around. A pair of green lace panties was draped on a dishtowel rack.

Upstairs it was better, much sunnier, with fewer wasps' nests. Stripped to their lathing in spots, the rooms were friendly, like rooms in a cartoon haunted house. Pearly scum on the windows scoured the light, making the house feel secluded and safe. No toilet, no closets, just four square bedrooms off a wide hallway, austere but built to a plan that had been lavish with space. The absence of sound rushed into my ears, carrying the faint shrieks of the first family moving in a hundred years before, the kids hooting out their windows, sturdy shoes banging on the stairs. On a windowsill I found something the last occupants had left behind, a red plastic comb. There were a couple long hairs still stuck in it. It was so explicit and plaintive, like an artifact in a museum dedicated to some holocaust I had miraculously survived. I was suddenly grateful for my life, and in that same peaceful instant I was ready to leave it. I felt half gone already, as if by standing there and becoming just a little more tranquil and willing I would slip through a crack in the opulent silence. I would leave a sandal behind, one of those inexplicable single shoes that litter the world, to make the next visitor shiver and wonder about me. I stayed a long time. I sampled the different views, discovering out the back a smeary, sunlit garden scene, accented with a slatternly trellis. Beyond that, strangled in vines, was a square one-room brick house with a slate roof. At some point it had been painted chalk white, even the big iron bars bolted over the windows. I knew what it was.

That house was like my basic primer. None after that was ever quite so plainly built or so compelling. By the end of that week I had probably been in twenty houses within a five-mile radius of Beasley. If the front door didn't open, another one always did. I soon realized I didn't need to bother hiding the car. Nobody cared. I got used to the wasps' nests, they were fairly common, but there were worse things. One house was empty except for a room downstairs where there was a double mattress, some neatly labeled cartons of kids' clothes, and a shopping bag overflowing with inspirational self-help tapes. Several years' worth of elementary-school photos of the same boy were strewn across the dirty floor. They documented his transition from a dogged freckled little kid to a pasty teenager with a perplexed fog in his eyes. In another house I saw a kitchen consisting of a sink and a hot plate, with a crib in the corner, lined with a grubby orange towel. Occasionally there were messages waiting for me, like YANCEY IS BEING GOOD penciled inside a closet. It got easier to ignore any qualms about snooping as my curiosity began to function as a built-in excuse for itself. I couldn't pass an empty house without doubling back and finding a way in.

It was easy to keep this a secret from Dan, once I was sure the UPS man would leave Dan's catalogue orders in the garage. I could be clean and fresh and have the house filled with dinner aromas by the time Dan came in. He never asked where I'd been, he never even seemed to notice the big bunches of hydrangeas I filched from the dead. After his shower he would want to have drinks in the living room, ideally while he demonstrated a new acquisition. One night he unpacked a canister vacuum cleaner that was supposed to have enough suction to pick up a bowling ball. It wouldn't pick up a large crystal ashtray. I watched from the couch as Dan took off his sneaker and tried and failed to get it to stick to the nozzle. It wasn't dismay in him, more like panic. He threw himself into the wing chair and put the shoe on again, tying his laces with shaking hands.

"Danny, how much does it matter?" I knew exactly how much. "Send it back. The one we've got is fine."

"You send it back. I've got better things to do." He flapped his legs open and shut, stirring up a sullen breeze. The vacuum, a retro thirties imitation like a chrome armadillo, had slunk under the coffee table. "I ordered a pizza oven today."

I didn't know if this was a defiant boast or a test of my sympathy. "Great," I said neutrally.

"It fits on the counter. You plug it in. I'm stupid. I'm a total sucker."

"You're not a sucker. You're just . . . ever hopeful."

"You mean, like actually hoping you'd ever care what I do."

"I like pizza."

"Don't go all chirpy. You don't have to *humor* me."

"I know. Honey, come over here and sit."

I patted the couch, like a nice mommy, noticing how genuine my solicitousness sounded, and how it stirred the oily pity that was always waiting in me.

"I'm making something you like," I said. I would change the menu. Dan hadn't moved. His head was thrown back, face slack, legs open, a big doll of a man.

"Spaghetti?" he said.

"Only the best. Chef Boyardee."

He gave me a slippery smile. He was so easy to please, too easy. I didn't believe him, not his appetites, not his requirements. It hadn't occurred to me yet that I didn't believe in his love.

The house was fifteen miles east of Beasley on the back route to Calhoun, set back from the road thirty yards or so. I almost missed it. It was being consumed by a scrabble of bushes grown halfway into trees. I braked and backed up and turned down the dirt lane. For some reason I was driving Dan's car. I had to walk in through the

tangled growth, feeling my way over a crust of dead nature that reminded my feet of frozen snow. It was very hot, mid-June. Drawing
closer I saw that Virginia creeper had covered several ground-floor
windows. Near the house the growth thinned out into sparse weedy
grass marked with traces of char. A bonfire had blistered the white
paint on the porch columns, not real columns but square posts set
on clunky brick pedestals. The style of the house was stodgy, circa
1920 or so, not one of my favorites. Behind a rusty screen door the
front door opened with a slight shove and I stepped inside and made
sure the door was shut behind me.

From an atypical window at the top of the stairs, old-looking light
seeped into the vine-throttled gloom. I paused to admire it, and then
began my downstairs pass. There were the usual four rooms, the two
in the front containing an old upright piano and overturned crates
that had been used as chairs. An empty vodka bottle stood on the
piano and other bottles were strewn here and there. There was one
of those wire contraptions that support a funeral wreath, and a plastic bucket overflowing with white rags I tried not to look at too
closely. In one back room, neatly spread out on the floor, was a
Christmas handkerchief or scarf. On it was a pyramid stack of Tupperware boxes, clean and empty apparently, although again I didn't
investigate. All these rooms were sprinkled with what seemed to be
wet ash. In the other back room a thin old brown mattress, the type
with buttons, was pulled onto a "dune" of real sand decorated with
branches and driftwood. I was deciphering the hieroglyphic stains
on the mattress when there was a bumping sound upstairs. Footsteps, oh God. *Coming down.* Then they stopped. I knew I could get
trapped if I tried to escape through the back. I made straight for the
front hall and was halfway across when I felt compelled to glance
back up the stairs.

He was there. He stood a few steps down from the top. Headless
from my vantage point, he was backlit by the upper window, almost
geometrically square-shouldered. Light T-shirt, dark pants. His arms
hung down in a loose self-assured way. He descended a couple more
steps and stopped, as if to let me see his face, but it was in shadow,
it was just featureless blackness. I could tell he wasn't smiling. Then

he clumped slowly down the rest of the stairs, and I came flowing back into my self and realized I was awkwardly twisted away from my feet, which were still pointed at the door. I angled my face at him on a rush of blood, not sure how much of me he could see. His face, his head, his whole body, were soaking up what little light there was in the hall, giving it back to me in clues. A soft rounded sheen on his forehead, a rim of light on his upper lip.

I said, "I'm sorry." I made an attempt to smile up at him but it fell short, into a smirk.

As he eyed me he began to scratch the underside of his forearm. When he rather fastidiously lifted his arm to peer at the itch I thought I detected a bluff. I relaxed just a hair.

"I shouldn't be in your house," I said. "Sorry. I'm going now." I stepped toward the door.

"My aunt's house."

"Oh. But she doesn't *live* here."

This produced a very small, amused gleam. I got to the inner door and opened it and glanced back. He was legible now but his blackness—his being black—forbade me to stare at him. "I just go in these old houses." I knew how flustered I sounded.

He compressed his lips and released them. "Got caught this time."

His face wasn't wide but there was a stretched aspect, the eyelids were ellipses, the nose was flattened as if by the taut thickness of his skin. His eyes were so dark I couldn't see the pupils, while his mouth conveyed nothing but its own particular fleshiness. It was very disconcerting, the mouth so still, refusing to smile, while a definite light was coming into his eyes now. I was trying to shoulder the screen door open but it was stuck. He stepped over quickly and banged the upper corner with the heel of his hand, trapping me under his upraised arm, giving me a whiff of cinnamon, then I stepped out backward into the sun. He came out to watch me struggle through the bushes to the BMW.

"You be careful in that thing!" he called. As I got in I managed to wave. "Don't you be speedin on me!"

With mushy hands I put the key in the ignition. As I reversed back up the track I glimpsed him through the overgrown bushes, stepping back into the house. I didn't know why I hadn't asked him what he was doing in there. No, better not to have shown any interest, not when he was so disinterested in me, amused by my whiteness and my inane remark about his aunt living there, which of course she didn't, any more than she owned the house. That was a lie. And then he had had to see me get into a stupid expensive car. He thought I was rich, if he had bothered to think anything about me at all. I drove back into Beasley, returned some videos and went to the Food Lion, waiting for him to recede. By the time I pulled into the driveway he was filling the whole sky, watching me punch in the alarm code, watching me unpack the groceries. I hadn't bought any food he would want. I had seen their shopping carts; potatoes and cabbage, boxes of macaroni and cheese, white bread. He would look at my frozen yogurt and laugh.

I ate on my lap in the living room, reading a *New Yorker* short story. It happened to be about a group of white people in Manhattan with nothing in common except their cleaning lady, a *treasure* who was now suddenly dead at the hands of an ex-husband nobody'd ever known existed. As I read this, a long body materialized across from me on the couch, matte brown muscles, slitty eyes, an impenetrable Gauguin nude posing for me on the chintz flowers. He had wanted me. That disinterest had been desire that I had misread, confused by his obdurate closeness. Or maybe not. Maybe when I was nervous I was still ugly. My vanity flustered me, as if he could see that too. I concentrated on practical questions. How had he gotten there without a car? Where did he live? Not anywhere nearby, there were no other houses around. He must have walked, one of those black men who just appear on a deserted back road or cut across a derelict parking lot.

Then I started getting ready for Dan, who was coming home that day. Yes, that was why I had Dan's car; he had taken my Volvo to the airport because it was less enticing to thieves as it sat parked for five days in the airport lot. Dan was in Minneapolis or Tampa or Denver, in a convention hall, standing around and ogling girls and jingling his change with his sales reps, his buddies. The one from

Chicago who could drink eleven Bloody Marys and pick up a dime with his toes; the New York guy who sent his steak back at Peter Luger's three times. I can't remember now specifically where Dan was, if I even knew then. I used to forget. I enjoyed that one week of every month when I was relieved of his clean reliable presence. I liked being in bed alone, I liked the strangeness of his leg not pressed up to mine. Sometimes I speculated about who he might be lying next to, but that was manufactured excitement since I didn't really think Dan was capable of that much adventure. When he was home I would supply him with mystery by watching him sleep, and then he would be off again for another week, leaving me to dust his bureau and handle the things on his little leather tray—his change, his mints, his Kon-Tiki figure—with conscientious wonderment, like a widow who wants to feel more aggrieved. That afternoon I rolled his clean socks into balls as compact as bombs, I folded a fresh washcloth the way he liked, in thirds like a towel, and generally urged our reconnection. When he walked in he was loud and jokey, promising me a "gross" story involving lap dancing, volunteering to make a marinade for the steaks. When we got in bed we were triumphant and drunk. We made love, and in the morning the black man was gone.

ELEVEN

ON MONDAY I was back at the house. I told myself I hadn't finished it. I was confident I wouldn't find anyone, but I winced up the
stairs with my heart thudding, calling *hello*, just in case. No sign of
him, and not much else to see. There was a small dirty bathroom
tiled in yellow and black, and four bedrooms. In one of them the raw
plaster walls had been painted a pink that was faded now, which
seemed to make it more intense. I had seen this pink before but always in houses older than this. In each room was a little rubble, bits
of clothing strewn around. The views out the back were tobacco
fields steaming in the sun.

This time when I left I drove further up the road until I hit a
stretch of very modest ranch houses. I was trying to spot one that was
definitely "black," a pointless exercise unless I actually saw some
black people. A certain tang to the color scheme—lemon-yellow
house with grass-green shutters—was not foolproof evidence. The
most reliable sign was a table and chairs under a shady tree; white
people never sat out in the heat unless they were riding something,
a lawn mower or a golf cart. Eventually I turned and trawled back,
feeling absurd when I reactivated the friendliness of a woman who
had waved when I passed her before.

That night I dreamt a black man was standing beside me in the
bus shelter at Burlington High School. He tried to put his arms
around my shoulders and I backed away and his skin started to unpeel off his hands like long inside-out gloves. I walked away, pre-

tending not to notice them stuck on my shoulders. A straightforward, repugnant dream, but as I was coming awake, it was my failure to return the gloves that seemed grotesque. I was still trying to explain myself to him, some wisp of him, as the dream faded.

I looked for him around Beasley, but not compulsively. Once or twice I mistook other tall men for him. After a couple weeks, I couldn't conjure him up anymore.

On a Saturday morning in early July I glanced out the bedroom window and he was there, next door in the Alligoods' yard. I thought, *My God, he's found me,* and flinched back out of sight. When I peeked again he was skirting their barbecue, carrying a rake now, heading away from their house toward the river. It was him, the squared back, the same work clothes. His bearing made the white T-shirt and gray work pants seem military. As I registered the new free-form areas of straw shaped around the Alligoods' azaleas, I realized I had noticed their yardman once or twice before. I was feeling stricken that I hadn't recognized him out at the old house, when Janet Alligood came out on her deck and called him in a light musical voice. "*Calvin* . . ." By the time I got down to the kitchen he was drinking a glass of water, his throat pumping, one long hand hovering by his breastbone. When he finished he swooped to pick his rake up off the grass, and walked with it to the edge of the deck. His arm reaching out to put the glass on the railing sent a flow back through his body, like a wave.

I don't know what my plan was. I didn't have one. I just stole out the front door like a thief and headed for the Alligoods', observing jubilantly that there was no truck or car in their driveway, as if this proved something. Janet answered the door.

"Hey, stranger! You don't have to knock, honey. Come on in, I'm feedin Dick."

Dick was standing by the kitchen sink, insouciant and English-looking in his well-bred bones and sunburn and khaki shorts, his hair blond as a woman's. Janet plunked down on a stool as Dick wolfed his sandwich. Beyond him, outside, he—Calvin—was standing with his back to the house, rake in hand, motionless. He seemed to be staring out across the water.

"Hey, pretty lady, what the devil brings you here? Oh, hold on." Dick stepped into the laundry room and came back with a stack of old *New Yorkers*. He put them on the kitchen table and gave them a baleful look. I knew what was coming. Dick was fond of emphasizing our Yankee-ness, not maliciously, I had decided, but as a way of making himself feel more deliciously Southern.

"Yankee rag," he twanged. "That's all a mite highbrow for me."

I made a highbrow face and thanked him.

"What's a Southern girl say on her weddin night?" he demanded.

"I don't know."

" 'Ouch! Daddy, that *hurts!*' "

Janet moaned softly. "How's things, honey? Everything okay at your house?"

"We're fine, we just need a yardman."

"Calvin's *it*, Calvin's the business," Dick said. "Punctual. Nice manners. Even has kind of an eye."

"Calvin Moore," Janet said. "We love him."

I explained I wanted his name and number in case Dan ever got sick of mowing our lawn. Dan was out at the moment, I said.

"Oh." Janet touched her throat. "I don't know if he has a phone. I'll go find out." She slipped out the back door. "Calvin! Stop admirin my view!" Dick turned and watched with me as Janet and Calvin met halfway across the lawn. Their voices were lost but Janet, in thick-waisted middle age, listened to Calvin with one hand on her hip, elbow coquettishly thrusting, and the other hand feeling the back of her hair. I wondered what Dick thought about this.

"Guy's a cipher," he said. "He's Janet's project, she found him. She's got the touch. That's one thing they really hate."

"What's that?"

"Bein patronized. They can always tell in a heartbeat."

Now Calvin's face was almost stony, but Janet was grinning as she stalked back up to the house. She slipped in the back door on a gust of heat.

Dick said, "And the upshot *is* . . ."

"Claudia, honey, he's booked. You can't have him till August and maybe not even then."

Dick cried, "My man! *Told* you he was good."

"Well, but that doesn't help Claudia, does it? Poor guy, his kid's sick again. Oh. Here he is."

Dick lunged at the door and Calvin stepped in. His eyes flickered over Janet. We watched as he put his hand on the counter beside a little gingham-lined basket of eggs and discreetly touched his mouth to his shoulder to tamp his sweaty lip. Then he straightened up and disengaged his focus, like an actor trying to act blind.

"Mrs. Janet said you got a friend." His voice was deeper than I remembered, blacker.

"In person." Dick flourished a hand at me. Calvin looked at me without expression.

"This is Mrs. Dryburgh," Janet said.

"How're you?" I asked. Just the palest emphasis on "you."

"Doin all right, how you doin?" He blinked, slowly, ostentatiously. I thought it might be a signal. He had looked away again.

Dick said, "She's fine, except for that horrible lawn over there. You know, I don't believe Dan *enjoys* doin his yard work. Y'all want it done, what, every two weeks? Mowin, edgin, the usual?"

"Dick, we get ours done every week," Janet said.

"My dear, Calvin is a very busy man." Dick's delivery had turned florid. "I am *tryin* to work a *deal* here."

"Why can't he just do them on Saturday after he does us?"

I glanced at Calvin and willed him to speak but he was staring pointedly at the floor. I understood I was the one expected to talk. "Would once a week be okay?"

He rolled me a drab look. "Be eighteen, for mowin and all. You got some stuff out front needs keepin up."

"That's true, we do."

"Calvin," Janet cried in a smiley voice, "*we* give you *twenty*!"

Calvin's gaze rolled back to me. "Be twenty-two."

"Fine. Great."

"When do you want it done?"

"Today," Dick said. "Right now." I looked at him. "Trust me, Dan'll love you. He'll give you a big smooch, soon as he gets back from wherever he went."

"Wal-Mart."

"Oh I'm glad you said that, I have to go there," Janet said. "Oh dear. Now what was it I needed?"

"Scuse me," Calvin said. "I'll be over," he announced evenly, to all of us.

Janet sprang up to open the door for him. "You let me know when you're done," she sang, and closed the door fast. As Calvin moved behind me through the yard the glare in the kitchen seemed to swell.

"Well, that was swift," Dick said.

"Hon, his kid's sick."

"It's fine," I said, "that's an okay price. I don't think Dan'll mind. I don't."

"I bet you don't." Dick eyes were a little shiny on me, his smile a bit warped.

"Dick, maybe now's a good time to get your new bug gadget up," Janet said. "Go on, Calvin can help you."

"Yeah, okay." He saluted us lazily, a finger to his temple, and went out.

Janet and I watched Calvin. He was raking again, unaware of Dick bearing down on him. "He seems nice," I said.

"He's a sweetie, he's fine."

Dick was talking to him now, gesturing with what seemed like unnecessary gusto. Calvin's expression never changed but his face was softening, or opening, kindly, as if to draw Dick's anxiousness out of him. I asked Janet how many kids Calvin had.

"Twelve, for all I know. I know there's a little girl, cause once when he was here, a friend of his came by in a big hurry and said she was in the hospital and his wife or girlfriend or whatever needed him. Poor Calvin. He doesn't want to put up another one of those damn things." Calvin was disappearing with Dick around the side of the house. "Fifteen hundred volts to kill a few little flies and some no-see-ums? I *ask* you."

———

Dan loved Calvin. He was bemused by his failure to hire a yardman himself, but didn't mind my having gone ahead. Dan always liked it when I found ways to spend money. He stood in the kitchen watching Calvin on the big red lawn tractor, while I sat safely below Calvin's line of vision and watched Dan. I was feeling ridiculous, embarrassed by Calvin's matter-of-fact presence, which made my speculations about him seem sordid now. He was black, he was here, so what? When the tractor finally cut off I was upstairs. I heard Dan go out on the porch and they conferred in low grumbles, in the midst of which Dan let out a whooping laugh. Later I asked him what he had found so funny and he gave me a sage look. "Guy thinks he's a philosopher."

Calvin came back the following Tuesday in midafternoon. Dan had warned me he would be coming—"Maybe skip the sunbathing while he's here, Clod"—but he was still just suddenly there, with a tremendous double bang on the front door. When I opened it, his elliptical gaze just clipped me and then cut away. Behind him on the walk stood a big plastic bag full of bark chips.

"I'll be trimmin round the sides and doin those bushes in back." He turned abruptly and went down the steps. I tried not to wonder why he was back so soon.

An hour later the thermometer said 92. Calvin had been very busy with the clippers. I was ironing in the kitchen when he started spreading the chips under the evergreen shrubs by the back porch steps, disappearing for minutes at a time until the instant I glanced up, which was when he tended to pop up again. Once he seemed to look straight in and I froze as he threw his gaze up, dug in his back pocket for a Chap Stick, and applied it, his face opaque and abstracted.

It was almost time to provide some iced tea, but in what kind of glass? Should I, remembering Debs-Anne's grandmother, do it with a flourish, in a Waterford tumbler with lemon and a sprig of mint? He would think I was insane, or worse. I cracked ice and dithered, decided on a plain glass, no lemon or mint, then at the door I changed my mind and went back and slit a slice of lemon to perch on the rim. I carried this out on the porch and down to the lawn, feeling I looked too suburban, but thankful for my sunglasses. I had on a black T-shirt and white shorts.

He was squatting down smoothing a hand over the grass when my bare feet entered his field of vision. For a long moment we seemed interlocked, with him staring at my feet and me at his hair. It *is* wool, I thought. But it was really more like a sprayed-on coating of damp sparkling sponge. He stood up smoothly and took the glass. Thanked me. Folded the lemon slice with one hand, squeezed it, and dropped it in. His knuckles were blacker than his hands, his big earth-rimmed fingernails reminded me of the smooth inner surface of certain seashells. He was standing a whisper too close, not on purpose, I decided, just without noticing.

"I'm goin down on the dock, sit for a minute," he said.

"Great." Did he want my permission? "Good idea," I overenthused, and turned back toward the house.

"Always nice to have some company."

He was striding toward the water. "You come down if you want." He threw this over his shoulder.

Unwilling to run to catch up, I had to traipse after him. When he got to the end of the dock he sat down, put the glass down, and ripped his T-shirt off over his head. I might have turned back then except my feet were suddenly, stupidly, on fire. In real desperation I watched him hastily spread his T-shirt out beside him. I leapt onto it and lowered myself clumsily into the narrow space, working hard not to touch him. He finished his tea with much rattling of the ice and rested the glass on his thigh. My mind was stripped, shut down to everything but his proximity, our volumes of flesh and muscle. I felt the dampness of his shirt under me. I could smell my body lotion, combined with sweat, as it wafted over us on a shred of breeze. I knew he could smell it too. His body was throwing heat along my left arm, but his nakedness was controlled in some way, he seemed less bare than a shirtless white man would have, as if he were still wearing his skin. My sunglasses were sliding down my sweaty nose but I couldn't move for fear of bumping him.

"I used to be scared of this river." He lifted the glass and flung his ice cubes into the river. "Terrified. Two inches of water in a bucket bout scare me to death."

"Really?" This was worse, we were sitting too close to talk. He was rolling the empty glass on his thigh.

He spoke straight ahead, to the water. "Yeah. They used to have to roll me in the dirt, give me a dirt bath, like I was a little puppy dog."

I tried to emanate amused skepticism.

I said, "What used to bother me was the wet grass in the morning, when it was full of cobwebs." I saw them again, the soggy nets with their trembling balls of trapped dew.

"Yeah, but I figure you like bein scared. That's how come you be slippin in all these houses. Snag yourself a little thrill."

"Well, it's not really that. I'm just amazed how all these places sit empty."

"I guess you like spyin on people. That must be it. You know, you got kind of a sad thing about you."

"Do I?" It was all I could manage. I was amazed by his nerve.

"You won't ever get tired of this. This is a real nice position here."

"Thank you. Didn't you ever spy on people when you were little?"

"People who were there. Spyin on ghosts, that's different."

"I don't really think they mind."

Silence. I couldn't tell if he was actually angry.

I said, "Well, maybe I'll stop."

"Oh, you don't want to just stop cold like that." His voice was almost smiling, he was easing it around a curve at me.

"No. You're right."

I thought, This is going okay. I wanted to ask what he'd been doing in that old house himself. I wanted to ask about his child's health, except that would reveal that the Alligoods and I had been discussing him. He had gone very still. I thought he might be eyeing a styrofoam cup bobbing a few yards out, and decided to hazard a glance sideways. His lips were lightly pursed. Diffidence veiled his whole face, a self-consciousness at odds with the powerful, slightly stubbled jaw and the sculpted, impossibly swollen lips. The line of his nose was lightly concave, the distended nostril melting onto his cheek like grainy brown butter. Around his eyes the skin was grayish. His eyes seemed to press outward painfully, constrained only by the thick lids with their simple oily crease like a child's. His curly lashes looked singed, making me think of dried-up spider legs. When he lifted a hand to his neck and his elbow just grazed my arm, I looked away, mortified at having seen too much. But there was so much there, all that texture and thrust. I didn't understand all that over-statement, it seemed pointless. I don't have the right kind of eyes, I thought. I couldn't give him his own face, it defeated me. Sensing the absurdity of this, I felt it confirmed by a sweet sting of shame. He was dragging his hand over his face as if to rub away the residue my eyes had left.

"Okay," he said. "Now that's over, I got to get on back to work."

His knees crackled as he got up. He set the glass down beside me and I steadied it with my hand as it jumped in rhythm with his progress along the dock. I took my time getting back, walking up to where he was working on his knees near the porch. He had his back to me, his head didn't turn. I flung the T-shirt at him as I hit the porch steps and saw it tick his shoulder. No response.

He was wearing it when he came to the back door to get his money. My thighs had pressed it into a crazy striation of wrinkles, making a rather comical contrast to his blank face. When I brought the money out to him, his hand swung toward me from what seemed like a great distance, with a deliberation calculated to express con-tempt for the transaction and me and Dan's house.

He didn't look at the money. He was staring at a point beyond my shoulder. "I didn't finish."

"That's fine."

I fixed my own eyes at a distance and noticed the empty bark chip bag wedged neatly between two flowerpots on the porch steps. Be-yond that was the opposite shore and the sun-crazed water and the pine trees, all pushing in, pressing him against me. There was no room, no place for my eyes to go. I smelled a sharp cinnamon tang. Why didn't he just leave?

"What's your first name?" he said quietly.

It seemed too overt, too sexy in my mouth as I said it. I might have blushed.

"I'll be back next week, probably Thursday. Wednesday I take my half day, go out to that old house. Wednesday after lunch."

He bunched his lips, ruefully, concisely, then turned and went quickly down the porch steps and disappeared around the side. I ran through the house and into the den to watch him walk up the road. He was straight-backed, almost rigid, throwing his legs from the hip, exuding an exalted self-regard that looked silly on a man with a head as round and earnest as a boy's. I saw all this. I was seeing right through him. I wanted to yell, Yoo-hoo, that act's not working. All that fierce posturing. He had thought I wanted him just because I had stared. He had no idea what an object of fascination he was. And then just before he disappeared around the curve he jabbed a thumb upward to get at an itch in the middle of his back and that bit of awkwardness delivered him to me. Like a wound his folly opened up in me. Soliciting a white woman, his employer? He was a fool, a fool to want me. No . . . no, not at all. He had only wanted what he'd seen, what he *thought* he'd seen. Or had he cleverly, blackly, sensed I wasn't the real thing? Something about me had revealed itself. Confusion clotted in my throat, and I felt a scalding, overwhelming despair. That's what had given him the nerve, I thought. My inferiority, my obscurity, signaling his.

I went out on the back porch and walked around the side of the garage. He had raked up some pine straw and turned a broad swath of earth near the foundation in preparation for a new bed. Out back by the porch the evergreen beds on either side of the steps had been tidied, the lawn clipped into two symmetrical arcs. The composition of his chips was flawless, his hand and eye had been aware of how each piece should be, relative to the others. He must have arranged each piece separately. The pattern twitched in the glassy light. I understood that I was crazy. I went inside and lay down in my cool bedroom, stared at Dan's trouser press, and chose oblivion.

When I woke up Dan was standing over me, grinning. "You're gonna meet Harley. He's downstairs."

The afternoon swam back to me, distant and absurd.

"C'mon Claud, let's hustle. Wash your face and stuff. We're meeting Debs-Anne at the club."

And I was glad. Happy to be released from the usual evening routine with Dan, believing myself saved.

TWELVE

HARLEY GOT UP from the wing chair as I came into the living room, and I was shocked. There's never enough time to prepare for a new face. Here was a snub-nosed baby-man. A spray of brown hair had been trimmed to flop sideways across his tan forehead, which gleamed welcomingly. He was chunky in the shoulders, with well-toned fuzzy arms and a soft roll of tummy above his striped canvas belt, the same type as Dan's. Harley was wearing a polo shirt like Dan's too. Harley's was a soft washed purple.

"Claudia, hey!" His strong handshake carried a whiff of soap. He was one of those men who remain redolent of their toiletries all day, whose surface is so scrubbed you can't help thinking about all the moist mysterious mess it contains. He was a touch drunk. Nothing serious, just a faint persistence to his smile, and when his head moved, his gaze lagged behind, lingering on my waist, my calves, and finally wandering back to Dan. Dan was standing by the fireplace, stirring his ice cubes with his finger.

"I think ole Dan musta been tryin to keep you all to himself. Hey Dan, you creep. How'd you ever get a girl like this?"

"Money. You want a fresh one for the road, Harl?"

"Nah, I'm still suckin on this. Claud might need one though."

He had raised his eyebrows at me. I said that maybe if we were late, we should go.

"Yowza," he said. "Let's do that. This is great, we're all finally gettin together."

Remembering Harley's enthusiasm, I always think I should have picked up an ominous undertone, like the anxiety you feel sometimes on too bright and gusty a day. I suppose the evening had already siezed me. I was ready for a drink, ready for anything.

Debs-Anne, slim in a new polka-dot dress, was waiting at the bar. Chester's only customer, she was aslant on her stool, cantilevered into the flow of her conversation. When we came in, she speedily summed it up—"but so *what*, you know what I mean?" She kissed Dan's cheek and ran her arm around Harley's middle. Chester seemed more shrunken than ever inside his white jacket. Starched collar up around his ears, he was discreetly standing by with one yellow eye trained on the credits of *Fresh Prince*. I heard Debs-Anne say, "*Yes*, she's pretty, I *told* you . . . hey, Claudia?" and her hand swung out and pulled me in.

Dan leaned over the bar. "Chester, my man. Things cool with you?"

Chester cracked a smile. "Oh . . . not *too* bad," he cackled. As Dan was ordering our drinks, Harley stretched his hand over the bar and Chester, standing sideways to it, gripped it in an odd clandestine way. We all found our stools, Debs-Anne and I side by side, flanked by each other's husbands. Chester brought us the drinks and two bowls of popcorn and moved away, back to the almost inaudible TV.

Harley lifted his glass. "To your new home."

"To their whole new *life*," Debs-Anne corrected.

"To our *wives*," Dan said, sounding embarrassed in spite of the irony he'd ladled on. "God, whose idea was this, getting *them* together?"

We laughed and clinked glasses a little self-consciously.

"Debs, you should see their place," Harley said. "You won't believe the job they did. You guys've done an incredible job."

"I *have* seen it, Harley."

"Oh yeah." He snuck a cherry from Chester's setup tray into his mouth, and glanced around behind him. "Where the hell *is* everybody, home washin their dog?"

"It's Tuesday, brainy," Debs-Anne said.

"Y'all think I'm drunk. Claudia, would you please tell em I'm not?"

"Harley's not drunk," I said.

Debs-Anne wiggled inside her dress. "Sugar, why don't we buy a home on the river? *Sugar.*" Harley's attention was fixed firmly on the start of the local news.

"Hold on, guys, there's a major downside," Dan was saying. "Mosquitoes the size of bats, flood insurance up the wazoo. Noise pollution from like a zillion jet-skis—"

"Oh God," Debs-Anne said. "I feel better now. Harley, did you hear that? Their life's a *disaster.*"

"Truly." Dan grinned. "It sucks."

"Look. Lloyd," Harley said suddenly.

On the TV a bald portly man in shirtsleeves and a loosened tie was talking into a reporter's mike. He kept interrupting himself to take hungry drags on his cigarette, clasping his whole lower face in his hand in a fondling gesture. It was compelling to watch, and slightly distressing.

Debs-Anne explained he was Lloyd Swanner, the local DA. "Him and Harley's mom are cousins, aren't you impressed? He's a very big cheese, accordin to him. That trial's over already? Boy, that was quick. Sound please, Chester? Thank you."

I realized we were seeing the grand portico of the county courthouse downtown, and that this was the end of the trial of the man who, after a two-day drinking binge, had gone over to his boss's house and shot him when he opened the door. The DA was gone now, replaced by a younger man in a blue tractor cap, who was surrounded by a huddle of people so determinedly plain-faced and severe they might have been painted by Grant Wood.

"That's the dead guy's brother," Debs-Anne said. "He found the body after two days, when it was all stiff and . . . oh Lord, what'd he ever do to deserve that? I could cry."

"Shhh," Harley said.

"Sir, can you tell us how you feel about the death penalty being handed down here today?" the reporter said.

"We believe justice was served," the brother mumbled, then cleared his throat and bent closer to the mike. "We think it was fair," he said loudly. "The DA did a great job. He proved Larry Bonner was just plain mean."

"May his soul rot in hell," Debs-Anne intoned softly.

The news item came to an end and Chester immediately turned the sound down again. He was trying to maintain a decorous tone in the bar, I decided. There was no way he would be interested in what any of us had to say.

"Claud," Dan said loudly, "ask Harley what you're always asking me, about how come there's all these murders here. Claud's a little weird. She likes anything . . . what's that great word?" He was asking Debs-Anne, who shrugged. "You said it about a smell in your car, from Harley Tom being—"

"Oh, *oogy*," Debs-Anne said. "Well, but let me explain. Baby spit-up is oogy. Dog do on your shoe is oogy. Findin a hair in your food, all that good stuff. Killin your boss just for somethin to do cause you're *drunk*? Well, I don't even know what that is, but not oogy."

"I could kill," Harley said.

"Oh, you could not," Debs-Anne shot back. Did she want to assuage his anxiety about murderous impulses, or deflate his macho bluster?

I tried to step into the breach. "Harley . . . ?" I said, showing him my profile. "Are you a killer?" My voice had just the right low, musical sound.

Harley was studying me. "You know, you could kill too."

I said I probably could. I said, "I think in the right circumstances most people could."

"I don't know about that," he said.

"Claudia, that is *disgusting*."

I had shocked Debs-Anne. It made me want to do it again. "Why?" I said. "It's just people doing what comes naturally."

"You know, in France, if you kill your wife they let you off," Harley said.

"Ha. That's why this is America." Debs-Anne stroked the points of her hair onto her cheeks.

"In Norway it's illegal to spank your own kid," Dan called back to Harley. "They put you in the slammer."

"Oh *please*," Debs-Anne said.

"Bonner's your basic schizoid," Harley submitted.

"Maybe he drank too much Coke when he was ten," Debs-Anne said. We all stared at her, even Harley. "That's a quote from Lloyd the other night on TV. He was makin fun of those shrinks they always get to say how screwy the guy is. As if we don't know that. Lloyd's not real big on those guys."

"No, he wouldn't be," I said. Dan gave me a significant look, gave a reminder that Harley was related to the DA.

"He doesn't hate shrinks," Harley explained, "that's just his job."

"Sending guys to the electric chair. Yikes. Well, I guess somebody has to do it. No offense." I realized I was starting to have a good time.

"It's not the chair here, it's gas," Debs-Anne was saying. "Is that what it is in Vermont, the chair?"

"They don't *have* capital punishment there." I said it rather curtly, warmed by a flush of righteous indignation.

"Course, you get more murders down here." Dan was applying his own brand of tact.

"Yeah," Harley said, "that's why it works."

"It's fair," Debs-Anne crooned sadly. "An eye for an eye. Specially when they just keep lettin em out all the time."

Dan, in his most offhand voice, said, "You know, all these so-called problems Bonner had when he was a kid. Being asthmatic and getting beat up and shit? Like, I'm sure the dead guy's really *concerned*."

"Poor guy," I said.

Harley touched my arm. "Bleedin to death doesn't hurt, it's supposed to be kinda dreamy."

"Yeah, that's what John Lennon thought," Dan cracked.

"No *no*, Harley." Debs-Anne was suddenly very crisp. "She's talkin about Bonner. She thinks the *murderer's* the poor guy."

Silence. Even Chester, I noticed, slicing lemons over by the sink, had suspended activity.

Debs-Anne cocked her head thoughtfully. "Well, maybe she's right. It won't hardly Bonner's fault. Poor guy. Heck, all he did was drink too much, just like I do sometimes." She demonstrated for us, lifting her glass and draining it. "And I'm kinda screwed up too. But now . . . isn't that *strange?*" Pause. "*I* never kill anybody. . . ."

She set her glass down and waited for this to penetrate our skulls. She was cool, collected, convinced of the eloquence of her rationale. A nasty disaffected chill trickled through me. How could she be so incurious, not to even consider what might make somebody violent enough to jeopardize his own life? I knew what her problem was. Lack of imagination. I was ready to help. I waited for Chester to fill her glass and step away, trying, it seemed to me, to make himself even more inconspicuous than usual.

"You know, Debs-Anne," I said, "I can see *you* with a gun, a really—"

"Nine millimeter he had," Harley said, "like *you* should have, Dan, I keep tellin you, bud."

"—a really *big* gun, and you don't have any idea what just happened, except somebody's on the floor dead, and you're standing there like a zombie, like Bonner was—"

"—he *says*," Debs-Anne snorted.

"—and then, bing, the fog clears. What do you do? You start begging for that one split second to be taken back. And nothing happens. The body's still there, still not moving. That's when you know. The worst thing that could ever happen has just happened. It's all over. It's like you're both dead."

"Fuck." Harley laid his head on his folded arms, tenderly, as if it were a baby.

Debs-Anne's face crumpled. "Ooh, that would be *awful.* Much worse than bein the actual dead body. Right, Dan?"

"But the body doesn't *know* it's dead," I tried to point out. I thought I might be getting a little drunk. "It's not really part of this."

"Duh," Dan said.

"It's just *you* there, Debs-Anne," I persisted, a little hoarse and breathless now. "Wife, mother, and—"

"No, actually not. Cause I would've given the whole idea a little bit of thought first."

This blind faith that automatically exempted her from the abyss, this privileged conviction, where was she *getting* it from? I was humming with the need to enlighten her, I was almost vibrating. "That's not how it works," I said.

"Oh no? Please tell us then."

They were all looking at me.

"Murder is like . . . when somebody's hanging in the air, like a safe. And the ropes are too weak and it's too heavy. So it's going to fall on the sidewalk and smash somebody." (*Heavy*, I thought . . . that was good.)

"Classic. Shit happens." Dan sneered. "You're not gonna buy into that, Debs." He rammed her with his shoulder. She ignored him.

"People just get fed the fuck up," Harley opined rather flatly. He wanted this to be over.

"But see, maybe *one* day," Debs-Anne piped like a little girl, "that ole safe crashes on *your* little ole head. Bet that changes things, hmm? Not just tough luck *then*?"

"Yeah, it still is," I said evenly. "Same as anything, like getting a brain tumor, or your child falls out of a tree. Any little boo-boo. You forget and leave your car in neutral and it runs over a—"

"Oh, so now it's *my* fault?" she cried. She was slicing the bar with her coaster.

"There's no fault, it's just how it *is*. We kill each other, we're human, it's all built *in*!" Around the edges of my anger I was monitoring Dan's anxiety.

"Like that's a *real* good excuse!" Debs-Anne snapped.

"It's just a reason. Cause people don't really *want* to kill each other, they just do. Right this minute all these different people, housewives and grandfathers and boyfriends and nice people like us"—Debs-Anne was making a frustrated grinding sound deep in her throat—"are getting out guns and knives and sledgehammers to use on their neighbors and parents. And *children*." I dropped my voice. "And strangers too, but mostly it's people we're close to that get killed, people we love even. As I'm sure you're aware, Debs-Anne. You do *know* about all this, don't you?" In the corner of my eye a dark hand wiped the bar, a slow listening hand, as helpful and intimate to me as if it had just smoothed a page I was reading from. "You know we're not like animals, right? Because animals eat what they kill, and we just"—Debs-Anne had her hands clamped over her ears—"kill and maim and *torture* each—"

"*Whoa!*" Dan cried. "Hey guys! Can't say I didn't warn you about her!" Chuckling hard, trying to make it okay.

Debs-Anne shook out her hair. "Well, *hey!*" She flopped a hand onto Dan's arm. "That's sure not what *I* need, not after the day I just had with my son. You want to get oogy? Let's get oogy! We're talkin potty trainin and baby poop, yellow baby poop all *over* my house. We don't need those two nut cases over there, do we, Dan?"

"Hey, we could kill em!" Dan said.

Harley lifted his head. I thought for a moment he was going to lay it on my shoulder. "It takes passion. Killin somebody takes passion. See, *she* knows."

"Chester!" Debs-Anne cried. "Get over here and save us from these maniacs!"

He turned from the TV, smiling.

"Hit us again, Chester," Dan said.

He came over with the wine bottle and filled my glass and Debs-Anne's. I waited for his eyes to lift, but he would look at none of us.

The happy hour wore on.

I was briefed by Debs-Anne on her sister-in-law's recent baby shower. Dan went and sat beside Harley and tried to jolly him into a more sociable form. As he and Harley were paying the bill, Debs-Anne and I went downstairs to a reserved table in the center of the almost deserted dining room. We sat down side by side to avoid each other's faces, but as Harley and Dan were settling in across from us, Debs-Anne leaned toward me, warm and whispery.

"Girl, are we friends again?" Her urgency was making me cruel, I just sat there. "I have this problem with violence," she said. "It's kind of a thing with me."

"Don't worry, Debs-Anne," Dan said, "nobody'd ever try to kill anybody as sweet as you." If he was being sarcastic, it didn't show. His gleam seemed genuine.

"Thank you, Dan." She batted her eyes at him. "Claudia? I think your husband might be *playin* with me."

Harley was smiling up at the waitress, a pretty teenager who was new to me. We all ordered the grouper, and Dan asked her to bring two bottles of Chardonnay.

"And a Diet Pepsi!" Harley called after her. He beamed at me. A fresh air of pleasantness, of trying to have a nice evening, had just rolled in like a fog. We were all still young enough to feel grown-up in a setting like the club dining room. Debs-Anne and I were both watching our waitress, who had stopped at a nearby table to reach over and straighten the tablecloth.

"Chrissy Teale," Debs-Anne murmured. "She turned out okay. She had a little problem with f-a-t for a while there."

Harley and Dan twisted around to look at Chrissy's rear end. "I don't know," Harley said. "I still like mine a little smaller than that."

"Me too," Dan said.

"Your wife's got a *darlin* little butt on her," Debs-Anne cried.

"Did I say she didn't? Harl? Did I?"

"Her butt's adorable," Debs-Anne added. "She's good all over. Look at that nose, I'd kill for that nose. And that little beauty mark?"

"You know what I like, that little cleft in her chin," Dan said. "Don't y'all love that? Look at that perfect chin."

I warned him with my eyes.

"Great nose," he said.

"Hey, I'm pretty too!" Debs-Anne pouted, making Dan laugh. Chrissy appeared and started setting out bottles and salads. "We've all just been sayin how pretty you are," Debs-Anne said.

Harley smirked up at her. "You have to be, if you want to work here. This is one of those ugly-free zones."

Chrissy gave me a wink. "Sure is!" she cried, sailing away with her tray.

"I thought all you had to be was white," I said, avoiding Dan's eye.

Debs-Anne stabbed her fork in the direction of the kitchen. "You need to go stick your nose in there."

"Don't forget Chester," Dan said pointedly, firing a warning back at me. "How old *is* he anyway? Should somebody make him retire?"

"Oh, Chester wants to be right up there pourin a drink when he goes," Harley said. "He told me."

"Chester's a dear man," said Debs-Anne. "A real wise ole soul. And a good listener. He always lets me rattle on about nothin."

"Yeah, like for half an hour while the whole town's standin around with an empty glass," Harley said.

"Oh, boo-hoo," Debs-Anne said. "He's referrin to this big lawn party Nan-Darlin had when we got engaged. It was a real big deal, she had Chester there doin her bar. And the party's goin, and I go up to the bar for a refill and I give Chester my glass, and he sees my hand shakin, and he gives me just the most wonderful smile. Tryin so hard to lift me up. And I burst into tears! Well, I had *nerves*, I was in a swivet on account of this one here, him and his mama, pokin at me and pullin me back and forth the whole damn week, makin me feel awful, and *poor*. Yes, you did," she reiterated, chipping Harley a glance. "So, I take my drink and I go over to this little bench and I'm there, feelin lonesome and mean and *scared*, and who comes over to sit with me? Chester. Leaves his bar, bang in the middle of the party, and plops himself down next to me."

"What for?" Dan asked, around a mouthful.

"To tell me secrets about Harley. Says he knew Harley ever since he came to their house to do their patio, when Harley was just little. He told me I'd do just *fine* bein married to Harley cause he wasn't like the other boys." She set her fork on the edge of her plate. "He was much nicer."

I noticed Harley seemed a little apprehensive; had he never heard this before?

"The reason Chester knew all this," Debs-Anne said, "was cause one day Harley and a bunch of his little friends got all curious about this scabby rash Chester had on his head? Askin him how come he had it, did it hurt, you know, just bein kids. So the next day Harley comes out in the yard with this big *collar* that their dog Beaumont used to wear. One of those big circular things, Elizabethan collars they're called, so the dog can't scratch at his head? And Harley

says to Chester"—Debs-Anne had hidden her face in her hand—
"Harley says, Now, Chester . . . you put this on and you *wear* it,
cause it'll help"—I thought, she's going to cry—"help heal your
head. So Chester does. He takes it, and he finally gets it fastened on
his neck and he . . . he . . ."

"Oh no . . . ," Dan said.

"*Wears it all day!*" she squeaked. "Can't you just see him, with his
little head pokin out and his . . . his . . ." She was incapacitated with
mirth. Dan and I looked at Harley.

"Not all day," he said. "About half a minute."

"That was nice. He was being nice," I said uneasily. "You both
were."

Debs-Anne, dabbing her eyes with her napkin, shot out a hand.
"Won't nice, it was nasty! This little butthole here planned it all
out for a *joke*, for his little friends all hidin in the bushes! See, I *knew*
the whole story, cause Harley had just been tellin it to me while
we were standin up in my window, watchin Chester get his bar set
up. Harley was goin on about what a *bad* little boy he was, while
he was tryin to cop a little tittie pinch. And now here I am gettin a
whole nother version from Chester. Oh Lord." She touched a corner of her napkin to each eye. "And Chester pattin my hand and
givin me his little worn-out hanky. It was *horrible*. Scuse me while I
blow my nose."

Harley had strewn saltine wrappers all over the table. Dan and
I watched him pluck them up and wedge them between the salt
and pepper shakers. I suddenly remembered Calvin's bark chip bag,
still out there—unless Dan had found it—out there in the dark,
folded up between the flowerpots. *Wednesday*, he'd said. Panic fin-
gered me. Wednesday. Did that mean next week? Or tomorrow?

"Anyhoo," Debs-Anne said, refreshed, "Chester made me feel one
heck of a lot better about that whole scene. That's what I wanted to
say."

"The important thing," Harley said, "is always makin sure Debs-
Anne *feels* good."

"Well, weren't you the little shithead?" Dan emptied the first
wine bottle into Harley's glass. "I'm gonna go up and tell him."

"He probably knows." Dan glared at me. "I don't think there's much you could tell Chester about white people."

"Claud's an expert on this," Dan said.

"No, hunh-uh. Chester's not like that." Debs-Anne wagged her head. Behind Dan, Chrissy was coming with the food. "You know what? They can be a whole lot nicer than us sometimes."

Harley hooted. "I'd be nice too."

Debs-Anne eyed the plate Chrissy had just put in front of me. "He means we'd all be adorable if somebody else was payin our way. Does this fish look dry to y'all?"

"Looks fine to me," Dan said. "Well, I might be on food stamps too if I could." He grinned up at Chrissy as she set his plate down, but failed to induce a smile.

"Yeah, that's always fun," Harley said. "Screwin people who go to work every day."

"Dan, you'd never take food stamps," Debs-Anne cried, "you've got too much pride!"

"Nah, I'm a bottom-line type of guy."

"Yeah, well. You're like this little gal waitin in front of me at the store today. Get this. Two giant packs of sirloin, couple hunks of smoked cheese, a Sara Lee cake, and a jar of maraschino cherries. Pays for the whole show with food stamps. I bout liked to have a fit, cept I've seen it a million times."

"Hey. Party on down at the projects," Dan said. "That's cool, who cares?"

"Me," Harley said hotly. "I care, I don't like gettin screwed. Maybe it's different if you can afford it. Uh-oh. Look at Claudia, smilin like that. Claudia, I'm not the bad guy here, okay? She thinks I'm a bad guy."

"No she doesn't," Dan and Debs-Anne both said.

"I've just got my own welfare system, Claud, it's called charity. That's why I don't need the government to send me a bill. I know what I'm supposed to do."

"How?" Debs-Anne murmured as if she were cueing a child. "Harley? Who tells you? God?"

Harley sawed his baked potato skin.

"Not just me, he tells everybody," he muttered, eyes down.

"Yeah, but Harley, he doesn't *talk* to everybody," I pointed out, rather neatly, I thought.

"Yeah, I know." Harley looked up at me. "That's my fault too."

"*Harley?*" Debs-Anne whined.

Harley put down his knife and fork and raised a hand. "Okay." He swallowed half a glass of wine. Dan and Debs-Anne chewed. The silence throbbed, like deep inside one of those movie space stations where the air shafts crawl with scaly monsters dripping gluey poison saliva. All around us the empty white-clothed tables waited for the complicities they would witness the next night and the night after that.

"Damn," Harley said suddenly. "What's the *good* news?"

He seemed to be asking me.

"You're white?" I said. As I stared back at him his lower face was rippling, contorting. He had made "black lips" with his tongue and his inside-out lower lip. His tight forehead glared at me.

"He's not white," Debs-Anne said, "he's just gross. Harley, honey, nobody's even lookin at you."

Harley adjusted his lips to say, "Claud is, she likes me," and made the mouth again, his eyes fastened on mine, the livid flesh of his lips and tongue glistening in the soft light. Dan, buttering a roll, elbowed him.

"Hey, you big jig, cut it out, that's my wife."

"Cut it *off*," Debs-Anne said.

"I love you," I told Harley. "I do. I really love you." The lips dissolved again and Harley's cool eyes held mine for a moment, then he lifted his glass and let his gaze tilt away.

"She does, she's not kidding," Dan confirmed, scraping up his last bit of fish. "Just give her some of that ole jive-ass shit and she's yours."

"Ugh. Not me." Debs-Anne stood up. "I'm not made that way. If that makes me a racist, I don't care. Scuse me, I'm gonna go borrow the little girls' room."

Abandoned, the three of us couldn't quite look at each other.

"Hey." Harley's voice had dropped an octave. "They got a raw deal, I know that. I feel sorry for em. I grew *up* with em, I know what it's like. I'm probably more liberal than you guys on a lot of this shit. But it's not my fault they're *here*. Okay? You know, it's like . . ." His voice trailed off and his eyes darted, seeking help. "I just get tired. As in, weary. I'm tired of seein those stupid *crowns* in their cars—"

"What *are* those?" I said.

"I don't know. Somebody said black power symbols. And babies everywhere. And that old burnt-out dude that sleeps on the Parkway every night? I don't need to see that."

Me, I thought . . . you don't want to see *me*. Then I remembered he didn't know I was ugly. Or wasn't. I must have been fairly drunk.

"Babies, yeah. Speed-breeding," Dan said. "Hey, let's just be glad we don't have to help em do *that*. But Harl? I don't like getting screwed any more than you do. You got that part wrong, bud."

"Yeah. Hey. That was dumb."

"No problem. Here, finish this up." He poured Harley more wine. "Did you check out who's over there?"

Their heads turned. At the table below the swordfish, a man in a shiny sports jacket was eating dinner with a woman in a sequined sweater. A guy they knew from the office? I didn't care. I suddenly felt ashen and drained, beyond drunk.

Harley's eyes had settled on me again. "You know, she's awful quiet. Is she always like that, when she's not talkin about murderin somebody?"

"She's thinking. She thinks a lot."

"She sure is a cutie. I like her."

"She's all right. Aren't you, Clod-Bod."

Things were very quiet and fluid. Harley was holding his head crooked, watching me. I seemed to have swum too close to him, like a fish in a tank regarding a human face, a blobby collection of fleshy protuberances and holes. His eyes shone dully and his lips stretched and parted. There was a wodge of food between two teeth. His mouth closed and opened again and no sound came out.

"This looks like a fun table," Debs-Anne said, not sitting down. "Let's go up and see Chester."

"Let's not."

I felt them all mulling me over. "She speaks," Harley said.

"I think *our* house, folks. Yes?" Dan distributed glances. "A little reefer, a little Jack?" His manner was supple, confident. I understood he had settled into Beasley as if he had slid into warm silk sheets. He sounded mature and relaxed, like an adult.

Back at the house drinks were found. They were all settling down in the living room—Harley supine on the floor—when I went quietly up the stairs, as if I were just going up to use the bathroom. I knew no one would come to retrieve me, but I still shut the bedroom door, then I raised the windows. I got undressed in the dark and lay down in the mumble of their voices, and the whole of that long evening heaved into the room, the twinkling fairy lights, the pink faces laughing. We had all been grotesque, I knew that, but they were gone now. I was separate, I wasn't one of them. The evening was coming apart, dissolving away into the river, the hollow gulp of it in the Alligoods' boathouse, its slap-slap against the wooden bulkhead, private night water washing over me, tugging at my body. I knew Calvin had meant tomorrow. I could feel him out there, a dark shape full of hopeful thoughts about me, waiting. Not knowing what he was really getting. And his not knowing felt like camouflage, like a safeguard, in the same way that everything I didn't know about him fortified me and gave me more courage. I wasn't being deceived in any way though, I knew that. He wasn't a frivolous man. He was strong. I felt loyal to some dark pure idea of him. It occurred to me I could catch something horrible. You could bring it back to the house, I told myself. You could make Dan sick too. But the threat of all that, that line of demarcation, was drawn on the water that was lifting me away.

THIRTEEN

HE WAS THERE when I came in, sitting on the bottom step. I got halfway across the hall and stopped, and he got up and stood there with that empty-handed ease, and roamed his eyes over me. Then he walked up and laid both hands against my cheeks. He was so close I had to shut my eyes.

"So. Here you are."

Then he was turning away toward the stairs. I followed him up, across the hall, into the pink room.

The floor had been swept and the windowsills wiped. The tall fumy windows stood open onto the ordered greenness of the tobacco fields below, way far below, inexplicably, as if we had climbed into a tower. The tobacco had flowered into white froth, like lace tossed over the long rows. In one corner of the room there was now a low square table covered with a blue cloth, with a brown paper bag on it. Beside it was a rusty lawn chair and on the floor next to it was a big plastic cooler. A thin mattress lay under one of the windows. I knew it must be the one from downstairs. It had been made up with a pastel flowered sheet and there were two pillows in light green pillowcases, their edges machine-embroidered with Chinese dragons and pagodas. One pillow had been indented by his head as he lay there listening for the car.

He hadn't been too worried about me showing up.

I shrugged my shoulder strap off and set my purse on the table, then just stood and watched as he sat on the edge of the mattress and took off his work boots and socks. His socks he rolled up and stuffed inside the boots before squaring their heels neatly against the baseboard. The way he was ignoring me seemed to give me permission to stare. He stripped off his T-shirt, tossed it at the chair, and settled back calmly with his hands behind his head, pretending to be unaware of the offerings of black moss in his armpits and the long ridge under his fly. He might have been alone if not for his eyes, too carefully not watching me as I started to undress. The first time pretty. Pretty girl, *pretty girl*. Easy: just be what he sees. I stepped out of my sandals and walked around the end of the mattress and knelt on it. I bent my head down to his chest and tickled my lips over his tiny circlets of hair.

My first look at his nakedness—his thighs and shadowy groin—is frozen in my mind like a photograph. He was half kneeling on the bed, pulling off his trousers and underpants; a reassuring glimpse, heartening somehow, not surprising, not shocking, I thought confidently, almost smugly, and I reached for him, just as he pulled himself away, and then we were alongside each other and we struggled for a minute. I felt a small wary prickle of recognition as his warm hands tugged my shorts down my legs and then the acknowledgment of him came, like a suppressed memory billowing up into my skin. Inside the indistinct amazement of this, there was no surprise about what he was doing or how he knew it all. Even his deliberation seemed familiar, it was like that first day, when he had come down the steps and paused to show me his face. But he was giving me too much now, I couldn't keep up. I was sluggish, stunned with desire, while he moved over me with a rhythm too heavy to shake into frenzy, as if he was burdened with too much pleasure to do anything but just tenderly bear it wherever it would go.

He didn't have any special tricks, there were no awkward diddlings and lickings with one eye open to monitor their effect.

I remember his throat, the cords silver with sweat. And the way he pulled back suddenly and looked down at me, way down, trying to get far enough away to watch what we were doing. And my body remembers him too, but not with any words, especially the usual ones—groan, thrust—I won't write like that about him. And the weight of his dick, I haven't lost that, the waxy feel of that long veined fruit, mauve-brown, almost too ripe to handle, oozing its bead of juice. But the picture that holds everything else is his face above me with his eyes shining on mine, while I try to keep my eyes open but they keep closing, dropping me into dangerous loose space where I clutch blindly and beg him to save me. But that doesn't even make sense. This is all enraptured *nothing*, no one can write about this, why am I even trying? Because I might still remember one new thing that would put me back there with him. Back in that day that was so smogged with humidity the sun looked like the moon. A pewter coin, framed in the window beyond his shoulder.

It sank lower into the haze, burning red and urging the color out of the walls, like pink steam. In this theatrical light Calvin slept, while I eased myself up and admired our props—blue plastic cooler, lawn chair, paper bag of provisions. His confidence that I would come charmed me now. He had trusted me to understand how important it was and I had. My bra lay on the floor like a dusty snakeskin. My breasts felt too heavy, my nipples were stinging softly. Calvin was on his stomach with his arm angled across the floor-boards, palm up, long fingers curled helplessly. In the rosy light his leg, flecked with barely visible hairs, was very dark—it was black— against the pale damp sheet. His unpillowed head was facing me, his nose almost touching my hip, his eyelid swimming lightly in its polished socket. I saw the reason for the physical extravagance. Its purpose was to please. It was form exceeding function, an almost un-bearable excess of sculpted precision embellished by the round shine of his forehead and his impossibly curly eyelashes. His beauty coated my eyes like a film. I only needed to *see* it, I thought, cher-ishing the distance we'd had to cover to get here, with him scoffing me at every turn, ushering me out of this very house, ignoring me in front of the Alligoods, insulting me on the dock, and all the time wanting me. I lay myself down beside him, resisting the urge to whisper, *And your aunt doesn't live here either, that was a lie . . . you were trespassing too.*

When I woke up the room was gray, with a taint of neglect. Just for a second I felt alone, in some danger. But there he was, still beside me, snoring lightly. He hadn't moved. As if he felt me staring, the snoring stopped and his eye clicked open. He rolled onto his back, slinging an arm over his face. I sat up and placed my hand low on his belly and stroked it.

"Late now," came from underneath his arm. "Water's on in there. You go on." His arm lifted and he cast me a sharp glance sideways. "What're you doin?"

"Nothing. I'm doing *this*." I sounded as sulky as a child. I removed my hand.

He sat up away from me with his knees drawn up, making his back into a wall. "Girl. Get your ass in gear."

I crawled over and rested my forehead against his back. Peeking around him I saw the long fruit standing up again, knocking between his thighs. When I reached for it he grabbed my wrist. "You spoiled enough already." Then he stood up, as embarrassed by his erection as a tree would be of a branch. He plucked my shorts off the chair and chucked them at the bed. When he bent down to reach for my bra I scrambled to get to it first. I found my underpants under a pillow. In the bathroom the tiles were still scummed and the walls were lacy with peeling paint, but the porcelain fixtures had been scoured to a domestic shine that scared me. The jagged crack in the mirror was like a warning to me to avoid it.

When I came out in my bra and shorts, Calvin had his trousers on, and his boots. He had his head stuck out the window and was absolutely natty, dressed in a fresh layer of skin. A beer can sweated on the sill. His studied idleness suggested he had changed mood again. I walked over, just close enough to share his view, which provided a dusky rectangle of terror. It was all still real out there, the floppy ornate tobacco stretching toward woods soaked in twilight.

"Girl knows *how* to, I'll say that," he said, lazily emphatic. He watched me with the side of his head. "Uh-oh. She doesn't like that." He sipped at his beer. Do nothing, I thought, make him look at you. I prepared an arch face, but then he turned and his expression was grave. I knew I couldn't match it but I tried.

"Stop that, you look crazy. Come on over here." I shook my head. His directness had reduced me to petulance again. "Come on now."

I went over to him and we stood side by side and pretended we could see through the overlap of dirty window.

"So, you probably think you know me now," he said. "Tell me. What you think's goin on in this house?"

I couldn't talk.

"Can't hear you," he said.

"Nothing's going on. I'm married, I have a husband."

"Yeah, name of Dan. Nice-lookin guy."

"My life's funny to you."

"You're a strange woman, you know that?"

"I thought I was supposed to be sad. You have children," I accused.

"I only got my girl. Be two and a half next month. Jamaica."

"Do you and your wife live around here?"

"She's not my wife. How come you don't have any kids?"

All I could come up with was a lie. "I can't."

He made a derisive snort. "Who told you that?"

"Doctors. How's Jamaica, is she still sick?"

"She's fine. She only got one kidney, she gets infections. So you and Dan left Vermont and come all the way down here to live."

"You must've had quite a chat. What else did he say?"

He turned away. "He told me he gets worried when you be goin in dirty old houses, fuckin strange men."

He found my pocketbook and shoved it at me. "Where's your shirt at? You need a comb." He was picking at my hair, trying to poke in the loose pieces. His hand was too close to my lips. I grabbed it and tried to press it against my mouth and he opened it up, like a spider fastened onto my face. I smelled myself on his palm. When he let go, dread sluiced through me and congealed in my stomach, dread of the late hour and the twenty minutes it would take to get home and the lies I still needed to invent. As the first one started taking shape in my mind, he saw it, his eyes shrewd and appraising. Everything speeded up. He used the bathroom and made the bed while I finished dressing and tried to apply some makeup in the waning light. When I closed my compact, I saw he had put his T-shirt on, a luminous patch I followed quickly down into the dim stairwell and out onto the porch. He took a moment to make sure the front door was secure and then led me through the bushes to the Volvo, nosed into the holly bush.

"You're gonna scratch your paint all up," he muttered, yanking at the door. "Don't even *lock* it?"

"I forgot."

"Get in. Go on, get in now." He leaned into the car. "I'm walkin. Look, don't drive fast. Get yourself smoothed out."

The cave of the car was frighteningly familiar, with its reproachful smell. He saw I was horror-stricken and reached in and pulled me back out. I stood as close beside him as I could.

"See that up there?" He tipped his head back and I stared miserably at his jaw, trying not to rub my face against it. "That's the evening star up there, see that? What does that star know about us? Doesn't even know we're here." He bent his head to me and put his arm around my shoulder. "Listen now. You hear all those people fixin their supper?" The stillness was absolute, like sponges pressed against my ears. "Sittin out smokin and talkin about all their little things that happened today?" Black people, he meant. "What do they know? There's not a soul knows about us. Nothin's different out here. It's just another pretty night."

"No. It's not. It *is* different. I can't go home."

"Uh-oh. Car comin. Go on, slide on back in now." He closed the door and thumped his hand on the roof.

I backed around in the lane and bumped up onto the long straight road that was waiting to reel me back in. As the other car passed me, it flicked its headlights to tell me to turn mine on. Behind me Calvin was out on the road, walking, shrinking fast in the rearview mirror until finally all I could see was his shirt, a white dot floating.

FOURTEEN

WHEN I PULLED into the driveway it was dark, and every window in the house was ablaze. Somehow I knew this wasn't about my being late. As I walked to the porch the lawn was black-edged and jagged in all that showy light, and I could feel the burden of drama tilting off me toward whatever excitement was happening inside.

"Here she is . . . !" Dan called back into the house. He was at the door, panting and predatory, like somebody poised to grab his baggage off a carousel. The irritation this aroused in me gave me an edge. "Danny, who *is* it?" He pulled me in out of the night and slammed the door; he had drunk more than usual. Footsteps clacked in the hall and a woman appeared, silver-haired, youthful in pale slacks, improbably wiping her hands on a dishtowel. She drew closer to me, faltered, and stopped dead.

"Da-dah! Guess who?" Dan cried, watching her.

"Hello, Ping," I said lightly.

She was shaking her head, an outright rejection. "No," she said, flatly, her husky voice stripped of inflection. Frozen, dishtowel held at mid-chest as if to ward off the truth. "No. It isn't. It's not." And then the first tug of that helpless little smile I hadn't seen since we left Vermont.

I unveiled my loveliest smile. Ping approached hesitantly, seized my shoulders and air-kissed both cheeks, and finally embraced me, then released me and held me at arm's length. She gave me a timid perplexed watery look and crushed me against her again with such force her Prince Valiant hair shook against my cheek. A quiet sniffle, and then she let go and stepped back with a huge gasping laugh, pure happiness lighting up her tight old radiantly made-up face. I just had time to wonder if she'd had a fresh lift before she turned away, reaching back to waggle a hand. I took it and let her lead me into the living room. The champagne bucket was on the coffee table, holding an open bottle of Moël. Quickly judging the lighting I chose Dan's chair and Ping gracefully collapsed onto the couch. Dan was slouched in the door to the hall with his arms folded on his chest. He said, "We were just about ready to call the cops."

Looking up at him, I showed Ping my profile and heard a happy croak.

"Oh Danny, I'm sorry," I said. "I was sick."

"Oh darling, sick how?" Ping cried. "Where?"

I told my story, about the crabs I had eaten on the way back from Raleigh, about feeling poisoned and getting off the interstate onto a back road, just in time to pull over and be sick in the grass; I had had to crawl back into the car to sleep it off. "I just woke up." In that glossy overcrowded room, my lie seemed so much more credible than the truth.

"Soft-shell crabs?" Dan was incredulous. "You know they're garbage. You still could've called."

"No she couldn't. *Could* you?" Ping beamed at me. "Darling, Danny and I have had a little light supper, but I want you to eat something now. I insist. A little scrambled eggs and smoked salmon."

"Oh Ping . . . no . . . please. Maybe I could choke down a little champagne."

Ping was candescent. "Darling, get Claudia a glass."

"Claudia," Ping said quietly, quickly, when he had gone, "I must apologize. This is not my style at all, to just come crashing in on you like this. But I've been eaten alive with curiosity about how it all turned out." I murmured apologies for never having sent any photographs. "Who would have *believed* them?" she cried. "Anyway," she rasped in her normal voice as Dan came back, "I thought, my gals on Sea Island can just wait a day or two, and I changed my ticket right there at the airport, just like that, mad thing that I am." Her eyes were flashing all over me, my face, my legs, my hair, adding it all up. "And of course there's your gorgeous house," she remembered, aiming a coy glance at Dan as he bent to pour me some champagne.

"Yeah, she thinks it'll do," Dan told me. I could tell Ping had managed to mollify him, maybe just by visiting. Their roles as mother and son seemed to have been reinvented. Saying good night to Ping a few minutes later, Dan was so affectionate and casual with her, there was no way of knowing it had been years since they'd seen each other.

"He's looking well," she said as Dan went upstairs. "But *you.*" She patted the cushion beside her. "Indulge me, darling." I sat down next to her as she started fumbling between the cushions for her glasses case.

I tried to deflect her. "Oh Ping," I said, too late.

"My dear." As she stared at me I stared back, at her fuzzy jawline, her faded blue eyes, the frosted sheen of her cheeks, like pink marzipan. I was suddenly sure she was about to notice I wasn't wearing my rings and then I remembered she'd never seen them before. Tomorrow she would want to.

"Claudia, I have to tell you, there are plastic surgeons and plastic surgeons. Believe me, I know. But this is quite new to me, this work you've had." I mumbled something prosaic about the new me and swallowed some champagne. "No." She lifted a hand suddenly. "It's not that simple, darling. I want to be clear, I want to be sure you understand me." The hand fluttered over mine like a tissue. "You're *here* now, that's all, darling. That's what it's all about. You're suddenly, gloriously, truly here now, with us. Claudia, you will be careful about the strong sun down here, won't you? I'm sorry, darling, tell me again how old you are."

"Thirty-three."

"Of course. That's a good time to start getting just a touch more rigorous. A few little tricks, that's all. Never pull downwards on your skin when you apply your cream. Try not to always sleep on the same side. You've got a good ten or twelve years before you even have to start thinking about other things. There are exercises you can do for your neck, I'll show you, they really do help. Of course, being fair means thinner skin, which . . . Oh darling, you look worried, I'm not trying to scare you, I'm trying to *help*." She reached up and closed her hand over mine, where it was hovering in front of my chin. "You've developed a nervous tendency." She gently lowered my hand into my lap. "You keep touching it, darling. Don't worry, we'll work on that. Tomorrow I want to see what you moisturize with. You know it mustn't be oil-based."

"Oh good, it's not." Resplendent in uncreased beige linen, pinned in a slant of sunshine, Ping stood in Dan's and my bedroom, reading my tube of face cream while I watched her, feeling exposed by the unmade bed. I yanked at the duvet and she sprang to help, crying *Let me*, smoothing the conjugal linen, making herself an unwitting accomplice to the crime I had redreamt all night, muffled and smothering inside my memories of Calvin. And all that morning while she admired the house and tried on my rings, and later when I was driving us around in Dan's car, her attention to me, her inability to leave me alone, seemed to drive Calvin further into me. Sealed up with Ping in our commingled perfume, I kept remembering his wrenched, sweating face while Ping was amusing herself with mine. I could feel in her stolen glances the fun she was having, superimposing my freshly carved profile on the old hopeless one, brimming the whole time with the ripe complacency of somebody chuckling to herself at breakfast over a particularly bizarre dream. As if by extension, this attitude seemed to encompass Beasley now too. "What a droll place for you to live," she growled merrily as Main Street slid by beyond the tinted glass. She was different with me now, more confiding and genuine. Like all women with husky voices, she gave the impression she relished its sound, but instead of the latent sarcasm I remembered lying at the bottom like sludge in a rusty pipe, a more discriminate irony laced her tone that day, an echo of the wry voice I liked to use in my head. I was actually starting to enjoy our excursion. Driving along the grander stretch of Market Street, Ping remarked on all the clear front doors. "I swear. Not a shred of privacy. People can see right into your house!"

"I know, especially at night." I didn't mention that one night when Dan was away I had driven to the historic district, parked, and slowly walked a few blocks, helplessly peering in at the irresistible spectacle of people begging to be stared at. "They're not like us," I said. "I think privacy might be a dirty word here."

I had made her laugh.

"My gals on Sea Island do love a good gossip. The old days, that's their thing. Who married who and who got the first divorce and didn't so-and-so have a miscarriage in a cab on V-J Day. They tickle me. But these ghastly stories they all tell. Some broker catching his daughter in flagrante delicto and *killing* the poor boy! And there was some judge's wife who was out in the barn with her lover and her two sons snuck up and killed *him*! And nobody ever goes to jail. I told them once, I said, 'Now come on, you just make this stuff up.' "

"What'd they say?"

"They screamed. They loved it. 'American by Birth, Southern by the Grace of God.' That's the bumper sticker on Penny-Lou's Mercedes. Very big on bumper stickers down here."

"I've noticed."

Like old pals we cruised down the Parkway. Ping was making appreciative noises when I realized I had neglected to drive her by the club. "Very swish," she pronounced it as we were circling the parking lot. Then she suddenly cried, "Oh darling, you know what I love? The way you've come out of your shell. I knew you would. Before you were just so . . . *brave*. And now you can just be yourself and have fun. Darling, let's go buy you some clothes. There must be a shop."

"Oh Ping. Really, you don't have to do that."

"Darling, I must. *Allons-y, vitement!*"

"*Tu es tres gentille.* Well, okay. We could go to Greenville." As I headed back through Beasley, I turned onto Fourth Street and saw Ping unfold the sunglasses lying in her lap and put them on. On the corner of Fourth and Reardon the usual group was gathered in front of the market, black men standing cock-hipped in conversation or staggering around under the weight of their jokes, gasping and slapping weakly at each other's hands. On the bench a couple older men sat staring quietly at the road.

"So depressing," Ping said. "Why aren't they all mad?"

"I don't know. Angry, you mean."

"*Bored.* I'd be out of my tiny mind. You know, you could carry a lot more color now. Women down here do that. Neutral is not a word in their vocabulary. Royal blue, chrome yellow. *Chartreuse.* I do love chartreuse. Chartreuse and black, chartreuse and navy. You never see it on blondes, it makes them muddy, but I think you could make it work. I told you, didn't I, what a success your hair is? Oh, it must be such *fun.*"

I said that it was. I was surprised and rather impressed at how freely Ping referred to my operation, but of course the surgery taboo didn't apply to a fellow veteran.

"Now, tell me about my son."

"Well, I think he really likes it here. I think he feels at home."

She flapped a hand. "Big fish, little pond."

I ignored that. "And of course we love being on the river."

"The light in your bedroom this morning was absolutely divine. It must make you both feel heavenly." Pause. "Literally." Sharpened to a small palpable point, her curiosity pulsed quietly as she waited for me to divulge what effect my transformation had had on our love life. "The whole house. Absolutely lovely. I adore what you've done." But here there was a shade too much emphasis.

"I think the house might have gotten away from me."

"Oh dear," she said in a voice that agreed.

"I kept picturing an older house. Big wide floorboards. Lots of French doors and slipcovers with big roses. All sort of faded and, you know, elemental."

"Ralph Lauren. That man is a genius. Snitches all those great classics I grew up in, marks it up ten times, and sells it to the Jews. He deserves to be rich, and of course now he's making antiques. That takes gall. Darling, what did you do, let Danny help with the house? You let Danny confuse you. Danny doesn't have any taste, never has had. He's a strange child of mine. George always called him the changeling. My God, that child was peculiar."

"Dan?"

"That summer camp business. That was unnerving, I have to admit. He could have used at least another year with Rosenthal after that. But who ever listens to me? No, George had suddenly had enough. Opened a bill from Rosenthal and threw a pluperfect fit. Not that Rosenthal wasn't odd. One time the door to his office wasn't quite shut and I could see him in there combing Danny's hair. Anyway. I'm sure you've heard more about that camp debacle than you ever wanted to."

"Mmm, not really," I said, stalling. "Not for a while."

"Children are monsters, I don't care who they are. Absolute little sadists. I imagine even you were."

"No. I mostly got bullied a lot."

What was all this about? I remembered a hideous story of Danny's that involved Super Glue, could this be something worse?

"That camp was very mediocre. That was where his whole food-fetish control business got started, by the way, not in our house." There was a pause. "I still think the counselors made half of it up. They were very *keen*, and that poor boy whose . . . who was damaged, you know he never actually named Danny."

"No." I was thinking very hard. "Maybe he was afraid to."

"Probably," she said vaguely. "Claudia, let's be practical now. I want you to envision your wardrobe and tell me where the gaps are."

This frightening item about Dan's childhood winks at me now, a shiny nugget buried in the silt of that murky day. I pick it up, I rub it, but nothing more is revealed. Throw it back in and go on. (Wondering now why I never asked Dan about it, I think maybe I didn't want any more details, certainly no explanations: all I needed by then was the crude stuff on Dan, the cruder the better, to counterbalance my treachery.)

Newton village was a configuration of white-plastered cinder-block buildings set into the asphalt acreage behind the Greenville strip malls. The marquee awnings must have been intended to distract from the steel window frames and the shiny plastic lettering screwed into the walls. Skimpy concrete walkways kept back the eager snouts of expensive parked cars. The place had the desolate glamour of a shopping center contrived in the Third World from a postcard of Beverly Hills. I pulled into a space in front of one of the biggest shops and turned the car off. Ping made no move to get out.

"I always forget," she said musingly. "Once you leave New York it's all like this now. Penny-Lou's favorite restaurant is in a shopping center, next door to a gym. Ah, well. *Tant pis.*"

Inside, the shop was like a large track-lit cave, full of bright fabric and the luster of leather, much of it gold. Accessories, jewelry, the shop was packed. As Ping worked her way through the racks, emitting low growls, the saleswoman stood back and admired a pro. "No, no rayon. . . . Is this navy or black? . . . Viscose is fine. . . . Oh, I *adore* houndstooth, always have. . . . Now, this is good. . . . Oh, this is darling. Claudia, here, try this on, and this, and this, and here's a belt."

She flipped up collars, she smoothed skirts, talking the whole time. She sounded like a magazine. "Enjoy your waistline." "Sheer is always fun." But underneath the horrible stiff young-matronly clothes, I could feel my body starting to smile. Everything she found for me became one more disguise. She didn't know she was trying to perfect a woman who had been perfected yesterday wearing nothing but musk and sweat. Calvin was there now, crouched in the mirror, watching me lift a plaid evening skirt and show him the bruise on my hip, when Ping yanked the curtain back. Smoothly dropping the skirt, I vamped for her and for the saleswoman peering over her shoulder. "My new daughter-in-law," Ping murmured, never even noticing her slip of the tongue.

The last ensemble I knew would be Ping's favorite. I came out of the dressing room into the shop, to show off in front of the big three-sided mirror. The chartreuse suit had faceted black buttons up the front of a collarless quilted jacket. The earrings were pearl disks encircled in gold braiding. A black velvet headband dented the blond blob of my hair. "Bag," Ping murmured, and a gold chain was slid over my shoulder. "Faux Chanel for now, I'm afraid darling, but you'll get there."

"Oh, now, *that* . . ." the saleswoman drawled. When my eyes met hers in the mirror she squinched her nose in jubilation. I glanced back at the mirror and the disguise was gone . . . but I was still there. The complete specimen, the platonic ideal of Anglo-Saxon power in its female form. I was bonded into the uniform as if I'd been vacu-formed. Everything about me was contributing to this phantom; my highlighted hair and Dan's diamonds and my own body. The well-made ankles, the determined chin. Trying to hide my disgust just made me look glaringly self-possessed.

And there was something else. This woman wasn't even young anymore. Where her head joined her neck there was a distinct bracket. Her neck skin had started coming loose. When, just this *morning*?

Ping had crumpled onto a banquette and was pawing in her bag for her credit cards. Her hair was askew like a wig. "Look what you've done to me, I'm a rag!"

We decided to have lunch in the gourmet shop–cum-restaurant a few doors down, and settled on a table in the big window that over-looked the parking lot. Ping, nestling in, asked me how I planned to keep busy. "Darling, have you a plan?"

"I thought I might try to do a book of drawings," I heard myself say.

"Clever you."

"I thought I could do some of these old houses before they all start to fall apart. If it actually made any money, maybe I could give it to the state historical society."

As Ping neatly springboarded from this into the nightmare Garfield was having restoring his eighteenth-century farmhouse in Connecti-cut, I could suddenly see my book, its worthy intentions sabotaged by my determination to reduce lovely old decorative woodwork to Hall-mark tat. I was rescued from this by Ping's description of Garfield's wife, Buffy.

"Sort of a stripy blonde. Bony. Not unattractive. Still skinny de-spite the three kids. She's one of those horsey girls. You know."

I did. I saw the flat chest draped in cashmere, the elegant bitten fingers, the lank hair pulled into a heavy expensive barrette. What to do with this portrait? I suddenly wanted to impress Ping with the spoils of my life as a voyeur. She was toying a little wanly with her salad. Maybe I could provoke a stab of shared laughter, a little naughty eye contact. The surface of my tongue was crawling. But Ping had found a distraction. On the other side of the window two light-skinned little black boys had just perched on the rim of a cement planter. They were dressed in matching shirt-and-shorts outfits printed with sailboats. Ping seemed transfixed. "Couldn't I just eat you up," she whispered, and horribly, as if they had heard her, their heads turned and they showed us their faces, like overlapped pennies. Ping thrust her head closer and waggled her fingers. Without even a blink they swung their attention back to the cars.

On the way out, Ping bought a tube of chocolate wafers. She had it open by the time we were out the door and when I noticed she wasn't beside me on the sidewalk, I glanced back. She was holding them out to the little boys. Silently they consulted each other and then each took one.

"Do we say 'thank you'?" Ping asked gaily.

"Yes, ma'am," they said gravely, as down the long row of shops behind Ping a door opened and a tall black woman, electric in a purple silk tank dress, rippled toward us. "Just admiring your beautiful boys!" Ping cried as the woman approached, brass earrings flashing. "I have boys too," Ping offered as the woman stepped off the sidewalk and unlocked a silver Mercedes.

"They're a handful," the woman said tersely. She slung herself into the car. The door locks popped up and the boys got up and climbed into the backseat. As their mother drove away, the younger one waved wildly at Ping.

Ping brewed her silence as I pulled onto the highway. "Why don't we stop at the nursery," I said. "You could take Penny-Lou a plant, if you don't mind carrying it on the plane."

"You know, I am so sick of it all, I could scream."

"She was okay, Ping, she was tired. That's what she was saying."

"No no, she hated me," Ping insisted levelly. "My fault. I was nice to her kids. Should have known."

"I wouldn't read too much into it."

"Darling. Aren't you nice. But you're a little naive. Oh I'm sorry, I forgot, you grew up in Vermont, you haven't dealt with this your whole life. Not that that helps. Here's a story for you. Beverly Wallis, she works with me at the Red Cross. Perfectly lovely. Big eyes, aquiline nose. Like Lena Horne. How old I have no idea, you know how they don't age, ever. Well, last week we all voted to let our new secretary go—extremely cute black gal—and Bev informed us that if we do this, we're committing—I forget what—moral indecency."

"Why do you have to fire her?"

"We almost published a newsletter where she misspelled the most critical word in fund-raising."

"Money?"

"Friend. Now, does Bev—*un*oppressed, husband's a patent lawyer—does Bev call me up and say, Ping, let's have lunch and talk about this? No, no. Puts it in a letter. Makes *a statement*. Makes us all feel ghastly. I can hardly look at her now. I'm flummoxed. I just feel like shaking her and saying, Bev I can't make you happy, none of us can. We're all so sorry, but *please*. And why, if they feel so unequal, do they keep pointing it *out* all the time? Don't advertise your flaws, disguise them, for God's sake. I don't mean flaws. They don't like us, that's what it boils down to. Even Beverly. They tolerate us. Tell me I'm wrong."

"Oh Ping." I needed silence. "I don't know."

What I knew was Calvin, always holding his silent laugh at the ready. Laughing more silently, more luxuriantly today. Celebrating his conquest. Where was he now? Surely his head was crammed with images from yesterday, like mine was. A quiver of hope shot along this connection to him and hurtled back to me, bringing raw footage of what he must have seen, the sweaty hair plastered to my pale scalp, my scrawny mouth begging him.

"Not that they don't hate themselves, God knows," Ping said. "Always doing all those things to their hair and trying to lighten their skin. Are we still on for the nursery?" I felt her eyes on me. "Claudia, please don't touch your chin."

In the nursery I followed her through the long greenhouses, stupefied by the seething extravagance of color and the dense sticky air, carrying my desire for Calvin like a stone slung in the web of my pelvis, making me ache softly with every step. Ping finally chose three orchids for the house and we drove home. I left her sitting at the kitchen table with a magazine and some iced tea and locked myself in the bedroom to remember Calvin. I was greedy and thorough, and guilt-free. There wasn't enough room for guilt left in me. I could barely remember Dan.

But later that day I stood in the kitchen and watched Dan and Ping together down on the dock. She was imperiously, superbly relaxed, Dan less so but taking a stab at simulating it, standing in his mother's orb with his hands jammed in his pockets, holding his elbows in close to make himself a smaller target for her attentive neglect. Their silhouetted bodies, chained by biological chance, strained against the airy brightness as they small-talked, and a little flame of affection for Dan flickered in me. He couldn't help being her son, the imperfect, inferior son. If he had been beloved like Garfield, confident and poised enough to be a more gracious man, I might have been able to love him better. We were all in her thrall. I hadn't withstood her either, I had let her torture me into a preppy Barbie doll. Now she was turning, making Danny follow her along the dock like a toy on a string. I was trying to sustain this benevolent useless connection to him when the phone rang.

"This is Calvin."

I was horrified. I said hello.

"How you doin?" Cozy as an old pal. "You busy?"

"Just watching the river."

"Yeah? How you doin?" So he was nervous too. "Got yourself back okay."

"Yeah, I did." I could hear traffic. "Where are you?"

"Exxon, River Road." So close. "You doin all right?"

"My . . . Dan's mother's here. No."

"I been thinkin, might be kind of a stretch till next week, you know?"

Dan and Ping were making their way to the house. "I don't know."

"What? That's fine. You don't want to, just *say* so."

"*When?*" I said as Ping and Dan hit the porch steps.

He let go with a deep chuckle I couldn't bear to interrupt. "Well, now. Lemme think. Maybe you . . ."

"I have to go. Please, can you—" but Dan was in the kitchen, his face curious. "Do you want to do the lawn?" I blurted, trying to warn Calvin as Dan reached out a hand.

"Ace, how ya doin? The place looks great!" Dan listened a minute, watching me. His eyes rolled. "You bet. We've all been there. . . . That soon? Okay, you're the boss!" He hung up. "Guy's trying to screw me already," he laughed as he went out. "Wants to come back tomorrow!"

"The yardman," I told Ping.

She was standing by the sink, giving me a narrow look. "I'd love to see you in the white linen tonight."

As Dan and I were getting ready for dinner, I told him his mother had spent upward of two thousand dollars on me.

"Good. It keeps her regular. Oh listen, she's got some present she wants to give you, some heirloom thing. Pretend you love it, okay? Go ape shit."

"Maybe I *will* love it. What is it?"

"I don't know. Some daughter-in-law thing. Something the other one didn't want."

Ping made quite a stylish presentation, in the living room while we were having our pre-club drinks. As she and I were chatting on the couch, I became aware of a small square purple velvet box on the cushion between us, pristine as a freshly laid egg. Dan, on his ottoman, watched closely as I picked up the box with a little cry and snapped it open. Inside was a small gold fleur-de-lis pin, the lily shape crusted with diamonds, its stem decorated with an oblong emerald. I was stunned.

"Mom?" Dan said. "Your grandfather's *pin*?"

"And his father's before him," she growled.

"I don't know what to say," I told Ping.

"Try 'thank you,' " Dan said. "That's what my insurance man'll say, for sure."

"Darling, I wouldn't even bother with that. Claudia can find her own hiding place for it."

"So tell her the story."

"I intend to, dear heart. I want to see her put it on first." They watched me pin it above my left breast. "That linen's not too rough for it, is it?" Ping said. "No. No, it's lovely on you. Now, this story. I warn you, it gets a little poignant.

"My great-grandfather, Carlton Dunn, was a lawyer in New York. He had a dear friend named James Gladding, also a lawyer. In fact they started out in practice together but then James had some problems and Carlton had to start propping him up. Apparently James went downhill rather precipitously. I think he was a good man, people *liked* him but somehow—"

"He was a loser," Dan interjected.

"Well, he didn't need to be. Anyway. One day James thinks he's figured out the perfect way to fix things and get another town house and get the wife back. It becomes known around town, to everyone's amusement, that James is now a professional card shark. He's playing blackjack all night and sleeping all day, way uptown in this little flat Carlton found for him. Well, before long, what do you know, James seems much brighter and all his friends are tickled, nobody more so than Carlton. Carlton, by the way, being a complete and utter dud at anything to *do* with cards. So one day James suggests a game or two, and Carlton thinks, Well, no harm there, I can't possibly beat him. And he rounds up some other boys from the good old days, with the idea that they'll all lose to James."

Dan made a derisive noise.

"*Darling.* As it turns out, James can't win a hand to save his life. He's the worst player there. Now once this becomes obvious, the friends all start begging off. Carlton too. But James insists the two of them keep on going. All Carlton can do now is try even harder to lose, but the opposite keeps happening. Finally it's getting a little dramatic. You can imagine. By now the man is monstrously in debt to my great-grandfather. Finally poor James reaches into his waistcoat and pulls out your lovely pin and puts it on the table. Everybody knows this has to be his rock-bottom last asset, probably his late mother's. Anyway. The final hand is dealt. Carlton declines a third card, as does James. Then this eerie little smile comes over James's face and everybody sort of perks up. Carlton lays his hand down and it's flawless. One ace, one face card. James lays *his* hand down and it's a dead loss."

"Like seriously dead. A two and a six or something," Dan added.

"Carlton picks up the pin and puts it in his pocket. He and James get up from the table and *fall* into an embrace. The next day James hangs himself." Ping swigged her drink. "He left a note for Carlton, thanking him for being a true friend and giving James the chance to repay him. The note really belongs with the pin, but I think I'd like to hold on to that, if you'll let me."

"That's fine," I said. I felt a little wobbly. "So . . . James knew all along what he was doing."

"Losing on purpose," she rumbled. "Going out with style, I'd call that."

"But why did Carlton let him? He obviously knew what James was doing, at least by the end. They all did."

"Darling, he had to. He couldn't embarrass the man further. James's humiliation was already torturous."

"Gentlemen have to honor their gambling debts," Dan announced. "It wasn't Carlton's fault he was lucky."

I said, "How was it luck if James was engineering it?"

"Darling," Ping sang out, "James was *trying* to make a *gift* of it."

"She doesn't get it," Dan said. "It's fine, Claud, just say if you don't want it."

Oh, but I did.

"Well," I said. "That's quite a story. God. Ping, honestly. Thank you." I studied the thing on my breast and smiled at it.

That was when I knew I could do it, live both lives. Calvin was back now with a vengeance. He was inside me at dinner that night, helping me watch Ping as she explained the relative merits of Jekyll Island and Sea Island, Georgia, her gestures rattling the big diamonds on her bony fingers. It was Thursday now, the club dining room was full. Ping drew glances with her sleek buffed hair, her gray shantung silk and real pearls, her impervious semigloss finish, produced by years of boredom and arrogance. She's a white witch, I remember thinking gladly, drunkenly. In that light her makeup was too strong, not dramatizing her patrician face but just lying on it, like the marks you make on one of those magic drawing tablets and then erase by peeling the plastic sheet away with that gratifying ripping sound. All right, I was cruel, I had to be. I was trying to impress Calvin.

FIFTEEN

PING MET CALVIN the next morning. She and I were carrying
her bags out to her cab when a battered white van, high and square
like an old bread van, stopped in the road. The driver was black, his
profile very long and flat. With his strong jaw and his immobility, he
was like an Easter Island carving. He never glanced at the house. As
he drove off Calvin came striding up the path and took Ping's gar-
ment bag. His presence fell on her like a shadow. I could barely look
at him.

"Ping, this is Calvin—" I got that far before his eyes flashed me.
He draped the bag in the trunk and disappeared into the garage.
Ping and I had just launched into our thank yous when he started
the lawn tractor and roared out onto the driveway. "You're a picture!" Ping yelled over the noise, seizing my head as if she could un-
screw it and take it with her. "I'm so proud of you!" She stabbed a
finger at the sun, pretending to cower, and I laughed.

As soon as I had waved the taxi down the road, I headed for the
kitchen to watch Calvin work, too concerned about Janet Alligood
seeing us to go out to him. When he had finished the lawn, he
stepped quietly up onto the back porch. Here we were protected,
screened by the Alligoods' garage. I opened the door and stepped to
one side.

"I can't do that," he said.

I had offended him, it was stamped on his face. But he threw a glance past me into the dining room. "I'll be out at the house in an hour." He bolted down the porch steps and I stepped back into the kitchen. I had forgotten to pay him.

That day the house felt like ours. It was our mattress, our sad lumpy pillows. Calvin drove himself into me until our bodies seemed to hang, hooked in the liquid light, and then ebb away to some crude physical place nearby where they carried on, leaving us alone with each other. A trace of some obscure sadness was mixed in, a shiver of grief, as if to warn against such joy. Some hours passed. We were caught in a storm of pleasure, letting it batter us and toss us around like toys and then as it withdrew he went so still all of a sudden. He scared me. Staring down, raining his sweat on me, drawing me into his eyes. He said I was his flower.

Later, when we were cool enough, we started an investigation of each other. His buttocks were stippled with pale stretch marks. He had an appendectomy scar. When I poked the wrinkled gray bag of his balls, he said, "Careful, those are my gentles." On one of my nipples he discovered a long hair, one crinkled filament waving at him like an antenna, and tried and failed to pull it out. He told me there was a snail living in my belly button. We spent a long time at this, locating every flaw, feeding our satisfaction that these imperfect bodies could be the instruments of such bliss.

"Okay, Miss Pleased With Herself," he said. He was up on an elbow now, petting my pubic hair. "Tell me somethin I don't know. Surprise me."

"Hmm. Well, you know, I was a very bad little girl . . ."

"That's good . . ." he said encouragingly.

"I used to try to pee standing up like a boy."

"My sisters all be doin that. What else you got?"

"They let you watch?"

"You open your eyes in that house, you be starin at a little girl. Five girls, three boys."

"Your poor mother."

"She only had two," he said rather shortly. "Colefax and me."

"Where is she now, do you see her?"

"She's gone."

"Oh. I'm sorry." But there was something in his face. "She died," I said.

A beat went by. "My father lives in Calhoun." He was tweaking strands of my damp hair in his fingers, rolling them into worms. "I bet you never been there."

"Sure I have. Whose truck was that you came in this morning?"

"Half-Gallon's old trash basket, you call that a truck? You already worried about gettin regular delivery? Or maybe you're thinkin I should have my own."

"You could," I said, and heard how that sounded. "You don't want one?"

"I had a truck, up till February. Last winter got tight. Things are pickin up now though." He ran a hand over his face, like a man suffering with a bad hangover. His cheeks had gone dusty. "Look at your eyes, bigger than your face. You're like this cat we had one time. Mobipsa. Pretty little longhair calico. That was an immaculate animal. Then all her fur starts fallin out and she goes slinkin down the street on her belly, lookin for a bush to hide under. Pitiful. Looked like a plucked chicken."

"Thank you."

"If you're scared of bein here, that's all right. That's reasonable."

"I'm not." I half sat up.

"Well, you must be made out of sunshine then. Tell the woman she act like a bald cat and she just as quiet and nice as she can be. Little too quiet, feels like to me. Where's your little spark, girl? Maybe you got somethin you want to discuss with the doctor." He was trying to get my pubic hair to stand up, combing it backward with his fingers.

"I'm just modest, like that other pussy. Mobipsa."

"Woman looks like you do? That'd be a first."

"Your experience of women is obviously vast."

"Nope, don't be touchin the doctor's dick. Listen, I'm just tryin to figure a couple things out and I'm not gettin a whole lot of help. Lie back down."

"No wonder your patients love you, if you always go to this much trouble."

"I don't."

"No? I suppose it's their tits. They're probably not as pretty as mine. Maybe they have those big bumpy nipples."

"Why're you talkin like that?"

"Like what? I can't help it if I'm a piece of ass who just likes big dick."

"With a ugly mouth on her."

"I was being *ironic*."

"Yeah, well, don't. I don't like it. What's the matter with you?"

"You tell me." I flopped my arms at my sides. "Go ahead. Let's have a diagnosis." I had a sudden image of myself as one of those people who invite a blind person to feel their features.

"Okay. We can do this. We're goin to set the looks to one side though, cause you heard enough about that." He glanced down my body. "What I see here? This is a woman got herself in a little bit of a squeeze. She probably figured she was smarter than that. Now she's tryin to think what the hell she can do to fix it." I wouldn't give him a reaction. "Hopin it's not too late." He laid his hand on my stomach. "You know when I saw you lookin up at me in the hall, twistin your little purse strap . . . you know what I thought? This is about the most sorrowful-lookin, downcast white woman I ever saw in my life."

"But that's what you wanted to fuck."

He cut his eyes away. "That what you think?" He compressed his lips and nodded to himself. "So that's it. I come here to fuck a *white* girl."

"*Pretty*. That's what I meant." I was whining. "You wanted a pretty *face*."

"Maybe, maybe not." He was measuring me now. "I got one though. And you got your black dick. That's what you wanted, fuck a black man, see what *that* was all about."

He was too close, too fearless. I covered my face with my hands.

"Look." He pried my hands away. He was kneeling beside me

now, curling himself over me. "*Look at me.* Am I black? Is this a
black man here? What you think, you goin to separate that part out
now? Okay, lemme see now. You done your black thing, think you
know all *about* that now, but I'm supposed to be here with some
skank. Isn't this nice? Isn't this a nice conversation we're havin?
Thing is, I *like* a plain woman. A plain woman'll just about kill you,
bein kind and whatnot. Give you a back rub, make a little joke every
other minute, cook whatever you want. You listenin to this? I don't
mean she's a slave to a man, she just tryin to use what all she got.
She might be the ugliest girl in the world but she's tryin. Tryin so
hard, she *looks good.*"

"You mean in the dark." My throat was closing.

"You got a real nasty little streak in you, why is that?"

"You just told me. My junky life that I'm trapped in."

"That's exactly right."

And then like a child I felt the storm break over my head, and the
hot relief of streaming tears. His arms closed around me. He bundled me up against his chest.

"Aw, Claudia, shhh. Be my sweet girl. Claudia, Claudia . . . you
need a new name. I'm gonna call you Bipsa, how's that?" He had me
clutched to him, rocking me. "Bipsa, shhh . . ."

But I squirmed in his arms. "All that money you see? That's not
mine, that's Dan's. Calvin," I whimpered, "I'm not like that. I'm not
stupid and mute either, except around you."

"I know that."

"My family doesn't have any money. Money's like dirt to me."

"Well . . . depends what you spend it on." I don't think I even
heard the weariness in his voice. "C'mon now. You're doin all right.
You never know. Sometime you might even jump out of that thing
you're in."

He stroked me. When I was finally calm, he unwrapped his arms
and disentangled himself and lay down again.

"I was just jivin you about those ugly girls. You know I like pretty
girls best. I like how you look. You just jump into my eyes." His voice
was casual but his eyes were hungry all over me, my mouth, my hair.
"So what you want to know about me? Go ahead."

He was thirty-six. He had been born in Calhoun, a little town farther downriver, about twenty minutes from Beasley. I had driven
through it once. A four-block downtown, a tattered sprawl of frame
houses, a seafood processing plant. The whole town smelled like fish.
He had lived there all his life. Until he was four, he and Colefax,
who was just a baby then, had lived with their parents. His father
fished, his mother was a picker. I had to interrupt at that point to ask
what that was, he said it was somebody who picked the meat out of
crabs. "You've seen those women, wear those plastic hats look like
shower caps." After he was four and his parents split up, he and
Colefax went back and forth for a couple years, between his father's
sister, Aunt Veronica, and his father, who by now was going out for
two weeks at a time on a big commercial fishing boat. Then his father met a woman named Ginny who had two daughters, and together they had four more kids, three of them girls. During his last
year in high school things "got skinny" and Calvin had to quit and
help his father on the boat, but then his father injured his back and
had to stop fishing altogether. It sounded like he had a small break-
down then, but he was "a believer," according to Calvin, so that got
him through. Calvin lived not far from his father and stepmother
now, out on the far side of Calhoun, in a house he shared with his
half brother, Donny, who fished for crab, and Kyla, one of his half
sisters, and Kyla's boyfriend, who was at home asleep most of the day
because he worked the third shift at a textile plant.

The house was a nice rental, very clean, he said. He clearly loved
Kyla, a hard worker who did hair all day and then collapsed on the
couch and "watched TV with her feet." She was very particular
about cleanliness, smells in particular. She was always making Donny
put his fishing hat in the dishwasher. Behind the house was a big
fenced-in yard for Jamaica to play in, when Jade brought her over,
Jade obviously being the unwife. Throughout this, Calvin never
mentioned his mother. His avoidance of her was noticeable in the
litany of the other names, other aunts, and an uncle he saw a lot, and
the brothers and sisters, all names I could tell he liked saying, maybe
liked it too much, as if he were pestering his mother's absence, picking at the itchy edges of a scab.

Later that day, just before I left, I spied on Calvin from the bathroom and saw him with his nose buried in my shirt.

The lushness of the early summer flattened into a smoky pall. The humidity seemed almost granular. Sometimes there was the rustle of a late-afternoon storm gathering on the horizon and bruising the whole sky an ominous yellow-green then moving away with a teasing of distant thunder. Only the crape myrtle trees were in bloom now, their molten silver trunks buckling under their loads of frizzy hot magenta.

But the heat eased a burden for me, it kept me from thinking. There were days when the anxiety evaporated from my mind, sucked away into the burning sky. I began to understand the allure of a climate where just keeping your skin the correct temperature qualified as an achievement. Locked up in the ice-cool house, I waited for Tuesdays and Fridays, my Calvin days. I was trying to draw the river now. I had revived the book idea but I had given up on drawing old houses and was trying to do some Southern scenes instead. It might still make money, I thought, and I could give it to charity. I had to remind myself of this as an antidote to my lethargy. Occasionally in midafternoon I could sense the heat pressing against the house, daring me to step outside for a minute, and it felt crazy and good to be out there alone in that soup. The only hint that the neighborhood wasn't a postapocalypse ghost town was the dull on-off roar of the relentless air-conditioning pumps. Strange days. Like hot and cold, time had become almost tactile, dragging by with a sensation of not quite standing still that was provocative, like a breeze on a feverish cheek.

Calvin had stopped doing the yard. The week after we had become lovers he announced he would quit coming and I didn't argue, having caught a glimpse of Dick Alligood standing in his yard watching as I handed Calvin a glass of iced tea, no doubt with too much animation. Calvin had also suggested maybe I could make myself scarce when he came to do the Alligoods' yard. After this was all agreed, I had to inform Dan that Calvin wouldn't be coming around again. I found him pacing the back lawn under the pine trees, trying to decide where to erect his new bug light. I was practically gagging with nervousness. "Danny, Calvin Moore called, he's really sorry but he's way overloaded. . . ." But Dan barely grunted, squinting into the trees, making his calculations. That night we ate in the kitchen to make sure the machine was working, our attention seduced away from the TV by that other blue incandescence throwing its jittery light up into the pines. Whenever Dan muted a commercial we could hear bugs frying.

Dan and I hadn't changed. Our feeble connection survived, sustained by the extra attention I was prudently paying him and the stock phrases we'd always thrown back and forth. The dependable treachery of language was coming in handy. When we were tired we were still "sleepy-deepy." Dan was still Dan the Man. When I was quiet for too long, out came his usual "You okay, Clod, you feeling good about things?" The routines I used to rein in my scorn festooned the house like trip wires. I took pains to stay well inside them. I wonder if we didn't even flourish a little bit in this artificial atmosphere. Every morning I watched Dan get up from breakfast, squeeze the contents of his pockets, checking that he was complete, and trot off to the office, to return exactly eight and a half hours later with an air of industry steaming off his back as he poked in the fridge for his beer. Once or twice a week we socialized with Harley and Debs-Anne, usually at the club. Once or twice a week we had sex— I was back on the pill—but Dan's body was so pallid and pelted with long hair I could treat it with a secret withering pity. I guess I was hoping I could preempt guilt. I felt much worse taking Calvin a body that still slept with Dan, although we never spoke of Dan now. I told myself Dan was fine; what I had with Calvin had never been available to him, so he wasn't missing it. He would never know that he and I had been subsisting on twigs and berries. He wasn't suffering, he wasn't out of pocket, he had the same wife he'd always had. I never quite identified this rationalization as one of the standard conceits treacherous lovers entertain, but even if I'd allowed myself that revelation I could have disregarded it. What consumed me other than Calvin was never Dan, only myself. Away from Calvin, I pursued myself with the same devotion I directed at him, as if my inner eye were a lens that, deprived of him, automatically zoomed in on *her*, the woman he loved, painting her toenails for him, or standing in the middle of a parking lot, trying to spot a white van. There was always the fond sensation that Calvin could see me. My voice on the phone—"ninety-nine in the shade today, Mom"— would trigger what I imagined was Calvin's delight at the sound of it, as if he were in the other room listening. The delight was all mine, of course. But loving someone connects you to your true self, so a side effect of that must be a low-level dose of self-love, a feeling of preciousness about yourself, because you're precious to him.

But that richness of ours, that we seemed to share when we were apart, deserted me when I saw him again and he overwhelmed me. The richness was all his. It hurt that he had been walking around in the world, showing the intricate knit of his eyebrows to anybody with eyes. He had a front tooth that butted the other at a very slight angle. There was a sheen across his shoulders like a dusting of pollen. I could have looked at him forever and not seen enough. He watched me too, in long flows I could feel, stroking me with his attention, drawing lines and circles on me, gathering me in. But I was always swaddled in my wretched self-consciousness. I loved hearing myself under him, distantly yelping, a woman being free with herself. But then afterward, washed up onto the hard beach of my mind, I would struggle to think of what to say, when all I wanted was to keep my eyes shut and sink into just being beside him, listening to him breathe. His serenity would ease my bewilderment. Until he stirred, I would be fine. I would be his.

Then after a little while he would shift his legs. Take a long breath, start in on something. He talked a lot about the boat, the water. One time he tried to explain about being out on the water at night.

"Say you're in the cabin and it's all real bright and cozy. Except maybe you stir your coffee and it feels . . . thick. And you start thinkin your hands don't look like yours. Maybe you been out ten, twelve days and you're gettin a little cracked. Knotholes lookin like eyes. So, but then . . . you step outside and the air cuts you, cuts you like a knife. Step out there like a big dumb piece of wood and in one minute, you're just a toothpick in the wind." A good line. I knew he would say it again. "A toothpick in the wind." He stopped again, to feel it. "Your runnin-buddy might be right there and you can't even see him."

"Your what?"

"That's the other boat that goes out with you. Can't see it now though, cause you're lost. You're gone. Then . . . there can be somethin else out there too, that makes me want . . ." He cleared his throat. "Somethin close. A big hole you could go through."

But I didn't want to follow him there, all I wanted was *him*, posed for me in the mist with his face polished like marble.

He kicked at the soggy sheet. "Dawn's always nice. The water gets that slick thing. Or else it looks like old crinkly tinfoil. I used to think. Like, obviously that was all the beauty in the world, right out there, but maybe not. Maybe there was a whole lot more someplace else."

"No."

"Hunh. I was wrong. How bout that."

He thought I had patronized him. "I mean, snow's beautiful, but not *more* beautiful. Just different."

"I've seen snow." He knocked his head gently against my shoulder. "You'd go out on the boat with me, wouldn't you, Bipsa? Jade, she hated the water. She didn't even like me likin it. She was never too big on bein by herself. That was part of why I finally quit."

"Didn't she work?"

"She did till she had Jamaica. She was a geriatric nurse's aide. She likes those little old people with six hairs on their head. She makes em laugh."

"Why can't she get somebody to take care of Jamaica?"

"Cause she got to be there and look after her child, that's what I give her money for. Jamaica's got special requirements. Can't have too much protein all at one time, can't get dehydrated. Any little infection, they have to run fluid through her for a week. Born on my birthday, February thirteen. You wouldn't guess she wasn't all right, lookin at her the night she was born, little pinched-up face like a rosebud. But then, I don't know, drivin back from the hospital, there was some weird ugly thing in the road. Big dead white thing. Kept on goin, here comes another one, broken wing stickin up. Dead white chickens fallin out the back of some busted cage, and Jamaica just been squeezed out into all this shit."

Danger, the horrors of life, one of my *interests*. I could have said something about that, why didn't I? Too interested in Jade.

"So you were there when Jamaica was born?"

"No. I was busy doin somethin else. You need a baby."

"No I don't. Does she look like her mother?"

"Yeah, little pixie girl. Jade's good-lookin. She's got a good brain too. Quiet like you. You two probably get along. You could have a nice visit and not say a word. She knows about you, I told her. I'll tell you about her." His fine head on the pillow, his eyes smiling, stretched sideways at me. "I'll tell you anything except what you want to know. How's that?"

Hidden away with Calvin, our disparity unobserved by other people, I stopped noticing he was black. His blackness would disappear inside him for long stretches until something reminded me, I don't know what, probably just the shock of remembering I was white. But what triggered that? I wanted to think he'd forgotten my color too. I was encouraged by how he let his talk get blacker around me.

But away from Calvin I was whiter than ever. I was suffering from an anxiety that only seemed to be assuaged by the sight of black people. I was always in the car. Sometimes I snooped through Calhoun—I thought I had discovered the gas-station poolroom he had described, but not his house—but mostly I cruised around Beasley. On the Parkway black couples strolled the promenade, holding hands, stopping to back each other up against the railing. They were cool, sagging into each other and laughing, relaxed into the conspiracy of pleasure at hand, but I could still see true hopeful tenderness stored in their bodies. When they were shy, that showed too, it wiggled around them and made them goofy, making me feel goofy as I sat in the car and watched, and tried not to look back down the Parkway at the white kids huddled around their pickups and jeeps all plastered with those NO FEAR decals, like hex signs. I could only assume they were flirting as they shuffled and stamped out their cigarettes like middle-aged strangers huddled in a stiff wind. Then the horrible suspicions would flit through my brain like pieces of trash; that I seemed that blighted and joyless to Calvin, and, worse, that every black man alive had that same measure of sweetness in him, so that every black woman knew what I knew. That was why Calvin had needed a white girl to impress. And these apprehensions burrowed in me until the next time I stepped onto the porch at the old house and felt him upstairs waiting for me.

Except usually he wasn't. The first time he was late, the heat lulled me to sleep, but I was so keyed up I dreamt I was still awake and getting more and more agitated as the afternoon dwindled away. Then I was sure I was hearing the van door sliding shut and Calvin really was coming into the hall downstairs, and his feet were on the stairs, slow and steady, not hurrying, not guilty.

"What happened?" I said.

He seemed mildly surprised. "Nothin." He knelt over me and paddled me with his hands. "I'm here. Here I is."

"Where were you though?" I caught a glimpse of his face. "With Jamaica?" I said hurriedly, urging a fake edge of concern into my voice. "Calvin? Is anything wrong? She's *okay*, isn't she?"

Silence. A couple of his slow beats. "Yeah . . . she's fine. . . ."

That was it, just that patient evenness he rolled into his voice as a sign that he was disappointed with my transparent bullshit, that it was crude and unworthy, as it had been crude to demand an explanation from a man who was skimming his cheek down the inside of my thigh, who had plainly gotten here as soon as he could. I was learning. I had also learned about the little gold crowns in black people's cars. They were air fresheners. Calvin had decided to be amused at my relief, which must have been apparent. "You could've just asked somebody."

SIXTEEN

THE PRESSURE OF life with Dan became more intense. Dan had been making new friends. We met people for dinner at the club, there was a pig-and-pearl party, even a wedding to go to. And I was branching out on my own; Debs-Anne was pregnant and at the various baby showers I met women who would expect to see me again. These were Beasley's young elite, born there, with no notion of ever leaving. Two of the women ran the lavish gift shops where their friends bought presents, and a couple more taught elementary school, but most stayed home with their small kids. The husbands sold real estate or worked with their fathers in the family business; there was a radiologist, a dentist, a lawyer. They seemed smitten with us. "Y'all said you got here in March? Where y'all *been*?" Dan felt flattered, but I suspected it was like the old joke. All we'd had to do was show up. We had been vetted, of course, for age, appearance, and income, and then the group—which in my mind was always standing in cocktail posture, laughing, heads thrown back, drinks in hand—had opened up, made a little space for us to scoot through, and then, still laughing, shuffled back and sealed the hole up. There were no dinner parties, just cocktail parties that ran late into the night, supplied for the long haul with hot crab dip and little cheese biscuits and pounds of shelled shrimp, all displayed in pieces of old family silver. With Dan installed among the other husbands at the beer keg, the women made an effort to include me, admiring my clothes, instructing me on where to find necessities, and discussing people I didn't know in an easy nice way I sensed they enjoyed having me hear. I tried to be as languidly frisky as they were, and as well dressed. Dan could wear shorts and a T-shirt but I needed to be what my mother would have called nicely turned out, and to pepper my compliance with a sort of put-upon sass. On the nights when I seemed to really have the hang of it, my sass could get a little crisp around the edges, but luckily the conversational style was so anecdotal it was hard to express too strong an opinion. Politics might come up in the form of a joke about somebody's brother running for the school board. Nothing ever approached an argument, although one debate—which birthday is worse, thirty or forty?—got surprisingly heated considering nobody had experienced both yet. Sometimes I decided sunshine must act like peroxide, bleaching out cynicism. It felt as if a shroud—of what, manners? apathy?—muffled these long nights. Or was everybody just young? The souls of dead *elders* hovered, and every once in a while they spoke. "They oughta move that Mason-Dixon Line farther south!" a woman cried out once, without irony. They tended themselves with an elated, saturating regard that even deprived their gossip of real venom. "Oh, Sue Carter's *like* that," a guy might say, making the woman beside him shriek gently, and that would be it; they were never in any real danger from each other.

At a certain late point in the evening, worn-out from hours of drinking and impersonating myself, aping surprise and agreement, I would stare at the last broken bit of shrimp floating in its melted ice water and feel vicious, almost decadent. Nothing had changed, I was still "my old self," as voyeuristic and judgmental as ever, only worse, now that I was free to mingle with these unfailingly innocuous people who would never guess how different from them I was. And of course then my old sly arrogance would kick in, and I would want them to know. That need would be ticking in me like a small bomb looking for a good place to explode.

At a pig-and-pearl party in early September, I picked on a guy called Steve Venable III. He and his father had a law practice in Greenville. I'd met him briefly once before, and then that afternoon,

Harley, bringing me another drink, brought Steve along too, rein-
troduced us, and went away to check on the pig.

"Claudia," Steve said. "I hope Beasley's been treatin you well?"

"Oh Steve, I love it." I had learned to use people's names. "I like
the diversity. In Vermont you never saw a black face, aside from a
few that were there at the university. I still remember the first black
person I ever saw."

Steve smiled. "Bet they hated the snow. Oh, here comes the wife.
Hey, wife." We were joined by a buttery blonde, heavily pregnant in
a yellow sundress. "Ellie, you remember Claudia. Married to Dan,
moved down from Vermont?"

She grinned. "Bet y'all are thinkin, how'd we ever pick this crazy
place!"

"She was just sayin how much she likes it."

"Is it possible to actually meet black people socially?" I inquired.
"Are any of the churches interracial?"

"Well," Steve said, "I heard the Catholics lost their priest a while
back and the black Catholics let em horn in, which was darn nice.
I believe one of the Baptist churches might be mixed, I'm not real
sure."

"Clubs?"

Steve looked pleasantly blank.

"Beaches." Like reading a list.

"Well, you might want to try theirs," he laughed. "I heard they fry
some great crabs."

I had been there by accident one afternoon. Curious about a sign
that said Billings Beach, I had turned off River Road and followed a
dirt road that ended in a field full of parked cars. Beyond it black
families in bathing suits milled around a cinder-block building. A
radio was playing. Through a breezeway onto the beach I saw, as if
through a telescope, a tiny girl in a bikini slowly pour a bucket of
water over her head. Back on River Road, it had seemed like a mi-
rage.

"But no, to answer your question," Steve said, "not a lot of that
kind of socializin goes on around here. I'll tell you somethin, and
this is lamentable. I've never eaten dinner with a black man."

"Half your clients are black," Ellie fondly reminded the side of his face.

"I believe *that*," I said. "Every time I go by the courthouse, it's all black people waiting out on that portico."

"Well. Not quite." Steve was twinkling at me. A man who would have been unable to *see* me six months earlier.

"It must be nice being able to help," I twinkled back. "You can be the guy who saves the old Negro, you know, like Gregory Peck—"

"*To Kill a Mockingbird.*" Dan was suddenly at my elbow.

"I sure can try!" Steve said. "Hey, Dan!"

"You're in the right place," I brazened on. "There was one of those guys in the Food Lion yesterday. Same faded overalls, straw hat, you know, checking over the pigs' feet. So Steve?"

"Madam?"

"What happens to all the really bright black kids in Beasley? There can't be enough jobs at Burger King for all of them."

"Well, you know, a lot of em sign up. They get recruited in high school at those army summer camps. I imagine the rest of em, if they're all that smart, just try to get their butts the hell out of town."

"I'm surprised how few interracial couples I see."

"Oh, they're there!" Ellie sang.

"I think maybe the Klan can relax a little bit about the master race getting mongrelized."

"You're probably aware this was the actual birthplace of the Klan," Steve said placidly.

"*Beasley?*" I was exultant.

"North Carolina," Dan said. "Y'all excuse us for a minute? We'll get up with you later."

Steve ceremoniously raised a hand. "Children? See y'all at the pig." Ellie gave us a rather bemused little wave.

Dan steered me off, away from the smoky drum where the pig was starting to attract a crowd, toward the water. When we got to the edge of the river Dan reached for my drink and I snatched my hand away.

"I'm not drunk," I said, "I'm just being pointed, which they can't stand."

"For the eight hundredth time, they don't *care*! You *are* drunk, by the way. You're obnoxious. You sound like an idiot. Talking about the Klan, for Chrissake, these people don't want to hear that. You're an embarrassment. What're you now, a civil-rights worker?"

"Would that be a problem?"

"I could give a flying fuck, except for one thing. The blacks *got* their civil rights already, remember? It was real big news at the time. They got every single goddamn thing they want, so don't even start with that shit. Harley's right. Hand em everything on a plate and they still can't be bothered to talk right."

"Maybe they don't all want to sound white."

"Hell no. They might have to get a real job."

"Why do you think they don't *work*? Do you have eyes in your head? Why do you think they're all lazy fools?"

"I didn't say all," he sniffed. "I said *some*."

"Any black person not on the Supreme Court is a slob."

"Why are we talking about this? I don't care about this." A revelation was stewing in his eyes. "Okay. Okay, I get what this is about now. You're all touchy-feely now with your new face. You love everybody, you're a saint. Got to get out and cheer up the poor black folk. *Whoa*, wait till those black boys see *you*. Course, you know it's a waste, cause they would've liked you fine the way you were."

"*You* did, for a while."

His arm shot toward me, he might have meant to hit me, but I pulled back and he lost his balance and flailed, then steadied himself by slapping a hand on my shoulder and keeping it there. We were an affectionate couple taking a moment away from the party. I swallowed the rest of my vodka. Dan crossed his arms on his chest and cocked his head at me.

"I guess it's a pretty good face for the money."

"I guess you get what you pay for."

"I make a point of it, actually," Dan said, as his eyes slid to the side.

"*You're not Margaret!*"

The woman's face was inches from mine, radiating amusement

from under a cap of pinched yellow-gray curls. Who on earth? "But I *am* Tassy Rankin! Least, I was the last time I looked!"

Remembering, Dan and I laughed expertly.

"I am just covered in shame! What was I thinkin, you're so much *prettier*! And *this* is my pretty friend Nan-Darlin Swain." The woman beside her was attractive, diminutive, bosomy in a pleated white tunic.

Dan seized her hand. "Harley's *mom*."

She beamed back and forth at us. "I have so wanted to meet y'all. You know, Harley's just besotted with you both and now I see why. We're so glad y'all have come to our part of the world."

We thanked her.

"Now, Claudia," Tassy Rankin said, "I hope you realize how very patient I'm bein, waitin for you to come draw my house."

"White, with forest-green shutters," Dan said, "at the end of the Parkway. The one with the cannonball!"

"That's us. And I so much want to be included in Claudia's little book."

"Dan, you come and flirt with me for a minute," Nan-Darlin said, drawing him away. "I promise not to hurt him!" she called back.

Tassy blinked expectantly at me.

I said, "You've heard about my book." I bitterly regretted having mentioned it to Debs-Anne.

"No secrets in this town!" And then somehow she was off into an explanation of how a Union Navy warship had fired a cannonball at her family's house on the waterfront. "It's still stuck right there, in the front, not that I mind. It's made my house quite famous."

"I've heard."

"You know," she stage-whispered, "my great-uncle Zak put it there. Got up on a ladder one night, him and a friend. They thought it was a sketch. Isn't that dreadful? Now don't tell anybody."

I promised I wouldn't.

"Not that my family didn't suffer during the war. My granddaddy was an officer, captured right down in New Bern and held there for two years, while his wife was at home, scared to pieces, stayin with their three little babies right in that house where John and I are now. That was a fearsome dark time. I was brought up on stories of just how grievous it was. Course, we all were." Her eyes were round with it. "But you know? That's what's made us so strong. That word, *solidarity*. That's how you know exactly who you are, so you don't give a hoot in hell whatever fix the rest of the world gets itself into. The world can just blow up around your ears and you'll be snug as a bug. That's how we feel. That's what real sufferin does." She squeezed out a thin exalted smile. "Aren't you precious to listen to me! And now even our black people, they're all comin back from up north. Quite a little exodus, I understand, and why not? It's their home too. I think they were a little disappointed up there." She paused suddenly to fiddle with her wristwatch and I saw the obligation she was under, the need she had to spell all this out to me. "I'm afraid there are still people up there who fail to understand about us and our black friends. They think the war was about slavery. And callin it a civil war! How *could* it be? We had our own *country* here, with a president and a cabinet and a congress, and an army and a navy! It wasn't a civil war, it was just the federal government tryin to force us to live like *they* wanted us to, which was just a pity, because this was the real America then. It still is. Oh, they're startin to serve! I'm *so* excited y'all are here! I just know y'all are goin to love it like we do. And I *know* y'all have never tasted barbecue like this before!"

The caterers, white kids with big aprons tied over their T-shirts and jeans, were lined up behind the long tables, scooping up coleslaw and hush puppies and shredded pork from the stainless steel pans. Tassy went off to find her husband. Looking for Debs-Anne I came across the oyster table just as the caterer was tipping a fresh load out of the steamer. They came thundering out in a great slosh and people grabbed them up and opened them, knives flashing, laughing at their own gluttony. Debs-Anne was there, off to one side, looking a little grim. In the barbecue line, we were both glum. I was worn-out from Dan and Tassy, and Debs-Anne was five months gone and not blooming. Her back was bothering her, her feet were puffy and purple-tinged. All she had to offset her discomfort was her conviction that the baby was a girl.

Debs-Anne's pregnancy was weighing heavily on me too. That she was living through an event so momentous stirred and depressed me. That night after the pig-and-pearl as the two of us were sitting in our kitchen with our noses in balloon snifters of Courvoisier, I thought she had a new limpid beauty, as if the baby were draining off all her succulence. I asked her what the baby felt like and she thought for a minute. "Gas." Then, maybe out of sympathy for my childlessness, which I had let her assume was painful, Debs-Anne seemed to search for more, and gave up. "Y'all'll get one. It'll happen." I sensed a change of subject coming.

"You know, I got a whole lot of time for that one in there," she said, meaning Dan. He and Harley had shared a joint down on the dock, yelling and baying, now they were in the living room with the bourbon. "Y'all are gettin along okay, aren't you, honey? I mean, I know you love him, but still you worry, cause you can't always remember why you married him. Aren't I right? Lemme see y'all's wedding pictures. They always tell the tale, don't they?"

"Oh no, I was too fat."

"You were never fat. But you know, y'all don't have any pictures of when you were younger and you must've been *darlin.*" She squinted down the years, envisioning me in my prime. "You still are."

"I was voted the prettiest girl in my class."

"Wasn't it *fun*? Oh Lord. Now look at us." She consulted her snifter mournfully.

"We've got a couple good years left."

"Who're you kiddin, girl?" As if to punctuate this, a mean cackle strayed in from the living room. "I don't know. Sometimes . . ." She poured herself more brandy, letting it splash into the glass. "That whole dumb number . . . do everything *but*. Make em marry you first. Kill yourself on the gear shift. *They* weren't waitin, it was just us. *Some* of us," she added darkly. She sighed. "I do love Harley. That's why I want to stay pretty. For *him*."

"You can always get a face-lift."

"Oh, that's cheatin, that doesn't count. Go on, get me your yearbook, right now."

"Debs, I don't have one. It's in Vermont!" I cried, as she jumped up.

I followed her into the living room, where the boys were stretched out on the floor on either side of the coffee table, apparently communing underneath it. Dan was lying on his hip, allowing Debs-Anne easy access to his back pocket. He let her slip the wallet out, he must have felt it, but he just rolled onto his back. I inched up behind the wing chair, watching Debs-Anne find the snapshot section.

"Okay. What have we got here? Danny and his big brother . . . that's adorable. You're much better-lookin than him. Danny and the biggest dog I have ever seen in my whole life. You kept this creature in an apartment?"

"He didn't exactly suffer." Dan's voice seemed strained to me, loaded with anticipation.

"Danny and . . . who is *this* person?" she squeaked, managing by the skin of her teeth to sound merely curious. As she flashed the picture down at Dan, I remembered he had carried it since our wedding, a snapshot taken by my mother of me pouting at him with my profile at its most acute angle and an ear peeping out of my upswept hairdo. The hat and wispy veil were unmistakably bridal. Dan wasn't bothering to see which picture it was, he knew.

"Go ahead," he said, "take a shot."

Debs-Anne consulted the photo again, in rabid silence. Her brow creased. I felt Dan watching me.

"That's his first wife," I said.

Debs-Anne, aware of Dan's eyes too, showed me the deadliest poker face of all time.

"Where?" Harley cried. "Lemme see." He sat up on the far side of the table and took the wallet from Debs-Anne. There was a long moment before he handed it back, with his face locked up. "She looks real nice," he said, lying down again.

"She's dead," I said.

Debs-Anne held the photograph closer, as if she wanted to smell it.

"I love her," came from under the table, strangled-sounding.

"Hey, bud," Harley said reproachfully, "you never *said* anything."

I think he was reaching for Dan under the table but Dan was struggling to sit up.

"Gimme that," he said to Debs-Anne. "Geezum crow."

"Here you go, Danny," she said softly, and handed him the wallet. He slid it back in his pocket and lay down again.

"I am so *sorry*, Danny." Debs-Anne's face was a tragic mask. "Harley? Time for us to go, honey."

I seconded this with a discreet tip of my head in the direction of the hall. They departed very quietly, just one stifled hoot coasting back. I went back in the living room and announced I was going up to bed.

Dan said, "No. Don't. Come over here."

I sat down at the end of the couch, near his head. The wallet was lying on his chest now and his eyes were open, staring at the ceiling. When he spoke he was solemn, as if death really were hovering there with us.

"Sorry about this afternoon," he said. Tense, holding it in. "I don't want you to leave."

"Danny. I wouldn't."

"I'm not a total dummy like you think."

"No, I know. Of course not."

"I get these ideas all the time. I wake up and I think . . . okay, I know they're stupid, but still. I don't know. I think maybe I could produce movies. I'm gonna start writing em down."

"You should. Danny?"

"What?"

"Where would I even *go*?"

"Anywhere." An accusation: *anyone* would have me now. He had curled himself awkwardly onto his side and was cradling the wallet like a little book he was reading. "You were a lot better before."

"No. I wasn't really. I was completely vain and self-obsessed. You have no idea."

"Now you're cured."

"Dan."

" 'Thank you, Danny,' " he singsonged. "Claudia?"

"What?"

"Where's the fucking *baby*?"

I was halfway up the stairs when the rest came, quietly. "You're still a real asshole, you know that?" I heard a gurgled choking sound.

I was still awake when he came in. He got his trousers off and fell onto the mattress with a snort, unconscious. I crept out of bed and took his trousers into the bathroom, found the wallet, and flipped through it. The photo was gone.

In the morning I waited for the phone to ring.

"Okay," Debs-Anne said, "I got me a fresh cup of coffee and all the time in the world. What's the story? Did you ever *meet* her?"

"No."

"Did he love her, d'you think?"

"That's what he says."

"Girlfriend, am I bein nosy? You sound funny."

"No, I'm fine. Go ahead."

"Well, it's just . . . I've heard of true love but . . . was it like a sex thing?"

"Who knows? Maybe he really did love her."

"Well, this is an extremely decent guy you're married to. Dan could spit the wrong way and I'd love him but . . . I don't know. Doesn't it give you the creeps? It would me. All Harley's old girl-friends were, you know, cute, give or take. You should've heard Harley last night in the car. He was a hoot." Pause. "Listen to me, I shouldn't say that. What'd she die of, anyway?"

"Childbirth. They both did, it was a real horror show. A blood-bath."

It was the weekend after that when I walked into the kitchen and saw the gun on the table. The first handgun I'd ever seen. It wasn't like a toy or a prop gun, it was real, the most real thing in the room. The floor creaked outside the door and Dan sidled in.

"Get that off my table," I said.

"Aw c'mon, it's pretty. That's all stainless steel."

"It's beautiful. I don't want it in the house."

"I got it for you, for when I'm away."

"Well, I'm never going to touch it. Really. So go put it somewhere where I won't have to see it."

"Yeah, but . . . *where*, though?" Pretending to be concerned, but hugely self-satisfied. "It's a SIG-Sauer. Go ahead, touch it." He went over to the table and picked the gun up, hefting it, trying out gun moves.

"Make it disappear," I said.

"Oh, cool your jets, will you? For fuck's sake." He took the gun and left the room.

SEVENTEEN

HAT DID DAN know? I couldn't tell, all my references were gone. The world was warping and straining at its edges, barely holding its shape.

One morning he caught me off-guard, suggesting a treat, a trip to the beach at Nag's Head. As we pulled out of the driveway Half-Gallon was just dropping Calvin off next door, and I was suddenly convinced Dan knew about Calvin; he was having fun with it, playing games with me. But then on the beach he was his sturdy acquisitive self, never lifting his eyes from the sand, selecting and rejecting and finally grabbing my hand and folding my fingers around a treasure, a small black conch shell. He was delighted with this gift, so sincerely thrilled that it made me feel, just for one horrible moment, that I deserved it. On the way home he was feeling intrepid and we took a road that was sometimes more like a causeway, cutting through dreamy thick wetland. In a little hamlet called Englehard, which was holding its annual fish fry, we had to nose our way through the lolling crowd. The white people were possibly even fatter than usual and the black people were blacker, blacker than in Beasley, blacker than on TV, blacker than Calvin. Dozens of slender, serene, impeccably alien silhouettes were strolling through the blear of country music and smoking fat. I put a hand up to my face, not wanting to be seen. I knew my eyes were too hungry. "Jungle fucking fever," Dan muttered, and I produced a snigger. I was shameless by then, trying to keep myself glued together. Every day I heard myself using the same lazy junk words Dan relied on—*no problem . . . no shit . . . whatever*—to phony up a feeling of control.

The days I spent without Calvin were wedged like chocks of wood between those few liquid hours with him. I remember once as he eased his body off me I panicked and whimpered, *No . . . don't go,* and then felt a stab of viciousness. "I *hate* this."

He was sitting at the edge of the bed, away from me, rubbing his face. "What? What do you hate?"

"The stupidity of being here like this. We're here and then we're not, and when we're not I can't *remember* everything."

"Don't try."

"You mean don't *bother*? Or do you mean trying makes it worse? I don't know what I'm doing."

"Hmm." He lay back down again and raised one hand and watched it twist as if it were turning in a breeze, a disaffected dilettantish gesture. "I guess you're having yourself an affair."

The next time I went to the house, I took a big sketch pad. My intention, I think, was to demonstrate that if I couldn't talk very well, there was one small trick I could do. I was scared of this too, but I forced myself. I would surprise him, I would do his portrait. He was scandalized when I told him. "What? You can't do that!" He decided to sit by the window so he could look out while I worked from the bed. I had him in the lawn chair in a three-quarter pose, the window frame sketched in quick and loose behind him. I got the shape of his head on the first try, and the tautness of his face, his convex *wrapped* look. The mouth even looked right. I wasn't afraid to make it too big, it looked fine. He could tell how it was going, he kept wanting to see, but I insisted on finishing. I started to darken his skin, to model all the planes and give his head its boldness, laying on more and more skin tone, shaping and working away, and I killed it. The page went flat and dirty, it was a mess of lead. I concealed my attempts to bring it back, making him hold the pose while I tried to highlight his cheekbones, erasing and smudging. He held still a minute longer, and then he got up and came over. I felt our gazes collide on the paper.

"Where'd you learn that?"

I gawked up at him. He was serious, he thought it was great, he couldn't tell it was clumsy and mediocre. My contempt for his ignorance burst through my misery like a fist. He took the pad off my knees and pulled the pencil out of my fingers and went back to the chair and sat down. Yes, I thought. Fine, you draw me. Draw a picture of me thinking how simple and ignorant you are, trying to guess what else you don't know. Names bristled in my brain. Karl Marx? Jung? Truffaut? Had Calvin ever read a book? He was glancing back and forth from me to the paper, lips compressed, hand and eye moving urgently, completely engrossed. The artist in his rickety lawn chair. Finally he stopped and chewed the inside of his cheek, adjudging. Waiting, I could tell, for me to come and look over his shoulder, while I sat and waited for him to get up and bring it to me. Finally he tore off the page and leaned over and handed it to me.

In the middle was my head, egg-shaped, a big-eyed pretty-girl head, with flaps of hair like a cocker spaniel's ears, and precise spiky eyelashes. Above the head, odd sketchy little clumps, quite skillfully shaded, were hard to interpret but suggestive, like cloud shapes. On top of them lines of black lozenges spread outward from the pretty head, like a crown of bullets.

"No body," I said.

He reached silently for the drawing and I handed it back. He started working again. "Those cloud things," I said. "Those are my unformed thoughts." My heart was thudding. "Aren't they."

A minute later he handed me the amended drawing. There was a body now, way too small for the head but itself in proportion. Skinny shapely arms stuck out at the sides, one hand holding a cat by its tail, all of this in the same feathery strokes as the cloud shapes, making the huge graphic head even more static. A caricature of passivity. Like the head emitting bullets, the body was radiating wormy lines, which made the face look more alarmed, with its big pop eyes. I felt it. I felt that it was me, thinking too much and staring and not talking. My eyes did feel like that, not just at that moment but often. It was shocking. It was too primitive and too real.

"People never know what they look like," Calvin offered consolingly.

"That's true. This is a little abstract."

He was studying my drawing of him again. "This is realism," he said, surprising me.

"It would be, if there was any resemblance."

"No, it's good. You didn't even have to go to school to learn this."

"Sure I did. I went all through high school, I took classes at the college museum. That's when I figured out I wasn't that good. So then I studied art history in college, so I could be a curator. What I really wanted was a job at that museum." I backed up then and described the echoing interior of the Fleming, the balconies lined with portraits of families propped like dolls on their horsehair sofas, and pioneer landscapes full of dust gleaming like gold, pictures I had haunted since puberty. "I think I thought they were mine," I said, and he grunted. I told him about helping out in the background at all the museum's contemporary openings, ingratiating myself, making myself indispensable, getting to know the curator. But the petulance was coming into my voice. "I was doing everything I could think of, so I could get an assistant curatorship when I got my degree in art history. With honors. I applied for the job. I went for the interview. I knew the curator pretty well by then." Calvin was austere and attentive in his chair, as sober as an interviewer himself. "I thought we got along pretty well. But I didn't get the job."

"She didn't think you could do it?"

"Well, a lot of the work involved trying to raise money, dealing with the public, hosting big fund-raising benefits. Schmoozing. All that." Careful, I thought.

"She just didn't like you. What'd she look like? Plain woman?"

I shook my head, cautiously, afraid that too violent a movement might make the words fly out like broken teeth. I shrugged, and leaned my back against the wall to feel steadier. "I don't know what it was. Things worked out in the end though. That's when I got the job at the paper. I liked that, doing layout and artwork, designing the ads." Calvin's face was thoughtful. He kept nodding.

I said, "You never know with people like that. They have too much power. They get weird with it." I suddenly knew I was talking about white people.

"Some do. Not all." He meant white people too.

"You don't think so?"

"People try, that's what I think." He recrossed his legs, completely at ease with the subject, like a guest on a political chat show refusing to take the bait. "Doin the best they can, most of em."

"No, they're not. They're not at all."

"People are just gonna be what they are." Meaning what, things were peachy? Race didn't count? Or was he dissembling, trying to placate my whiteness? I didn't know who was comforting whom. "One thing for sure, the past is always goin to prevail. You can't get free of what you come from. You can *try*."

"Those people don't even think about that. They're having too much fun being their wonderful powerful selves."

"What you want em to do, fly?"

"No. I just appreciate a little imagination sometimes. There but for the grace of God. Remember that? When was the last time you heard that one?" Calvin just sat there, watching me. "Don't you think it's amazing when people can actually manage to put themselves in somebody else's shoes?"

His smile was weary. "You're a cold woman, Bipsa."

"I'm not."

"Yeah you are. You know, everybody got their little hurt. Some sad secret thing. If that makes you feel any better. I don't care who it is, they all got some mistake they made or maybe it's somethin they lost. Somethin they're gonna wait their whole life for, even though it ain't ever comin and they know it. Somethin's supposed to join us all up and that must be it. All I can think of . . . all that hurt goin on. Everybody doin the best they can with it though, most of em." He gave me that thin smile again. "That's the *bad* news."

"Right. Meaning it's okay if people are thoughtless and cruel."

"Why're you so happy about it?"

"You *do* know they hate *you*."

He turned his head and threw his gaze way out, as if to carry himself away on it. Stillness shimmered out of him like heat.

I was too appalled even to form an apology in my mind.

He made a sound, p-p-p-p-p . . . and vibrated his hand in the air. "Dominoes, that's all. Like, if you come from a liar, you might be a liar. Strange thing about you is, you ain't got no movement sometimes. I see that. What *is* that? Like somethin stopped in you." He was looking at me again, hard. "What'd you do?"

"Nothing. I'm just a sad person like everybody else."

"Yeah, you are." He dragged his hand over his face. He looked sallow-eyed. "You know, we got to get ourselves out of here."

"We could go for a walk."

"We could do that."

He didn't really want to walk in the tobacco, that was my idea too. The plants were almost shoulder high, rows of green splashing fountains. We walked with a row between us, the jungle-sized leaves lashing our skin. The fragrance we stirred up—the fumes—were exactly like unfiltered Camels. When my sandals got slippery in the dirt I took them off and carried them. Calvin was trudging rather doggedly.

"This is a real pretty plant, but you try pickin it. All these Mexican boys they got doin it now . . . maybe you don't get so sick if you think you're gettin rich. They tell you it's the heat. These white boys I used to work with, thought it was like holiday fun pickin for two weeks. They all be sayin, Shit, man, this is some *heat*. Whew! Ain't this some dismal heat today? Wasn't no *heat*. Your whole skin and your hair be all gummy with tar, won't even come off in the shower. Poison, glued on you. Rain makes it worse, people all be passin out, throwin up. Can't move, can't sit up and take a drink of water. Just . . . *ill*."

"It's the devil's crop."

"See?" He grinned over at me. "You *do* know somethin. Somethin besides how to make me hang on and *suffer*."

"Oh, poor you. You'll probably live." I felt a little delirious, dizzy from the novelty of being with him outdoors.

"Oh, I'm into it now," he agreed darkly, as we ran out of field.

We had just turned around to go back when I realized I was alone. I stopped and looked back and he was standing like a statue, right up to his chest in the bright tobacco.

"I'm doin it," he said. "I *been* doin it, all this time. Lovin you." The light jangled, great chunks of light crashing, and then Calvin's face changed and he lifted his arm in a salute. I twisted again toward the house and saw a black man waving back, his shirt lavender against the dark wall of ivy. Calvin said, "Half-Gallon, bein early the only time in his life."

That silenced us. My mind was empty anyway, scooped out into the warmth of the sky. It was enough to be slogging together through the big leaves toward Half-Gallon, watching him grow bigger until I could make out his grave Easter Island features. Burrowing his hand deep inside a paper bag, he seemed to belong to us, as if he were our child.

"He's got some more of those cookies," Calvin muttered. "*What you doin?*" he yelled as we stepped clear of the tobacco. Half-Gallon was chewing in a concentrated fastidious way, watching us closely.

He was shorter than I would have guessed from seeing him in the truck, about my height, and younger, maybe not even thirty. He was long-necked but short in the leg, as if the weight of his long head had compressed him at the other end. A slender, almost feminine hand emerged from a dangling unbuttoned sleeve to lift a broken piece of cookie to his mouth.

"This is Claudia," Calvin announced.

Half-Gallon dipped his head. As I slipped my sandals back on, he slung his gaze into the sky, rummaged at the bottom of the bag, and produced a perfectly whole cookie. Holding it between two elegant fingers like a cigarette, he handed it to me and then put another broken piece in his mouth. I thanked him and asked where they came from.

"You tell her, she won't eat it," Calvin said.

Ignoring him, I gave Half-Gallon my full attention and felt our triangular connection tighten happily, like a little party.

"This is a great cookie," I said. Half-Gallon was munching steadily. "Chocolate chip. With . . . pecans?" He was starting to unnerve me.

"What kind of cookies you make?" he said.

"None. I can't bake anything except brownies."

"You cook fish?"

"I can cook fish pretty well."

"You cook steak? How you cook it?"

"I put it on the grill."

"Spaghetti?"

I glanced at Calvin, who was applying his Chap Stick and pensively taking this in.

"You got to put two different meats in your sauce," Half-Gallon said. "You know about that?"

"No! I don't!" I was trying to laugh.

"I think we had about enough of that." Calvin sounded too firm, as if he were scolding Half-Gallon for trying to flirt with me. What was going on? Half-Gallon's smile was sly as a cat's. When Calvin put an arm around me, the smile split wide open. A side tooth was missing.

"So, what you think about *this*?" Calvin asked him, giving my shoulder a squeeze. What was all this jolly crudeness, was it black men being *black* together? Eyes downcast now, Half-Gallon's whole face was shining. "Yeah, but this here's mine," Calvin said with that same forced lustiness. "You go get your own."

"I did," Half-Gallon said, serious again, his face flat as a shovel.

"You think Serafina *Nelson* goin to entertain your spooky self? Let's ask this woman. Claudia, would you say Half-Gallon is good-lookin enough to get himself hooked up with the finest woman in Calhoun?" Calvin pulled me closer, with a nudge, some sort of a cue, and I got it.

"Hmm." I let a beat go by. "Well. He does have a nice smile." Half-Gallon had gone limp. He had thrown his eyes up to heaven, like a saint. "His hands are beautiful." I searched, intent on being truthful. "Pretty eyes," I said, and he lowered his gaze and leveled it at me, unclouded, and heavy, but not with desire. His curiosity was drilling a hole in me.

"Sorry I asked," Calvin said. "Okay, boss, we got to make our move."

Half-Gallon held the cookie bag out to me. I accepted it. As he turned to go, Calvin tipped my face up and kissed my mouth, then we trailed Half-Gallon out to the lane, drowsy and reluctant. I asked Calvin if it was really okay for Half-Gallon to drive.

Calvin said he was fine. "People all call him simple, but he's just like that. Nothin wrong with Half, except he ain't ever gone with a woman yet. That could be it. You got to stir him up once in a while, like crabs in a bucket, that's all. He's got a sister Melanie, she's the same way." He said Half-Gallon painted houses and worked mostly for his brother, who owned the van. He had gotten his nickname when he was two years old and drank a half gallon of buttermilk. Half-Gallon had started up the van.

I stood in the lane and waved them away, and then went back in the house to get my purse and my sketch pad. It felt even dirtier in there now, forlorn and used up.

I started resenting it, not just the secrecy and the strictly prescribed hours when I would be jerked back into life, but sometimes even the pleasure itself, quarantined in that room. I resented getting in the car and driving to it. But I did take a distinct pride in what we achieved without any of the standard diversions like money or places to go or friends. Once, coming up the stairs, anxious that he wouldn't be there, I thought I smelled food. A big platter of fried chicken sat on the table under a lid of crumpled foil. Calvin was sumptuously naked on the bed.

"That over there is the dessert."

When it was time, he arranged the pillows behind my back and pressed a neat row of overlapped napkins on my sweaty body, from my ribs to my knees. He balanced a plastic plate on my pubic bone, handed me a knife and fork, spread a dishtowel on the sheet and set the chicken platter on it, and then retired to the end of the mattress. "That one there," he said, pointing out a breast. Of course it was fantastic, the crust light and spicy and still crisp, even though it must have been cooked hours before. Calvin watched me gnaw it.

"Take some yogurt, thin it out with a little milk. Some egg if you got it. Dip it in that. Shake a little cumin and some hot flakes in with the flour and roll it good. Got to have your fat not quite smokin, lard and butter, two to one." He reached over and wiped my chin for me.

"It's the best I ever ate," I said. "It's unbelievable. Too bad we have to eat it locked up in here."

Calvin was meticulously pulling the chicken off the bone in long delicate strips. "Yeah. That is too bad."

"Imagine us in a restaurant. What would that be like, I wonder."

"Claudia, what'd you think this was goin to be?"

"I'm just getting so I can't *breathe* in here."

"You sound like an actress."

"You sound like Dan." No response. I said, "Why'd you split up with Jade?"

"I was lonely. I was lonely when she was right there. I remember one time she had on this sweater with red strawberries all over it, little frippery thing. I was thinking how much I loved those strawberries. Then I thought, Yeah, you love em, you love em more than her. You know when you want to feel it, but you want to get *rid* of it? It was like that. She was havin a bad time too. In the daytime she was okay but when she was asleep she had a voice comin out of her just like a man." He dropped his voice. " 'In the mud. No, in the *mud.*' Five, six times a week. Eyes shut tight, mashin her head against the wall, curled up like it was somethin filthy peckin at her feet. Whatever it was."

"You."

"Yeah, I was floatin in there. And her father that used to make her kneel on rice. And Jamaica's kidney." He was unfolding his body, getting up. "What about you, Bipsa?" Taking his plate to the window, dipping his knees to fling the chicken bones out with an arm like a whip. "Why're you doin Dan like this?"

"He doesn't know."

"You call that a reason?"

"He wouldn't mind."

"He wouldn't mind. How well you know this man?"

"I'll tell you how well. I ask him if he's hungry and he always has to look at his watch. He sees me out on the dock and every single time he says, Hey, whatcha doin? He can't go to sleep unless he's heard the weather report. Except when he's full of bourbon."

"All he's got is you."

"I don't care."

"Yeah, I see that. Eat some more chicken."

The week after that, the last week in September, was going to be one of Dan's weeks away, at a trade show. The Friday beforehand, I kissed Calvin awake and announced this to him. His face flared.

"What you goin to do?" he said.

"I thought I could spend more time here."

"Nights too?"

"He might try to call me."

"Hm. Up to you."

Calvin would still have to work, so it wasn't as if we'd gained more time, it would just seem that way. But then I think we started to feel we were about due for a reward. Monday we spent all day at the house. The tobacco field was just sponging up the last light when I got in the car. Tuesday we met there early, around eight. Around lunchtime Half-Gallon beeped his horn in the lane and Calvin went off with him. I had decided to gamble and meet him that night. I brought a picnic and we ate it on the bed. After that we made love for the first time in the dark, turned into tougher, greedier people. It was around midnight when I got home. I had just shed my clothes on the bedroom floor when the phone rang. I had to force myself to answer it.

"Hey! How's my girl?" Dan was drunk.

"Fine! How's it going?"

"Fucking great! Claud, listen to this! Oh shit. *Rick!*" he called. "What was that thing you said—remember?—that I said my wife would freak when she—" A mumble in the background. "Oh yeah! Listen to this, Claud. 'Beat em like you own em. Beat em like you *own* em!' Get it?"

"I get it." I was staring at my reflection in the window, a specter holding a phone to her head.

"It's a thing they *say* here! I'm in Montgomery!"

"Dan . . . I know." I understood, unwillingly, that he had hoped to earn my approval with this piece of ugliness.

"Fucking great down here, you'd really love it. Say hi to Rick. Hey, Rick, my ole lady wants—"

"Dan, maybe you should go to bed?"

"Fuck you, it's early."

The line went dead. I watched as the woman in the window put the phone down slowly, entranced by her nakedness.

EIGHTEEN

ALVIN WORKED ALL the next day. The heat had relented and
I spent a few hours on the dock, using up page after page in botched
attempts at drawing water. By late afternoon I had managed to
imbue the Spanish moss overhanging the Alligoods' boathouse with
the same hint of menace I remembered from an illustration in an
old edition of *Uncle Tom's Cabin*, and felt a little pang of renewed
hope for my book. I was having a glass of wine and watching the
news when Calvin called and asked me to pick him up on the Calhoun road near the Handi-Mart.

By the time I got out there he had gotten past the Handi-Mart and
was sitting by the side of the road, up on the bank. Sitting next to
him was a small black boy with a ball cap on sideways. As I pulled
over they stood up and I saw the boy was a very petite woman. She
scuttled down the bank on her rear end until Calvin swooped her up
by the armpits and swung her over the little ditch and set her down
on the road. As soon as her feet touched the ground she started walking, but he grabbed her back and pulled her toward the car. He held
on to her hand as he thrust his head in the window. This was Melanie, Half-Gallon's sister, he said. Melanie was keeping Calvin between herself and the car, but a circumspect gleam of curiosity—a
weaker version of Half-Gallon's—shot out from under her soft hat-
squashed hair. I said hello but she was trying to squirm away again,
and Calvin let her go.

"She doesn't want a ride?" I was relieved.

"She's a walker," he said, getting in. He made it sound like a vocation, and she seemed to be confirming this, arms swinging, feet chugging in their huge purple-and-white lightning-bolt sneakers. As we drove past her Calvin leaned his head out. "Don't you forget what I said!" he yelled, and she scribbled both hands in the air and giggled. "This is *her* road," he told me, "back and forth, back and forth. She's all right, I keep an eye out. You know where her rest stop is." I did know, as soon as he said it, in that fond voice. He said, "That's where she hangs. *Used* to hang. I told her she had to give us some privacy."

"She was there that first day." I had just remembered the little Tupperware shrine. "Was she?"

"Hidin behind the kitchen door. You bout scared her to death. Scared both of us."

Sometime around midnight we were lying limp and peaceful, the candles guttering in their wine bottles, crickets creeching, when something rustled in the ivy below the window. "One of them real *big* crickets," Calvin muttered. He started to reach for me again, and a shout came, intimate, low. "Hey! Hey man!" Calvin's hand froze. "Calvin!"

"I'm goin out for one minute, see who that is."

It was obvious he already knew. He was hurrying, hopping on one leg to get his pants on, still pulling his T-shirt on as he went out, banging his shoulder on the door frame. I tracked his footsteps down the stairs and out the front door and lost them. Under the window I heard the ivy thrashing, the sound heading away around the far side of the house. I bolted down the hall into the corner room at the front, where a side window stood open. As I stared at it, the voice came again, higher now, cajoling and a little hoarse.

"You know what I'm thinkin? I'm thinkin, this here's a *tired* man. Got his dick in a *sling*!" Silence, or perhaps Calvin answering in a voice too low to hear. Then, "You been at this awhile now, what I hear, you and Missus *Bee-Em-Double-Yew.*"

"So what's up, man?" Calvin was forcing a restrained coolness into his voice. "Where you been? I got a child now. Bobo, man, stop swingin that thing."

"You got a *child*? You know how many I got? Seven. *Eight*." Something cracked violently. Metal on wood, it sounded like. "I got eight fuckin kids, man, what you think about that?" *Thwack.*

"You hangin at Jimmy's? Where you hangin, man? I'll get up with you tomorrow."

"Fuck you *think*, man? I'm over at Jade's, gettin some of what you owe me. But that's cool! Cause I know you and me's still friends. Friends forever."

"Ain't nobody scared of you now, Bobo. I reckon you been gone too long. How long you been gone?"

"Fuck you know about it, nigger nose stuck up a white snatch? *Hey!*" The voice suddenly shot up past me. "*Ain't like he never ate light meat before!*" Then it was wheedling again, almost whining. "Come on, man, come on out with Bobo. You know where I been? Up in Philly, man! People *made* of money up there and they all dyin for it. Like sellin em butter and bread, and I'm *in* there, man, I'm in there *tight*. You know what I was thinkin, comin over here, man? I was thinkin bout that time at Jimmy's when you smashed the bar all up!" Hee hee hee, he laughed, high, like a girl.

"That was Colefax."

"That was *you*, man! And Jimmy tryin to roll a blunt big as his dick? That was *you*, rubbin your ugly lips all over my face, kissin me and cryin bout how much you be needin your little Jade? *What a juicy fat pussy she had?* Course you didn't put it like that. No, cause your shit always come out smellin like poetry. Yeah, that musta been just before you threw up all inside my Firebird."

"Whose car is that you stole now?" Calvin said.

"Stacy *give* me that car."

"That ain't Stacy's car. Stop jigglin like that! You been smokin that shit too long. Why don't you go get a drink and cool down. You a mess, Bobo, you hurt my eyes."

"How's the leaf business, man?" The insane cackle again, then it broke down into choking.

"I'm doin all right."

"Yeah—hee hee hee—I guess you are. I guess you a rich man by now. That must be *your* car, hidin in the bushes. Shhh. Calvin got a big *secret*. Shit. You think *I'm* gonna mess you up? Don't you be issuin me that shit. You got a bigger problem than me, man. That white pussy gonna fuck you over and not even know she doin it and that's how it is. And you know it too."

I knelt on the gritty floor and inched my head out as far as I dared. He was just below me in the burnt clearing, compact, foreshortened into stacked muscles, bullet-headed in one of those black nylon stocking caps. No shirt, just a leather vest, a shade darker than his meaty dull skin. Suddenly he thrust out his arms and a length of pipe glinted in his hand. *Bum-bum-ba-doo, bum-bum-ba-doo* . . . I didn't know what it was at first, the sound was so soft, but it was him, head down, feet planted, muttering a thumping drum boogie that was getting louder, more insistent, bum-*bum*-ba-doo. He was shrugging, making the vest flap, snapping his hips, waving the pipe like a baton. "Bum-*bum*-ba-doo . . . yeah, Jade been treatin me fine. Had to get some of what you *owe* me, man! Bet you thought I forgot! I don't forget nothin! Bum-*bum*-ba-doo. *Hey girl!*" he screamed up at me. I cringed back. "Look at Bobo dancin! Bum-bum-ba-doo. Your ole man know where *you* at tonight? Do he know what you like doin *best?*" Something moved in the corner of my eye, crawling toward me on the floor . . . a sock. It was red in the daytime, I had seen it before. Under the window there was more thrashing, moving away from the house, toward the lane, but where was Calvin? There was just the cricket screech, then a thundercrack of metal on metal and glass smashing, and I scuttled into the room overlooking the lane in time to see Calvin leap off the porch and then stop in his tracks and stare hopelessly out at the lane. Bobo's tires whined in the dirt before they bit the paved road. I ran back to the pink room and lay down as Calvin came slowly up the stairs. He undressed and flung himself down and I waited, trying to match my ragged breathing to his.

"He's nothin. I'm tellin you that so you don't have to ask me. He's a dead man. Climbed out of his grave and don't even know his feet already rotted off. He took out a taillight, that's all. I can cover it."

"It's insured." Why was I whispering? "Who is he?"

"We did some business. Once. One time."

"When was that?"

"When I was stupid."

"He's not really staying with Jade?"

Calvin hiked himself up on one elbow and with an attitude of studied patience wrapped his hand over the top of my skull and held it there like a sponge to soak up all the terror foaming inside. My mind withered gratefully. After a minute he flung himself back down with an arm over his eyes like a bandage and we lay there, listening to all the things I wasn't saying.

"Yeah," he said finally. "He's the bad nigger, I'm the good one."

I fumbled for him and found his hand and we breathed together, exhaling Bobo, trying to move on past him. We tangled our arms and legs together and still Bobo lingered. Even his children were there with us in their jumbled purgatory. But not a particle of this knowledge about Bobo clung to Calvin. He was purer to me than ever, and stronger, and more honest. Healthy, full of love. Everything Bobo wasn't. That was all I knew, all I wanted, and Calvin wanted it too, it was pounding around us quietly. I was like his filter, the part of him that could receive his trouble and purify it, now that I knew. I tightened my arms around him and he tightened his. It was a miracle that he was here where he should be, lying in my arms, pressing his ear against my cheek. Bobo was like a task we'd accomplished together, and now we were slouched down inside our one skin, safe, washed in our sweat. All that was left of Bobo was the feeling of being way beyond his fury, being inside thick invisible walls that were amplifying every little sound we made together. The night folded us in.

The dawn was gray and hot, another soggy day. Calvin and I stood in the lane and stared at the smashed taillight, then I drove him to Beasley. He directed me to one of the older black sections, still closed up asleep except for a couple older women watering their plants and a little girl sitting on her front porch steps with her cat. On a corner near a boarded-up grocery store Calvin asked me to stop, and he got out and walked quickly down the street. His plan was to stop at a cousin's house, pick up some breakfast, and wait for Half-Gallon.

At home the answering machine was waiting, red light blinking. Sick with apprehension, I pressed the button and out curled a male voice, a long fat snake of white dough.

"Good *morning*. I'm calling from the Beaver Creek Church of God. I just call people and tell em Jesus is precious and you're precious too, and may God bless you real *good* today! The purpose of this call is to win souls to Jesus Christ. If you're a sinner, please call in. Praise God, a savior to rejoice in. He's so good and wonderful, we can't praise Him enough. If you're a Christian, you know this! The more we can win, the less we'll have to burn, so win all you can and hear Jesus say, Well done, my children. So win all you can!"

The machine clicked off. That was all. No message from Dan.

I ran a glass of water and stared out at the river and Bobo came back to me in a kind of vision, flouncing on his toes, his head knocking side to side like he was caught in a cloud of invisible punches. He was more real in that moment than I was.

That evening when I got to the house Calvin was asleep, still dressed, curled up on his side. A large bottle of Colt 45 stood by the bed, empty. As soon as I sat on the windowsill his eyes opened but he didn't seem to notice me, he just drew his knees up to his chest. His face had that dusty look.

"Bipsa. You know what I need right now? I need a cigar." I realized I had never seen Calvin drunk. Was he drunk? "What you been doin with your cute self all day?"

"Nothing. Petting the dog."

He flopped onto his back. "You got a dog? You ain't got a dog! Come on over here with that cuteness."

"I'll go get you some cigars. What kind?" I was suddenly edgy, and afraid he would notice.

I was just reversing the car when he flailed out in his unlaced boots, got the door open, and threw himself in.

"Now *darlin!*" For some reason the South had flown into my mouth. I twanged at him. "Does this make good sense to y'all?" He was hunched over, squeezing his hands between his knees. We bounced up onto the road.

"Be dark in one minute," he muttered.

The Handi-Mart was squatting in its stale yellow glow, with half a dozen cars and trucks parked in front and a couple more at the pumps. One had a Confederate plate. "Lively tonight," I said, and pulled the car back around the side by the kerosene tank.

"People all got their numbers in now."

"What do you mean?"

"People play the numbers. You know. Got to do the number voodoo, get it to the man by seven, then you can do all your unimportant shit, like go buy the kids some frozen dinner." It was hard to hear him, he was turned away from me, staring out at the pampas grass. "Go on now, I'll be fine. Box of Tampa Nuggets and a forty-ounce Colt."

As I got to the door a man was approaching, bathing trunks, muscle shirt, one of those rawboned rubber-band bodies. He made a show of hustling to open the door for me, forcing me to wait for him to do it. "Lemme get that, *there* ya go!" All smiles, staring at the tops of my breasts. "*Two* Colts!" I heard Calvin yell. The man's squinty sun-bleached eyes looked beyond me, out to the pumps, as I slipped past him.

At the refrigerators I hauled out the bottles and carried them to the girl at the counter. She was pretty and hugely overweight, her blond head immobilized by a surgical collar of fat. Working alongside her was a fair heavyset young man who might have been her brother. Watching the girl go off to find the cigars, I could feel myself being stared at. I tried to ignore it.

"Maybe that's what *I* need."

It was Tassy Rankin, staring pointedly at the malt liquor. "Would that put some spunk in my poor ole tired blood?"

I forced a little laugh. "How *are* you?"

"Well, I'd be fine, if y'all would ever come see me." She set an ant trap and a drum of cashews on the counter. "Y'all don't mind, I'll just be a minute," she told a woman behind us. As I paid the girl, Tassy dangled a scrap of broken shoelace in front of her face. "I need some just like this, dear. Brown, thirty-six inches. Well, you better come soon, cause I'm liable to die first."

"Oh, never!" I picked up my bag and shifted it heartily.

"How nice to bump into you. Here, of all places! I *thought* that was y'all's car out there. What happened to your taillight?" She watched me backing toward the door.

"Vandals."

"Oh, for pity's sake, don't you wonder where they get the nerve. Bye-bye now. Say hey to Dan!"

As I got in the car Calvin grabbed at the bag. He was swigging before we were out of the parking lot.

"There was somebody in there," I said.

"Old white lady in a blue dress."

I looked at him. "Did she see you?"

"Stuck her head in the window."

"Oh God, what'd she say?"

"Said 'hey.' "

"And what, you had a *chat*?"

"I said, 'Hey, how you doin?' She say, 'Fine.' That'd be about it. She seemed kind of pleased to see me. You want to slow down?"

"Shit. What's going to happen now?"

"Looks like it did already."

I veered into the lane by the house and rammed the car into the deepest part of the brush in the yard. Sticks and leaves thrashed in through the open windows. The car finally ground to a halt in a tunnel of branches and leaves jammed against the windshield.

"You just wrecked your paint," Calvin said.

"That's okay, the car's already been trashed."

I shut off the lights. The darkness was oppressive. Calvin neatly snapped off a twig in front of his face and dropped it out the window. "Yeah. Might as well throw it away, get you a new one." He nudged the bottle at me and I drank some beer and nudged it back. I could just see him, positioning the bottle between his thighs. "This is stupid," he observed, as if to himself.

"I wanted to ask you. A blunt is a joint?" I knew I was annoyed; I had not identified my anger as fear.

"Joint, spliff. Reefer, yeah."

"Did you see Bobo today, so he could bully you some more?"

"Bobo can't hurt me. And he wouldn't, even if he wanted to." He took a drink. "Claudia, why don't you just *tell* the man?"

"Oh, I couldn't do that, he might shoot you." Dignified silence. "With his new gun."

"Mmm. Well, he bound to find out now."

"Why?"

"Cause that woman back there is a ghoul." He drank some beer and when his voice came again it was sugary and scolding, with the same breathy inflection as Tassy's. " 'Oh honey, you're not black . . . you're *Calvin.*' "

I didn't even get it. "She *knows* you?"

"Look. It oughta be you that tells him. Be a whole lot smoother that way." He was shaking his head. "You think I'm not nervous too?" He made a sound with his breath, a huff of astonishment. "I look at you sleepin and I think, Man, what are you doin? This a *white woman* lyin here."

I covered my face with my hands, my perpetual instinct.

"Don't do that, I hate it when you do that." He gathered my wrists in one hand and pulled my hands away.

I was thinking, Talk, this is just talk, I'm in a car, I can drive away.

"This is a big event, you and me doin this," he said. "But we been keepin it goin. This is just the bad part, that's all. I just about had it with this part. Time to get on to somethin new." He was handing me the bottle. I drank some and gave it back. "We got to start gettin serious. Got to think about money now. All that."

"I don't have any." I would never have any. But then the little fleur-de-lis pin suddenly glimmered in front of me, a gold spider dropping down its silky thread. "I really don't."

A feather of light lay on his eyelid. His hand reached out and a knuckle stroked my cheek. "That's okay. We get some."

Then he was feeling around the console, finding the lighter and pushing it in. He rummaged in the bag at his feet.

"Calvin." I made my voice deep and practical, hoping to stop my heart knocking the breath into my mouth. "How would we live?"

He was getting his cigar going, stoking it. I filled my lungs with the smell. "Well, we can't go too far. I can't take Jamaica and I can't leave her. Maybe five miles. Ten at the outside."

"Too close," I said, and a world of joy ripped open in me, like a wall blown off a house, and inside I could see us eating in a room crowded with all our shared things.

"Claudia." Calvin pulled on the cigar and his face smoldered and died away again. "He'll be okay."

"Why do you say that? You don't know him."

"Oh, I know the man." He pushed the bottle at me and I pushed it back. "He likes a drink. Likes a little smoke too, I reckon. He's got a little bit of cruelty in him. Not a bad man though, and he loves you, that's for sure. Loves you the best he can. You make his life pretty. Everything got to be smooth and pretty with a man like that. Can't even *see* it if it don't look like him. Smell like him, talk like him. That's fine. That's his business. That leaves a lot of stuff out though. You know what I'm sayin? That leaves a whole lot of stuff out." He flicked his ash out the window. "Hear that? No crickets." It was true. It was dead quiet, we were buried together in a hole in the ground.

"So. Can't leave the man high and dry. Can't leave the dick husband." He took a long pull on the cigar. "I guess I don't understand what we been tryin to do here. See, now I'm *scarin* you. I scared a little kid today, little white boy waitin in the car for his mother. Takes one look at me and starts lockin all the doors up tight, eyes like fried eggs. But see, you *like* that, and I never even told you all my scary stuff yet. Lemme see. I went with this little girl one time, sixteen years old she was, and she tells me she's pregnant, and I'm cold. I'm cold like ice. Finally I think, Okay, go take some money over there to her house. I get over there and her brother comes out the door and spits on my truck. His fists come up, he's gettin all ready to come into my mouth. I say, *Now what the hell's the matter with you?* And he say she's dead. She's lyin inside the house, dead. She got so worried she stuck somethin inside herself and died in her mama's bathroom on the hard floor. I was a grown man. She thought I was a prince. That was Kyla's money, that she didn't have, that she got out of thin air for me. I didn't pay her back one dime."

"You will. Calvin. You don't have to tell me all this."

"Now wait. I got to pay the hospital, that comes first. Three hundred and twenty-seven dollars and fifty-three cent every month, for Jamaica's upset last winter. Got to stay cool with *them* now. Then I got a loan outstandin, for the up-front money I gave em on it. That's a loan for two thousand and five."

"From who?"

"White guy I know. Cause what'd Jamaica ever need insurance for? Child of mine's gonna pop out perfect, right?"

"She has it now though."

" 'Pre-existin,' girl. What country you been livin in? And now here comes Bobo, back from the outskirts of Hades, wantin what's his."

"You don't owe *Bobo.*"

"Well, now, this matter is under some discussion at the moment. See, I was in business for a little while, after the boat. Little reefer now and then, help get the bills paid. Then Bobo come back home with this rat poison he's tryin to peddle to all his old friends, and he tells me I'm a small-time boy. Little country boy. Nickel and dime. Now, I can't *stand* hearin that. So I sit Bobo down one day and I tell him about these people I know in Greenville. I knew it was a shaky deal. I knew it the whole time. Bobo lost all his money and a lot of other people's money. Bobo almost got killed."

"That wasn't your fault, it was his. Bobo's stupid."

"Nope. Bobo ain't stupid. He just sick with that shit. Guns and drugs. They got him now, he's done. He did a flip on me. He be dead before too long, that or worse. You didn't see him before. Bobo was sharp."

"But you had to do that for the hospital bill."

"Nope. This was before. See, you keep tryin to pretty it up. But this load ain't that heavy, not for a man loved to lick his own ass like I did. Or maybe you thought that was just Bobo shit-talkin. You know, I fucked a cripple girl once on account of a dare. Crippled and white. Sounds like a joke, don't it? I made her beg a little bit too."

"Calvin, stop it. People change. You changed."

"This a story, that's all. Just so you don't have the wrong idea. So you don't think I'm some *fool* slidin through, smilin, rakin up leaves. Puttin his dick where it don't belong. Or maybe that's not what you thought. I never did know. You never did give me too much to go on. Just don't start now. Anyway. You got my high points now. You write it down, dig a little hole, and bury it out in the yard, for all I care. I'm spic-n-span. I feel pretty good now. Why don't you go on home."

He laid the empty bottle in my lap, being careful not to touch me.

Light streamed down when he opened the door. He shoved with both hands to push the door open against the crush of branches, holding it open and reaching back down for the paper bag on the floor. That was when I could have touched him, I could have put my hand out and touched his arm. He was getting out, shutting the door, that solid thunk. Nothing moved. I waited for him to help me, but there was just silence, then the first sounds of him making his way back to the porch.

I had just bumped up on the road when blue lights flashed in my rearview mirror and seconds later the police car sliced past me, rocking the car. *Good,* I remember thinking. That was what I wanted, mayhem everywhere, a filthy tangle of other people's tragedy and turmoil for my own weakness to hide in.

NINETEEN

ALL THAT NEXT day I moved in a stupor. I cleaned and ironed
and shopped for Dan's homecoming, stocking up on his hot dogs
and ice cream. A kind of convalescent lassitude swept me along.
The house felt especially tranquil and sunny, and my hands were ex-
quisitely sensitive to textures; a cool white ceramic bowl, a little mustard spoon made of yellow bone, just the sort of plain useful things
Calvin and I would have in our house. Our house. Yes, we would
have one.

At 5:30 Dan bounced in and tried to obliterate the five days I had
just lived. So glad to be home, glad to see me, completely unsur-
prised to find me waiting for him. His innocent hug nailed me to the
hall floor. But then he bounded upstairs and I was fine, walking on
back to the kitchen, energized by the lie I had accomplished just by
letting my hand linger on his neck. In the kitchen I dribbled back
into reverie, mesmerized by a sheen of sunlight lying on the river
like cream. I was in a sickening drift, a wooze of half madness
that had to be edged back with exaggerated details and desperate
split seconds of conviction. While Dan took his shower, I remember
going out on the dock and looking down toward the end where
Calvin and I had sat together the first day. White butterflies were
swarming, commemorating the spot like a handful of thrown blossoms. As I watched they turned into mindless trapped insects.

While we were having our drinks I told Dan his car had been
vandalized in the lot of the Beasley Mall. A swarthy glow came over

him. "You're shitting me." He went out to see and came back with a faint swagger, like a cat dragging home a dead thing. I served dinner. We watched a video Dan had brought home, its violence as numbing as a warm blood-filled bath. Afterward, moving around in the bathroom, flossing his teeth as I watched him from the bed, Dan looked unfinished, his arms and legs dirty with hair, his genitals like pasty uncooked meat. He came padding in, vigorous and expectant, and stopped a few feet from the bed, put his hand on his hips, and began to whip his hips to make his penis slap up and down, which made him laugh like it always did. I knew he would keep laughing until I groaned. I groaned, and he gave one last savage thrust. *"Hey girl!* Let's get it *on."*

He was rough that night. There was something high-handed about him, even coarse, which I didn't bother to analyze. It suited my purposes.

"Something juicy for you on the front page," he said in the morning, slinging the paper at me from the bedroom door. He waited for me to sit up in bed and read how two nights before, during a robbery at the Douglas Crossroads Handi-Mart, a male clerk had been shot in the shoulder. With Dan's eyes on me, I calculated that Calvin and I must have been there twenty minutes before, maybe less. That explained the police car that had barreled past me just as I was leaving the house. "Enjoy. I'm going to Harley's," Dan said.

I remembered the clerk. As distinctly as in a dream I saw his big soft back, the childish eyes, the freckles that had matched his sister's. She *had* been his sister. The paper said she had been locked in the storeroom. The suspects were two black men in their twenties. I couldn't imagine how all this had gone on in that crowded store, although by then the place must have emptied out. It seemed crucial to find Calvin and talk about this. It must mean something. It was Saturday, he would be working at the Alligoods' soon. By the time I got downstairs I understood it had nothing to do with us, and I would still have to honor my promise to be away while he was next door.

I got in the car and wandered along the highways lined with acres of cotton, ready for the machines. Fully ripe it looked burnt, as if it had been killed by the white lumps my mind kept registering as wet snow.

When I pulled into our driveway Dan's car was parked in the garage and Dick Alligood was in front of his house, using a weed whacker. I was trying to slip out of sight when I heard the machine cut out.

"Look at me!" Dick's face was maroon, his hair brassy with sweat. "Bustin my goddamn gusset! You know how come? Ole Calvin stood us up this mornin! That ain't the big news though. The *po*-lice were here and they were lookin for *you*, young lady."

"I didn't do it!" Bad choice of words: I felt instantly scared.

"That's exactly what I told em!"

I found Dan in his den, half hidden behind his computer. He was busy with his bills, shuffling papers around importantly. "Claudia, you know you can always come to me with your little problems."

I could tell the stern tone was an affectation, to add to the fun he was obviously having.

"Dan?"

"It's okay. Danny fixed it."

"Dick told me about the police." My mouth felt like a hole cut in leather. "What's up?"

He peered around the monitor. "Just one police. One little ole Officer Oden. Wanted to know where you *were* the night that Handi-Mart thing happened." Dan's eyes were just merry with his obscure little joke, I decided. Now he was pretending he was busy again. "I told him I was very sorry, but I was away on business at the time and didn't have a clue where my little wifey was. That frosted him. He really wanted you, his gun was throbbing. Their efficiency is impressive, I must say. Running registration checks on all the red Beemers in Beasley County? Must be at least two. Probably took em all morning."

He looked up and saw my face.

"*I* don't know, Claud," he said, mock-wearily. "Somebody saw a red Beemer at the Handi-Mart so now they're all out trying to find it. God, that guy pissed me off royally. I always forget what assholes cops are. Tells me we're supposed to have North Carolina driver's licenses by now. Then he keeps going, 'Sir? Sir, I need to speak to your wife, *sir*,' like a broken record. But anyway, you don't have to go see him. He thinks he's seen you already."

"What do you mean?"

"I showed him your picture. You know, that one you like so much."

"Dan, but that's . . . not me anymore. That's fraud or being an accessory or something."

"Every time I said you weren't home he goes, 'Sir, I'll come back later.' I said, 'Hold on, bud, I'll go get you a picture.' Bingo. Couldn't leave fast enough." He tapped at his keyboard. "I guess you didn't fit the description."

"But Dan, people here all know each other. What if somebody finds out you lied?"

"Fuck em if they can't take a joke. Anyway, they're cops, how would they know us? What's for lunch, now that I've saved your ass? Oh. By the way." His voice was rich with sarcasm. "If you know anything, you're supposed to *call* em."

He was eyeing me again.

Maybe a touch more profanity than usual. Maybe he was a little uglier than he needed to be. I can see that now. But then, all that next week, he seemed normal. There was nothing there. Once or twice our eyes met for an instant and then blinked away, one of those witless accidents of timing that can connect two strangers at a bus stop. There was only my inertia, verging on muzzled hysteria, my certainty that I was going to act, *any minute now*, while all the time I felt immobilized for hours until, like the need for oxygen, some internal mechanism would bring me gasping up to the surface of life and I would find the car keys in my hand, with no idea of where I was going.

On Thursday before he went to work Dan reminded me I had to be at the BMW place in Greenville by noon, to get a quote on the taillight work. Five minutes later I was upstairs disassembling the hall closet, tearing through the shoes and boots, trying to find the boot with the fleur-de-lis pin hidden in the toe. *Only to check it*, I kept re-assuring myself, convinced it would somehow be gone. Its delicacy stunned me all over again. I snapped the box shut and slipped it in my pocket. By now, with the adrenaline kicking in, the idea of driv-ing along every street in Calhoun to search out a brick house with a fenced-in backyard seemed entirely reasonable, in fact guaranteed to produce Calvin, until it dawned on me he wouldn't be home. Mi-raculously remembering which churches he worked for in Beasley, I circled each one without spotting any sign of him. I was on the road to Calhoun when I decided to stop in at the house. It was as close as I could get to him.

Grit I'd never noticed before was sifted in the corners of the stairs. I stood at the bottom and let Calvin's absence scorch a throbbing hole in the middle of my throat and then went up, feeling the dia-mond pin rubbing my hip in its little box, turning into a useless trin-ket. The door to the pink room was closed. Inside, the few pieces of furniture were still there but the table lay on its side just inside the door. The bed was bare. The sheets he'd taken home to wash every week had been ripped off and balled up in a corner like old rags. The mattress was as stained as I remembered, only more so now. Ex-amining the stains, trying to guess which ones were ours, I started crying, and stumbled into the table on the way out, scraping my shin. I hobbled down the stairs and let myself out the front door.

He was sitting on the porch floor with his back against the house, rolling a leaf between his fingers. I didn't surprise him, he would have seen the car. He didn't look up.

"Just waitin for Half-Gallon," he said.

I wiped my face and took out the little box, and held it down be-side his shoulder. He threw a glance at it. "And here comes the man now," he said. Half-Gallon's fender had eased into view beyond the holly bush. He couldn't see us, he gave the horn a tap. Calvin said, "You shouldn't come around here now."

He stood up, and his face was chalky and dull, the whites of his eyes bloodshot. I bent to rub my banged-up shin.

"What'd you do there?" he asked sharply.

I straightened myself and held the box out again. "I can sell this.

We could live on it for a while, maybe even pay off some of your debt." He wouldn't take it. "I know a place in Raleigh where I can sell it. Calvin, please. Look at it."

He took it then, and snapped the lid open, being careful with his face. Half-Gallon beeped again.

"What's this worth?" Calvin said.

"I don't know, maybe a lot. *Something.*"

He snorted and closed the box.

"It's mine to do anything I want with."

He was staring full at me now. "I'm just askin you this one time now. This is it. You can't be changin your *mind* all the time." His eyes were suddenly silver with tears.

I grabbed the box from his hand, took out the pin, and flung the box away into the weeds. In my pocket I found some old kleenex and wrapped the pin in it. Reading my plan, Calvin shied away and his hands shot up, like a man trying to exempt himself from an accusation, and his head gave one sharp shake, like a flinch. But I was determined. I jammed the pin deep inside his pocket, then snuck my hand around to the small of his back and pushed it under his damp waistband, and his arms came around me. He pulled me against him. It had just started to rain. As we huddled together it started coming down hard, drawing a heavy curtain around the porch. We ignored a long bleat of the horn and clutched at each other, his head bent down and my mouth tearing at him. "Claudia," and again, "*Claudia.*" Dragging my head back. "You do it right, it'll go fine. Don't give him any hope. You flip-flop on him, he'll get crazy. You got to be straight. Keep it *simple.*"

I was trying not to hear how nervous he sounded. I said, "Calvin, don't go, wait till the rain stops," but it was thundering onto the porch roof, I don't think he even heard me.

"He's not used to any surprise shit, you might have to help him a little bit. Sunday. I be right here. Five o'clock."

I lifted my arms again to hold him but he had turned away. He ducked his head and hunched his shoulders, and he stepped off the porch into the rain and never looked back.

II

Sunday, October 6

It's over. They shut down the ventilator around 4:30. Mom was there and Ping.

Ping said not to wait for George to come from Hong Kong. Garfield and his wife are on a trip somewhere, been notified. Daddy couldn't travel because of his knee surgery.

Mom and Ping are downstairs together. I'm in the bedroom. I'm "lying down." It's 7:25. I think they opened some wine. I smell Mom cooking onions. There's not much talking, they're too stunned.

I'm not stunned. I know exactly what happened. I didn't *tell* Dan. My mouth wouldn't open and because my mouth wouldn't open, Dan got in the car and I took a bath and felt good that he still didn't know anything yet, so nothing terrible had happened and now it has. All I had to do was tell him and he would have raged and howled at me and kept drinking but he would have stayed home and been safe.

His face was so exposed, everybody could see him, he was so help-less. I kept wanting to pull the sheet up, but then a nurse did it as we were going out. She was gentle. A *cascade* of bad effects, they said. Can't repair a liver, can't stop the bleeding, a cascade. It changes him. It means he was always capable of this—*dying*—and I never knew. I didn't know he had this power and now he's taken it and left me. He's escaped.

Mom just came up to give me Debs's love. I can't go talk to her,
I have to stay here.

He was a simple good man. He loved me. He wanted me to have
his baby and I wouldn't. All I did was try not to. Selfish pig.

He died terrified. I should be dead instead. I can't live now.

Monday, October 7
Morning

Mom just called the hospital to ask about Danny's things. She and
Ping upset to hear we can't have them yet. I know why. The sheriff's
office needs it all. They have the car too.

The obituary ran without any errors. The New York addresses and
his prep school, Ping's work, all very correct. But then the other, on
the front page. Local man found dead. And the location. Making
Ping distressed, but she's right, people will assume he was there to
get drugs. I was in the hall and I heard crying, and Mom saying,
Now Ping, that's just in this little paper down here, and Ping, *Oh, I
know, it just galls me, that's all, silly of me.* And Mom, being staunch
and a little distant, *No, not at all.* Sounding a little scared of Ping, I
thought, then I peeked in and Ping's head was on Mom's shoulder.
Which I was glad about, and thought if they could be mothers together, consumed by the loss of a child, I could be alone, but Mom
never stops bringing me things. Cheese and crackers, tea, Vaseline
for my sore nostrils. A minute ago she came in with a fresh Band-Aid
for my shin. Touching my shoulder, begging me to forgive her for
letting this happen to her little girl. Poor Mom, when all I want is to
be alone in all this clarity of detail, black lines around everything.

Sticker on the door of the funeral home, going into the office:
FRIENDS OF TOBACCO. Ha ha, you bet. A morbid joke to help me
while the funeral director kneaded my hands and begged us to come
into the other room. Apparently we went in the wrong door. But
Ping had already sat down in her navy silk suit, surrounded by his
homey knickknacks. An old-timey cardboard calendar from a heating company. Things were very bright in there but also underlit, due

to some recessed fluorescence, making the red plastic roses on the desk look grimy. My eyes all over the place, like Danny always said. *Claud, you're staring. Don't stare.* So I looked at the big wall safe and we sat there and let Mr. Dixon pour his syrup over our heads. A big man, mottled face, steel eyeglass stems biting into the bristles in front of his long red ears. He had a small white smudge on his tie, toothpaste, or maybe some material he uses in his work. I thought about all those white bodies he touches and whether he still distinguishes the quick from the dead, or are we just the pre-dead to him? Skulls, not faces. This idea was a comfort, I liked him for it, but then I noticed his compassion was stopping and starting as if he were pressing a button somewhere on his body and I knew he was aroused by the violence, by *the crime*, and I was glad we didn't want very much from him. We had slender requirements, as Ping called them. She asked for a very low-key nondenominational service. He was hurt and squeezed his forearms. Wanted to show us the "chapel." Ping said she was sure it was lovely. She said we'd order the flowers ourselves. No music. He asked about visiting hours and Ping said there wouldn't be any. He asked if we were ready to see Dan, and Ping said, *I think not.* He looked at me, I said, *Maybe later.* She chose the display coffin and the cremation coffin and the urn, juggling a sheaf of laminated photographs as if she had a giant hand of cards, her diamonds splattering sparks against the wall behind Mr. Dixon's head. She wrote him a check. That was it. We were back outside in the sun, by the car, and she fell into my arms like a bundle of sticks.

It turns out they never went to church when he was little, Danny made all that up. Last night when I mentioned us going to St. John's sometimes, Ping's face went flat. She said, a shade coolly, that she'd been surprised to hear Mom talking in the living room to the minister. She said, *I didn't realize you were religious.* I explained it was Dan, that he even went on Wednesday nights a couple times. *Really? Where'd this come from?* I told her it had just been social, to fit in, and she made a small mouth and kept shaking her head, so I tried to make it into a little joke, like, it could have been worse. *At least he never put a chrome fish on the car, or a bumper sticker.* She seemed confused. *You know,* "*God Said It, I Believe It, That Settles It!*" Then I gave her my favorite. "*My God's Alive . . . Sorry About Yours!*" But I was too busy injecting the necessary sneer into that one, I didn't notice she was on the verge of tears. She said, *But there are some quiet good Christians.* Trying to make a place in there for Danny. I found some unused kleenex for her in my pocket and she finally collected herself, then started to pick hairs off my sweater.

I came up here and cried and watched myself. Eyes bleeding mascara, snot like taffy, tragic little poke hole of a mouth. Poor thing, she was never that ugly when she cried before. She was too ugly already. But that's gone, she's gone. Nobody misses her. No—stupid and selfish. Cry for *Dan.*

Hold him in your head, be true to him. Be his own true one.

This morning Mom made waffles. She was just pouring in some batter when Ping came in and saw it and almost looked happy. Wanted to help. While we ate she told how when Danny was a teenager his father would make waffles—*yes, I know, hard to imagine George cooking, but he did!*—and then he would take a big smoldering plate into Danny's room and wake him up. *George didn't care how much Danny wanted to sleep, sleepiness was not part of the plan, Danny had to wake up and eat those damn waffles!!* She was crying and laughing, wiping her eyes. I thought, *Yes.* All those times when his food rules made me insane and I knew he couldn't help it, but I got mad anyway. Why couldn't I have been kinder, would it have killed me?

4:00 P.M.

Sheriff Hines came again, with the same deputy. They both seemed even more apologetic. It was difficult. They met Mom but said they didn't want coffee. Hines was gruff but in a nice way, droopy and burdened. The deputy, Woolard, was blushing throughout all this, trying to ignore me, staring at the rug when Hines started asking me about the possibility of drugs again. Hines so pained I could see his young puzzled boy's face underneath his old loose skin. Then more repeat questions: Did Dan say anything "significant" when he left the house, what time did we eat dinner? Which parking lot was the taillight vandalized in? Said I couldn't remember. Did I know whether Dan had taken his gun with him that night? That was new, I never mentioned a gun, have they been talking to Harley? Said I didn't know. Every question blows a hole in my mind and I sit on the edge of a windy crater and look way way down at my hands. Twist them in my lap, play with my rings, feel like a widow on TV. Make my eyes faraway. *No*, I say, *no enemies, no debts, no marital discord, no disgruntled employees, no problems at work, no, no, nothing like that.* Secretly convinced that if this goes on long enough, Dan will burst in and say, *Don't you guys have anything better to do?*

Then they wanted Ping, so I stayed in the kitchen with Mom and tried to listen. Hines wanted to know how Dan and I got along. *Just beautifully*, Ping said, with that emphasis, that touch of hauteur. They won't have liked that.

Tuesday, October 8

All these people around. Write. Maintain objectivity and quietude. *Anne Frank.*

Debs was here in the bedroom, waiting for me to wake up. I saw her head suddenly, she was sitting right beside the bed on the floor. She started saying how much she loved Dan but how he was in a better place now. She started to cry. I got up to brush my teeth and came back and she was on her knees. I got back in bed and she prayed for Dan's soul to be at peace with God and for him to be accepted as God's servant for being loving and good. (I was not going to cry while she was praying, I was refusing to.) Also that Dan be reunited in heaven, oh please God, with his little dead baby. And then she was crying harder and I started too, just a little, *hating* myself. Then she prayed for Dan's beautiful wife who needs God's help, who's in torment from all the world's evil that makes her so confused. I touched Debs's hands to get her to stop but her head stayed down, and it all flooded out, she prayed and prayed for me, God's poor lost soul who needed to be filled with the joy of understanding. I felt desperate to stop her, as if God's understanding were incubating in me already, I said—gently—that I didn't want this and she grabbed my arm. *But you do! Let Jesus come in and he'll forgive you*—crying again—*he forgives me every time and I'm a mess, look at me! It works, just do it, please.* I told her I didn't think she was a mess. *It's okay, the Lord Jesus has compassion for you.* Her head came up. *We all do.* Eyes on me now like shining bullets. *I have so much compassion for you!* She was aglow, hot with it. Then we heard Mom moving in the hall and Debs got up and collapsed across the bed. Came back to herself with a bang. *They'll get em, they'll get this trash that did it and they'll die for it.* Rubbing my feet to reassure me. I said Dan didn't care, Dan was dead. *Yeah, but you do, you care.* I knew we were both remembering that horrible night at the club. I said—treading carefully—that revenge was maybe a little crude. I said it only *feels* good. *Maybe to you!!* she cried. She said it wasn't up to us anyway, just up to God, because when people live by the sword they die by the sword. I said I didn't need for anybody to die, and her face bloomed. *Claudia, it's not about you or me, it's about Dan, about him being moral and pure, and if this scum just goes to jail and watches TV, then what's the difference between Danny and them?!* She eased off the bed. Went to the mirror to rub her swollen tummy and admire it. *You know, everything that's awful happens for a reason,* she said. Came back, leaned over to give me a kiss, saying how tired she is all the time now because the baby kicks her all night. Chelsea, it's called. She knows it's a girl, because God always answers her prayers.

Noon

Told Mom and Ping I was going to the drugstore but I went to Dixon's. Mr. Dixon was at his desk with his glasses off, rubbing his puffy eyes. Brightened when he saw me. I couldn't say why I was there, but he knew. He was nice, sat me down in a chair, and excused himself. Came back and ushered me across a big hall hung with curtains, to the door of a small room. Nothing inside but the coffin like a giant caramel. Flowers standing near it. Lid open. He said he'd be just outside.

There was the end of a nose, it looked powdered, and then his forehead, it was a man with lips that were too prettily pink, a man like Dan, but dead. I went closer. He seemed to be sleeping and then his eyes started moving under his eyelids, his eyelashes rippled. I didn't make a sound. Kept myself from running out but I left very fast. It was weak, but I was scared because it wasn't Dan. It was Dan's husk, like that horrible cicada shell, when Patti said close your eyes and hold out your hand. It was what he shed on his passage to nowhere. All his funny goofy rubberiness dripped out into a steel pan until he was bloodless, chemically preserved, I can write this because he was gone, it was vacant, a shell, wearing a J. Press suit he never liked. Ping insisted and I gave in. White shirt, blue-and-gold rep tie, he looked like a banker. I won't cry again, it's like masturbating next to a body. Dan doesn't care. He doesn't even understand he's dead, he thinks he's still going off to work, coming home, eating ice cream. He doesn't know his movie ideas are just dried-up crumbs rolling in his head.

My guilt can't even help. It's an insult to him.

Night

George came, midafternoon. Whiskey-eyed and baggier but still full of bluster. Sky-blue shirt, gold collar pin, lustrous-headed on the porch, holding his hand out.

George Dryburgh, Daniel's father. I'm sorry, you are . . . ?

Kitsch in that ugly shirt . . . a specialty item.

I wasn't going to help him.

Then he realized, and stepped forward and gripped my shoulders. He held me so close I could feel the squirm of our joint relief that the enigma of my identity had helped defuse the sadness. I watched him oversee his bags being taken out of the cab. When he paid the driver his hands were shaking. He came into the hall and stood too close, glassy-eyed. I noticed he had nicked himself shaving. Then we heard Ping coming downstairs. *What do you think of our new little beauty?* George stared past me, shocked all over again. Ping's finally aged, she's like a silver relic tarnished overnight by all the grief in the house. She and George embraced gingerly, like stick figures.

They're too exotic here, their aromas clash with the smells of Mom's chicken potpies and clover-leaf rolls, Dan's kind of food, not theirs. What will they eat? Debs brought a crabmeat casserole, they might like that. There are three fruit baskets now and a key lime pie, must be from Janet Alligood. Why is the bustling domestic part so repellent?

Searched the house while everybody was taking a nap, all Dan's desk drawers and closets and bureau. All his color, his rainbow of polo shirts, red pants, two identical lemon-yellow sweaters, waiting for him, still hopeful. No gun. I was in the garage when George found me. I told him what I was looking for and he said I should let the sheriff's office handle it, but then he lifted the lid off the garbage can, peered in. I was going through a box of Dan's old running shoes when I realized George was dismantling the toolbox, I didn't have the heart to tell him I'd just done it. We went back into the kitchen and he insisted on doing the cupboards, made me sit. George in his suit pants on his hands and knees, pulling out bagel slicers and asparagus steamers with his hair coming unstuck on one side, hanging down in a gummy slab. Then he wanted a hand mirror to check the tops of the cupboards, up on a stool in his sock feet. He finished that and started grilling me. *Laundry hamper? Attic? Desk?* I kept shaking my head. He sat down and discovered the loose hair. He tried to fix it, staring at me the whole time. I averted my eyes.

Well, this is all very Daniel. Always keep em guessing, that was the game. I never knew what was going on. Nor his mother. I suppose you did.

I said I did sometimes. Said I didn't think his gun was in the house. I suggested he had taken it in the car with him.

He agreed. *And you have no idea what he was doing out there.*

Shook my head.

Drugs. He had a weakness, we all knew that. Marijuana certainly. Well. My God, you look great. (Sort of nodding to himself.) *You do, you look terrific.* Just the faintest summary, practical note in his voice, like, At least you've got *that* solved. I said thank you.

Ping came in to say it was time for him to go downtown to talk to Hines.

Official cocktail hour tonight. Mom served onion dip and Ritz crackers. George sat in Dan's chair and talked about his meeting with Hines. No suspects and no leads. There's talk of a reward being offered. Ping wanted to know how much it might be. George said, *Two.*

Two? My God, George, surely we can—

You don't put out filet mignon to catch slimeballs. This is Hines's show. Let's just wait for him to see what crawls out of the woods. He's not completely asleep. He likes Claudia. You've made a conquest there, Claudia.

Silence. Mom got up to go to check on the meal, wobbling a little, crying and trying to hide it. George sat drinking angrily, thinking. Ping set her drink down too hard, with a loud crack.

She said, *It was the car. They saw a fancy red car, they wanted a joyride. . . .*

George said, *Chérie, darling. It's a race thing.*

No. We don't know that!

George started speaking like a machine. *They got him to stop, God knows how. Made him drive out in the middle of that goddamn field. Got him out, shot him. . . .*

He was measuring my reaction, then both our heads turned toward Ping, who was peering at us through her fingers.

There was urine, George said. *On Dan's clothes. Urine on his clothes.*

Ping was hiding behind her hands. I was all right. Felt floaty, got up and went to the couch to sit beside her. She grabbed my hand and pinned it to her knee and held it there, hands like ice. Mom came back in and Ping looked up and said, *Time to eat? Doesn't that smell divine.* George came over and gave her his hand and I followed them to the dining room. Saw their clothes dissolve and their bare bodies were firm and young, thrashing and groaning in the effort of producing Dan. Ping suddenly turned back and whispered to me to wear the fleur-de-lis pin tomorrow. Tomorrow I can say I forgot that Dan put it in the safe-deposit box.

My precious pin.

Wednesday, October 9
Morning

Condolence mail. Ellie Venable, Harley's parents, Dan's boss. A very sad, sincere note from Mary Rose, who seems to feel bad about selling us the house. Melissa his secretary wrote that he was "precious and a genius with people and we'll never forget that big gorgeous smile." The other two were from women I don't even know. One on good paper with a deckled edge, offering condolences, and "the hope that as a new arrival you won't judge us too harshly. The whole world is like this, all so frightening now." The other one was on paper printed to suggest denim, with a border of orange stitching: "I did not know your husband, but I feel assured that he was a very outstanding person. Emphasis should be made upon you that this is a loving place where I have been living for sixty-three years in God's perfect glory. I am not without faults, I know this from self-experience, man's greatest teacher after God. Perfection is only mine through Christ our Savior. Vengeance is mine saith the Lord."

Harley dropped all Dan's office stuff by. Mom dealt with him.

I finally accepted one of Ping's Valiums last night. I feel almost ready.

10:00 P.M.

It all just rolled along. That knowing, slightly sinister confidence of people performing a ritual, the oily slow motion and safety of it. Nothing more can go wrong. No imperfections other than my hair squashed in back from hours on the pillow, I didn't care, and it gave all those watchful eyes something to go on. So much pity, the air stiff with it, like walking through jello. Couldn't bear to look at anybody. Harley gasping, mouth open, his whole face wet. Ping and George dry and upright, holding on to each other's old beautiful hands, exempt from the mess. Ping's calla lilies so beautiful next to the coffin, like trumpets. Mr. Dixon called him Dave at one point. Then we bustled out in our clothes and came home to Mom's unstylish food and Dan's body traveled on to become ashes in New Bern.

Now it's like a sanitarium, everybody shut in their rooms, the flushings and spoon-clinkings finished, Ping and George drugged and sleeping, and all the molecules of this day wavering upward through the ceiling, emptying into the stars, looking for Danny.

Thursday, October 10

Ping and George and I to the bank. Ping wept over the safe-deposit box as if Dan's papers were mementos of him. No surprises apparently, except at one point George snorted and muttered, *Smart,* and thrust some shares or whatever at Ping. She said *Hmm,* then they both looked at me pointedly over their glasses. Later Ping said, *Darling . . . the pin?* I was ready for that, said I was sorry, I'd forgotten Dan had taken it to the jeweler's because the pin part was coming loose. She frowned but then George poked her with an envelope and she didn't bring it up again.

There isn't a will. George says that aside from a small mortgage, Dan's debts are "zip." They would be, Dan was always so scornful about people carrying debt. Ping and George don't even seem to care about the money being mine, they're being almost relentlessly decent, although I did catch George, when he didn't know I could see him, watching me in the hall mirror, avidly, appraising the new upgraded goods. Ping wants to take me shopping before they go.

Monday, October 14

Alone.

Ping and George left two days ago, George kissing my cheek and then his old wet thin lips sliding around, groping for mine.

Mom left this morning, distraught at the airport, crying, *I can't just leave you here.*

Mr. Dixon came this afternoon, suave with his gravitas. I took the urn, thanked him, and closed the door. Carried the urn to the kitchen, planning to go straight out to the river, then decided to freshen up first, so I brought it upstairs and put it on the bedroom floor, feeling nothing. Efficient, busy with my important job to do. Started to change, then felt the need to go do it immediately. It was clean and windy out, having rained around noon. I squatted on the bank and took the top off and upended it. Nothing came out. Then they plopped out in a clump, with bits and pieces of bone mixed in. Not Dan. The urn went in too. Some ashes sank, some stuck to the surface, some blew back on the riverbank and stuck in the seam of my jeans.

I've always had this coldness in me. I'm paralyzed on the surface of everything, can't go *under* anymore. Cold woman, he called me. Bipsa, you're so cold.

I just have to be alone with her, this harsh uncomforted person.

A man just drove by, this is the third time, in a new dark green car.

Tuesday, October 15

Well, of *course.* Because he's black and he worked here.

I need to keep track of this now.

9:30 A.M. Hines and the deputy Woolard and a new man, from the State Bureau of Investigation—Tasker, tan narrow face with deep accordion cheek creases. He said there were questions about a former employee. We all sat.

Calvin Moore.

I think I stayed blank.

You and your husband employed him.

I said, *Yes, then he quit.*

Why was that?

Said I had no idea. Tasker opened a notebook and read that "Moore" worked for us in early July for three weeks. I knew it wasn't that long but didn't contradict. Tasker asked if we fired him.

I think I just explained that he quit.

The tone was a mistake. My heart was pounding but I smiled, casually, and caught Woolard's eye and he smiled back.

Tasker said, *He was a good employee?* I said he was.

Reliable? Punctual? Any problems like that? Altercations about money, any unpleasantness? Said no to all of that. Tasker wanted to know how Calvin had gotten to work. Said I thought "a friend" drove him and picked him up, I had no idea who he was. Questions about his equipment. I said if people didn't have their own mowers and trimmers, Calvin had his own, that he brought. (Would've known that just from being his employer.)

Had Moore ever been inside the house? Said no. Tasker said, *So y'all didn't have much background on him.* (Implying what, exactly?) I said he had been highly recommended by neighbors.

My only big lie was about whether he was ever in our cars. When I said no, Tasker pressed it. Had Dan or I ever given him a ride? Said, *No, absolutely not, and what is all this about?* (Too brisk.) They all hunkered down in their seats and I thought, Calvin's dead.

Hines told me. They were all watching. I went dumb immediately, I'm sure I didn't give them anything, I smoothed my lap or something. Hines said not to worry, Calvin's "safe and sound," waiting to be arraigned tomorrow. I willed myself to stay mute but my face was changing without me even trying, I could feel it getting girly and big-eyed. Hines said, *I know you're in a world of hurt, but we're right sure this is the man and we believe he acted alone. I'm just sorry it was somebody in y'all's employ.*

Yes. I'm just so tired.

And they stood up, good Southern gentlemen, and I did too, and gave them each my hand, but they wanted more.

He was . . . so nice. Immediately knew this was wrong, way too transparent. Hines's mouth wilted into a slit. *That's all we hear about him, is real good things. I'm just sorry I never had a chance to meet the man.*

He thought I meant *Dan.*

I said, *I appreciate it.*

We walked to the door, their sense of accomplishment squeaking in their shoes. Hines said they might have to come by again. Would I be here?

I surely will. This is my home now.

Hines looked cheered up, making me remember what George had called him. My "conquest." He said *There you go,* and rested his hand on my shoulder as he passed out the door.

So. He's here with me now, we're together. He was never not here.

Stay alert but slightly "dazed." Don't volunteer anything. Don't ask the wrong questions, like, *Where are the other suspects??* Don't protest his innocence. How long can this last, what can they have? No confession. No gun. No motive. (They could hardly believe me capable of an affair with a black man.) They liked me, they *believed* me, their concern was genuine. I was the only fraud.

He'll know they came here, but he'll trust me. He can't be scared, this is always happening to black men. Pick em up, let em go. This is not 1939 in Mississippi. I don't even know where the jail is.

11:00 P.M.

Debs and Harley came. We sat barely talking in the kitchen, windows black and dead because the bug light wasn't turned on. Debs was holding my hand, admiring my rings in a knowing, mature voice. Harley gave her a look, like maybe she was overdoing it, but she ignored him. He sank lower into his drink and blew ripples on it.

Fuckin sons-of-bitches. I could cut their balls off.

Harley, Debs said.

I told her it was okay. *In fact, they've already picked up a black man.* (Both of them gawking.) *A yardman who worked here for a while.*

They were horrified and thrilled, their gazes slinking toward each other.

Debs said, *You knew him?*

I tried to say his name and my mouth shook, and Debs saw.

Oh honey! She got up and crouched down by my chair and patted me.

I said it wasn't him.

Harley said, *Tall guy? Never talks?*

I said, *It wasn't him, he didn't do it.*

Honey, we hear you, Debs said softly. Then, even with my eyes closed, I could see her imploring Harley. His ice rattled.

Okay. Here's how it is. Here I am, in my buddy's beautiful home, drinkin his Jack, that he loved (I opened my eyes—he was raising his glass to Dan) *but like . . . is he here? I don't see him. Y'all see him? No. You with me so far? Now you're tellin me the yardman did this, killed my best friend in cold blood? What the fuck, I'll buy that. Just fry the guy's balls off, all right? Cause this whole thing is fucked. This is total total bullshit. End of speech*, he croaked.

Held up his glass to salute Dan again. *Here's to you, bud.* He poured some bourbon down his throat and choked on it and hacked, and used his fist to wipe his tears, like a little kid.

Debs leaned her head on my shoulder and said Harley was upset. *He's just sayin it can be real hard to tell about people. I mean, this guy seemed normal, right?*

No, Harley said between coughs.

He didn't? Debs, I noticed, was consulting Harley about this, not me. She eased back into her chair, keeping one hand attached to my wrist.

No, Harley said. *Weird. Sulky. Big.*

Debs gaped at him. *Muscle shirt show-offy, like with a strut, or what? A blue-gum, right?*

(Blue-gum??)

No, Harley said. *More like Little Jimmy at the marina, the one who creeps you out. Quiet and superior, thinks the sun shines out of his butt.*

Uppity, I said.

Really? Debs said, rapt, dazzled with horror.

I got up, becoming firm, pleading exhaustion, moving them on down the hall. Harley's face under the chandelier looked bruised. Pummeled. *So they've got a case on this guy or what? What went on, what the hell was Dan—*

I explained I hadn't asked a lot of questions.

You didn't ask?

Harley, she didn't ask.

I said, *It was dumb. I guess I was tired.*

Debs shushed me. *You're not dumb, don't you ever say that. It'll all be in the paper, Harley.*

Harley said it better be.

Honey, we love you, we're prayin for you.

They both kissed me.

Love you too, I said.

They terrify me. And look how it all skids around. I break my rule and protest his innocence and they just think I'm in *denial.* It's like a bad joke.

Be more careful. Take notes, write down anything at all. This is working so far. I can do this.

Wednesday, October 16

Another item in the paper, reporting "new leads." Still nothing in the letters column. A letter complaining about the Christians getting the yoga class at the community college shut down because yoga is un-Christian, and a letter from a woman writing to thank a neighbor for giving her daughter a ride home in the rain. No calls for justice or revenge, nothing, not a word. Surprised. Relieved.

Lunchtime

The DA called—Swanner, that relation of Harley's—asking me to come in to see him. Sounded fine. Courteous, courtly, etc.

The courthouse is dopey. All those steps up to the big portico with the soaring Ionic columns and twelve-foot-tall double doors and then inside it turns into a fifties high school. Linoleum floors, staircase set the wrong way so you walk in looking at the underneath side. One of those big round school clocks with the second hand clicking the miserable seconds. It was deserted except for two white country people with their heads wrapped in smoke and a swank black couple draped over the water fountain in sharp outfits, they looked like matadors.

I was dressed for Swanner, white blouse and dark skirt. The low heels were good, he's not very tall. He's not bald like I thought, he has the most optimistic comb-over ever, about five hairs. Tried to interpret what this capacity for self-deception means, does it bode well or ill in a DA? Felt cautiously cheered by his rather shiny blue suit and dusty brown loafers curling at the toes.

It took him a long time to get going. Had to locate his pen, then there was the polishing of the glasses, then a search for his lighter, finally discovered under one of six legal pads. He pulled a pack of cigarettes out of his shirt pocket and waved it at me perfunctorily. *Bet you don't smoke.* Then the lighting up, the delectation of the exhale, a final professional shooting of the cuffs, and he was ready to bestow his condolences and reassurances. Things are proceeding "in a timely manner." There's another problem. I'm sure he means to sound sincere, he may possibly *be* sincere, but he speaks with so much repetition and so *exceedingly slowly* you can barely follow him. Your mind flits away into a thin silence where you just hear

your own breathing and a few snide frivolous thoughts, like whether
he could speak normally if he had to tell his wife the house was
burning down. All right, I don't like him. I didn't like him that time
on TV.

He said Calvin's been arraigned and is being held without bond.

I asked where. He seemed perturbed, perhaps at the unseemly
proximity. The county jail is in the courthouse, in the basement.
Calvin was two floors below us.

*Mrs. Dryburgh? I'll call you Claudia if I may, and I want you
to call me Lloyd. There's somethin I want you to know. I want you to
know this, and I want you to know it beyond a shadow of a doubt.
There's not a chance in the world that this man won't be indicted day
after tomorrow. Because that's Harry Tasker's job, and Harry's a man
who knows his way around a grand jury.*

I said I liked Mr. Tasker.

We all do. We all like Harry. Harry's a good man.

I asked how strong the case was.

He took his glasses off and threw them down so manfully they slid
off the pad. A pause to think. Long pull on his cigarette, his whole
jaw disappearing into his hand, only his eyes showing. I finally asked
if "Moore" had confessed.

*Doesn't have to. Doesn't make a speck of difference, in light of other
circumstances.*

A pause, to allow me to ask what they were.

Mr. Moore left some fresh fingerprints all over Mr. Dryburgh's car.

I didn't speak but must have looked sick because he started saying
he hadn't asked me there to "rile" me, just reassure me. I thanked
him. I knew I was too shaken to try saying more but then did, I asked
him why Moore would *do* it?

Well now. Motive. If I can speak frankly.

Please. (Always be obsequious to this man.)

*Straight and simple, juries always want a motive. Otherwise they
tend to stray over to reasonable doubt. But I don't want you worryin
about that! That's not why we're here! We'll dig and we'll find it.
Those pieces'll come. Mr. Dryburgh may have accidentally stumbled
on some drug kind of mess. Moore's been in some trouble that way be-*

fore, that's how come his prints were on file. (Was it that thing Calvin got into with Bobo? Obviously it was no big deal anyway.) *But now we're gettin a little ahead of ourselves. All I want to say to you is, this is a bad one. Two surface wounds, then a bullet to the liver, leavin him out there to die, blood leakin into his abdomen . . .* Then he seemed to remember me. *I'm callin for the death penalty. It's not the norm with a defendant who doesn't have a big record but we'll get it. We'll win it too. Won't be hard.*

My head felt scorched. Sour scum on my tongue, I can taste it now.

I said, No? Sounding feeble, I guess, sounding *unconvinced* maybe, because then he started saying how when the court selects a jury, first they try to get rid of everybody who doesn't believe in capital punishment. Anybody who feels they might not be able to send a man to the gas chamber is automatically *excused.*

(This can't be right? Maybe he was making this up in order to "cheer" me??)

Kinda squares it up a bit. Levels the playin field. So I want you to just go home with that, and feel easy and peaceful in your mind.

I said something about being glad.

Well, now, that's a good way to be.

He said if there's no plea bargain and it goes to trial, I'll have to be a witness. He outlined what that would involve. *Just some plain, simple, real easy questions you won't have a speck of trouble with. How long y'all been livin here. How y'all were gettin settled into your new home. Things to establish your lifestyle. Then there'll be questions about Moore. How long he was in y'all's employ. How he was never inside y'all's car. Nothin you can't handle, trouper like you are and all.*

I am an idiot. Why did I tell them Calvin hadn't been in the car? A serious misstep. But what do fingerprints on a car prove?

Then he asked me to go to the sheriff's office with him. Didn't tell me what for, so I had to say yes, being *helpful.* It was just across the parking lot, he walked me over, basking in the glances we got, steering my elbow. *Hey, Junius, what d'ya say!* He might as well have just yelled, *Hey, looky here what I got!* And the men looked, obliquely,

politely, strangers in their shirtsleeves who all seemed to know who
I was.

When we got there he put me into a little office and went out and
came back with a young deputy, like a little boy in a uniform. The
deputy had a box, he put it on the desk, and Swanner asked me to
come over. It was all little plastic bags, full of what Calvin had had
in his pockets. A small packet of bills and some change. An old black
key. Some receipts wrapped in rubber bands. His Swiss Army knife.
A small studio photograph of a black baby in a turquoise top and a
little white sunbonnet, the picture was crumbled at the edges from
being handled. It was upside-down. I couldn't really see her, couldn't
turn it *around*.

Then Swanner was holding up the baggie with the fleur-de-lis
pin, asking if I'd ever seen it. I was shaking my head, trying to stay
detached, still trying to see all his things in their official government
sandwich bags. Why didn't he ever show me her picture?

Swanner said, *Billy? I heard this pretty little piece nearly got
throwed clean away.*

Billy said, *I was standin right there when they brought him in.
Empties out his pockets and here's this wad of kleenex and darn if
Deputy Fennell don't take it and throw it away. It was only cause the
wastebasket was empty we heard this like, clunk. I fetched it out again,
I was standin right there.*

Y'all are takin good care of it now though?

Billy said they were, *yessir.*

During this I recovered a bit. *They're not allowed to keep photographs?*

Swanner said they don't always want to. *Somebody might try to
take it off em for fun.*

He awarded himself a cigarette and steered me out past a clot of
deputies, all deferentially standing back to make way for us. Out in
the lot Swanner, all chipper and obliging, asked if he could find
somebody to drive me home, and I thought—as loud as a scream if
I'd had the courage to scream—*I'd let it get thrown away too, to save
my ass if I were an innocent black man!* A long compressed moment,
Swanner's smoke-squint eyes playing over me. I said I was fine to

drive, thanked him. He exhaled politely, trying to keep the smoke off my face, blowing it right at my clean hair.

It's me oughta be thankin you.

My connection to Calvin is invisible. It's all inside out. I cry for him and they think I'm crying for Dan. This is fine, it's protection for us. But I was wrong about Calvin. If he let them throw that pin away, he's worried. But he didn't have any choice. He did it for both of us.

Late

There was a delivery for Dan, an electronic blood-pressure monitor that you stick on your finger. I wanted to try it out, I was already crying and I knew if I put it on, I'd cry harder. There was also a pen with a light on the end, for making notes on his movie ideas he got in bed. He had ideas and plans and he yearned to feel important and I scorned him. I used to think the only interesting thing Dan ever did was marry me instead of an attractive woman. And then I killed her off, his wife. He loved his poor dead wife, he said so—stoned but he said it, they both heard him. He didn't CARE what she looked like. Dim dull needy man, that's what I thought, even while he was carrying my picture around. Wishing and hoping for me to get pregnant. Oh Danny, I didn't know. I need you now, please. I'm so sorry. I can hear you coming in. Put your keys in the silver dish and come up. You forgive me, you're coming up, I hear you. Let's go back. Danny please.

Thursday, October 17

It didn't go that well.

I had felt so poised going in, restored by Ping's last Valium. He was at his desk in his shirtsleeves, and I just said it. *Mr. Swanner, I'm sorry, but I think maybe Dan might have given Calvin Moore a ride once or twice.*

I wish you'd start callin me Lloyd. Waving at the chair.

Thank you . . . Lloyd.

Well, I appreciate you comin in here with that. You're an honest woman and I like that. I like an honest woman. But what'd I tell you yesterday? Didn't I tell you not to worry? I don't want you to compromise yourself in any way. If you have to testify about Moore ever bein in that car previous to the night of the murder, all you say is what you just told me. You just can't be a hundred percent sure that he wasn't in the car. You can do that now, can't you?

I had to say yes. *But Lloyd, fingerprints? They can't mean all that much.* He said it depended on where they were and, with apologies for going into detail, he explained with a certain gusto how Moore wiped the door handles but "clean forgot" the glove compartment. His prints are on it, even on some maps and stuff inside. Naturally. He went through the glove compartment when I was in the Handi-Mart. Exactly what I would have done, bored, waiting for somebody, especially being itchy and keyed up like he was that night. Just knowing all this boosted my confidence, and I asked what had made the sheriff look for a fingerprint record.

Swanner pulled a face. *Well, they get lucky sometimes. Don't tell em I said that.*

It was a phone tip, somebody called in with some tidbit on Calvin. The yardman did it. Nice try. Too bad they won't be getting the reward.

Swanner kept eyeing me, stroking his chin. *Claudia,* he said . . . *Claudia . . .* Testing the sound, approving it. *It's nice, innit? Not a name you hear every day.*

I agreed with him, then excused myself as nicely as I could.

Two guys waiting in the driveway when I got home. SBI, they said, like I'd know what that meant. Excuse me? I said, but politely. State Bureau of Investigation, same as Tasker, I should have remembered that. They needed to "dust" the Volvo. Fine, please do, I said, help yourself, that's great. Then I wrecked it by slamming the front door.

———

The most important thing so far: *lack of motive results in reasonable doubt.*

Without a motive, Calvin is safe. This is infernal and crazy. Every step I take feels like a trap, everybody is dangerous to us. I don't know what I'm doing. I'm afraid of myself.

More condolences. Two from Dan's sales reps. Also a special communiqué on folded-up notebook paper, in pencil. NIGGERS KILLED YOUR HUSBAND. AFRICAN PORCH MONKEYS SUCK DICK, this accompanied by a crude drawing. Then an ugly made-up word, FUCACOON. It wasn't the shock—I didn't feel any—it was just the helplessness, the degradation of giving the writer the satisfaction of holding his dirt in my hand. It reminded me of those anonymous notes somebody stuck in my locker, except they were worse because at fourteen I could still be shocked.

Mom and Daddy keep calling. I don't tell them anything except that I'm better. Daddy's knee is mending.

Ping has had a simplified version of events. I told her there was an arrest but I doubted it would stick. I started getting into telling her about Swanner, what a hambone, etc., but she interrupted, asking about the "suspect."

I said, *A black man who worked here once for a couple weeks.* (Didn't feel the need to remind her she'd met him.)

That big somber guy? I heard her drinking. *It's not him.*

Dear Ping. *No, I don't think so either. I think they're crazy, that's what.*

I have to run, darling, my boy's here.

She meant Garfield, but for a second my heart burst.

————

7:00 P.M.

Swanner was here, just waltzed in about 3:00. I showed him into the living room, got him settled, ashtray, etc.

Claudia, I got a problem. There's a police officer name of Freddy Oden, just happened to see you down at the sheriff's office yesterday. (I must have looked completely innocent, it meant nothing to me.) *Seems like somebody pointed you out to him in the parking lot.*

Said I didn't know Officer Oden.

Well, that ain't the problem. (Purposefully bad grammar, used to reinforce down-home camaraderie.) *Problem is, Officer Oden don't know you. Comes to me, says he's mystified. Says the lady he knows as Mrs. Daniel Dryburgh is—how'd he put it?—kind of a . . . "unfortunate, funny-lookin little gal."*

And then I remembered who Oden was. And Swanner was digging in his shirt pocket and holding it out to me, that wedding picture Dan loved.

This is her. This woman here.

I could hardly bear to touch it. There wasn't time to make up a new story but I thought if I told it right, Dan wouldn't sound any worse than a scofflaw.

Yes. That's my husband's first wife. Dan told me about this. Officer Oden kept insisting he had to see me, about that Handi-Mart robbery, and I think maybe Dan got a little impatient, and went and got this picture and showed it to him. Really just to enable the officer to get on with his business. Sort of a bad joke.

Probably some of that Yankee humor.

Not really. Just Dan's.

But now, help me out here. Where's the fun? Givin a false ID to a police officer investigatin a felony?

I looked bashful, like of course I knew it was naughty of Dan. Said, *Sometimes Danny could be kind of disrespectful like that, but of course he knew it wasn't me they were after.*

No. Course not. Cause that wasn't you in the red BMW.

Exactly. Maybe I should have a word with Officer Oden. (Knowing from the paper this wouldn't be necessary because they've just arrested both the Handi-Mart guys.) *I don't want him to think Dan was being rude to him, or sneaky.*

Swanner's hand flew up and he tapped his strands of hair, then he stroked his head, fast, like that's his real speed and the Southern molasses is fake. It scared me.

Oh, he don't think that. No, Fred says Mr. Dryburgh was real helpful. Askin all manner of questions. Wantin to know all about the BMW mystery lady and her boyfriend.

I reached for my bag on the chair. He waited till I had just tucked the picture in before he said he needed to have it back.

The utter helplessness of this, like moving in a dream, with images flashing at you, then dissolving as you reach out to touch them. Jamaica in her little white hat. My own wedding picture. Swanner put it back in his shirt pocket, gave it a businesslike pat, then looked around, wanting to see more, wanting a house tour. I invited him as far as the dining room, ostensibly to see the view, and watched him take it all in, the useless luxury bouncing in microcosm in his eyeballs.

Claudia, did you ever meet your husband's first wife?

An unnecessary question, prompted only by the usual titillated curiosity. I told him no. *I know he loved her though,* I added, and there it was, that slimy flicker of amused skepticism. His head kept going up and down.

Beautiful home y'all have. Beautiful. He said it heavily, like a malediction.

So far: The policeman, Oden, told Dan that the BMW woman's passenger was a black man. But then why didn't Dan tease me about it, why weren't there any cracks about my double life? Maybe he really did think I was having an affair. Did he? All that week he suspected and never said one word or gave me any strange looks? Did Dan have that sort of restraint? Maybe. Maybe I can't remember him. But even if he did believe it, he would never have guessed who it was. Never.

Swanner *knows* it was me at the Handi-Mart. How? From Tassy

Rankin? But no, because Tassy would also have given them my name and they wouldn't have needed to use the BMW registration to find me. It wasn't Tassy.

Okay. Feeling sharper.

Jade. What is she thinking, what is she doing?

Friday, October 18

Spent all day waiting for Swanner to call about the indictment. Started getting hopeful when I didn't get a phone call but resisted calling his office, not wanting to appear too ravenous for information. Then decided it might be more suspicious for me *not* to be foaming at the mouth with blood-lust revenge, so I called the county clerk's office and a woman told me Swanner "got his indictment." I don't think she had any idea who I was, I stretched my vowels.

Ran out to the Food Lion and just missed Half-Gallon, glimpsed his van going the other way as I turned into the road. What on earth? A message from Calvin? He left a calling card, a little V-shaped branch stuck upside-down over the doorknob.

Tuesday, October 22

Still hot, must be low eighties. I guess it just goes on like this, though the nights are cooler now, that's a relief.

Out to the Christian Community School in Terra Ceia to pick up some bulbs, thinking it would be an event to tell Mom to prove I'm functioning. Land of the Sky. I could just imagine the Dutch settlers standing on their raw land, grateful to feel crushed and small again. The light today was banged down hard against the fields, making the shredded cornstalks glitter like broken glass. I knew I was speeding, didn't care. My eyes went streaking over all that flatness and I was flying, ripping Calvin out of his cell, and we were lifting, flying into the sky.

The bulb woman had a thin cotton dress and wool kneesocks and sneakers and grim wire spectacles. Her hair was bundled into a muslin cap that tied under her chin in a bow. She was my age. The sun slatted through the barn roof and made stripes on her soft old-young body. So self-contained, but not self-conscious. She made me remember being simple, which I never really was, not like that, I was never that wise or humble. But watching her I seemed to think I had been or I would be again, and the coldness of the earth floor snaking into my legs was like strength. Her whole mysterious life came out through the grimy lines in her palm when she gave me my change, with that astringent smile I could read, that said, I don't give much away to painted fluffballs. She would never have guessed the strength of my emotion. We carried the crates out side by side like sisters and put them in the trunk, and when she turned and tramped stolidly back to the barn I felt almost equal, and worthy, and I thought, *Find Jade.* Just like that. I stopped at the meat place in Acre Station and phoned the jail up.

I got to the courthouse fifteen minutes before visiting hours started and parked facing the other way, but with the rearview and side mirrors angled at the entrance to the jail. When the first visitors started to come, I realized I didn't know Jade, all I knew was she was small and liked old people and had nightmares. A woman the right age pulled in and got out, black as bitter chocolate, cheap purple jumpsuit, high heels. I hoped it wasn't her. Then a woman came on foot, urging along a toddler probably too old to be Jamaica — prettier than the first woman but with a comb stuck in the back of her hair, and all worked up, yanking at the child. Twenty minutes passed with nobody except older people, parents. Then a dusty blue hatchback pulled in two spaces over and I knew.

Very small, all in proportion. Unprocessed hair pulled back in a braid. Round earnest forehead. Big eyes, no makeup except lipstick, that splash of wet red paint on black skin. Black jeans. Dainty like a ballerina, with her small neat head and that trim hip-flexed planting of her feet, in black flats that were cheap and sexy. Darker than I expected, but not as dark as him. One of those high round impossible asses as she leaned back in to get Jamaica, lifting her out, slinging her onto her hip, the capable mother. Breasts bigger than mine but

soft, moving inside her shirt, which was white with the sleeves rolled
up above the elbows. Little silver-coin earrings. Pretty. Pulled together, trying to bring him some cheer, bringing him Jamaica, who
didn't seem sickly at all, but teeny like he said, in a plaid hat and
denim overalls, little red Keds dangling. Mother and daughter, in
charge, going in to see their daddy.

I waited. They came out well before three, didn't even use up the
allotted visiting hours.

I just learned from Swanner's secretary that Calvin's court-appointed
lawyer is Sam Midyette, Jr. He'll be assisted by a Mr. Van Dorp.

Friday, October 25

No sign of Jade today, but I think I saw Calvin's father, and Colefax.
Colefax shorter but with the same head and neck, putting a little
jumped-up snap in his walk for anybody watching, like, *This is
nothin, man, he'll get out.* Their father is quite tall and gray, a slow
man with a cautious face. He had on a gray work uniform with a
sewn-on name tag but he was using a cane.

The Halloween spirit is heating up. All these elaborate arrangements in people's front yards. Bales of hay dragged in, potted
chrysanthemums and decorative cabbages, pumpkins, scarecrows.
Cardboard skeletons dangling on the front doors, plywood cats
everywhere, and goblins in the trees, made from sheets wrapped and
tied around something small like an orange. Such a hearty pagan appetite, it's like the Day of the Dead.

The Alligoods are still away. Don't know for how long, or where
they went, I never saw them leave. I'm glad. I couldn't handle their
horror over Calvin. Nor did I miss Dick when I was putting the iris
bulbs in today. They're that strange pink-brown, with some purple
ones mixed in, two swaths on either side of the walk. I tried to think
of my hands as gloves Calvin was wearing. We pushed each bulb
way down in and tamped the plug of earth back. The air very warm

and dry today, and sad, like in an old attic. Even sounds were more plaintive, the hammering from the new house going up seemed so distant, like crackles from an old radio, and there was a woman who kept calling her dog in a long thin wail.

I talked to Ping again. Not much to say, but a connection was there. She sounds pretty good, she's in Connecticut with Garfield and Buffy, then off to London with them next week to find furniture for the new house. I'll miss her.

Looked up Sam Midyette in the phone book and drove by his house, only about three blocks away. A big house, not pretentious. His wife was in the yard, what you'd expect, pretty with ash-blond hair tied with a fat red yarn bow. She was pruning vivaciously. I liked her.

I keep fighting the thought that this is not happening. Or that it's happening without me. Which it is in a way. I don't matter. To his father and brother I'm the token white woman in the nightmare. I could be anybody. It's like instead of crawling through a tunnel, I am the tunnel. It passes through me.

Tuesday, October 29

Jade left the jail about 2:00 and headed back to Calhoun. I thought she hadn't seen my car but halfway there she suddenly pulled over. I pulled up behind her and waited but she just sat there, so I got out and ran up to her car. Her window was down but she wouldn't turn her head, then a truck went past and she had to yell it—*Stop following me!*—then she jiggled the gear shift, like, okay, message delivered, stand back, I'm going now. I said, *I just need to talk to you!* Her jaw clenched but she told me what to do, turn left at the Texaco, etc., and not to follow so closely. I thought, Good, she's scared too, maybe I'm not crazy.

It was a little yellow ranch house. She was at the back door, waiting to check me out, anonymous white woman in a dumb turtleneck, tripping over a root sticking out of the driveway. Then we were going through the kitchen into a small living room, neat as a pin, crowded with furniture all in matching silver-blue plush, even the carpet. Whopping TV, magazines displayed in a fan shape, dish of foil-wrapped candy on a glass coffee table. Gift-shop plaques on the wall, including an almost blond head of Jesus. Overpowering aroma of fresh-brewed coffee. No sign of a child. I decided it couldn't be her house we were in. We sat opposite each other, almost knee to knee, too busy collecting information on each other to bother even pretending politeness, taking turns with our eyes on each other's faces and legs and breasts. She finished first and wrapped her cardigan around her, it was the sweater with the strawberries. Short red skirt. Legs freshly shaved.

I asked how he was.

How you think? A fierce rewrapping of the sweater, then she glared out at the road.

Knowing whatever I said would be wrong made me reckless. I asked if he was comfortable at least.

She looked at me awestruck, examining my stupidity.

Oh, he's fine. He's cheerin me up. Tellin me don't worry. Ain't no evidence! Midyette gonna get him out! That's right, everything gonna be just dandy. Cause what-all has he done? All they got him for is killin a man had a wife he was—

She didn't say *white* man. I was just thanking her for that in my mind when her mouth skewed open and her hand came up to hide it, her eyes teary and wild around the room, everywhere but at me. She wiped them and glowered at the table. Her legs a little open, with downy fuzz on the insides of her thighs. *You know they put a tap on your phone.*

I said, *Oh, I don't think—*

She rolled her eyes and buried her face in her hands.

I suggested getting him another lawyer, maybe one from Raleigh.

Where'd he ever get the money for that? What's that gonna look like? He got to stay with Midyette now. Look. You know why it's dangerous for us to meet like this, you know that DA's guy is all over the place.

(What DA's guy? Is that the guy I always see in the green car?) I just said very calmly, *Yes. That's why I made a point of following you out of town.* Then I asked her what Midyette's like. She said he's "all right." Then suddenly she squinted, maybe remembering something Calvin had told her about me, like almost a verdict, then it was gone.

I asked if she knew who called in the phone tip to the sheriff. She didn't seem to know about that. I asked if anybody had talked to Half-Gallon yet. She thought not. Apparently he lives there on that same street. Then she said everybody else was "okay." I asked who she meant.

People who think they all know his business. People got a big eye out for him, ever since he was little. They all watch him, see where he goes. What he goes. Who he goes.

She had this tight blind little smile, chin up, crazy around the eyes. Proud. She adores him.

He's not gonna plea down, she said, in this low warning voice, like, no matter what *you* might be expecting of him.

I said I knew that. I said, *He would never—*

Kill anybody?! Oh, thank you! Thank you so much! That why you came here today, to tell me the father of my child ain't a killer?

I kept my voice quiet. *He wouldn't plead guilty to something he didn't do.*

A long acid minute. I could hear water running—a toilet flushing. I asked Jade if she knew where he'd been that night. She said he was playing poker. I must have seemed distressed. She said, *Midyette says that's good.*

I suggested maybe a good character witness would be the guy who'd loaned him ("him"—we never once said Calvin's name) the money for Jamaica's operation.

What guy is that? she said, and I felt a little stab of triumph. *Medicaid,* she said tartly. *Medicaid paid most of that.*

Change of subject. I asked how his sister was.

Kyla, she said, filling it in, as if I couldn't possibly be expected to remember the name. But there's a problem with Kyla, some friction. Kyla's refusing to visit Calvin. Jade said this was because Kyla was still mad at Calvin for "Bobo floppin at his house."

I was lost. What house? Jade spelled it out for me. When Bobo was in town, Calvin had let him stay with him. At *his* house. Calvin has his own house, he doesn't live with Kyla. Jade carried on about Bobo, sputtering about Calvin wasting time on him, feeling sorry for him. She called him a piece of human garbage.

Maybe it was Bobo, I said, and she gave me a wince, like, You're only just thinking about that *now?* She informed me Bobo had already left Calhoun by then.

I said what about Bobo's friends?

Bobo ain't got no friends, anybody was Bobo's friend is dead. Then she heard what she'd said and looked stricken.

I couldn't get over the house business. I wasn't tracking too well now, I kept trying to think why he wouldn't ever have told me he had his own place. I asked Jade when it was that he moved out of Kyla's.

He wasn't ever there, not to live. Having her own triumph now, I could see. And then maybe she half pitied me in my ignorance. *Well, he was there for about two weeks once, right after we split up.*

Oh, okay, last year.

No. This year. June.

No, because by then I knew him, and you and he had already—

Those big round eyes, going dead on me, then she slammed them back out at the road and turned a shoulder on me.

Calvin left her for me.

A door opened down the hall and a heavyset black woman about thirty, with close-cropped hair, came in. She had on a shiny orange shorty kimono and huge fuzzy rabbit slippers with ears. Jade gave her a cool face. *We're havin a meetin. This is the guy's wife, Claudia.* She looked back at me and said, *This is my friend. Maddy,* she tacked on.

Maddy wanted to give me a cup of coffee, but Jade reminded her she was late for work. Maddy rubbed her arms inside her sleeves, acting worried, like she didn't want to leave us alone together, but she went on back down the hall and started the shower.

Maybe the water sound eased me. I said, *When you visit him, do you talk much about . . . the situation?*

Through that plastic screen? In all that racket? she cried, proud, like knowing about jails gives her an edge. Then it poured out. *I told him when it happened, I said, You got to get out of here, just go away now, but he say he can't, cause they be tryin to find anybody ever did work at y'all's place. Says he got to just stay calm and sit tight. Didn't leave us alone the whole week. Had to be with his baby. Touchin her, feedin her, changin her clothes ten times. Sniffin her head. I'm sayin, You just put her in those overalls, now you takin em off again?* She shot me a new look, soft and streaky. *They can't ever find out about you and him.*

I said I knew that.

You can't be comin to the trial.

I told her I'd have to, to testify. Then I said, *How would it look if I wasn't there?*

Who cares how it looks? Who's that gonna hurt, you lookin bad? You just be cryin and starin at him and what's that jury gonna think then?

I said people would think I was crying about "what happened."

But that's bad for him too. Ain't no way it works with you bein there.

She thinks I should go away, take a vacation and not come back or something. I tried to explain I have to stay in town to answer questions. I explained I'm supposed to be helping. She seemed mollified for a minute, but then suddenly crazy and wired up. I thought it was time to go.

She said, *You talk to that DA. You might hear things, like about what they know, stuff they're plannin. Stuff I could tell Midyette. You know they got some secrets.*

Very, very smart. Of course. I blinked at her and felt idiotic.

She stood up and led me out the back door and it was too much, like we'd been in there for days. She pointed to a big flat rock set in the corner by the stoop and said if I had any information, not to use the phone but just write it down and put it in a baggie and leave it under the rock. She stepped down and showed me how to jimmy up one edge.

We stood there for a minute. I was thinking about Calvin lying to me and why he would do that. Pride. He wanted me to think he was paying off that hospital bill without any help. He didn't want me in his house, probably some little crummy place.

I don't know what Jade was thinking. Leaves blew across the driveway off a little tree and she hugged herself and I suddenly felt Calvin watching us there, glad we were together. We were doing some good work. I was thinking how, just before I left, I would touch her shoulder.

We don't need any money. All of a sudden, in a rush. *I'm still workin.*

I said, *But he supports you.*

In a very patient correcting voice, she said, *He helps me out some.*

I wanted it to end on a positive note. I said we had to remember all they have is a couple fingerprints on the car and some bullshit story somebody made up to try to get the reward.

She said, *Yeah. I'm cold, I got to go in.*

I didn't want her to go, I kept talking. *He's got his dignity. You know? That belief in himself.* The word *valor* came into my head.

She went on in.

I got in the car, turned it on, and looked over at the swing set in the yard next door, with the swings empty like the kids had died. I turned the car off and went back in the house.

The living room was deserted. Somebody called, *Back here!* and I went down the hall to an open door, Maddy's bedroom—a dusky gold cave, curtains still drawn, bed not made. Jade was sitting on the bed, beside a white uniform laid out there. Maddy was standing by the bureau, her body divided by a thick white bra and skimpy see-through panties. They both seemed so tranquil, there was this heavy slow thing about them. Maddy said for me to come in and I stepped into a smell of sleep mixed with the fragrance of the talcum she was patting in her armpits.

I said, *I'm sorry, I just have a question.* Maddy was rummaging in her jewelry box, then holding up a gold chain, to get Jade's opinion. *I wanted to ask about his mother.* No response. *He's so angry about her, but . . . is she dead?*

Jade was remote now, staring away into a corner. *No. She ain't dead. He still remembers her. She was sittin under a tree. She was holding Colefax, he was just a baby. She had her plastic hat on, from work, and some kind of red dress. He remembers how she smelled too.* Jade was watching me now. *Yvonne. That was her name.*

Maddy was motionless, with the chain between her hands, its little gold medallion was quivering.

I said, *So where is she?*

Jade adjusted her skirt, taking her time. *People say she went over the line.*

You mean she's in jail.

Some commotion was going on between their bodies, some ripple, anger I thought. I wanted to show I could be just as angry on Calvin's behalf about anything that had hurt him. *For thirty years? What on earth for?*

They were so still, so watchful, and nothing moving, just that sparkly medallion. That musky flower smell was stuck down the back of my throat.

Jade wagged her head. *No. This a free woman I'm talkin about.* (Pause. Dragging it out, crossing one leg over and kicking the air, making me watch.) *This woman just got up one mornin and looked in the mirror and thought, Hmm. I bet I could pass.*

And just leave her children?

It happens.

She wouldn't do that!

I was hot with outrage, full of blind argument, anything to keep it back, away from me. Maddy was coming over to me, coming close. She turned her back and her hands came up around her neck and handed me the ends of the necklace. On the nape of her neck a grainy pattern of hair. I was fumbling with the clasp. Over her shoulder I saw Jade holding herself folded over, clenched. She was flicking her nail at a button on the uniform. Maddy put her kimono back on and led me — I think she took my hand — to the kitchen. She poured us both some juice and nudged a plate at me on the counter, corn muffins.

I said, *I disturbed you. I'm sorry.*

Maddy smiled. *That's all right.*

I said, like I was choking, *Calvin's dark.*

Calvin and Colefax favor their daddy. Their mama was light. She watched me struggle with that, not pointedly, just with a kindly interest. *Nobody knows where she went, it's just something to talk about. Honey, you ought to eat somethin.*

I said, *I'm sorry but do you know if he's ever said anything?*

About me. She knew instantly what I meant. She shook her head no, and then she settled her sad eyes on me and they spoke to me, plain as day: I'm sure he's thinking about you though, I'm sure of that.

Out loud she said, *I'm sorry about your husband.*

Just that, nothing else in her voice, not a whisper of innuendo. No reproach. Knowing everything about me, she could still feel that toward me, that untainted pure sympathy. And then she cocked her head and sorrowed over me and all I wanted was to be small enough to creep into her arms. I thanked her and turned away. When I was backing the car around, she came out and stood on the back stoop in her bare feet and watched, looking worried, rubbing her arms.

I stopped at the old house, taking pains to park way around at the back, feeling treacherous for not having come before, for not even *thinking* of it. But it was all done. Clean as a whistle. Maybe Jade helped him, she loves him enough. It was like no one had ever been in that room for years. The windowsills were covered with dust again. I did my bit. As I left I wiped the doorknob.

What did they tell Calvin when his mother disappeared? Did they say she was visiting a friend, but not to worry, she'd be back? Or she was sick in the hospital? They must all have agreed on some story and thought, we'll stick with it and just let time go by. We'll protect him, we'll distract him. That was when he was so afraid of water. The first thing he ever told me. But the kids would have known, the older kids would have picked up the rumor, a dirty secret they could pester him with. And he would have heard the grown-ups talking about her, Yvonne, Yvonne, in low voices that stopped when he came in the room, silence gathering around him. And all that time he'd be trying not to believe it. Accepting it maybe, just for one instant, in bed in the dark, then denying that he even missed her. Being brave, growing bitter, hardening himself around her red dress.

Of *course* they don't know. She might have had an accident. Maybe she fell down a well. People just talk. I bet they talk a lot when a light woman marries a dark man, I bet they don't like that. She probably wasn't that light. How does Jade know anyway, she never laid eyes on her. People don't have to pass anymore. Do they? Don't know, can't ask. I'm on the outside and Jade knows everything, she knows all the black stuff. That's what we were arguing about today, who really knows him, who his *real* woman is. Who loves him *best*. She was glad when I asked about his mother, glad to dish that out. Like it was my fault, for being white. She wanted me to despise his mother, but I don't. Even if it's true. If it is, her lie's worse than mine. What would Jade make of that? Everybody lies. I don't care about his lies to me. Just the one. I wish he'd told me he'd taken Bobo in. He didn't think I'd understand about him still feeling responsible for Bobo, but I do, more than Jade does, more than Kyla. They don't know what I know about him or where we've been together. They don't know I'm way out here with him, where I want to be, past the point where I could even choose to go back again.

"Victim's gun found."

Swanner could have called to tell me before I read it in the paper. It would have been nice. I had to call the office. The secretary when she was calling him to the phone referrred to me as the Merry Widow. She didn't care if I heard. What's that about, what are they picking up?

The gun was found by accident in Calhoun, during a raid on a crack house. It was in a plastic bag, stuffed in some bushes in the backyard. They already did the tests. It was the same gun that shot him. Dan was shot with his own gun. No news on prints yet but Swanner says "don't worry," some of them will be Calvin's. Hah.

Another forked twig stuck on the doorknob. Why can't Half-Gallon carry a paper and pencil?

Thursday, October 31

Debs and Harley came by for a "Halloween drink." They seemed dismayed I hadn't put out so much as a bowl of Mars bars for the trick-or-treaters, until I pointed out there hadn't been any. *This is a shunned house,* I said. This went past them, they were wound up about being invited to be on the Christmas house tour this year. Debs is determined to do this even though Chelsea's due in January. She's going to gild three hundred pine cones, she's got Harley out collecting them.

When I presented my fresh news about the gun tests, Harley didn't really react. It seems he had naturally assumed Dan would have had the gun in the car with him that night, because that's where he kept it, in the glove compartment. Apparently this was because I wouldn't have it in the house. *You mean, you didn't know?* Harley said this too innocently, overacting. I played along, just trying to seem a trifle regretful about not knowing that particular item of info. I was seething. Harley by now was thinking out loud about whether or not Dan had gone out there "to score," this in a practiced voice that suggested he'd presented this theory before, like to the sheriff. I said I thought Dan was too nervous of black people to do that, and Harley looked bland and cunning both. Finally I asked Harley if he knew whether Dan always kept the gun loaded and he explained—patiently—that that was the whole point of having one. He was blushing though. Debs started crying quietly, and then really bawling. Harley pointed out it wasn't good for the baby and took her home.

I can't absorb this new thing about the gun. I don't care what Harley thinks, I can't put Dan and his gun together out in the world.

Friday, November 1

Nothing's really changed. It just means I'm better informed. I'm glad really.

Swanner didn't accuse me himself. No, he called to tell me he was sending over his "assistant" (not to be confused with an assistant DA) to "go over some things." Farris Lewis. Tall, with droopy brown hair, big feet in tan Hush Puppies, the rest of him more stylish. Oversized white cotton shirt, expensive floral tie. Slouched his way through the living room, bending down to look at all the photographs, grinning to himself. I should have known then.

We went in the kitchen and I got the coffee going while he went all mellow, letting his spine slide down the chair, playing with the pepper grinder. Calling to me over his shoulder. *What do you say we take it from the git-go?*

I came to the table. *Fine.* Sat down opposite.

You know about Lloyd's theory.

I said no.

Shootin at the Handi-Mart, end of September. You and Moore are both at the scene when it occurs, or close to it anyway, cause a witness saw the car with you two in it. The officer who checks it out speaks to your husband and your husband tells him a whopper. He shows Oden a picture ID of his wife, which later turns out is his first wife. Meaning, y'all musta got married on the moon, cause there's no record of him ever bein married more than the one time.

And here it is again, coming out of another pocket. Farris pressed it on the table and spun it helpfully in my direction. A copy this time, a color xerox.

So now, who is this?

I shrugged.

The theory is, this is you.

I looked scathing.

It is you! Lisa had that figured. Damn . . . she's good.

So I had to ask who Lisa was.

Farris got out his credit card holder and flopped it open on a studio shot of a big-hair brunette—thin cruel magenta mouth, spiky lashes, crucifix propped askew on a mammoth cleavage—his fiancée. Lisa is apparently "addicted" to makeover magazines and therefore had no trouble with the conundrum of an extra wife there was no record of. She must be a genius. I couldn't stop staring at her.

That sure must be somethin to go through. He mumbled this.

I suggested Lisa would probably want to know all about it.

Not if you don't want her to, he said primly.

It's like being a sinner your whole life, stumbling around in the darkness and then being saved. Like you've been touched by the light and made whole. Tell her that.

He frowned, said that would offend her. *Okay, now when people find out, how's that make you feel? That bother you at all? Cause I think Lloyd might could play some ball with this. Get ole Fred Oden up there, take him through the false ID business. "Officer Oden, please look at this photograph of the woman Mr. Dryburgh said was his wife and point her out in the courtroom." And old Fred, he'll ham it up. Look all around and say hmm . . . no . . . golly, he can't see you anywhere. With you sittin right there in the front. Kind of a cornball Perry Mason moment but you have to give the jury some fun. Course, they'll like the picture, they'll take it and pass it around. Not this one though, it'll be a big nine-by-twelve glossy. They'll take their time, compare it with the real you.* (Faintest emphasis on *real.*)

I got up to get the coffee.

Okay, what's Lloyd got? He's got—turning to watch me, leaning back, all rhetorical and expansive—*a new glamour-girl wife who's messin around on her husband whenever he leaves town. The husband either knowin about this already, or else he didn't before but he does now, for sure. Okay. Big question is, what's the husband gonna do?*

My back was to him. He waited until I was there with the coffee, sitting down.

He's gonna go get five thousand and some dollars out of the bank and then, the next night, he has to make a run down to Calhoun.

I was too shocked to be cautious. Stunned and outraged. I think I might have been smirking. *You think Calvin was blackmailing my husband?*

Farris shrugged. Twiddled his spoon. Looked thoughtful.

I said, *So when Dan supposedly takes him all this money, Calvin shoots him anyway. That makes sense. And that's why his prints are all over the gun.*

He wiped it, obviously. But then there's the matter of that little pin he was holdin. Your pin.

Who ever said that?

Your mother-in-law.

She's in London.

Leaves tomorrow.

Moore stole that pin from the house. Stupid stupid.

Farris dropped his chin on his chest like he'd been shot, then hauled his head back up. *Look, people do it. It happens. They take a trip to Boonesville—*

I beg your pardon?

Take a trip to Boonesville. Do the wild thing with a black. That's not the crime. The crime is protectin your lover that killed your husband. Christ, I don't fuckin believe you. Here's a guy actually willin to marry you and pay for you to look . . . He stared past me at the river. *Course, you know what Lloyd thinks.*

I said I could imagine.

He doesn't have a racist bone in his body, if that's what you mean. No, Lloyd thinks maybe you helped the boyfriend. Maybe set it all up for him. At least gave him some inspiration. Didn't you? C'mon, sure you did.

I slashed my eyes at him and he stood up. Jammed the xerox in his pocket, slammed his chair in, slapped at his floppy hair, all flushed and ham-fisted.

What'd he do, blow you away with a coupla new tricks?

He stalked out through the house. I started to feel better, like I'd just thrown up, that same detached accomplished feeling. Went in the powder room to see how I looked. Not bad enough. Went and creamed off my makeup and now I'm nice and gooey with pinched red eyes.

I look good.

12:45 P.M.

Dan's Merrill Lynch statement just came. It says his debit card was used on the fourth, to withdraw $5,100. They would have found the VISA slip in his wallet.

I need to talk to Calvin. I need something, a connection. Anything.

Melanie might be out there.

I saw a McDonald's cup on the porch, upside-down. I picked it up and there were things underneath. A baby pine cone, a nugget of blue glass, a Ramada Inn matchbook, and a half-smoked cigarette. She was crouched in those little bushes, going to the bathroom, I thought, but then I saw she was just investigating, poking around in the undergrowth. She was overdressed for the heat, red nylon windbreaker and puffy nylon warm-up pants and a different baseball cap, white this time but set at the same sideways angle. She could tell somebody was watching her. She stood up and turned, cigarette in her mouth, trying to be tough. I waved the cup and called, *Mel, hi! I didn't know it was yours!* Made a show of putting it back to protect her things and felt such a surge of tenderness for her, saw her at home with me, eating with me, giggling like she did for Calvin. I called, *How you doin?* She stretched herself, to show me how unimpressed she was.

Starting to feel better, calming down, writing it down always helps.

She came wading through the weeds, angling in on the diagonal, keeping me in her sights. She stopped a few yards from the porch and stuck her lip out. I smiled and gestured at the cup.

It's all there, you can count it. We met before, remember?

She threw her cigarette butt away, savagely, with a whip of her arm, and I saw she had a thin unclean T-shirt on underneath the windbreaker, her nipples pricked against it, no underwear.

I said, *I hear you like this house. I do too.*

She dropped a hip, bored. In a soft lispy voice, *He ain't here, he's in jail.* She pulled Ping's purple velvet box out of her jacket pocket and positioned it very precisely at the corner of the porch floor.

I know he is. He'll get out.

I sat down—hoping this was a conversation—and leaned back against the house. The cup was by my foot and she came swishing over in her nylon pants to retrieve it. She dropped her collection of objects inside it, including the velvet box, then went to the corner of the porch but she wouldn't sit down.

Maybe you could visit Calvin. Friday's a visiting day. Or maybe you'd rather walk there. I don't know how you do all that walking. I'd be a little scared.

A quietness came into her body, a listening.

I said, *I hope you're careful out there on the road. You are, aren't you?*

She said, *Wasn't about no money.* Very insistent.

Oh. What was it about?

She considered this. *See . . . you can't always tell. Signs might be all right, but you just never know. Like this guy in particular? I heard him, I heard the car sneakin up like that. Real real slow.*

Some guy snuck up on you in a car.

She did an angry head shake, like trying to clear her head. I thought, Who's she mad at, me or this guy? Then I understood: both. The guy was white. I said, *This was a white guy.*

She shrugged and hiked herself up onto the porch. She was looking out at the brushy yard but watching me with her whole body. *Hat was drippin. Rain be runnin down my back. Shoes all slushy.*

Your purple shoes, the ones you have on?

Shirt had stripes.

Your shirt?

His. Then she seemed stuck. I said she didn't have to go on. She pulled out a stick of gum and started unwrapping it. *His finger? Nothin wrong with that. He was pokin at his radio, turnin it off, and I saw his finger and it looked okay. Not scary. Not like no bone, you know what I'm sayin? And he's laughin cause I'm messin up his nice car . . . just laughin. So I'm laughin too and I'm thinkin, poo, he's okay, you can relax, girl. He's askin me, where am I goin, do I know it's rainin out and I ain't supposed to be out walkin? Boom. Locks go down.*

Fidgety now, chewing her gum, one foot drawn up. She stroked the toe of her sneaker over and over, smoothing the rubber with her finger. *He had them four-way locks. . . .* She turned her face away because it was crumpling.

But he was just a creep, that's all. Melanie, it's not your fault. You only got in because it was raining.

She sat up straighter. Looked down the front of her windbreaker, pulled at it, trying to tidy herself. Still not looking at me.

Said my cigarette was funny cause I had it in a baggie. But it still got wet anyway. I couldn't get it goin, but he didn't notice that. Too busy gettin it out. Showin me, hunh, like I ain't never seen one before. I says, Hunh-uh, that ain't for me, and he says, Yeah it is, look at it. And he already got the money out, brand-new money, I saw it.

A lot?

Twenty.

Where was this, by the side of the road? Did he pull over?

Talk talk talk talk. Nasty like that, got to be talkin to hisself all the time. Dirty dirty, you a dirty little girl, ain't you a dirty—

She turned her face to me and her mouth was open. She pulled her gum out. Then she worked up some spit, I saw her pink tongue, and then she let the spit run out. Telling me, *I didn't swallow it.* She touched the back of her hand to her lips, remembering, savoring, *Yeah.* Popped her gum back in and drew her other leg up and wrapped herself up tight, a little ball of misery, and I wanted so badly to do something. I wanted to hug her. I almost had my arms around her when she jabbed out her elbows and we rolled off the edge of the porch into the weeds. She was underneath me, trying to get up, struggling and pushing against me, my weight was crushing her, it was horrible. Her hat came off and my hand skidded into her cloud of hair before she squirmed away and bounced up. She started laughing but not making any sound, slapping her knee, showing me she was fine and dandy. Didn't need me. One more dry giggle. Then she found her hat, slapped it on her thigh, put it on, and did a little knee dip as she cranked it around to the right spot.

She pretended not to hear when I invited her to have lunch with me. Just pushed her gaze sideways. I said, *I heard the food's not too bad at that Carolina Diner place.* She put her chin up, sidled over to her cup, and brought it with her to the car. When I opened her door she wavered but then she got in. When I got in the other side she had her huge rubber shoes propped against the dashboard. I could hear her nervous breathing. But out on the road she seemed calmer. She started a long story about some money she was owed, that a friend had given another friend to keep for her, but which had been stored in a plastic box that got left on a stove and melted. A lot of different people were involved and I got confused and asked the wrong questions, which ruffled her, but we were doing all right, we were doing fine till the dog ran out. She shrieked. I swerved, and she got socked against the door. When I got the wheel straight I glanced over and she was still cowering.

It's okay! Wow! I forced a loud laugh. *What a lucky dog!*

But she was rigid, with her eyes frozen ahead at the road.

Mel, he's fine. We missed him!

I braked and snatched at her but the door was open and she was out in the road screaming. *Dumb dog! Dumb fuckin bitch! You bitch, geezum fuckin crow, geezum fuckin crow—*

Dan. My Dan.

Out in your car, cruising. Hey! This is cool. Let's go find one, see what all the fuss is about, see what she'll do.

Did you feel hard and mean, was it like being back in high school again?

Bingo, there's one. Walking in the rain. And she climbs in! And she does it for you. Well, you knew she would—dirty little bitch—no surprises in your world, Dan. At least not till she spat it out. Well, never mind. Just tell me, how did it really feel with her, and don't say it was no big deal because I know you got an extra-rich squirt of disgust. Admit it. And then you drove back to your phony house and kissed the faked-up wife. *Hey Claud, what's for dinner?* What *was* for dinner? A rainy day . . . maybe it was my last day with Calvin. I have no idea what I cooked. Let's say chicken. I roasted a chicken and we took our plates into the living room and watched whatever. Aerial police chases, videos of children flying off seesaws. I didn't care, I was worn-out from fantasizing and crying and masturbating. You might have been feeling a little shaky too, maybe not quite like yourself, but eventually you were soothed by the buttery rice and the gravy. You were deep in the TV groove now, and the world around you lay small and dim and easy and you drank some more and you thought, Geezum crow, if I just gave him some money, I bet I could get him to leave town. Didn't you, Dan. Hey, who doesn't like money?

Next day, straight to the bank.

Maybe you felt a little anxious getting the cash, so you joshed around with that pretty teller you like. *Hey Rhonda, your husband ever buy you that Cadillac yet?* Rhonda, wowed by the amount you need, has to make a special phone call but you don't mind waiting, you can wave through the glass at all your new buds. Rhonda has fun counting the money out, feeling your eyes on her. Okay, Dan the Man, what's the plan? Zip on out to Calhoun tomorrow? We'll see. Don't rush it, stay loose. Yours to blow, dude.

And on Saturday night, sure enough, you're in the car, feeling good, feeling pretty psyched. Clod-Bod's home primping and you're out driving around, downshifting, revving at the light to make sure the schmuck in the Camaro notices your car that cost more than his house did—don't worry, he doesn't know you earned the money by being born, sliding out of Ping's body. Plop. Man, that was tough, and you're *tough now too*! Waiting for the light, *vroom vroom*, gonna go out there and show this guy what *white* power is, not dick power, no, just a big hard wad of cold cash rolled up in your pocket. Burning down the old cement highway, shadows whipping by like in all those old fifties movies, film all speeded up, *classic*. Your car's the wrong kind but never mind, you've got a real gun. Let's think now.

Show him the cash first, then let him see the gun. No no. Show him the gun first and he'll be out of there. Shit, here we are, okay, slow it down. All these dumb little houses, half of em dark already cause they're all in there fucking like rabbits, churning out babies *you'll* have to feed. That's better, now you feel big. And what's wrong with their women anyway, that they have to fuck ours, sniffing around with their . . . sticking their . . . ugh, okay, settle down. Who said white guys aren't cool? This is just a transaction, that's all. Fuck. What is this, a gas station that's a pool hall? Typical. Bodies moving that sluggish way. Maybe somebody'll know where he is. Just pull up and keep the motor running. And here's a dude stepping up to the car, helpful as can be, except he's never heard of Calvin Moore. Yeah sure, you jive-ass mother—No, be cool. Here comes another one, loping up, keeping himself way clear of the car, good. This one says Moore ain't around tonight. Oh but look, he *is* . . . he's in the doorway, coming out slowly, coming to the car.

Mr. Moore? (That sounded okay.) *Get in the car, let's take a ride. How bout a walk? You can leave the car here, be fine.*

How dumb do I look? No, calm down, people are watching, show em who's white here. *Moore? Just get in the car.*

Cake. He's doing it. What is he, a moron?

In the car, back on the road, speeding back into the county, Calvin quietly said, *What's goin on?* and you yanked the wheel, I can see it, the arrogant *slice* of the wheel as you cut the car into the field and braked and threw the door open, and there was the BMW key chain swinging and your khakis knife-creased from the cleaners and your Docksides and yellow socks and the signet ring, they were all adding up big-time, they told the right story, but not to Calvin. Calvin just thought how pathetic it all was, when the man couldn't hold on to his wife. But he wasn't about to let Dan see any of that, he was too smart, and too busy worrying about whether Dan had a gun, and where it was. And wondering what I'd told Dan—*nothing* yet but he didn't *know* that—and thinking why hadn't we just run off together when we had the chance . . . and what the hell is this man pulling out of his pants, *money?* He thinks the woman's for *sale?* And that's when Calvin's fear and pity mixed and all he felt was the condescension, cold and oily, but he thought, *No, don't let him see that, don't antagonize him, and don't say her name.* But he has to say something, quick, before the guy feels dumb with his money burning a hole in his hand. Poor guy, his hand's shaking.

Hey man.

Don't start with that shit. This is five thousand here. A lot, yes or no?

Be crazy to argue with that.

Yeah, that's what I thought. Go see the world, I don't care, just go. Here. Take it.

Look. Why don't you take her, go away somewhere. Try to get it together.

Yes, Calvin might have tried that, something flat and reasonable to get Dan chilled out, to distract him from his money. Or he might have meant it, the contempt faded now into weariness with these helpless white crazy people. But Dan heard insolence, that's all, the outrage of Calvin's tone so cool and niggerish it made his brain burn. He screamed at Calvin to get out of the car.

Very slowly Calvin did, trying to force composure into his body while there was still time, but not liking the way his boots were rolling in the dirt. And when his feet got firm, what does he see? A white man with empty eyes holding his gun in the headlights, stiff with that thing Calvin recognized for the ten millionth time, that thing he was going to have to rescue him from. Just go easy. *Hey man, my ass is gettin cold! What're we doin out here? Why don't we get back in the*—

And Dan wobbled that big silver gun at him. *Get the fuck out of here!* Meaning, why aren't you running yet, I want to go home. And Calvin lifts his hands but Dan fires. And it crackles through Calvin's legs, the sound of the fear he's got to disarm every single day. And he starts slogging toward Dan, thinking, *Lemme stop this poor fool before he kills me,* calling, *Hey man!* And Dan fires again. And again, screaming his ugliness, anything, desperate, throwing the gun down now, *see, see?* But it's too late, too late, Dan. Cause here he comes, here comes the big scary black man, stooping to pick up the gun and fire it and it feels okay, feels fine, doesn't even feel wrong.

And a few hours later at first light, other men are straggling home after a night out and see the lit-up car like a boat out there in the mist, scary as shit. They walk on out there. There's a body. Dead, they assume. White. Rich. What's peculiar was how much it changed the longer they looked, dying there under their eyes until it was just shriveled and sad inside the old preppy uniform. Just a played-out white guy, sorry now for his sins, maybe, almost, and the three of em standing there with their bladders on fire, nobody around.

Like a piece of film, Dan. And it's light out now, big man. It's morning, it's Saturday. Hey Clod, what's for breakfast?

Sunday, November 3

Notes from the bathroom. My new makeup is great. Be the Best You Can Be? This could be it. Blusher on the cheekbones and under the eyebrows, eye sockets sooty purple, in a domestic violence sort of way, not inappropriate. The eyes themselves are still red and positively rheumy, not much I can do about that. Lips are grape-brown, loaded with gloss, like two strips of liver. And the lighting is splendid this morning, crashing around my head like big glass waves.

With fresh admiration I remember Dr. Kurth, how he peered deep down inside the well of a woman's soul and saw what she wanted. Legibility! That *click* that you get with a good logo. Oh, there it is, *the little polo player*. Calvin was just too simple, he didn't have enough *sophistication* to suspect I could be a trick. Or maybe he just got trapped in my one brief shining hour of true loveliness, my weird overlap period when I was a pretty woman who didn't quite know it yet. A fairy tale for sure. Like the woodcutter's gorgeous daughter, humbly sweeping the hovel because she's never looked in a mirror. Except he did know something wasn't right. Strange, he called me, strange woman. That first time. Maybe he'd just caught my smell. Mutant mucus, not normal pussy juice. Digging away at it, working over that tight white thing, fishing for that stuff he knew was in there till he finally snagged some of that old shame festering in there. What's *this*, Bipsa? Bipsa, what's the matter with you, tell me, tell me, tell me.

I can't stop thinking about the alibi guys, the "poker players." What if they blow it, get all twisted around on the witness stand, nervous and cowed in their cheap suits?

12:30 P.M.

Harley and Debs just left, they stopped by after church. Debs has gotten him to be a Baptist, he's going to be baptized again. We stayed out front in the sun, by the new 4×4, with a chrome fish on it already. Harley Tom was locked inside, some punishment was going on. He was in there inside the smoked-glass windows, howling, like a tiny criminal in a prison van. Debs wasn't impressed. *They gotta learn sometime.* I think my makeup spooked them. Debs said rather uncertainly, *You seem better.* I told her I was.

She said, *You're makin the adjustment. I guess we all are. You know, we always planned on gettin a black nanny for Chelsea, but then, you know, after what happened. But yesterday I had this great interview? Big girl, all straight and starchy. Sweet though. But I was still so nervous. And then she said somethin that just helped me so much. Somethin about, quote, those* other *kind of lazy trash that think the world owes em a livin. She hates em.* Debs was chuckling. *You should've heard her.*

She got the job. Harley sounded almost sarcastic.

I know what to do. This will work. I'm not afraid at all.
I'll start with Swanner.

———

Monday, November 4

Swanner's out of town till tomorrow. Be patient.

I saw what they do with cotton these days. It gets compressed into giant white rectangles, they must be the exact measurements of the bed on an eighteen-wheeler. They're lined up along the road, they're like mobile homes without any windows or doors, waiting to get carted off.

Tuesday, November 5

He was at his desk, already slapping his cigarette pocket when I came in, sensing some excitement. Or maybe he just liked my new makeup, though I've refined it since yesterday. That Fellini kewpie doll had to go, but I kept the lip gloss, very Southern. It was candy pink today. My getup was good too. A white silk blouse just sheer enough for a lace bra to show through, trashy wide suede belt, that green fake suede skirt Ping made me buy, "suntan" color tights. Heavy on the perfume. I even dug up an old taffeta slip, to slither when I walked in.

Lloyd. Smiling, slinking into the chair, crossing my legs, nylon rubbing.

Claudia. (A little overwrought and anxious?) *Let me get you some coffee.*

We waited for the woman to bring it in. She wouldn't look at me.

Swanner said, *You came here with somethin for me. Unless I'm imaginin that, and I don't think I am.*

No, you're sure not. Not that you don't have a good imagination . . .

He looked dubious, not sure if I was teasing. Decided I wasn't. *Well, that's part of my job. I'm always puttin myself in somebody else's position. It ain't enough for me to know what happened. Why'd it happen? That's my job. Why were these two guys fightin? Why'd so-and-so pull a knife?*

But Lloyd? Tell me. What does make people kill?

He slumped under the weight of his knowledge. Squeezed the bridge of his nose, hoisted a buttock to extract a handkerchief from his back pocket, took off his glasses, and started polishing.

You want to know what makes people kill. Well, there's all different ideas about that. Some people talk about wickedness. Criminality bein the devil's work. That's one theory. Then you have a psychiatrist type. Says the reason so-and-so's a rapist is cause his mama spanked him too hard one time. But it all boils down to one particular, and you don't need a guru-shrink to tell you what that is. Common sense'll tell you. It's arrogance plain and simple. The me-disease. The disease of me. I want it? I'll have it. A comb from the ten-cent store? A human life? I'll take it, and I won't think about anything else on God's green earth. Not the people I'm hurtin. Not my family that tried to raise me up right. I'm not even thinkin about goin to jail. No sir. I'm a feel-good person! And Claudia, you know, those feel-good people are laughin at us. We're fools to them. They hold people like us in contempt, all us dummies who are moral and self-responsible. We're bein sneered at. Did you know that? I bet you know how that feels a little bit. (His glasses were back on, he was watching me closely to see the effect of this.)

You see, down here we like people to be responsible for themselves. Do the best with whatever God handed out. That's all we ask. It's a kind of love, to expect that. A caring. There's some people might even say we care too much. It's not complicated, is it? Two little words I'm talkin about now. Free . . . choice. Nobody holdin a gun to anybody's head, is there? Aren't they all just free as a little bird to do what's right, just like you and me? And if they don't . . . well, we got to pay for what we get in this life. Last free lunch I know of was when God provided manna for the Israelites. And they still had to pick it up off the ground, didn't they?

Yes. And that seemed almost the correct word, so easy—yes yes yes—I could almost feel it too, the helpless joy of being sure.

Expectin people to be their best. I know you know what I'm talkin about. Bein your best, that was what you wanted.

I laughed, I twinkled. *Well, sure. But I cheated.*

Well now, I don't believe that. I believe you were just tryin to shine.

*Nobody here'd blame you for that. Musta been kinda like Christmas
and the Fourth of July all rolled into one. Wannit kinda like that?*

*Yeah, that's pretty close. You know, I never congratulated you on
discovering my double identity.*

Nothin's hard if you got a mind for it.

She was a sad little thing, wasn't she?

*But see, maybe that's how this all happened. Maybe in all that ex-
citement, you led Moore on just a little bit. You probably didn't know
how little it took. And, maybe too, you were just a mite bored. It's hard
bein married sometimes, no matter how much you love em.*

I didn't love Dan.

It was what he wanted, why did it seem to throw him?

Is that so? Trying to look calm and failing.

*I love Calvin Moore. You know that. We've been together since
June. That's why I gave him that pin, to keep for me. I wanted him to
know he could trust me. I told him I wanted to be with him. We had
a plan to meet that Sunday, the day Dan was in the hospital.*

Dyin . . . your husband was dyin, he prompted, to remind me, to
keep me going.

Yes. Dying.

And you want to tell me who did it.

I let a beat go by. *Who?*

He checked his strands of hair, stroking and patting, like a man
reaching out to be reassured by his dog. I said, *Not Calvin. I know,
because I was with him almost that whole night.*

A fever came over him, which he instantly hid, like slamming a
lid on a flaming pan. Gave his legal pad a casual little poke.

I said, *I went to meet Calvin that night after Dan went out.*

Went to your rendezvous house, did you? (So he knew about the
house, and what else??) *You say this was from about ten till . . . ?*

I said it was just starting to get light out when I left.

*And you weren't scared of what your husband might do when you
got home?*

I shrugged.

*And there's Moore, never said a single word about it. I guess he was
tryin to protect you. And now you're tryin to protect him. Sounds like*

*true love. Well now. I guess that makes you a witness for the defense.
Is that what you wanted to tell me?*

I got up. "Smoothed" my hips. *Yes. But Lloyd, you're an intelligent, decent, God-fearing man. You can probably still figure out some way to get this man gassed to death.*

I wanted to study his reaction but I had to go, I was too afraid I would self-ignite with sheer satisfaction.

We'll have to leave here now, Calvin will see that. Jamaica can come visit us. You can put a child on a train when she's five, or I could even send somebody to bring her. I need to do some research. Prognosis for being born with one kidney, is dialysis inevitable? Possible transplant?

The pure relief of not carrying this around anymore, to let it go. Let them all know what I did, even my parents. I don't care, except about Ping, but it's too late for that, she's known about Calvin ever since Swanner grilled her about the fleur-de-lis. Ping.

I can't think about Ping.

Sam Midyette sounded easy to talk to, relaxed, quick. He didn't want to get it on the phone but he's curious for sure. Three o'clock at his office tomorrow. I think I should leave a note for Jade under the rock, not to tell her about the new plan—she wouldn't understand the necessity—but just that I'm meeting Midyette. I can take it out there after Maddy's gone to work, maybe take some money too. She won't like it but money's money.

Such portentous power in all this. Like when you're dreaming that you're reading a book and of course in order to do that, you have to compose the words in the same instant you're reading them, line after line rolling out like magic. I feel like I'm telling the truth, as if just by saying the words, I'm making it true. I *was* with him, in my heart. My beautiful black man.

If Calvin believes his mother left home to pass for white, think what that means. Think what he had to overcome in his heart to love me.

Wednesday, November 6

Almost time to meet Sam Midyette, I just came back to change my clothes. Just saw Jade talking to Calvin's father in front of the jail, talking with so much animation I thought she might have been telling him she was a thousand dollars ahead, then both their heads turned and seemed to look straight at the car. It must have been an illusion. From stress. I think she was carrying a new red bag.

5:00 P.M.

Sam's young, just two or three years older than me. Smooth, middle-handsome, relaxed in the old collegiate manner, as if still flopping around the frat house. Hands seem to be in his pockets even when they're not, etc. Unfazable, with a little bit of boyish eagerness to please thrown in. Although that may have just been part of his come-on, eyes up and down the front of me like a yo-yo. But there was definitely a little welcoming beam, I thought, as if he might be about to say, *Claudia, what took you so long?* After the condolences he gestured me to the chair and sat down behind his desk and waited, getting serious under the tan.

I apologized for not having come sooner, and he hitched his ankle over his knee. I told him I'd been with Calvin that night and he just stared at his sock. Then finally he talked, started telling me about Calvin. Said he's "depressed but sustaining himself by the force of his will." He said there's a lot of family support there. I said I knew that.

Then he wanted to hear more about that night. I had worked out the right answers so that was smooth—did I leave the garage door open, did I leave lights on in the house. He wanted to know more about Calvin and me getting together. I had to admit my compulsive trespassing but by then he was sort of smiling, he seemed to like that. Told about the process of getting to know Calvin over time. I made it sound like a long time. It was good to be talking about it, like describing a worrying intimate disease to a doctor, and Sam was absorbent like a good doctor, nodding to imply he knew everything I hadn't told him yet, which of course made it come out. I said how much I loved Calvin.

Well, that's not too surprising, he's a good man.

I felt teary. Wanted to kiss him. I said, *You don't seem very surprised about any of this.*

He said no, said Calvin "*doth protested a tad too much.*" Kept insisting he barely knew me, couldn't really describe me even. My Calvin. A quiet moment, Sam and me sharing him. Sam said Calvin hadn't been too helpful in the preparation of his defense. First he claimed he found the pin, then he said he won it in a poker game.

Those poker players again. I tried to look wry.

What's he gonna think about all this?

That caught me off-center.

He said, *So your idea is just admit the affair and preempt all that forensic mess of theirs—fibers, fingerprints, all that.*

I said yes. Suddenly remembered to ask if Calvin would have to testify.

No, we try to avoid that. Claudia, you don't really want to do this.

I said I did, and anyway it was the truth.

It's way too risky.

Then he called it "unnecessary." I was starting to quake a little. He explained how the evidence against Calvin was basically a joke (his exact word). It felt like being back at the beginning of everything, being placated again but with everything switched around. In the beginning there was an airtight capital case, now suddenly there's no case. Now it's all "circumstantial." No witnesses. No weapon to speak of, because there's no way to connect Calvin to the gun. According to Sam the only reason it's a capital case at all is because death-prone jurors are more apt to convict anybody of anything and Swanner needs a big conviction to get himself reelected DA next year. Also, Dan's cash withdrawal is meaningless ("maybe he was goin shoppin") and so is the fleur-de-lis ("maybe you lost it"). Sam was pretty scathing, said the state doesn't have so much as a footprint. Calvin's only crime is "snoopin in his employer's car." I explained about how he'd had the chance to do that, but Sam interrupted then, like summing it up. Said again that Swanner's got "squat." Sam thinks he's scrounging.

He said, *That's how come he's all over you like a rash. Probably been tappin my phones again. How do you like the DA?* He was grinning by this time.

I don't, I said shortly. Sam was starting to strike me as a little too cavalier. A bit glib.

I bet he likes you. Sliding into flirtation, with business being over.

No, not much. But at least he believed me when I told him where I was that night.

I admit it gave me pleasure when he finally unhooked his damn ankle and sat up and stared at me.

You should have come to me first.

I tried everything, pouted, cocked my head.

He was chewing his lip. Then he said Swanner could really make life miserable for me. That old TV line. I responded in the same vein, told him I didn't care.

No, I guess not.

Suddenly I really wanted to leave. I got up but he sat there a minute, preoccupied. But then, showing me out, his little self-assured smile was back and his hand was on my shoulder. I remembered to ask about the jury then: Sam and Swanner can each reject fourteen potential jurors they don't want, and Swanner will try to offload the black people, but we should still end up with enough.

We're meeting again next week. By then he'll probably have found Half-Gallon. I gave him a rough idea where to look. He likes having somebody black to corroborate it, the "romance," as he called it.

All I have to do is pray Calvin doesn't say anything that contradicts all this. But he won't, he'll see what I'm doing.

I have just seen a pelican skimming the river. My first. Ugly-beautiful, a deformed egret by Hieronymous Bosch. I'm brain-dead. Let's go drink that Côte-de-Whatever that George and Ping found in Greenville.

Thanksgiving, late

The frenzy of that night after my meeting with Sam. And the heat, like being trapped inside a sack of hot air. It's all too distant from here, with the snow piling up outside and Mom and Daddy snoring away on the couch downstairs. The plow just clanked by, wiping its yellow light over the walls.

I'm fighting a longing to describe myself in the third person, that crazy wild woman stripping her house down that night in a lather of sweat. Everything, all the mess of my life, was sticking to me. Garbage bags out on the driveway, the garage starting to overflow with stuff, lights on, music. I don't know how Half-Gallon found the gumption to just come in. I was on the floor unplugging a lamp when I saw brown feet in those black canvas slip-ons. From that angle he was like a totem pole Indian. I stood up, said hello. Nothing. *Do you want to sit down?* I went and turned the CD off.

I saw he was too distracted, perusing the chaos. He asked if I were going away. I said no, not yet, just throwing out a few things. I said if he saw anything he wanted he should tell me.

He nodded. *You want a change.*

We sat down like patients at the dentist's, either end of the couch. Stared at the coffee table, which was the repository for items I felt I couldn't heave—Ping's Steuben bowl, some "heated beauty mitts" Dan ordered for me once, a digital rain gauge still in its box. It occurred to me to offer Half-Gallon the aluminum can crusher but he seemed so expectant and elegant with his hands placed just so on his knees, shirt cuffs hanging open. I saw buttons on the cuffs, the unbuttoned thing is part of his look. Offered him a drink but, thinking I meant alcohol, he said he never took a drink on a church night, meaning a Wednesday.

I said, *That makes us both sinners, missing church tonight.* Trying, I admit, a little too hard to make contact.

He cleared his throat. *Jesus is in your heart.*

Now I was feeling too anxious myself to ask why he'd come. I was relieved when he asked for a glass of water. He followed me out to the kitchen, ignoring the mess, gracefully high-stepping and maneuvering. While he was drinking his water I chucked out some coasters. Thinking I could make a reference to my new life with Calvin, I said, *We won't be needing these.*

He don't even like guns.

He said it with such conviction I glanced around at him.

He hates em, he added for good measure.

I said Calvin was going to be fine, and decided just to leave it at that.

Look like you want some help, he said, with a bit more spirit, as if the crisis had somehow passed. I asked him if he wanted to help me move some furniture and he said yes, a little lukewarmly. Then, thinking he might want to eat first, I took a steak out and turned the broiler on, but he said no. He wanted to fry it. Big to-do about pans. I think all the variety threw him. He wanted potatoes and olive oil and onions and garlic, rejected my broccoli and eggplant. He consulted the freezer and dug out an ancient bag of corn. I cleared off the table and left him peeling potatoes and went back in the living room to finish taking all the photographs out of their frames. When the smells started coming from the kitchen, I was thinking I might sneak in and make myself a sandwich when all of a sudden he was in the doorway. *You want to eat,* he said like a mind reader.

The steak was dished up on two plates, set on place mats. He had used the sunflower dishes for the potatoes and corn, and gone back into the freezer for some of Dan's rolls, which were in a basket lined with a paper towel. Steak knives, ketchup, mustard, Worcestershire sauce, butter sliced onto a saucer. For napkins he had folded paper towels into triangles, but I got out some linen ones, making a fuss, being appreciative. My headache dissolved at the first bite, and I remembered I hadn't really eaten much in days. We ate with precision, eyes down. I finally recovered enough to ask after Melanie, and he said she was fine. I asked him how he had made the potatoes so crisp—like lace, I said—and was just starting to hear about the addition of little bits of water to the pan when we heard a noise in the hall. As I stood up he ate steadily, diplomatically, on.

Debs had left the front door open for a speedy exit. Beyond her I saw the 4×4 in the driveway and Harley in it with the engine running. *Debs*, I said gaily. She looked good, flat-footed and stricken and huge in a washed-out denim maternity dress, bangs standing up on end. Panting slightly. I longed to be casual but I was too keen, too excited, watching her peer horror-stricken into the dismantled living room and then back at me, trying to refocus.

Just tell me. Just say. You didn't do it.

But I did.

She threw a glance back at the truck and Harley gunned the engine.

He doesn't believe it, she confided, almost cozily, as in the old days, and then, remembering, screwed her eyes up. *You really did, you fucked him?*

I wondered how she knew, then remembered Swanner being related in some way to Harley.

I said I loved Calvin.

She didn't seem to hear it when Half-Gallon's chair scraped on the floor. She leaned forward and whispered slowly, struggling to make me understand. *He killed . . . your . . . husband.*

No. He didn't do that.

Then why are you tryin to SAVE HIM?

I just told you why.

You knew the whole time it was him! I knew that was funny, you not wantin revenge. Oh no, too high and mighty for that, way way above us. I always knew that was phony. You know, I am so sorry for you.

But now her eyes moved beyond me, bulging nicely. Half-Gallon was taking up a position just behind me, making himself a helpful presence. Harley must have seen him, the horn bleated, anh anh *aaaaaanh.*

Food's gettin cold, Half-Gallon advised quietly. Debs was marveling at him with her mouth open.

I ran into the living room and grabbed that big gold-plated cork-popping contraption. When I bounced back into the hall with it, they were both bug-eyed.

I said, *Harley always loved this. I want him to have it. Give it to him for me, will you? From Dan.* I shoved it at Debs.

She turned and made for the porch, lumbering down the steps.

Halfway to the truck she stopped and turned. Harley was watching, moon-faced.

Harley doesn't want your damn stuff! Give it to your friend! He'll take all your old crap!

Half-Gallon was in the doorway now and I was out on the porch. Harley, being extremely careful not to look at the house, leapt out of the truck and came running up to grab Debs. He tried to get his arms under her armpits but she was in a lather, a fury, crying and squirming away, slapping at his hands. Eventually he grappled her back to the truck, around the far side, they disappeared for a minute but then suddenly she was back, drenched red from the taillights, hands fisted on her knees, bending double to spew out her curse— *I'll pray for you!*—then Harley seized her again and bundled her in and slammed the door. He scuttled around to the driver's side, head down, still refusing to look at me, muttering, *You're into some deep shit now*, then he climbed in and rammed the truck into gear and they were off.

I said, *Hmm . . . I'm not too sure Jesus is in her heart.* I turned to see how Half-Gallon had taken this but he was gone too. He was inside, sitting at the table again, decorously dishing himself up some more corn. I stood near his chair and apologized for the interruption. After an awkward pause he announced dessert was vanilla ice cream with maple syrup. I said great. I felt great. Sat down and cleaned my plate, even had another roll. But Half-Gallon was finished, and he seemed almost immediately to become anxious again, gnawing me with his eyes. I said to him, *Half-Gallon, it's going to be fine, I know it. You'll just have to trust me.*

Silence. Eyes downcast, hands folded in his lap.

Can't be lyin, he said miserably.

I said, briskly, that I didn't intend to lie. I said he wouldn't have to either. *Anybody who asks you, just tell them. It's fine. You know all about Calvin and me, you took him to the house all those times to meet me. That's all. Remember that?*

He was so glum I knew he'd told a few people already.

I said, *Calvin was there with me that whole night. Did you know that?*

Silence.

I got up to clear the table. He didn't move. Coming back to the table I did something I shouldn't have. I rounded his head in my hand, like you would a child's, just for a split second. I knew immediately it was wrong. He endured it, probably even more embarrassed than I was. Then I cleared the rest of the dishes. After a minute he stood up.

He didn't want any ice cream.

We went on into the living room, the plan being to take the couch out to the curb. I lied and said the Salvation Army was coming to get it in the morning. He lifted his end but I couldn't get mine two inches off the floor. I was desperate to get rid of something big, so we moved on to the leather wing chair. I gestured it was going out the back. When we got it into the kitchen I told him it was going in the river. He sort of blanched.

I know it's a waste, I don't care, it's ugly, I hate it! I might have been screaming.

You don't want it, I take it.

I pleaded. *Half-Gallon, I'm sorry, it's going in the river. With my husband's ashes.*

Yeah, all right. Very neutral.

When we finally got it set down at the end of the dock, faced out into that humid darkness, it was like a river god's throne. I really wanted to see Half-Gallon sitting in it. I invited him to, but he refused, so we tilted the top toward the river and tipped it in. There was a lethargic splash and it floated briefly, then the water closed over it, and just for a second oblivion poured through me, cool as mercury.

I ran back for the ottoman, met Half-Gallon in the kitchen, and pointed out what still had to go. He grabbed a towel rack. We kept crisscrossing on the lawn, loaded down with anything we could carry. I even managed a bedside table. I took down some curtains and the house started to echo. Finally I was upstairs, packing Dan's clothes into garbage bags, taking intermittant breaks to go to the window. In the long light from the house Half-Gallon was distinct against the black river and I could watch him bend over, choose a pizza tile or a clock radio from the collection at his feet, test its weight, and hurl it. Not all of it sank. Bits and pieces of expensive junk were floating out in the middle of the river.

I was squeezing a garbage bag through the window when I saw him, mid-dock, talking to a black woman dressed in white. Just as I recognized her they both looked sharply up toward the house and saw me, but the conversation went on. At one point Jade took hold of his shoulders and gave him a shake. When she let go he had to grab at her shirt to keep from going off the dock. I watched them in a trance, hypnotized. Then she looked up at the house again and I managed to wave.

When I got to the dock she was down at the end, alone.

I called out, trying to keep it light. *Jade, what'd you do with him?* I was halfway to her when I heard splashing and saw a big blot appear on a floating carton. It was Half-Gallon's head. Then I noticed I had just walked on his folded-up clothes.

Jade ignored this, loose and cool in her big shorts and shirt, which I could see now weren't solid white but printed with big spindly dragonflies. She was holding out the blue envelope I left for her under the rock, saying *I can't take this.*

Yes you can. Please?

She sagged herself and turned away upriver, exasperated, agitated, fanning herself with the envelope.

You're not givin it to Half-Gallon either. We both automatically glanced around for him. She said, *Look at him . . . swimmin.*

This was said with some force, the implication being that I had overworked him. Then she asked me how it had gone with Midyette, and her eyes were wild. And suddenly, dissembling just seemed like too much trouble, too much work for everybody.

I said there'd been a change. *I'm going to say we were together that whole night, at the house.*

She just stared at me.

I said it was all set.

But . . . that's not true though.

Sam Midyette thinks it is.

I can tell him.

*It's too late, and anyway, he was glad. He has to have a better alibi.
Jade, this is one of those times when the truth isn't actually going to
work. Truly.*

No. (And she looked terrified, even had a quavery hand in the air,
to ward me off, big white lying she-devil.) *Please. Don't tell about
you and him. Just leave that alone, he be fine, he will. Y'all ain't got
to worry about him.*

I had to explain certain things had changed. Gotten "a little complex," I said.

Complex? she cried. *What's complex? And what's Half-Gallon
doin here? You tryin to make him think he's your friend?*

I explained that he *was* my friend, that he'd come over to help me.
I said to her, *All I did was tell him to just be truthful and answer all
their questions. Because otherwise that creep DA's going to make him
look simple.*

You just tryin to control him.

Jade, that's not it. Half-Gallon can't lie, he's not smart enough. And
the water slithered and there was his head looking up at us, back and
forth one to the other. And I said, *Half-Gallon's great, he cooked the
best dinner tonight.*

I felt her eyes go icy on me.

Don't do that, he ain't a child, she muttered. Then she squatted
down at the side of the dock and I thought for a minute she would
show him the money, maybe even offer it to him, but she just leaned
down to speak to him in a velvet voice.

H-G, you hear how she say? His head swam a little closer. *She
talkin down to you, baby. You know why that is, don't you? She thinks
we all criminals! Baby, you know, she say for you to just tell the truth?
But sometime the truth is in a strange place and we got to go to that
place to find it. We can talk about this some more later on. H-G, you
had your swim, don't you wanna get your black ass out of that water?
Maybe she be nice now and turn around, so you can do that.*

I plunked myself down a few feet away on that side of the dock
and let my legs hang over the water. Jade sat down where she was
and glared at me. A smell of rotten garbage floated over the river

from somewhere. Half-Gallon drifted backward, then slowly sub-merged himself up to his eyeballs.

I sugared my voice like hers. *Jade? I know you want Half-Gallon to lie for you, but how can he? He's a Christian. He can't tell a lie on the Bible.*

But we were alone, staring at two waterlogged cardboard boxes stirring on the current of his departure.

Her voice came out choppy. *You crazy. Look at all this crazy mess. This is your mess. What you doin? And what's he gonna think?* Mean-ing Calvin. I was watching her sandal, hooked on her toe, getting ready to fall in.

He knows what I'm doing. Jade, believe me. He'll get it.

She was nodding to herself. *I always knew. Yeah . . . didn't I always know that?* Slumped now, staring blind over the water. Her hatred felt toxic, like I shouldn't breathe too deeply. *You think he did it.*

I said, *He did what he had to. You don't understand because you didn't know my husband. Dan made it happen.*

She made a *tch* noise, offended, snapping her head back so hard her sandal almost fell off. I watched her snatch it and jam it back on her foot. I felt overcome with weariness, just smothered in fatigue. My whole body was crusty with stale sweat.

I said to her, *Jade, it's fine. You believe whatever you have to.*

She stood up.

I was turning, I think, twisting around to look for Half-Gallon on the other side of the dock. She only had to give my shoulder a shove to tip me in. I came floundering up into a shower of brightness that seemed to be flying out of her, out of her white clothes—she was ex-ploding. And then in a flash I saw what she was seeing, as if I were beside her, looking down at the patchwork of ripped-up money and that head stuck in the middle—a wet lump of misery smeared with hair—and then I was back in myself, treading water. I registered the coldness of it. I heard Jade's car door slam. I watched the shredded money float away, then the corner of my eye caught something mov-ing on the bank, Half-Gallon dragging himself out of the river. His footsteps hammered the dock and I caught a glimpse of him, sleek, every lean muscle wrapped in wet shine. He was just above me, hunched over his pile of clothes. I sank lower in the water and watched through my lids like a crocodile as he picked up his shirt and hurriedly slapped it against himself. Huddling a little, crouched and tensed, then suddenly motionless, holding the shirt in an armpit as he searched the river, worried, looking all around for me. But I was too close, right below him, all his blackness rippling down on me. I wanted to tell him I was all right. But first I just needed him to turn. And he did, his flank gleamed and there was a dark hollow where his penis hung, just tipping into the light. Then he saw me and used the shirt to cover himself. I lifted an arm to ask for help, throwing him into a panic, torn between his modesty and my predicament. He turned away again, threw down the shirt, and pulled his pants on. As he knelt and stretched out his arms, I got a foot on the underpinnings of the dock and let him haul me up. I sort of fell against him and his arms went around me, just enough for me to feel the anxiety in him. His jaw rasped my cheek before he pulled back. I was chilly now, that's why I clung. He pulled back harder and started rubbing my arms, roughly, violently. *Get you all warmed up now.* Muttering to himself. More vigorous rubbing. He stopped and turned his head away, avoiding me, and my arms flew around his neck. I was anxious too, I shouldn't have done it. I wasn't thinking— all that naked blackness, too close, and his warmth. His hands squeezing my waist. His breath getting ragged. I knew his eyes were closed. I said, *Don't lie for Jade, lie for me. Say you took Calvin to the house that night to be with me, and you can save him.* I tore my wet shirt over my head and pressed against him hard and put my arms around his neck. *You took Calvin to the house that night to meet me. . . . It's a good lie, to help Calvin. . . . God'll like it*—he started to struggle— *and he won't care anyway because he can't even hear you!* . . . And he was gone, thudding down the dock. I stood and watched in a stupor, bouncing lightly as his weight shook the boards. He hit the lawn and kept going. I looked down and saw his shirt and picked it up. Heard him start the van. He turned the ignition switch too hard, desperate to get away. It screeched.

Telling him God wasn't real, that was ugly. And careless. Sam would kill me if he knew I had messed with one of his witnesses. Poor Half-Gallon.

Maybe he's forgotten already. More probably, Jade's been getting at him with her black sweet talk, reminding him I'm the devil. Which I am, I know that. White devil meat.

It'll be fine. They'll believe *me*.

Half-Gallon's shirt is rolled up in the bottom of my suitcase. I suppose I thought it would be a talisman. A connection. He'd be surprised to know how far it's come, farther than he's ever been in his whole life.

I'm glad now that Sam doesn't want me at the trial until I have to testify. (Says he doesn't want the jury watching Calvin and me and getting "overly excited.") It may keep Mom and Daddy from feeling they have to go down there to keep me company. The state of the house would upset them, although to me it just looks spartan. I keep telling Mom about Dick and Janet, emphasizing what good neighbors they are, all refreshed after their month in Hawaii, etc. This is especially true of Dick, he's always asking how I am and making a fuss. He invited himself over the other night for a drink, then he had another one and he asked me if I knew why Southern women were such "ball busters." I admitted I was in the dark on that one. He claims it all started when their husbands were "doin the dirty" with their slave women. The wives knew it, and the men knew they knew it. So the deal was, white Southern womanhood, in return for turning a blind eye, got hoisted on a pedestal. Which was fine, except then the women took the ball and ran with it, they started to abuse the privilege. I found this extremely convincing and fascinating but wasn't about to say so, and by then he was into another incest joke anyway. Janet on the other hand seems a little remote these days, which may be the result of Dick's attention to me. I certainly don't feel they are judging me in any way.

Here comes the plow again. Winter already. Still no Christmas decorations up yet, but in Beasley the party's in full swing. When I left yesterday there were Santa Clauses up on the roofs, risking sunstroke, reindeers pawing the brown grass. Whole acre lots are strung with fairy lights, every shed, every bush, every birdbath outlined in twinkles, an orgy of Christmas.

I love the sound of the plow, how intimate and cozy it makes everything. The busy roaring and scraping, the jangling chains. They said we might get two feet tonight. I hope so.

III

So, THAT'S IT. I couldn't get out of bed this morning after I finished the journal. I just lay here, staring through the diamond panes that cage this particular view of the hedge. I could hear the women moving around downstairs, cleaning supposedly, although since the dirt never accumulates, what they're doing is ministering to conditions of pre-dirt. They're mimicking cleaning. Shaneen, assuming I was hungover, brought up some tea and wanted to know if I could eat some toast. What I wanted to say was that I didn't need a single thing, I was replete, as Southern ladies used to say, having just supped on my own vomitus.

I had expected to sound young, a little unformed. I didn't expect to sound quite so obsessed with myself. In the old days I used to tell myself that any awareness of my failings was proof that I wasn't a monster. Which must mean that the despair overwhelming me now is a memorial to my impeccable character.

Must finish this in the manner in which I began.

April. The whole world was in bloom.

My moment in court arrived after lunch on the third day of testimony. Jury selection had used up the three days prior to that, resulting in an overload of women. Sam said this was good. Not so good was the fact that Swanner had used nine of his preemptive dismissals to dismiss black people, leaving only two on the jury. Sam felt this

could still work for us, that these two black jurors might feel out-
numbered and beleaguered and more inclined to vote for acquittal
of a black defendant, regardless. When I said "Regardless of what?"
Sam looked sheepish and said there was a remote chance the black
jurors might think I had put Calvin up to it.

Sam had briefed me on the prosecution witnesses who had pre-
ceded me. There was the farmer (white) who had discovered Dan's
body; the coroner with his evidence about wounds, time of death,
urine stains, etc.; Dick Alligood, testifying about my meeting Calvin
in his kitchen. Dick being a witness for the state didn't devastate me
because of course by then I'd discovered that the person who had
phoned in the "anonymous" tip was my neighbor. Then the jury
heard the forensic evidence involving the car. Finally, Swanner had
used Dan's Merrill Lynch withdrawal to tender his blackmail-gone-
wrong hypothesis; I had caught a glimpse of the bank teller,
Rhonda, going into the courthouse that morning, curvaceous in
powder blue. But all this information struck me as rudimentary,
even haphazard. There didn't seem to be anything that resembled a
"body of evidence." It wasn't until I got the transcript months later
that I understood how, during those first two and a half days—aside
from the stark moment when the clerk read out Ping's affidavit iden-
tifying the fleur-de-lis as mine—the connection between Calvin and
me was only ever implicit, like a lethal gas being delicately pumped
into the courtroom.

I remember my terror. An absolute dread of seeing him. As I went
past the defense table I stared straight ahead. I managed to be sworn
in without looking over at him. Only after I said my name did I turn
my head and just for an instant he was black again, black as a
stranger, and I was shocked, and then shocked again: it was Calvin.
He was looking at me, without any real difficulty it seemed, without
any expression at all. He was thin. His dark gray suit jacket hung
from his square shoulders as if from a hanger. White shirt, narrow
dark tie. He looked important and obscure, proud and doomed. He
was beyond distress or desolation. One of his hands was on the table,
empty, useless. It appalled me that he was on display. I looked away,
felt a rush of consolation that we were together in this, and then felt

I had contaminated him by thinking such an arrogant thing in his presence. I was sniveling by now. To keep my eyes from spilling I looked at the ceiling, while everyone waited, barely breathing. I felt my dress become transparent. I had chosen it not for Calvin but for the jury, a plain undramatic black dress meant to express nothing but my sadness. When I looked at Calvin again he had bowed his head. How squeezed, how *compressed* he seemed, sitting between his lawyers. "Hiding behind his lawyers," as Swanner would put it at one point. Somebody brought me a glass of water. The judge was generous with me, everyone was—keen to coddle me, gripped in their silent communal rapture of anticipation.

The guy who'd grilled me that day at the house was in the front row directly behind the prosecution table. Across the aisle was Jade, in a long salmon-pink dress, sitting next to Calvin's father, with Colefax on his other side. I think his stepmother might have been missing. There was another young black man, maybe his half brother Donny, and a plain-faced woman in a hard shoulder-padded white suit. That was Kyla. I took in the two front rows, crowded with his family, with their dressed-up clothes and their layers of sorrow. They startled me, they were like fictional characters I had, out of sheer laziness, failed to imagine in enough detail. No Half-Gallon; he was at Sam's, being baby-sat by the Midyettes' black housekeeper. For the first time in months I saw, just behind Swanner's assistant, Harley and Debs-Anne. Debs-Anne kept adjusting blankets and fiddling with Chelsea, who was snuggled between her parents in a baby carrier. I barely glanced at the jury. I never looked back at Calvin. The whole time I testified, I looked at the clock on the back wall of the courtroom or at Sam.

I was like an instrument Sam was playing. Meeting Calvin, becoming his lover, giving him the pin—together Sam and I produced our answers. There was no audible reaction to any of it, just a turgid silence. I duly mentioned Half-Gallon as a witness to the affair, to preempt the possibility of him clamming up when it was his turn to testify. There were questions about the opportunities Calvin had had to finger the glove compartment and shed his "Negroid" hairs in the BMW. To refute the blackmail hypothesis, I stated that at no time had Dan ever given me any reason to think he suspected me of adultery. As for what he might have been doing in Calhoun, I announced that Dan had at various times "used drugs recreationally." Then, lugging all this splendid frankness like a pregnant bride, I arrived at the actual night and told how, about an hour after Dan had gone out, I had gone to meet Calvin at the house and stayed there with him until it was almost light.

Swanner began his cross-examination by asking me to "refresh his recollection." His tone was one of respectful smarm just barely touched with sarcasm. (Referred at one point to Calvin as my "gentleman.") *So you left the house about ten . . . did I get that right? And that was cause you wanted to go and meet Mr. Moore at the rendezvous house on Route 32, wannit?* Over and over, I reiterated my previous testimony. And then it was finished. As I went out I didn't look to either side. It was like bursting through a bloody membrane into the air again. That was it. My big chance was over. I was convinced I had missed some vital point. But then Sam came out and rubbed my shoulder and told me I had "done good." He said Swanner was grabbing at straws and coming up empty; we were cruising. But then why was Sam's face so shrunken and why did he keep toying with his little gold tennis racket tie clip? I went home and ate something and threw up and watched junk TV. Then Sam called to say Half-Gallon, in his unfortunate brown cardboard suit, had come through fine, been credible and alert. He would be cross-examined in the morning.

The next day it was over. Dick Alligood got to deliver the ultimate blow when he was recalled after lunch. He testified that he had "observed" me on the night of Dan's death, at home alone, out on the lawn. I had been looking up at the sky, he said. I had seemed drunk. (Sam gallantly "objected.") Dick's sighting of me had been at the exact midpoint of the period the coroner had calculated as the time frame of Dan's death. (Classically, convincingly, Dick said he had stepped onto his deck just as Letterman was ending.) It was now obvious I had been quite willing to perjure myself to try to save my guilty lover. Of course this trump card of Swanner's was something of an anticlimax after Half-Gallon's revelation, which had come first thing that morning.

As soon as the judge reminded Half-Gallon he was still under oath from the day before, he started to cry. The moment that had tormented him for months was at hand. Swanner probably still thinks it was his sheer tactical brilliance that drew Half-Gallon out; the transcript shows how incredibly deft he thought he was being, with his grotesque obsequious delicacy. I can just hear the tone he would have used to summon up that box of kleenex for Half-Gallon. But basically Swanner just got lucky. He sensed Half-Gallon's distress and started taking pot shots at it. Had Half-Gallon driven Calvin to the house that night? No sir. Had Half-Gallon seen Calvin that night? No sir. Had Half-Gallon ever seen Calvin *with a big silver gun?* "It was raining." That was Half-Gallon's answer and Swanner pounced. "It was, was it? When was that?"

All down to the rain. *It was raining.* Our last day together, our last minute, and the sky opened. If it hadn't started to rain, Calvin wouldn't have gone into the glove compartment, because I would have been with him, we would *both* have gone out to the lane when Half-Gallon honked. I would have said hi to Half-Gallon, and Calvin and I would have grinned and been shy because we were back together. We might even have told Half-Gallon about our running-away plan. And Half-Gallon would have looked at us and looked away and then showed us a smile like a bird flying out of a cage.

I remember Sam wouldn't come in the house that evening when he came by to tell me about Half-Gallon's revelation. He stayed out on the porch with his hands in his pockets. He delivered the news with pained stoicism and then apologized, which was decent. He said that even though we had to brace for a guilty verdict, it still wasn't "all over." He spoke about the mitigating circumstances, adding them up again by rote. About Half-Gallon he said, *I always had a bad feeling about him.* Which left unspoken what he thought about Calvin. And if he thought Calvin was guilty, what was I—his accomplice?

Or just a dummy with a bad case of hot pants who had gotten in way over her head? I'm not even sure now whether Sam ever really bought my story, not that I gave him any choice. But I wasn't thinking about any of that then. I just remember Sam's trousers being bagged out at the knees and his loafers looking small and boyish, and I saw that he was just a small-town lawyer who'd had a bad day and wanted to get home to his wife and make himself a huge drink. I do remember in the midst of this bafflement, one thought came into my head, crisp as a sound sharpened by fog. I *had* been right about something, Calvin really had rifled the glove compartment that night when I was inside the Handi-Mart. That was how he had known that day in the rain to just open the car and grab the gun.

Mom and Daddy called that night. I remember telling them—obviously I must have—and their proud relief coming out of the phone in a gush. Then my mind slips out of gear again. A nauseous stream of images from the local news. I actually sat on the couch and watched it, Colefax and Jade squinting in the garish TV lights, holding on to each other as they limped down the courthouse steps. Jade sobbing. I registered that. I thought, *Black people in trouble.* Yes. There she was, that pretty black woman whose man had premeditated the murder of mine. Oh yes. Calvin was all hers again. Calvin was evil.

How long did that last? I remember opening a fresh bottle of vodka and crying—crying with the shame of having slept with my husband's murderer—and thrashing around the defiled conjugal bedroom, falling onto the marital bed, trying to bring back the feeling of Dan's fingers on my nipples, pulling and squeezing them, trying to be Dan's wife, *trying.* Then a long blackness descended, as if I were lying under a dirty blanket breathing my own stink, and Calvin was like an animal who could smell it, a black thing moving around the room. I hid from him in the dark and my brain chattered . . . no . . . I can't . . . how would we live. . . . *I don't have any money!* And I could feel that fearless hand stroking my cheek again and that low voice, reassuring me, telling me not to worry. *We get some.* So confident. Nothing to it, do *both* of em. Get her worked up, fuck her till she squeaks, and then angle for the guy's money. Do it, do a stupid-smart nigger thing. They were all big hot animals underneath the sneaky pomp and swank muscle tone. I *reviled* them, I was panting with it, my loathing gathering in a fug I could taste on my tongue. But then, with a strange sideways feeling of falling, that taste burned away, like menthol spreading up and scouring my skull. And the residue of my revulsion floated like hot ash and just dusted the faint outline of what had happened. But I still didn't *see* it. I was back with the facts again, struggling away, recharged, refocused on his rescue. I knew now that he had taken the gun from the car that day in the rain, I believed that. But I also knew he hadn't killed Dan. It was not possible. There was more to it. Something was wrong, *missing.*

It wasn't too late. We could go back to the beginning, to his own alibi, the real one. Find the poker players. Calvin could refute me and tell his own story. As soon as I was capable of speaking, I would call Sam and wake him up and explain the new plan. I would have to explain *why* Calvin had taken Dan's gun. I'd say it was for my protection. . . . He did it to protect me, because he was worried Dan would get violent when I told him I was leaving. Calvin *had* been worried that day, that was true, I *remembered*! I would go back on the stand and apologize for confusing things so badly. I would wear a different dress, less dramatic, more flattering. I only lied to save him, how stupid of me. . . . He really was playing poker, I would confess, humbly. *He loves poker.* I heard the simple true voice I would use. I would say that he was a good man, a good father. I would tell them I knew he could not have done it. Maybe wear white . . . I lay there, drifting.

The prosecution summed up first, starting at 9:00 A.M. Knowing both he and Sam had to sum up on the same day, Swanner droned on all morning and into the afternoon, lugubriously circling the same points like a warped 78 record set on 33⅓. Calvin was a cold-blooded killer, Dan's only crime had been trusting his wife. The judge, in a display of perverse patience, or maybe just apathy, didn't ask Swanner to wrap it up until a quarter to five. The jurors were required to call their families and tell them they'd be late, then they returned, rumpled and weary, to hear Sam's summation. Aware that they were too bloated now to take in much—one or two had been struggling to stay awake after lunch—Sam had no choice but to throw his notes away. He had to ad-lib Calvin's defense.

The guilty verdict came in very quickly the next morning.

After the midmorning break, the sentencing phase began. The character witnesses were a minister who'd known the family since Calvin was a baby; a white man who said Calvin had been a peerless employee who had performed miracles for him after the last hurricane; Kyla, stony with dignity, who said he was a loving brother and a good uncle to her kids and a good father. I think Sam told me Jamaica was there too, sleeping on Jade's lap, an accessory to Calvin's goodness.

Swanner feasted on the psychologist, a guy named Blunkett, starting with his credentials. "But now, you're not a real M.D., you can't write prescriptions." It was all trotted out. Calvin's high IQ, his feelings of abandonment and inadequacy. ("Knew right from wrong though, didn't he!") Wading deep into corn pone, Swanner had fun with the doctor's language ("that big word of yours that I can't pronounce!") and his methods ("now on your little graph here, where you got all these stars . . ."), whipping the old country mule like an itinerant preacher, exhorting the jury to discard all that newfangled science and embrace the plain common sense of the Bible.

Being interviewed on the news that night, Swanner had the soft bluster of a person trying to conceal a sense of accomplishment, but not trying very hard. There was a triumphal radiance to him, as if his nimbus of cigarette smoke were charged by the essence of enlightenment seeping out of his head. His was a singular achievement. Calvin had been sentenced to death.

The Alligoods must have been relieved when they realized I was gone. I rented the house in Salvo over the phone, sight unseen. It was a typical beach house, a shingled box up on stilts with a faded sky-blue door. Every gust of wind made the bed wobble. Nothing worked except the plumbing, belching brown water. The oven was defunct, the linoleum floors had buckled, the plastic veneer on the bedroom wall had been peeled off in long dagger-shaped strips. The place teemed with the ghosts of the people before me, crashing in and out with their packs of kids. My only true companions were the miniature green frogs that gathered in the bathtub at night, twitching like Mexican jumping beans. There was no season out there, just sand. No ripening tobacco, just sea oats, and a warm wind the exact temperature of my skin, sighing straight through me. My dreams were about animals walking on bloody stumps, needing me to reattach their legs. Then that crime happened. She was on TV every day for a week, the sobbing, dry-eyed, scraggy young woman whose two kids had been abducted by "a big black man." When it became apparent she had killed them herself, the country howled with outrage. Everyone felt used but it was black people who felt sullied. Demonized. I was appalled right along with them, nauseated by such a calculating deception. She had recruited a black man to do her killing.

There was still no revelation, not even a dull gleam of recognition. But that was when the rubble of my mind started to shift. Slowly, gently, I was possessed of the knowledge that I had used Calvin to commit my murder. My murder. It had been me killing Dan in that imaginative seizure, me wanting to witness my husband's terror.

I think this happened near the end of July. That's how long it took me to understand it. Three months. That doesn't seem possible. Almost immediately I needed to confess to somebody.

I saw Warner and Reed a day or two later, on the beach. A dedicated father and his son. Warner was trying to get Reed's kite to fly, slogging down the hot sand trailing a limp plastic lizard. Warner's ex-wife had vilified him during their divorce; I must have seemed relatively undangerous, too wounded myself to do him any real harm. After Reed had gone home to his mother Warner began courting me, very graciously, probing sensitively to find out what was wrong, pouring more wine but keeping his distance. On the third night everything—almost everything—came out. He didn't try to tell me it wasn't my fault, he was wiser than that, kinder. I was too exhausted to go home, he put me to sleep on the couch, but during the night I blundered my way into his bed, with the intention of redeeming myself, I suppose. Although it felt more like a penance, letting him handle me. Faking my desire. Not that he was fooled. In the morning, after administering a back rub, he told me I should have some therapy, maybe contact his psychotherapist brother in Raleigh.

Things carried on. Warner delayed leaving for another week, then one more. He e-mailed his clients and nursed their portfolios over the phone, leaving me to myself but keeping one eye on me as I drifted between our cottages like a wraith. It was Warner who first raised the question of what to do with the house and finally called Mary Rose. But it was too soon. I couldn't face it, I couldn't think about moving. Mary Rose told me to take my time. Poor Mary Rose with that tragic house on her hands again. In August Warner finally went back to Atlanta. It was a relief to be alone.

In September I went back to the house for a few hours to check on things. Mildew coated the porch columns and inside the front door was a landslide of catalogues. Calvin's letter was buried in there, I almost missed it. It had been waiting there for three weeks. I was shocked to see his handwriting for the first time, uniform and masculine, slanted hard to the right, on a page torn from a small spiral notebook. There was no heading and it was unsigned.

> This is why I took the gun. So Dan couldn't use it when you told him and he went crazy. I told Half-Gallon but he thinks I was lying. Then I saw Bobo that night and he said he was going out of Calhoun for good. I sold him the gun to get the money. Thank you for trying to help me, you didn't know. DON'T WRITE. Jesus spoke to me. He is our redeemer. He loves us both.

Of course I would write! I just needed paper. I ran to Dan's desk and rifled his drawers, a woman possessed, wiping back her hair, sobbing, frantic to write to her lover to explain, to tell him she always *knew* that was why he took the gun! I watched her scrabble for paper, and knew I was watching, multiplying my frenzy and feeding on it, and humiliation overcame me. I didn't know it as that, it was just a sudden, overwhelming dislocation. Time jumped, I lost a few seconds. No, I couldn't write, he didn't want me to. I understood. I was listening! And then more pictures came, of us, united now in our isolation from each other. Calvin in his cinder-block cell, me in Dan's den, with the tweed love seat and the teak desk. And this time shame finally found me, saving Calvin from whatever self-aggrandizing drivel I might have contrived. He was unreachable, he was beyond me, and I was alone with this new information, working backward from it. Now I saw why, when he was first arrested, he hadn't just *told* Sam about taking Dan's gun and selling it. He didn't dare reveal our connection. And anyway, he reckoned Bobo and the gun were both long gone. And he had a lawyer who kept telling him it was all fine. No case, no evidence. Calvin figured the only person he had to fear was Half-Gallon, and his friend wouldn't do him any harm. Who would even bother to question Half-Gallon? No, what he had to do was stay strong and calm and believe in the power of the truth to prevail.

And what was the truth? That it was Bobo, equipped with a new gun, who had fatally botched an attempt to blackmail Dan? *You know what your wife likes to fuck, you know what she likes doin?*

That fall Warner proposed. I was with him in Atlanta as the appeals process dragged on. Warner must have had half a dozen people out looking for Bobo, in Philadelphia, New York, Miami, even L.A. But Bobo had vanished; he was more than likely dead. It was very decent of Warner to do all that searching. He had already been advised it was pointless. I've never been sure in my heart that Warner was completely convinced of Calvin's innocence. I think he only wanted to believe in Calvin because I did. He would have done anything to prevent what he calls, tactfully, my "crisis."

I'm not convinced it *was* Bobo.

Maybe Dan was so demeaned by his brush with Melanie he needed to pump up his ego. What if he went to Calhoun to score some big bad black reefer, and the dealer he found was somebody who'd just bought a fancy stainless steel gun from Bobo?

I don't have any idea what Dan wanted all that cash for.

Swanner did get reelected. Following that, he had a few years of running unopposed for DA, then I lost track of him. I still dream about Lloyd Swanner. In the dreams he's always extravagantly unperturbed, the same as he ever was, especially the last time I saw him. I was rushing through the last few chores that would get me out of town when a nasty bit of timing put me in front of the newspaper shop just as he emerged with a take-out coffee. As our eyes met I became rooted to the sidewalk, swimming in a tingling moment of pure horror, while he merely lifted an elbow to steady his sloshing cup and continued on, turning back just long enough to deliver an expansive slow-motion wink, laden with good humor.

Swanner has attached himself to me, he's clamped to the wall of my stomach, his microbes pollute my bloodstream. For years I talked to him in my head. I still have the occasional conversation with him in the middle of the night. It always takes the form of a kind of bantering interview. I initiate it by admitting I'm curious. I appreciate that somebody has to do his job, but why him? What were his influences? For instance, why prosecute a man rather than defend him? Swanner is immediately insulted and says he doesn't have any interest at all in helping human scum escape justice. I apologize for asking. Then he tells me he believes in the efficiency of capital punishment. I counter with a few statistics that refute this, and Swanner switches tack and says that becoming the county DA was never a lifetime goal of his, he just kept his nose to the grindstone. I suggest he's being too modest, which opens him up like a flower. He allows as how the first time he ever won a capital case, it really was pretty damn hard on him; he had some gastric distress that night in bed. His imagination (I provide him one) played some bad tricks on him in the wee small hours. What if the man was innocent? I nod, encouragingly, but he tells me you can't start letting things like that get to you. I say no, of course not. It hasn't been easy for Swanner. There were moments when it might have been easier just to quit, but he was never a quitter. The implication is that, as with other kinds of work, it got easier. He never looks back now, he has no reason to. He's good with facts, good at making the tough calls, proud of upholding the law of his state. He's giving his kids all those fancy lessons he never got, and still managing to build their college fund. Strange how life turns out. This wasn't anything he ever intended (he wanted to play pro baseball) but God must have had His reasons.

Shit happens, as people used to say. Whatever.

In short, he has *no idea* how his life led him to that place. So I speculate on the current of cause and effect that ran underneath his youth like an open vein seeping upward: a God-fearing father strict to the point of cruelty, shadows jumping on his boyhood wall, true distress surfacing among the general insecurities of law school; clichés, all of which may be true. My own influences are much more interesting, of course, more obscure, more *profound*. But at least I can claim to be innocent of that kind of obliviousness. (You were right after all, Debs-Anne, evil really is out there, nestling inside every variety of oblivion. Individual, collective, accidental. But willed oblivion is the worst, the human craving for blindness. We really believe what we don't see can't hurt us.) Even now I enjoy mentally dragging Debs-Anne, kicking and screaming, through each step of my crime, illuminating for her all the various shades of my contempt. For my mother, with her overweening merciless pity; for Dan and Calvin. And Jade. Ping and George. Half-Gallon, and even Half-Gallon's Jesus. This has meant my having to explain to Debs-Anne how it all started, which of my dominoes was pushed over first. I have had to admit that it was me with Dan in that wedding picture. Over and over I explain how it felt to be ugly, to meet other eyes that looked hastily away in shame, when it was me that felt shameful. *Contemptible,* in fact, I hint, a little too broadly. But Debs-Anne always has her reply ready. Oh, so what, she says. Big deal. Lots of people are ugly and it just makes them nicer.

I'm glad I've never told Warner. He's always thought of me as genuine, not just physically but psychologically. He would be very disheartened to know how scheming I am, how in every snapshot of his appalling sister and me, for instance, I look affectionate only because I read a book on body language once and always make sure to cock my head toward hers just before Warner takes his picture.

Warner's proud of me, proud of our life here, in the midst of this antiseptic spotlessness that people with money find so pacifying, as if it signifies innocence. We have our anti-allergen carpets and UV shades, our lush lawn, and the enveloping lushness of the other magnificent lawns in our little enclave here. We like feeling protected, especially from the passing of time. Warner's had a little work on his eyes, but I'm repelled by the idea of more surgery. My neck is coming undone, but the skin on my sagging pretty-girl face is almost suspiciously unlined, as if Dr. Kurth's contributions were impregnated with some special time-release preservative.

So I still have my secret. Secrets plural. No one here knows anything about my connection to the case, if anybody even remembers the case now. Sometimes I regret telling Warner so much about it. I don't ever mention any of these "new" memories that have started surfacing. Not long ago Warner and I were out in the garden discussing some planting and I remembered what Dan said to me that night before he went out. I was suddenly hearing the whole sound track of those last minutes, starting with the sound of him in the hall, picking up his car keys from that little silver dish. I called down from the top of the stairs to ask him where he was going, worried because he'd been drinking. No. Not worried. Just wanting to calculate how much time I might have to be alone. He shouted up, *Nowhere!* and slammed out. I heard the car start. Then he came back in, and I came back to the head of the stairs and looked down at him. He didn't ask me what he may have been wondering, which was why his gun wasn't in the glove compartment as usual. He just stared up at me, until I finally asked him what the matter was. *Nothing! Go stick your fucking head in the mirror!* His last words to me, a stab of real humor there, a play on Go stick your head in the oven. He was driven into that corner of bleak wit by the force of his anger. Because he *was* that angry, and disappointed, and repulsed by me. I understand that now. But of course, I understood it then, and didn't care.

And then Dan went back out to the car and I went back to my bath, eager to sink in and continue being a woman on the verge of running away with her lover. Would I ever have done it? Did I love Calvin enough? Maybe I didn't love him at all. I loved the beauty we had. We were inside that beauty, it was a kind of glory around us. And I know that was real, but I wouldn't have it to remember without my changed face. I wouldn't have had it at all. So where is the lie? Maybe just here, on this page, adjusted like all the others not to reflect the most flattering angle or the most truthful, but the most "genuine," the one that sounds the most tortured and *realistic.* Maybe I've just been clever, making myself lifelike, when in fact I've been dead all along to everything except my own suffering.

But Calvin says it's the pain that hooks us up to each other. I believe that, that's what gets me out of here. Maybe I'll go out tonight. I've gotten pretty good at deactivating the alarm and slipping past Burton, snoring in his guardhouse. Beyond the wall the road seems paler and I walk more confidently, everything sliding off me into the creaking darkness and the magnolias' greasy luster. This is my own strange land. It still feels like mine, a place of so much prevarication and beguilement. When I walk at night Calvin is out there, still alive, waiting for me. I believe he can hear my footsteps coming and the pain that rushes into me then is exquisite. I could never leave him.

SALLY MACLEOD was raised in Burlington, Vermont, and, after studying at the Rhode Island School of Design, worked in New York, Milan, and London. A subsequent five-year interlude in a small North Carolina town inspired this novel, her first. She now lives on the coast of southeast England with her husband, painter and filmmaker Marcus Reichert.

A B O U T   T H E   T Y P E

This book was set in Electra, a typeface designed for Linotype by W. A. Dwiggins, the renowned type designer (1880–1956). Electra is a fluid typeface, avoiding the contrasts of thick and thin strokes that are prevalent in most modern typefaces.